MURDER IN THE BOWERY

A Gaslight Mystery

Victoria Thompson

BERKLEY PRIME CRIME
New York

BERKLEY PRIME CRIME
Published by Berkley
An imprint of Penguin Random House LLC
375 Hudson Street, New York, New York 10014

Copyright © 2017 by Victoria Thompson
Excerpt from *City of Lies* copyright © 2017 by Victoria Thompson
Excerpt from *Murder on Union Square* copyright © 2018 by Victoria Thompson
Penguin Random House supports copyright. Copyright fuels creativity, encourages
diverse voices, promotes free speech, and creates a vibrant culture. Thank you for buying
an authorized edition of this book and for complying with copyright laws by not
reproducing, scanning, or distributing any part of it in any form without permission.
You are supporting writers and allowing Penguin Random House to continue to
publish books for every reader.

BERKLEY is a registered trademark and BERKLEY PRIME CRIME and the B colophon
are trademarks of Penguin Random House LLC.
The Edgar® award is a registered service mark of the Mystery Writers of America, Inc.

ISBN: 9781101987131

Berkley Prime Crime hardcover edition / May 2017
Berkley Prime Crime mass-market edition / April 2018

Printed in the United States of America
1 3 5 7 9 10 8 6 4 2

Cover art by Karen Chandler

To Liam, Ryan, and Keira,
my favorite playmates.

Murder in the Bowery

I

"I NEED TO FIND MY KID BROTHER, MR. MALLOY."

Frank Malloy leaned back in his office chair and studied his newest client across the expanse of his desk. The young man had introduced himself as Will Bert. He was a handsome fellow, sporting a fairly new suit of brown, checked fabric and a pristine shirt with a fresh collar. He had settled his smart-looking derby on his knee instead of leaving it on his head, as too many young men did today. He wasn't the usual sort of client who came to Frank's detective agency, but then his agency was also fairly new, so he really couldn't claim to have a "usual" sort of client.

"How did you come to lose your brother, Mr. Bert?" Frank asked.

Bert shrugged almost apologetically. "Well, I didn't exactly lose him. It's kind of a long story."

"I'm not going anywhere."

"All right then. Well, you see, Freddie and me are orphans. After our folks died, we had to look after ourselves, so I started selling newspapers to support us. Freddie did, too, even though he was still really small."

A common enough story, Frank knew. "You were street arabs?" he asked, referring to the hundreds of orphaned and abandoned children who lived on the New York City streets.

"Yes, sir. We stayed at one of the Newsboys' Lodging Houses whenever the weather was bad, of course, and I always looked out for Freddie, but it was a hard life. That's why we finally decided to go out West on one of those Orphan Trains."

The Orphan Trains had been taking children from the city out West to find homes since before Frank was born. "I guess you were hoping to be adopted by some farmer out in Iowa or something."

Bert smiled a little at this. "I know it sounds strange, especially for a city boy like me, but those people from the Children's Aid Society make it sound like a fairy tale or something."

"But it wasn't a fairy tale for you and your brother, I guess."

Bert's smile disappeared. "Not exactly. We went to Minnesota, not Iowa, although I don't guess it makes much difference. We wanted to go with the same family, but none of the families wanted me. I was too old, already sixteen, but Freddie was eight by then and still real cute, so he got picked right off. I ended up in another town with a storekeeper, Mr. Varney."

"That was probably easier than farm work."

"I guess so. Mr. Varney, he never had any children, and he wanted somebody to take over his store when he was gone, so he trained me to do that. He wasn't going to adopt me or anything. He just put it in his will that I got the store when he died."

"And did he die?"

Bert seemed surprised that Frank had guessed. "Yeah, he did, as a matter of fact. He just keeled over one day after we'd unloaded some heavy boxes. The doc said there was nothing could've been done. His heart gave out on him. So now I'm a businessman, Mr. Malloy. I've got a bright future ahead of me back in Minnesota, so naturally, I wanted to find Freddie and bring him to live with me."

"I thought he'd been adopted."

"Well, they don't always go through with the legal adoption. The families, I mean. That's what I was counting on, anyway, but when I went looking for Freddie, I found out the family who got him decided not to keep him after all. He'd been sent back to New York."

That seemed harsh to Frank, but he shouldn't be surprised at how cruel people could be. "And nobody told you?"

Bert shrugged again. "Of course not. They probably didn't even know where I was. At least the family wouldn't, and the Children's Aid Society, what did they care?"

"And Freddie didn't write to you or anything?"

Now he had the grace to look embarrassed. "We was never much for writing letters, and I figured he was in a good place, being looked after, so what was the need? But when I found out he'd been sent back here, I came to find him."

Finding one small boy in a city like New York would be a daunting task indeed. "Have you looked?"

"Of course I looked. I figured he'd be selling papers in the old neighborhood, but now . . ." He gestured helplessly.

"Oh yes, the strike." The newsboys had gone on strike a few days ago. They'd done it last year when they thought the newspapers weren't treating them fairly, and this time they were trying to force both William Randolph Hearst and Joseph Pulitzer to pay them better. The struggle between a gaggle of children and the two most powerful newspaper moguls in the country promised to be very interesting.

"Right, the strike," Bert said. "The newsboys are giving lots of speeches, but they aren't selling many newspapers, and none of them are on the corners where they usually are. They aren't even staying in the lodging houses."

"I guess they aren't making as much money as usual with the strike," Frank said. The lodging houses charged the boys six cents a night and the same amount for dinner and breakfast if they chose to eat.

"And with it being summer, they like to carry the banner anyway."

"Carry what banner?" Frank asked, confused.

"Oh, that's what they call sleeping out on the street, *carrying the banner*. It's a matter of pride for the newsies."

"So you want me to help you find your brother, Mr. Bert?"

"That's right. I can pay. I told you, I own a store back in Minnesota, and I have money. Even still, I'd do it myself, but with the strike, I figure it's going to take some time, and I can't be away from my store very long. I've got someone minding it, but you know how it is."

Frank didn't know how it was. Luckily, he didn't even have to worry about his own business and getting paid like other private investigators did. Because of an accident of fate, he was now rich enough to only take the cases he liked, even if he didn't get paid at all, and Frank liked this case. He felt sorry for these two boys, being separated like that. He'd let Bert pay to save the boy's pride, but Frank would give him a reduced rate. "All right, I'll give it a try, Mr. Bert. I can't make any promises, though. You must know how hard it will be to find him. Do you know how long ago your brother came back to the city?"

"It's been a couple years now."

"Then you know anything might have happened to him." Life in New York was uncertain at best, and for the boys who made their own way on the streets, it was downright dangerous.

"Freddie's a smart kid. I know he's out there somewhere. I want to give him a good home, Mr. Malloy, the home we never had. Will you help me find him?"

"I'll certainly try. What can you tell me about him? You said he's eight years old?"

"Not anymore. That's how old he was when we went West. Now he's thirteen, I reckon. I don't have a picture of him, of course, but anybody who's met him will remember. See, when he was a little tyke, he almost got run over by a trolley. It cut off part of his foot, so now he only has two toes on his left foot. Makes him walk a little funny, and the other boys, they called him Two Toes. All the newsies, they like to give each other nicknames."

Frank had noticed that, although he'd never given it much thought. "When you said 'the old neighborhood,' did you mean where you lived with your parents?"

"Oh no. Wouldn't sell many newspapers there, would we? I meant the corners where we used to sell our papers. Newsies are real jealous of their corners. If you try to horn in on another boy's spot, you'll likely find yourself beat up pretty good."

"Thanks for the warning," Frank said. "So where were these corners where you used to sell?"

Frank wrote down the streets on the pad he pulled from his desk drawer. "And your brother's name is Freddie Bert."

"That's right. I'll be much obliged to you, Mr. Malloy, and so will Freddie, when you find him."

For once, Frank might have a case with a happy ending.

THE HOUSE SAT IN THE MIDDLE OF ONE OF THE WORST slums of the city, mere blocks from the notorious Five Points neighborhood and surrounded by boisterous saloons and teeming tenements and places so wicked they didn't even have signs. The house itself was dilapidated and filthy, and the roof had holes. Rain had ruined one of the bedrooms, rats had taken over the cellar, and pigeons roosted in the attic.

"I'll take it," Sarah Brandt Malloy said.

The owner, a rather rascally-looking fellow in checked pants and a threadbare suit coat, looked her over in disbelief, taking in her expensive gown and stylish hat. "Are you sure, miss?"

"It's perfect, isn't it, Gino?" she asked her companion.

Gino Donatelli, her husband's partner in the detective agency, was functioning as her bodyguard today as she toured the latest offerings of ramshackle houses available for sale on the Lower East Side of the city. The young man looked around doubtfully. "If you think so, Mrs. Malloy."

"Of course it isn't worth half of what you're asking, Mr. Bartholomew," she told the owner. She'd been looking for months, so she was an expert now. "I saw a larger place over on Mulberry Street for only a thousand."

Mr. Bartholomew began to sputter his outrage, but in the end he happily accepted Sarah's offer, as she'd known he would, and made an appointment with her the following week to visit an attorney to sign the necessary papers.

"May we drop you somewhere, Mr. Bartholomew?" she asked when they'd concluded their negotiations.

He eyed her carriage longingly. "Thank you, miss, but I wouldn't want to be seen in such a fine vehicle on this street. People would start asking me for money."

Gino helped Sarah into the carriage, which actually belonged to her parents, and instructed the driver to take them to Sarah's home. When they were safely away, Gino turned to her with a perplexed frown. "Are you sure you want to buy that place?"

"I know it looks horrible right now, and it didn't escape me that someone had obviously been living in several of the rooms, so we'll have to deal with that, but it's the perfect location. We aren't going to live there ourselves, remember."

"I know, and I guess you're right. If you want poor women to find it, then it really is the perfect location. Is it going to be a hospital?"

"We're going to call it a home for unwed mothers, so they can come to stay as soon as they need to, have their babies there, and stay until they're well again. We'll have a matron living in to watch over the girls and several midwives who will be available. They may even live in also and serve the rest of the community as well. I haven't figured that out yet."

"You'll have plenty of time to do that while you get somebody to fix the place up."

"Yes, and I'm thinking I'll put Maeve in charge of that."

Gino grinned. He was such a handsome boy, and he was so obviously enamored of their family's nursemaid, Maeve Smith. Sarah was pretty sure Maeve felt the same way about Gino, but Maeve wasn't one to give herself away. "She did a pretty good job of managing the workers when you were fixing up your own house."

"Indeed she did. Without her help, Malloy and I would probably still be waiting for them to be finished." Sarah opened the fan hanging from her wrist and began to flutter it, trying to stir up some air inside the carriage.

"You were right about bringing the carriage," Gino said. "I'm glad we don't have to walk in this heat."

"Or try to find a cab. My mother insisted we take it, and she was right, although I think she was more worried about our safety in this neighborhood than our comfort." Sarah glanced out the window at the street urchins running alongside the fine carriage, shouting for a handout. Her heart told her to throw some coins out the window, but her head told her that would only draw more children and encourage them to be bolder, endangering life and limb as they ran perilously close to the wheels and the horses. In the city, even charity could be dangerous. "Thank you for coming with me today."

Gino grinned. "I know you would've been fine on your own, but Mr. Malloy worries."

"I know he does, even though I used to travel these streets alone at all hours of the day and night when I was called out to deliver babies."

"He didn't have the right to worry then, but now that you're married . . ." He shrugged.

"I have to admit, it's very nice to have someone worrying about me. Oh dear, what's going on here?"

They both leaned to look out the window at a crowd of children gathered on the street corner. One boy stood on a box and appeared to be giving a speech while the rest of them cheered. Adults were stopping to listen and enjoy the spectacle.

"Newsboys," Gino said.

"Newsboys? Oh yes, I'd forgotten. They're on strike, aren't they?"

"That's what they call it. They aren't selling the *World* or the *Journal*, although I guess all the other papers are still available."

"But it looks like that one boy is giving a speech." Sarah stuck her head out the window to keep the newsboys in sight as their carriage pulled away from the corner.

"He probably is. They have to keep the boys stirred up or they'll give in and start selling the papers again."

"Why are they striking?"

"Because of the cost of the papers. The boys used to buy them in bundles of ten for five cents, then sell them for a penny apiece, but last year during the war with Spain, the *Journal* and the *World* raised the price of the papers to six cents for ten. The boys didn't mind then because people were buying more papers during the war, so they were still doing well, but the war is long over and the two papers haven't lowered their prices."

"That's not fair to the boys."

"I guess it would be if they could charge more for the papers, but nobody is going to pay more than a penny for a newspaper, so they're stuck."

"You know a lot about it, Gino."

"I used to sell newspapers when I was a kid. It's a hard life. I was lucky because I had a home and a family to go to every night, though. A lot of the boys are orphans."

Sarah nodded. "Or even worse, they've been abandoned by their families. I used to think all the children on the streets were orphans. I just couldn't believe that people would turn out their own little ones to fend for themselves. Then I came to understand that sometimes they have no other choice."

"It's amazing how many of the kids seem to do all right, though. I've seen boys as young as six or seven managing on their own. Of course, some of them end up in gangs, but the rest of them look out for each other."

"And the lodging houses help, too, I suppose. At least they don't have to sleep on the streets in the dead of winter."

Gino shook his head. "The boys actually prefer sleeping on the streets. They like being able to come and go as they please. The lodging houses make you come in by nine thirty, but the boys like to stay out late and go to the theater."

"The theater?" Sarah exclaimed in delight.

"That's right, and then they go to a diner and have supper and smoke cigars and talk about the show."

"I had no idea!"

"The boys also don't like the way they're always preaching to them in the lodging houses, trying to make them take classes and giving them lectures and even trying to convince them to go on the Orphan Trains out West to get adopted."

"Do a lot of them go on the Orphan Trains?"

"Not as many as you'd think. They like their freedom, I guess, and city boys are a little afraid of living in the country and doing farm work, too. The Orphan Trains have more luck with the really small kids who are too young to know what's going on."

"I expect the families like getting younger children, too."

"I don't know. Maybe they do if they really want more kids in their family, but a lot of them just want free labor for their farm, so they choose the older children and then turn them loose when they get too old to manage, or else the kids run away on their own."

"Not exactly the happy ending the Children's Aid Society claims, is it?"

"Not many orphans have happy endings anywhere."

Sarah supposed he was right.

* * *

"SO SHE FINALLY FOUND A HOUSE TO SUIT HER?" MALLOY asked Gino when he turned up at their office. "I was starting to think it would never happen."

"The houses in that part of the city aren't . . . Well, there's not a lot to choose from."

"So I've heard, over and over again, every time Sarah goes looking."

"This one is pretty bad, too, but it's the best we've seen, and it's big enough. And Mrs. Malloy said she's going to put Maeve in charge of supervising the repairs," Gino added with a grin.

"If you think I'm embarrassed because Maeve did a better job of that than I did at our own house, then you're crazy. She can have that job and welcome to it. Now, we've got a new case, and it sounds like it might be fun for a change."

Gino perked up immediately. "Fun? Did somebody get killed?"

"Gino, I'm ashamed of you. What would Maeve think if she heard you say a thing like that?"

"She'd wonder why you were ashamed of me for telling the truth."

Frank sighed. "I guess you're right. But no, nobody got killed. We're just looking for a missing boy." He gave Gino a summary of the story of the two brothers.

"I always suspected those Orphan Trains weren't a good idea. I was just telling Mrs. Malloy about them this morning. But you say this Will Bert wants to take his brother back to Mississippi?"

"Minnesota. That's what he said, so it can't be too bad out there."

"Mrs. Malloy and I saw a bunch of newsboys on the way home. They were all gathered on a street corner, and it looked like one of them was giving a speech. The strike is going to make it harder to find this Freddie."

"I know, and even without the strike, we might not find him. A boy alone like that, there's no telling what might have happened to him in two years, but the missing toes should make it easier to identify him. The boys remember things like that."

"Where do you want to start?"

"I thought you could ask around at the Newsboys' Lodging Houses, and I'll check with the Children's Aid Society just in case they sent him back out on another train or something."

Gino pulled out the pocket watch he'd just started carrying. "I should have time to visit at least a few of them this afternoon. They don't serve supper until six, and not many boys will come in on a hot night like this anyway, even if they weren't on strike. They'll get supper from a street vendor and find a nice, cool rooftop to bed down. But like you said, if this Freddie ever stayed there, they'll remember him, so at least we'll find out if he's been seen around lately."

"They also might know where he usually works, which would give us an idea of where to start looking."

"Maybe I'll get lucky and find the boy tonight," Gino said.

"If you do, hang on to him. He seems like he might be a slippery one."

FRANK FOUND THE CHILDREN'S AID SOCIETY OFFICES IN the United Charities Building on 22nd Street. Many of the major charities had taken office space in the building in order to more efficiently coordinate the distribution of charity in the city. What that meant in practical terms was that the charities were able to keep a master list of everyone who had received aid, so the poor couldn't "abuse" the system by applying to more than one charity. Frank didn't think that sounded very charitable, but nobody had asked his opinion, nor were they likely to.

The Society's office was a busy place with several clerks typing or filing. One of them took his name and escorted him in to see a Mr. E. E. Trott. The clerk described Mr. Trott as an agent for the Society. Trott was a tall, slender man with a shock of white hair and a matching goatee. His eyes were kind but a little suspicious.

When the two men had shaken hands, Frank said, "That young man said you were an agent. What exactly does an agent do?"

"I have the best job in the world, Mr. Malloy," Trott said, motioning for Frank to take a seat in one of the chairs placed in front of his desk. "I help gather up the children here and escort them safely to their new homes out West."

"Is it difficult to find homes for the children?"

"I wouldn't say it was difficult, although it isn't easy either. You see, another part of my job is to identify the leading citizens in each of the cities where we stop. I do this a few months before we bring the children out. Those individuals know their communities, and their task is to recruit the right kind of families who would be willing to take a child. Often, the families themselves will state their preference for a girl or a boy and the age of the child they want. Sometimes they even specify hair and eye color so the child will look like the rest of the family. When that is the case, we can sometimes match a child with a family even before we leave the city."

Frank thought that sounded a bit too much like ordering a child out of a catalog, but he kept his opinion to himself since he couldn't afford to offend Mr. Trott. He still needed more information. "I see, and do you keep records of the children you place?"

"Of course we do. We have a file on every child who has received our services. Is there a specific reason you're asking, Mr. Malloy?"

"Yes, a very specific reason. You see, I'm a private investigator, and I've been hired to locate one of the boys you placed out in Minnesota about five years ago."

Mr. Trott frowned. "Mr. Malloy, may I ask who hired you?"

"Ordinarily, I don't reveal my clients' names, but in this case, I understand the matter is sensitive because it involves a child, so I'm going to make an exception. My client is this boy's older brother. Your agency placed both of them in Minnesota, but in different towns."

"That does happen from time to time. Siblings don't want to be separated, of course, and we do try to place them together, but that isn't always possible."

"I can understand that. The older boy was about sixteen, too, and he said not many people wanted a child that old."

"This is true, unfortunately. With a boy that old, you never know what his background might be, and people are afraid to take them into their homes."

"The older boy was placed with a storekeeper who recently died and left the boy his property. He was anxious to find his brother and share his good fortune. The younger boy is about thirteen now. But when he went to find the child, he discovered that he'd been sent back."

"Back here, you mean?" Mr. Trott asked with a puzzled frown.

"That's what he was told."

"And this happened recently?"

"No, I believe the boy was sent back shortly after he was placed, so it would have been several years ago."

"Ah, I didn't remember anything like that happening recently, although it does happen from time to time. We always try to find another family locally to take the child, of course, so the child doesn't actually have to return here. I'm surprised that didn't happen in this case. And the older brother didn't know the boy had been sent back?"

"The boys didn't keep in touch."

Mr. Trott nodded. "The families would discourage that, of course. They'd want the children to forget their past. Even still . . . Well, I must tell you, Mr. Malloy, that children are hardly ever returned to the city."

"But you'd have a record of it if they were?"

"We should have a record of both boys, and I'll want to update the older boy's record to record his good fortune. We like to tell stories like that to the children we're trying to recruit. In fact, if this young man is in the city, perhaps he'd be willing to tell his story at the Newsboys' Lodging Houses. The Society operates them as well, and they have proved a fruitful source of children for whom we have found homes. We like to have special visitors from time to time to convince the boys they can have a bright future if they leave the evil influences of the city."

"He might be willing, since he and his brother were both newsboys. I'll certainly ask him, but meanwhile, I'd just like to find out if the younger brother stayed in the city or if he went someplace else."

"That is another possibility, of course, and there is also yet another possibility, although I hesitate to suggest it."

"What's that?"

"The younger boy, well, the family said he'd been sent

back, but it's possible he simply ran away. We've had that happen a few times, I'm sorry to say. Perhaps he thought to join his brother or even come back to New York on his own. If that's the case, we would have no way of knowing what became of him."

"I understand that. There's also the possibility that the boy is dead, but I'm not going to even think about that right now."

"Of course not. Let me check our files. What are the boys' names?"

Frank told him, and Mr. Trott frowned again as he wrote them down.

"Is something wrong?" Frank asked.

"No, but I suspect the name *Bert* is not their real name."

"Why wouldn't it be?"

Mr. Trott shrugged. "Sometimes the children change their names to disguise their ethnicity. People might be reluctant to adopt an Italian child, for example, or one they suspected of being Jewish or foreign in any way. I'm not saying this is true of these boys, but it's possible."

"But if that's the name my client gave me, it's probably also the name the boys gave you folks."

"That's true." Mr. Trott was smiling again. "Let me take a look. Our files are very well organized, so this should only take a moment."

It took longer than a moment, though, and when he returned, Mr. Trott was empty-handed. He also looked very unhappy. "I'm so sorry, Mr. Malloy, but it appears that we have no record of either of these boys."

"Then maybe you were right, and they used a different name."

"I thought of that, of course, and my clerks and I searched the records for all the boys whose names started with *B*, but we did not find any that could possibly be these two brothers. I don't have any indication at all that either of these boys rode the Orphan Trains."

Gino STARTED HIS SEARCH AT THE DUANE STREET LODG-ing House, since it was closest to Newspaper Row, where the boys picked up their papers. Located on the east side of Williams Street between Duane and Chambers, it stood seven stories tall and filled the entire block. Uhlig & Company Cloth House occupied the basement and first floor of the building. Gino figured their rent went toward support of the lodging house, which probably cost a lot more to run than the pennies the newsboys paid would provide.

He found the newsboys' entrance and climbed the stairs to the third floor. The place was eerily quiet, with no boys in sight, but even under ordinary conditions, they wouldn't have started to arrive yet. Afternoon and early evening, when the afternoon editions came out and people were heading home from work, were the busiest times of day for newspaper sales. Besides, the boys had to leave the lodging house by seven o'clock in the morning and weren't allowed back in before six o'clock in the evening.

Gino stepped into the empty classroom with its neat rows of desks where the boys would take lessons after supper if they were so inclined and where all of them would register for the night with whoever was sitting at the table on the riser beside the door. No one sat there now, however, so Gino called out a greeting. After a few tries, he heard footsteps, and a middle-aged man appeared, pulling on his suit coat.

Tall and a bit gangly, he greeted Gino with a warm smile. "You wouldn't be one of my boys come back to say hello, would you?"

"No, sir, I'm afraid not."

"You're about the right age to be one, and you wouldn't be the first. They come by all the time to tell me how much they miss the place and how well they're doing."

"That must be nice to hear."

"It is, it is, but you didn't come here to listen to me babble. What can I do for you, young man?" He eyed Gino's tailored suit shrewdly. "I'm pretty sure you aren't looking for a bed for the night."

"No, I'm not. My name is Gino Donatelli, and I'm a private investigator." He handed the man his business card.

"Private, you say? I would've taken you for police, except they don't wear suits that nice."

"I used to be with the police."

"Ah, that explains it then. I'm Rudolph Heig, the superintendent here. I hope this doesn't mean one of my boys is in trouble."

"Not at all. Just the opposite, Mr. Heig."

"Call me Pop. That's what the boys call me, Pop Rudolph. And what exactly is the opposite of 'in trouble'?"

"Getting a family, I guess," Gino said with a grin. "You see, a young man has hired our firm to find his kid brother so he can give him a home."

"Now that is good news. Why don't you come downstairs so I can get you a cup of coffee and you can tell me all about it."

Heig took Gino to his private apartment on the second floor, where he introduced his wife, known to the boys as Mother Heig. A plump, pleasant lady with a toddler perched on her hip, she welcomed Gino and made the two men comfortable at the immaculate kitchen table, serving them coffee and some cookies.

"Now tell me about this boy you're looking for," Heig said.

Gino told him the story. "So do you by any chance know

this boy, Freddie Bert? His brother said he lost part of his foot in a streetcar accident, and the other boys call him Two Toes."

"Oh yes, streetcar accidents are far too common, I'm afraid. Too many boys are maimed and even killed from trying to hang on to the side of the cars for a free ride. And I do know the boy you're looking for, I think. A lot of the boys who come here don't even know their real names because they lost their homes so young, so all they know are the nicknames they've picked up in the streets. Others lie about their real names for various reasons, so I guess you could say that you're lucky the boy you're looking for is so distinctive. I remember him well, because of his foot, of course. We ask the boys to give a name when they register, and Freddie always says his name is Bert, although I've suspected it wasn't his true name. Perhaps I've been wrong, though."

"And he went out West on the Orphan Train?"

"That part I don't know about. It's possible Freddie didn't start coming here until he returned from out West, in which case I might not have heard about it, although the boys do talk about the trains a lot, especially those who've gone and returned for whatever reason."

"Are there many of those?"

"No, not at all. The Children's Aid Society doesn't like to send children back. They make every effort to place them somewhere else, so it's possible Freddie returned on his own and didn't talk about it because he didn't want to be sent out again. But even without that, there's a good chance the boy I'm thinking of is the one you're looking for."

"When was the last time you saw him?"

"I couldn't say exactly. We have hundreds of boys come through here every year, and it's impossible to keep track of all of them, so I don't even try. I'll check my log book before you leave to give you an exact date for the last time he stayed here, but it wasn't long, I'm sure. Not more than a month or two at the most."

A lot could happen in a month or two, but at least Freddie had been alive and in the city then. Gino wanted to whoop with glee, but he didn't want to frighten Mr. Heig. "I don't suppose you'd know where I could find him."

Heig shook his head. "Even under ordinary circumstances, I don't know where his usual corner is or where he sleeps when he doesn't sleep here, but now . . . Well, I guess you know the boys are on strike, so they aren't coming here to sleep because they aren't earning any money. Most of them wouldn't anyway, not this time of year. When the weather's nice, we only get a fraction of the boys who show up when it's snowing."

"I know. I figured it wasn't likely I'd find him here. I'm just glad to know he's in the city. Will you send us word if he does come in?"

"Certainly. I'd be only too happy for you to find wealthy brothers for all my boys, Mr. Donatelli."

2

"**What's an Orphan Train?**" Maeve asked, interrupting Malloy's story.

Sarah was always careful about discussing cases in front of the children, so Malloy had waited until Malloy's son, Brian, and Sarah's foster daughter, Catherine, were in bed, and their nursemaid Maeve had rejoined them in the parlor before telling them about his latest case. Malloy's mother had already retired to her own rooms.

Sarah smiled at Maeve's question and turned to Malloy. "May I?"

"Go right ahead," he said, happy to let her explain.

"Years ago, long before I was born, I think, the Children's Aid Society decided that orphaned children in New York would be much happier if they were living on farms out West."

Maeve frowned her disapproval. "What made them think that?"

"Everybody knows that country air is better for children," Malloy said with a twinkle. He loved teasing Maeve.

"I don't know it. You couldn't get me to live in the country for anything," she said.

"Then it's lucky you're a little too old to be adopted," he said.

"Adopted?" Maeve cried, horrified.

"You're getting ahead of the story," Sarah chided them. "Yes, adopted. The Society decided to place the children with families in the country who could then adopt them, and through the years, they've taken thousands of children out of the city."

"Don't people in the country have their own children?"

"Of course they do, but not everyone who wants a child can have one, and sometimes a child dies or maybe the family is just willing to open their hearts to an orphan with no family."

"You make it sound like a fairy tale." Maeve didn't believe in fairy tales.

"Don't forget Catherine is adopted," Sarah said.

"Or at least she soon will be," Malloy corrected her. "And we couldn't love her more if she had been born to us."

"No, we couldn't," Sarah agreed, thinking they should really get started on the process.

"And I wouldn't have a job if you hadn't decided to take her in," Maeve admitted with a grin. "All right, I suppose it's possible for families to adopt children and for everyone to be happy. Were these boys happy, though?"

"If you let me finish my story, I'll tell you," Malloy said. "But the answer is probably no. The older boy was sixteen, so nobody really wanted to adopt him." He told them about the shopkeeper who took the older boy and the legacy he left Will.

"But was he happy with the man who took him in?" Maeve asked.

"He didn't say, but I got the impression the man treated him more like an employee than a son."

"That's what I thought."

"Don't forget the boys would have been much worse off if they'd stayed in the city," Sarah said. "They didn't have a family or a home, and they lived on the streets."

"The younger boy had it worse, though," Malloy went on doggedly. "It didn't work out with the family who took him, and he came back to New York, or at least that's what the family told Will when he went to look for Freddie after the storekeeper died."

"Smart boy," Maeve said.

"That's sad," Sarah said, thinking about how hard that must have been for such a young child. "He must have been terribly disappointed."

"Maybe he was relieved to get away from all those cows and chickens," Maeve said.

"What makes you think they had cows and chickens?" Malloy asked.

"Because they live in the country. So this Will hired you to find Freddie?"

"That's right. He's pretty well fixed now, I guess, and he wants the boy with him."

"So it will be like a fairy tale," Sarah said, "if you can find Freddie. Have you had a chance to look yet?"

"I sent Gino to ask around at the Newsboys' Lodging Houses."

"Is he coming by tonight to give you a report?" Maeve asked with elaborate casualness.

"I don't think so," Malloy said, pretending not to notice her frown of disappointment, although Sarah was sure he'd mention it to Gino. "Whatever he found out can wait until morning."

"And what about you?" Sarah asked. "Did you do anything?"

"I went to the Children's Aid Society's office. They're in the United Charities Building."

Sarah made a face. She'd had a bad experience with a charity located in that building. "What did you think they could tell you?"

"For one thing, if Freddie really had come back and if they'd sent him someplace else."

"Could they do that?" Maeve asked, outraged this time.

"I suppose they could, although I don't know if they'd force him if he didn't want to go," Malloy said. "It doesn't matter, though, because they didn't have any record of either of the brothers."

"What do you mean, no record? You mean they don't keep records of the children's whereabouts?" Sarah asked.

"They keep very good records. They claimed to have a file on every child. They even get annual reports from the adoptive families, or they're supposed to, although I'm told not all the families send them."

"Of course they don't," Maeve muttered.

Malloy ignored her. "But they didn't have a file for either of these boys."

"What does that mean?" Sarah asked.

"It could mean several things, but I don't think it means the Children's Aid Society lost their records."

"Do you think the boys really weren't on the Orphan Train?" Maeve asked.

"That's certainly a good possibility."

"But why would this young man make up a story like that?" Sarah asked.

"I have no idea, but I'm going to ask him the minute I see him. But to give him the benefit of the doubt, the people at the Society told me the boys might've given them a false name."

"Why would they do that?" Sarah asked.

"That's easy—so they couldn't be found," Maeve said impatiently.

Sarah always tried to give people the benefit of the doubt. "But who would be looking for them?" Maeve gave her a pitying look, and Sarah sighed. "I know, I'm hopelessly naïve."

"In spite of everything you've seen in the years since you met Mr. Malloy, too. I'm just glad you have him to look out for you now."

"Maeve, that's the nicest thing you've ever said to me," Malloy said, marveling.

"Don't let it go to your head. So these boys either didn't go on the Orphan Train or else they did but they lied about their names."

"And maybe Will forgot he'd given them a different name," Sarah said, still hoping for the best.

Maeve shook her head. "Either way, this Will Bert is a liar, Mr. Malloy. Maybe you shouldn't try to find his brother at all."

"Oh, I'm going to find him, but don't worry, I won't turn him over to Will unless he wants to go."

Sarah had a quick vision of a small boy all alone in the city. "What will you do with him if you decide not to turn him over?"

"I'm not going to adopt him, so don't even think about it."

Sarah laughed at that. He knew her too well.

As HE ALWAYS DID, FRANK PAUSED A MOMENT TO ADMIRE the gilt letters on the frosted glass of the door to his office, which said, FRANK MALLOY, CONFIDENTIAL INQUIRIES. When he'd started the agency—or more correctly, when he accepted that Maeve and Gino had started it before he and Sarah were even back from their honeymoon—he'd hoped for enough business to keep him from being bored. So far, he'd accomplished his goal, and this case was shaping up to be far from boring.

Gino was already at his desk, his nose stuck in a dime novel with a fictional detective rescuing a lovely young lady pictured in lurid color on the cover.

"What are the Bradys up to this time?" Frank asked, naming the popular detective duo featured in that particular series.

Gino looked up, a bit chagrinned at being caught out. "A lot more exciting things than we are. I think I found the boy, by the way."

"What?"

"Well, not actually found him, but about five weeks ago, he spent a night at the Duane Street Lodging House. Apparently, there was a bad thunderstorm that night, and a lot of boys came inside."

Frank dragged over one of the chairs they'd placed against the wall for waiting clients and straddled it in front of Gino's desk. "You're sure it was him?"

"Pop Rudolph—he's the superintendent—knew who I was describing immediately. We were right, the missing toes are pretty distinctive. The boy has a bit of a limp, so everybody knows about his accident."

"Did this Rudolph know where the boy works?"

"His real name is Rudolph Heig, and no, he says he doesn't even bother to keep track of that stuff, but at least we know the boy is alive and in the city."

"Or he was five weeks ago, anyway."

"One strange thing, though. Pop Rudolph didn't know Freddie had been on the Orphan Trains."

Frank's nerve endings started tingling. "Did Heig think it was strange that he didn't know?"

"Yes, as a matter of fact. All the boys know about the trains because the Children's Aid Society is always trying to recruit them to go out West and get adopted. It's pretty rare for any of the children to come back, though, and Pop thought there would've been a lot of talk about Freddie if he had."

"Did you know the Society operates the lodging houses, too?"

"No! I guess that explains why they use them to recruit orphans for the trains, though. So did you find out anything interesting at the Society?"

"Indeed I did. They keep careful records of all the children they put on the trains, but they don't have any record at all of Will or Freddie Bert."

"Why not?"

Frank shrugged. "I can think of a few reasons. Maybe they used a different name when they went on the trains."

"That's possible. Pop Rudolph told me a lot of the boys use fake names and sometimes they don't even know their real names. In fact, he said he always thought Bert was a fake name."

"The people at the Society said the same thing. The kids try to hide it if they're Jewish or Italian or something. But they searched their records for any brothers that were the same ages, and they didn't find anything to match them."

"Maybe the records got lost or something," Gino said.

"That's possible, but I saw their files. They go back to the fifties. They're very careful, and what are the odds that the only files they've lost in fifty years are the two we're looking for?"

"But what other reason could there be . . . unless they didn't ride the train at all."

"That's what I'm thinking, but why would Will Bert have told us such a wild tale if it didn't really happen?"

Gino didn't need more than a minute to come to the same conclusion Frank had after thinking about it overnight. "He wanted to give us a good reason to find the boy, one that would keep us going even if it got hard. But didn't he realize how easy it would be to find out he was lying?"

"He probably never thought we'd check to see if they really rode the trains. Why would we? He told us the boy is in New York, and Will probably knows he is, so we wouldn't have any reason to look anyplace else. He's not a detective, so he doesn't know how we do things."

Gino sat back in his chair and thought about it for a few more minutes. "I know you'll say I read too many of these." He flicked the book lying on his desk. "But I don't think he wants the boy so he can give him a home out in Michigan."

"Minnesota."

"What?"

"Nothing. I'm afraid you're right. And he couldn't tell us the real reason he wants the boy because, well, it's not a reason we'd sympathize with, I guess. So he made up this sad story about the Orphan Train."

"Which he probably knows a lot about if he really was a newsboy himself. So what are we going to do?"

"We could tell Mr. Bert that we've decided not to take him as a client, of course, but—"

"—but he'd just hire another detective," Gino said in disgust.

"Exactly. So I think we should take Mr. Bert's money and find the boy and then see if the boy knows why Will Bert, or whatever his name is, is looking for him and if he wants to be found."

"And what if he doesn't know why Bert's looking for him?"

"Then we'll ask Mr. Bert some more questions, but we're not going to just turn the boy over to him."

"Good. So what do we do next?"

"I'm assuming you asked this Pop Rudolph to let you know if Freddie showed up at the lodging house again."

"Of course."

"Good. Then I guess the next thing we need to do is walk around the city until we find a bunch of newsboys and ask if any of them has seen Freddie."

Gino winced at the magnitude of such an undertaking. "Where should we start?"

"I'm figuring Newspaper Row. I hear a lot of them are hanging out there and trying to prevent other boys from picking up papers from the *World* and the *Journal*. The Duane Street Lodging House is just a few blocks away, so if Freddie stayed there, his corner was probably in that part of the city, too. A boy doesn't travel any farther than he has to when he's ready for supper and a warm bed."

"And with any luck, the boys will remember him as well as Pop Rudolph did."

"With even more luck, they'll know where we can find him."

"I'M SO GLAD YOU FOUND A HOUSE," SARAH'S MOTHER SAID. Elizabeth Decker had stopped by to visit with the children that morning. Now Maeve had taken them back to the nursery for lunch while Sarah and her mother ate in the dining room.

"I had no idea it would be so difficult to find a suitable place," Sarah said. "I decided to open a maternity clinic almost five months ago. I thought we'd be delivering babies by now."

"What is the house like?"

"It's a disaster at the moment, but it's enormous. It has two parlors, a library, a dining room, a kitchen and butler's pantry, a servants' dining room, five bedrooms, and three servants' rooms in the attic."

"I'm surprised someone isn't renting it out."

"Apparently, they did for a time, after the family who originally built it moved uptown to a better neighborhood, but the owner died, and nobody could locate the next of kin for several years, so the tenants moved out. People have been squatting there, I'm sure, but no one has taken care of it, so it's a mess."

"How long do you think it will take to make it usable?"

"Ordinarily, I'd think it would take a year to make so many repairs, but Malloy and I agree we're going to put Maeve in charge."

"So you'll be up and running in a week or two," her mother said with a grin.

"Well, a few months, anyway," Sarah agreed. "And this time I'm letting her hire the workmen so they know they have to answer to her."

"Have you told her yet?"

"Yes. She's anxious to see the place, but there's no sense in going down there again until we've taken possession."

Her mother sighed dramatically. "I guess it was too much to hope that after your marriage, you'd become a respectable society matron and content yourself with visiting friends and doing good works."

"Delivering babies for poor women is a good work," Sarah pointed out.

"Not to society ladies, I'm afraid. They'd find it entirely too . . . messy," she said.

Sarah couldn't help laughing. "Do you find it *messy*?"

"I try not to think about it at all, but I know it's important.

You do know that once you start delivering babies for unmarried girls that the married women will stop coming."

"That's why I plan to hire some midwives to live in the house. That way they can go to the women's homes if they don't feel comfortable coming to the hospital."

"I suppose you'll want me to help you raise money to support this project."

"Of course, and I'll have to come to your parties to talk about the hospital, so I'll be mingling with all those society ladies after all."

"That's a small step, I suppose."

Sarah decided it was time to change the subject. "What do you know about Orphan Trains?"

"Nothing at all. Does this mean you're adopting another orphan? Perhaps you should wait and see if you and Frank have some children of your own first."

"We aren't planning to adopt any more children, at least not at the moment," Sarah said, choosing to ignore the hopeful expression on her mother's face at the prospect of more grandchildren. "It's part of a new case Malloy is working on."

She told her mother what she knew about the two brothers. "Oh my, that does sound suspicious. And I had no idea that all those boys selling newspapers were orphans."

"Not all of them, but far too many are. There must be hundreds of children in the city with no homes or family."

"You can't save everyone, Sarah, and it sounds like the Children's Aid Society is doing a good job of finding homes for these children."

"For some of them, yes, but how do they know what happens to the children after they're left? I'm sure many of them find loving homes, but certainly not all. And if a child were beaten or starved or abused in any way, who would know? And how frightening it must be for them to be taken hundreds of miles away from the only life they've ever known. I can't even imagine."

"Then don't imagine it, Sarah. Leave it to those whose calling it is and worry about your own affairs. You've set yourself a formidable task with the maternity hospital. I should think that is quite enough for one lifetime."

Sarah was sure that it was, but she couldn't help thinking about poor Freddie Bert with his maimed foot and no home. Was Will really his brother? Did he really want to give the boy a home? At least Malloy would make sure the boy wasn't forced to do anything he didn't want to do.

But if the boy didn't go with his brother, what would become of him?

F RANK HADN'T REALIZED HOW DIFFICULT IT WOULD BE to find newsboys if they weren't selling newspapers. Where did they all go? He'd seen boys sleeping in stairways and alleys and under bridges, but he'd never paid much attention. A large city, he now realized, provided millions of hidey-holes where a boy could escape notice.

Even when he did find a boy or a group of boys, his plan to ask if they knew Freddie Bert had also failed miserably. The first boy had gladly taken the offered nickel in exchange for information and then darted away without completing his end of the bargain. The next time Frank tried telling a group of boys that Freddie had inherited some money, which led every one of them to claim to be Freddie. None of them could show a mangled foot, however, and they'd run off laughing, leaving Frank feeling like Cinderella's prince must have felt at the beginning of his quest with the glass slipper. He was starting to agree with Maeve about fairy tales.

He and Gino spent the entire morning "under the bridge,"

searching the neighborhoods in the shadow of the imposing Brooklyn Bridge, which included Park Row—commonly known as Newspaper Row—where the major papers had their offices. Frank and Gino had arranged to meet at noon at the foot of the bridge to compare notes and grab a bite to eat from a street vendor. They were also glad to find a shady spot in the shadow of the bridge where they could escape the summer heat.

Gino hadn't had much better luck than Frank, but he'd learned one important thing. "There's a meeting here at the bridge in about an hour. I heard one of the boys telling some others. Kid Blink is giving a speech."

"Who's Kid Blink?"

"From what they said, he must be one of the leaders of the strike, which probably means there'll be a big crowd."

"How will that help us if none of the boys will talk to us?"

Gino shrugged. "We might see a kid with a limp, for one thing. And if not, maybe we can get one of the leaders to help us. They'll probably be older and more reasonable, at least."

Frank wasn't so confident, but it seemed like a good idea to watch the gathering crowd to see if they could at least spot a boy with a limp.

The boys began to gather well before the appointed time. They stood around smoking cigarettes and antagonizing each other the way boys do. Frank found it disconcerting to see boys so young smoking, but with no parents to care, the boys were bound to pick up all sorts of bad habits. Before long, they proved his theory by breaking into small groups to play craps. This was truly living dangerously, since shooting craps in public was a crime that could get them arrested, but only if the police caught you, of course. With no police in sight, the boys weren't too worried.

Frank and Gino had split up to watch the assembly from

different vantage points, and Frank had bought one of the newspapers still being sold from a nervous boy who scurried away when he saw the other boys gathering. He was right to be skittish. Reports of newsboy violence covered the front page of this rag. Boys were overturning news stalls where vendors were still selling the *World* and the *Journal*, and beating up boys who dared hawk the offending papers on the streets.

While pretending to read his newspaper, Frank watched the boys streaming in from all directions. Although he saw one boy hobbling on a crutch, he saw none limping, not even a bit. At last the crowd started to stir as if from some silent signal, and a half-dozen older boys marched up in a cluster. The crowd parted for them and then closed and followed, crap games and cigarettes forgotten as they gathered around. The tallest boy wore a patch over one eye, and he hopped up on an overturned crate. Kid Blink, Frank thought.

"You know me, boys!" the Kid shouted.

"You bet we do!" the boys called happily.

"Well, I'm here to say if we are goin' to win this strike we must stick like glue and never give in. Am I right?"

"Yes!" a hundred voices replied.

"Ain't that ten cents worth as much to us as it is to Hearst and Pulitzer, who are millionaires? Well, I guess it is. If they can't spare it, how can we?"

"Soak 'em, Blink," yelled one of the boys.

"Soak nothin'," the Kid said. "I'm tellin' the truth. I'm tryin' to figure out how ten cents on a hundred papers can mean more to a millionaire than it does to a newsboy, and I can't see it. Now, boys, I'm goin' to say like the rest: No more violence. Let up on the drivers. No more rackets like that one the other night where a *Journal* and a *World* wagon was turned over in Madison Street. Say, to tell the truth, I was there myself."

"You bet you was, Blink, an' a-leadin', too," another shouted to much laughter.

"Well, never mind. We're going to let up on the scabs now and win the strike on the square. Kid Blink's a-talkin' to you now. Do you know him? We won in 1893 and we'll win in 1899, but stick together like plaster."

The boys cheered, and the Kid went on, cautioning them against violence and encouraging them not to give up. Frank couldn't imagine Pulitzer and Hearst giving in to a bunch of powerless children, but the strike was already five days old, and virtually no copies of the two newspapers were being sold. He'd heard the strike had spread to Brooklyn and Staten Island. How long until the moguls began to feel the pinch?

A few more boys got up and spoke, each one stirring the boys to even greater excitement, until Kid Blink took to the crate again and finished up. "Now, you all know me, boys, don't you?"

"We do! We do!" they shouted.

"Well, we'll all go out tomorrow and stick together, and we'll win in a walk."

After the cheers finally died away, most of the boys ran off, eager to do whatever was left to them, since Kid Blink had requested no more violence. Soon the leaders were left with just a small group of hero worshippers anxious to bask in their reflected glory. Gino approached the group, waiting until it had dwindled down as much as it was going to. Frank waited in his spot, still pretending to read his newspaper.

"Great speech, Kid," Gino said.

The Kid looked him over. "And who are you?"

"He's a copper," one of the boys said.

"No, I'm not," Gino said, his smile never wavering.

"A reporter then," the Kid said with approval. "You want a story? I'll give you a story."

"Not a reporter either. Private investigator." He handed the Kid his card.

"Told you he was a copper," the first boy said.

"I don't want to cause you any trouble," Gino hastily explained. "I think what you're doing is great. I was a newsie myself, and I know how hard it is. Those millionaires have a nerve trying to squeeze you boys."

"You're right about that," the Kid said. "So if you're not a copper and you're not a reporter, what do you want with us?"

"I'm looking for a newsie. His family is trying to find him. His brother has made good, and he wants to give the boy a home. The problem is, the brother doesn't know where to find him, so he hired me."

"And you don't know where to find him either," the Kid said, and the other boys laughed appreciatively.

Gino grinned, happy to be laughed at if it got him the information he needed, Frank knew. "But I'm hoping you do, or at least that you'll help by spreading the word."

"So who is it you're looking for?" the Kid asked.

"Freddie Bert. He goes by Two Toes."

The boys exchanged glances.

"Walks with a limp?" one of them said.

"That's right. Do you know him?"

"I've seen him," the boy said.

"Me, too," another admitted.

"Any idea where I could find him?"

Some head shaking and shrugs.

"Well, if you do, there's a fiver in it for you." That was as much as boy could make in ten days selling papers. Gino gave one of his cards to each of them who would take it. "Good luck with the strike. I'd sure like to see Hearst and Pulitzer taken down a notch."

He shook hands with Kid Blink and walked away, but

slowly, so the group of leaders was gone before he was. The rest of the boys drifted off, too, but one drifted much more slowly than the rest, and when he was the last one left, he drifted over to where Gino had stopped, waiting.

Frank put down his newspaper and strolled over.

"Hey, mister," the boy called to Gino.

"What is it, son?" Gino asked, giving the boy his friendliest grin.

"Why are you looking for Two Toes?"

"His brother came into some money, and he wants to give Freddie a home," Gino repeated.

"No, I mean the real reason."

The boy was small, but Frank judged he was older than he looked. His hair was blue-black, shining in the bright sunlight, and his sun-browned face was handsome. Gino stared straight into the boy's big, brown eyes.

"That is the real reason."

The boy frowned impatiently. "I ain't no rube, mister, and Two Toes ain't got no brother that I ever heard about."

"Maybe he has one you didn't hear about," Gino suggested. "You could ask him when you see him."

"I could do that."

"What's your name, son?" Frank asked, earning a suspicious frown.

"Who're you?"

"That's my boss," Gino said. "We're both trying to find Freddie."

"And if you find him, what're you going to do?"

"Ask him if he's got a brother, I guess," Gino said. "If he does, ask him if he wants to see him. After that, it's up to him."

"I'm Raven," the boy said, satisfied enough to give his name. "That's what they call me, Raven. Because my hair's black."

"Of course," Frank agreed.

"You have another name?" Gino asked.

"Saggio. Raven Saggio. That's the only part of my real name I remember."

"Well, Raven, I would be happy to pay you the fiver if you help us find Freddie Bert," Gino said.

"I'll have to ask him."

"Sure," Gino said. "I understand."

"Would you like to bring him to our office or can we meet you someplace?" Frank asked.

Raven frowned. "I don't expect Two Toes would go to some office."

"Then tell us where to meet you and when."

Raven considered the matter for a moment, scrunching up his handsome face in a way that Frank knew Sarah would think was adorable. Better not ever let her see Raven.

"How about I meet you outside of the Devil's Den Saloon. You know it?"

"Uh, no," Gino admitted with a grin.

"It's on Chrystie Street between Broome and Grand."

"We'll find it," Frank said. "This time tomorrow?"

"Fine with me. If Two Toes don't want to come, though, I can't help it."

With that, he was gone, clutching Gino's card in his grubby hand.

"Should I follow him?" Gino asked.

"Good luck with that. Do you think you could keep track of him for twenty-four hours?"

Gino chuckled at the thought, then his smile died. "That saloon is in the Bowery, isn't it?"

"Yes, but at least we'll be there in broad daylight. Don't wear your good suit, though. That's just asking to get robbed." They started back toward City Hall and the nearest elevated train station. "Let's get off the El at the Bowery station and take a look at this place before we go back to the office."

Gino pulled a face. "Why?"

"Because I'm thinking there's a reason Raven chose it. Maybe that's where Freddie has a spot where he sleeps when he's not at the lodging house."

"Carrying the banner."

"Right, carrying the banner. Maybe we can figure it out and find Freddie without Raven's help."

"To save five dollars?"

"No," Frank said with a grin. "To make sure Raven doesn't warn Freddie off."

3

THE DEVIL'S DEN SALOON WAS FAIRLY QUIET IN THE middle of a hot summer afternoon. Even the usual Bowery bums had disappeared from their spots along the sidewalk, probably in a quest for shade somewhere. Lined with the usual dives and seedy brothels, the street offered nothing that looked like an inviting spot for a newsboy to hole up, though.

"Would it even be safe for a boy to sleep anywhere in this part of town?" Gino asked. "Seems like the drunks would rob him every night."

"You're right. He'd have to have protection of some kind. Maybe he runs errands for one of the madams and she lets him sleep on her porch or something." Frank let his gaze wander up and down the street again, looking for some likely shelter.

"A kindhearted madam?" Gino scoffed.

"I know, it's far-fetched, but there must be some reason Raven chose this spot to meet us." Frank's gaze returned to the saloon. It was the sturdiest-looking building on the block. No broken windows, no peeling paint. The front door stood open in the heat, and suddenly the opening filled with a very large man in plaid pants and shirtsleeves, lazily fingering his red suspenders. He had a head like a bucket and his eyes were as cold as marbles.

"Can I help you gents?"

"Yes," Frank said, figuring the man was the saloon's bouncer and that he'd take Frank for a cop. People always did. "We're looking for the newsie who lives here. His name is Freddie Bert, but the boys call him Two Toes."

The bouncer took a long minute to size them up again before he said, "Ain't seen him for a while."

Ah, so they were in the right place, although Frank figured the bouncer was lying about not having seen him. He'd protect the boy from the police from pure instinct if for no other reason. "He's not in trouble," Frank said. "His brother is looking for him."

"Says you. Black Jack looks out for him."

"Black Jack Robinson?" Gino asked in surprise.

The bouncer gave him a pitying look and spat on the sidewalk. "He owns the Den and most of the buildings on this block. You want the boy, you'll have to ask Black Jack."

"I don't suppose he's in," Frank said, faking a bravado he didn't feel. Black Jack was notorious.

"Come back tonight," the bouncer said with a grin that revealed a gold front tooth. "If you're slumming."

"Do the swells come here to slum?" Gino asked doubtfully.

"Willy Arburn brings 'em. You can find him at the boardinghouse on Sixth Street and Second Avenue."

"He's a guide?" Gino asked.

"Yeah," the bouncer said with a knowing grin. "You don't wanna visit the Bowery at night without one."

"Thanks for the tip," Frank said, figuring they'd learned all they could for now. "Come on, Gino."

They walked back to the train station in silence and climbed the stairs up to the platform. The tracks ran beside the first-story windows of the buildings along Bowery. Not many people were waiting for the train at this time of day, and Frank led Gino as far from them as he could. "What was all that about slumming and a guide?"

"It's a new thing the swells are doing. People with money and no brains, I guess. They hire a guide to take them on a tour of the Bowery and the Tenderloin and other parts of the city where decent people don't go."

"That doesn't sound like a good idea. I can't imagine the customers in those places like to be gawked at by people from Park Avenue."

"They don't, but the guides don't take them to real places. It's all fake."

Frank considered this amazing information for a long moment. He hadn't thought anything that happened in the city could surprise him anymore. "I wonder if Black Jack has that whole block set up for the tours," Frank said.

"Could be. I can't imagine he'd make enough money from it, though."

"Oh, the swells wouldn't just look. They'd be customers, too."

"I guess you're right. They could impress their friends with tales of drinking and gambling and visiting a brothel in the Bowery."

"And they'd have more money to spend than the locals. Still, I can't imagine that many rich boys want to visit dives."

Gino grinned. "Maybe you're wrong about that."

"Maybe I am. And Black Jack owns more places than this,

I know. At least we found out we're in the right neighborhood to find Freddie, though."

"Did you notice the windows on the second floor of the saloon?" Gino asked.

"Yeah. Lace curtains over a saloon doesn't make much sense."

"Unless somebody lives there," Gino said. "Somebody with a wife."

"Or a lady friend. Black Jack's got quite a reputation when it comes to the ladies."

"And when he wasn't using the flat, a newsie might watch it for him."

Frank smiled. "Let's ask Freddie all about it when we find him tomorrow."

THE NEXT AFTERNOON, FRANK AND GINO CHOSE TO WAIT for Raven on the corner, so as to escape the notice of the bouncer at the Devil's Den. A few bums approached them for a handout, but in general, Frank's practiced glare kept them away.

They spotted the boy trudging down Chrystie Street, shoulders hunched, his dark head swiveling this way and that, obviously looking for them. They waited until he stopped in front of the saloon before they stepped out, but before they had gone more than a few paces to meet him, the bouncer emerged from the saloon and spoke to the boy.

Frank and Gino stopped dead, waiting to see how the boy reacted. He hadn't spotted them yet, and if he felt threatened, he might run. But he merely looked up and replied to whatever the bouncer had said. The bouncer nodded and retreated back into the saloon, leaving Raven alone on the sidewalk. This time when he turned his head, he saw them.

Gino waved, and the boy came running.

"I was afraid you wasn't gonna show."

"Did you find Freddie?" Gino asked.

"Yeah, but . . ."

"But what?" Frank asked.

"He's a little nervous. He don't know why you're trying to find him."

"Did you tell him what we said about his brother?"

Raven glared up at them indignantly. "Yeah, but he don't have no rich brother what would hire no detective to find him."

Frank and Gino exchanged a glance. "Did he agree to see us anyway?" Frank asked.

"I told him he better because I could really use five dollars, and he said he'd do it if I split it with him."

Frank grinned at that. "If you take us to see him, you'll both get a fiver."

Raven's dark eyes gleamed. "We will?"

"You sure will," Gino confirmed.

"All right, I'll take you to him, but he don't want nobody to know where he's staying."

"Doesn't he usually stay at the Den?" Frank asked.

"How'd you know that?" Raven asked in alarm.

"Everybody knows that," Frank lied.

That placated him a bit. "He ain't staying there now, though. Something happened."

"What?" Gino asked.

"He wouldn't say, but he can't stay there right now."

"Then where is he?"

"I'll take you to him, if you still want to see him."

"Oh, we do," Frank said, holding out his hand in invitation.

Raven nodded and took off up Chrystie Street with Frank and Gino in his wake. Frank glanced back to see the bouncer watching them from the saloon doorway.

The boy led them down side streets and stinking back alleys for about ten minutes until they came to a ramshackle structure leaning precariously against the back of a rear tenement building. Rear tenements were the worst housing in the city, constructed behind the ordinary tenements on any strip of vacant land available. They got neither sunlight nor air, even on the best of days, but the poorest of the poor had no other choice if they wanted a roof over their heads. Orphaned newsboys were even poorer than the poorest, however, so they constructed their own dwellings out of scraps of wood and tin and whatever else they could scavenge in a city where people regularly picked through the garbage in hopes of finding something of worth.

They were expected, and a boy had already emerged from the hovel, pushing aside a filthy, ragged piece of fabric that served as the door.

He looked them up and down the way the bouncer had, although his glare wasn't nearly as fearsome. He stood almost five feet tall, rail thin with a smattering of freckles across his nose and sandy hair falling into his eyes. His pants reached only to mid-calf above his bare feet, evidence of a recent growth spurt. He looked to be the right age, at least, and there could be no question about his mangled foot. A good portion of it was missing, along with three of the toes. "Are you the private detectives?" he asked.

"That's right. I'm Frank Malloy, and this is Gino Donatelli." Frank handed the boy one of his cards. He purposely chose one of the engraved ones to impress him as much as possible.

"Why're you looking for me?"

"Like we told Raven," Frank said. "Your older brother Will is looking for you."

Something flickered across the boy's face, but too quickly for Frank to read the emotion. "Will?"

"That's right. He told us how you two went out West on the Orphan Train and got separated. He wants you to know that he got placed with a storekeeper who died and left him the store. He's well-off now, and he wants you to come live with him out in Minnesota."

"To come and live with him?" the boy echoed doubtfully. Frank tried to judge the boy's reaction to the story—was it the truth or the outlandish tale they suspected? But the boy gave nothing away.

"That's right," Frank said. "He didn't know you'd come back to New York until he went looking for you, so he hired us to find you."

"Did he hire you himself?"

"Yes. He came to the city to look for you, but then he realized he'd never be able to find you without help."

"You said you'd give us each a fiver if I found him for you," Raven reminded them impatiently.

Freddie shot him a black look, but instantly returned his gaze to Frank and Gino. "Will, huh? I thought it was about the girl."

"What girl?" Frank asked.

"Nothing. Did you tell him where I am?"

"No, because we didn't know until just now," Frank said.

"But you're going to tell him, ain't you?"

"Not if you don't want us to."

"But he's paying you, so you'll tell him," Freddie said reasonably.

"Look, Freddie—"

"It's Two Toes."

"Two Toes," Frank said agreeably. "If there's some reason you don't want this Will to find you, just tell us. We won't tell him anything at all."

"And if you're in some kind of trouble," Gino said, "we can help."

"I ain't in no trouble, and I don't need any help," Freddie said.

"What about this Will fellow?" Frank insisted. "Raven said he didn't think you had a brother."

Freddie sent Raven another black look. "He don't know nothing about me."

"Then is Will your brother or not?" Gino asked, and Frank winced. Gino hadn't yet learned the importance of patience.

Because that wasn't the important question. The important question was whether Freddie wanted to see Will, brother or not.

Freddie glared up at them both. "That ain't any of your business."

Before Frank could even think of a reply, Freddie was gone, darting away into the dark alleys that had no name. Gino started after him, but returned almost instantly. "He crawled through a hole in the fence, and there was no way I could get through."

"You said you'd give me a fiver," Raven reminded him petulantly.

Frank dug a greenback out of his pocket and handed it to the boy. "Any idea where he went?"

Raven shrugged and shook his head, and then he was gone, too, off in another direction. Gino made no attempt to chase him.

"Now I'm more confused than ever," Gino said. "Is Will his brother or not?"

"I don't know, but whether he is or isn't, I don't think Freddie wants to see him."

"Two Toes," Gino corrected him.

"Right, Two Toes. A hard-earned nickname, to be sure."

"Poor kid, although it doesn't seem to slow him down much."

Frank sighed and headed back the way they'd come, hoping they didn't get lost.

Gino followed. "What do we do now?"

"Will is supposed to pay us a visit this afternoon, isn't he?"

"That's what he said, although now that I think about it, why couldn't he just give us the name of his hotel or something so we could contact him when we had news?"

"He said he didn't want to waste more money on a hotel and was going to try to find a rooming house, so he'd just come to us. It sounded true at the time, but now I'm wondering if he just didn't want us to have a way to find him."

"Nothing about this case is adding up. Seems like the more we learn, the less we know."

"They're all like that, Gino. You just never noticed it before."

WILL BERT ARRIVED AS SCHEDULED AT FOUR O'CLOCK that afternoon. He greeted Frank with an expectant smile when Gino escorted him into Frank's office. "Have you found him yet?"

"Have a seat, Mr. Bert."

Bert's smile flickered a bit, but he sat down and waited expectantly.

"I've asked my partner to sit in. He's been assisting me with the case," Frank explained as Gino took a seat in the corner of the office. He'd be making notes, sitting out of Bert's line of sight so hopefully, Bert would forget he was there.

"So you haven't found the boy?" Bert asked, obviously puzzled.

"We found him."

Bert perked up considerably at this. "Where is he, then? Is he here?" He looked around as if expecting Frank to produce him out of thin air.

"I said we found him. And we talked to him. The thing

is, he didn't seem nearly as interested in seeing you as you are to see him."

"What do you mean?"

"I mean I told him about your good fortune and how you wanted to give him a home."

Bert's smile was completely gone now. He almost looked wary. "And what did he say?"

"Not much. He didn't act very happy to get news of you, and when we mentioned you, he ran away."

Bert scratched his head and frowned as he considered this information. "I should've known he'd be mad. He blamed me, you see. He blamed me for us being separated, that is. Maybe he blames me because he got sent back, too. He'd know I wasn't sent back, I guess. I thought he'd be happy I was looking for him, but he probably doesn't like the idea of going to Minnesota again."

Frank leaned back and studied Bert for a long moment. "Did you know the Children's Aid Society doesn't have any record that you and your brother went out on the Orphan Train?"

Bert didn't look particularly concerned. "They don't?"

"No, and they keep pretty careful records of all the children."

"That's strange. How'd you happen to find that out?"

"I checked with them to see if Freddie had been sent out again after he came back from Minnesota. There's no use looking for him here if he's in Texas or someplace."

"I didn't think of that. I guess that's why I'm not a detective." Bert smiled his winning smile. Frank figured it had gotten him out of trouble a time or two, but it wasn't working today.

"In fact," Frank said, "Freddie's friend said he didn't even know Freddie had a brother."

Bert was instantly wary again. "What friend was that?"

"A newsie. We've been asking around, and this boy knew Freddie."

"And he's the one who told you where he was?"

"That's right. We also found out Freddie's been living in Black Jack Robinson's saloon in the Bowery."

"Who's that?" Bert asked, but Frank had seen the momentary shock of recognition at the name.

"He's one of the biggest gangsters in the city."

Bert feigned amazement, and not very well. "That's terrible! I need to get Freddie away from here as soon as possible. Can you tell me where you saw him? I'll go down there myself. I know he's mad at me, but I'm sure I can make it up to him if I can talk to him for a minute or two. Just tell me where he is."

"That's just it," Frank said. "The place where he met us was down some alley. His friend set it up, but that's not where you'll find him. After we scared him, he'll probably never go back there again."

It was an exaggeration, of course. Frank was pretty sure Freddie was living in that shack with Raven, or at least he had been.

"Maybe I can find this friend, then. I can convince him I only want to help Freddie. What's his name?"

But Frank had no intention of getting poor little Raven mixed up in all this. "I don't know. The boys never call each other by their real names. And you don't have to worry about this anyway. You hired us to help, and we're not finished yet. Give us a few more days, and we'll see if we can't change Freddie's mind."

"I thought you said he ran away," Bert said doubtfully.

"He did, but you know how boys are. We know he's around, and we know he's connected with Black Jack Robinson, and—"

"Don't get him involved!"

Now, that was an interesting response from someone who claimed to never have heard of Robinson. "Why not?"

Bert made a visible effort to collect himself. "You said he's a gangster. He might do something to Freddie."

"I got the idea Freddie is his pet or something."

"Oh well, but that can't be safe. For you, I mean. To go bothering a big gangster."

"Don't worry about us. Let us take care of this for you, Mr. Bert."

Bert nodded miserably. He'd apparently thought Frank would tell him how to find Freddie and then be finished. This did not seem to be what he'd planned at all. "Just let me know when you've got him."

"And how will I do that? You haven't told me where you're staying."

"Oh yeah, well, I'm still trying to find a place. How about if I check back with you tomorrow at this time?"

When Gino had shown Bert out, he returned to Frank's office. "That was strange."

"Yes, it was. It seems like he really doesn't want us to keep trying to find the boy."

"But he kept trying to get information out of you so he could find him himself. Maybe he really thinks the boy will be more willing to go with him than with us."

"Or maybe he knows the boy will never go with us if we're taking him to Will."

Gino nodded. "I think he knew perfectly well who Black Jack Robinson was, too."

"You couldn't see his face. He definitely does."

"But why would he pretend he didn't?"

"Because he's supposedly been living in Minnesota for

years. I've got a very bad feeling about this. Freddie's in some kind of trouble, and he knows it, so that's why he's hiding."

"And this Will fellow is part of it, so Freddie is hiding from him."

"He might be hiding from more than one person, too. Remember Raven said something happened?"

"That's right. And Freddie mentioned a girl. Do you think that's part of this?"

"Maybe, but it could just as easily be something else. We won't know for sure until we talk to Freddie again. We just have to make sure we find him before this Will fellow does."

"Do you think we should take one of the Bowery tours?" Gino asked.

Frank shook his head. "I don't know how that would help, and don't get any ideas. There's nothing down there you need to know any more about."

Gino shrugged innocently. "It was just a thought."

"Well, stop thinking. We'll give Freddie the night to think things over, and then we'll go looking for him again tomorrow. At least we know where to start now."

"With Black Jack Robinson?" Gino teased.

"Maybe. If we have to. But I'm thinking Raven will be helpful."

"I hope so," Gino said. "I didn't like the way that bouncer looked at us."

"WE HAVEN'T SEEN MUCH OF GINO LATELY," SARAH remarked at breakfast the next morning. Maeve had taken Catherine and Brian upstairs after their own breakfast, and Frank's mother had eaten much earlier and retired to her own rooms.

Malloy didn't take the hint. In fact, he didn't even look up from the newspaper he was reading. "I see Gino every day."

"Yes, but we don't." She waited again for him to look up. He didn't bother. "You mean Maeve doesn't."

She snatched the newspaper away from him and tried to look angry. Apparently, she fell a little short because he just laughed. "Do you really think those two need a matchmaker?"

"Of course not. All they need is a little time together."

"All right. I'll invite him for dinner tonight. Will that do?"

"For a start."

"Can I have my newspaper back, please?"

She glanced at it. "What's this?"

"It's the *Times*. I know, it's not up to my usual standards, but it was the only one Hattie could find this morning."

"You sent Hattie out to find you a newspaper?" Their maid was entirely too accommodating.

"She offered because she knows how much I enjoy reading it in the morning. The boys from the *World* and the *Journal* usually come to the door, but they're on strike, remember."

The newsboys came to their door because they knew Malloy tipped well. She handed back the newspaper. "I think it's very brave of the boys to strike."

"Brave or foolish. I just hope they don't regret it."

"I know. I can't see either Pulitzer or Hearst backing down. If they give in to a bunch of children, no one will ever fear them again."

"According to the *Times*, the strike is spreading, though. The newsboys in other cities won't sell the papers either."

"Really? I had no idea. How did they even hear about it?"

"Who knows? They probably read it in the newspaper."

The telephone shrilled its jarring alert, startling them both.

"I don't think I'll ever get used to that," Sarah said.

"It's early for a telephone call," Malloy remarked, rising to answer it.

Sarah could easily hear him out in the hallway, shouting into the mouthpiece of the candlestick phone.

"What . . . ? Are they sure . . . ? Yes, of course . . . No, I'll go myself. You stay in the office in case someone comes . . . Yes, I'll telephone you."

Sarah laid her napkin on the table and walked out into the hallway where the telephone resided on a small table. "What is it?"

Malloy rubbed a hand over his face. His eyes were bleak. "It's that boy we've been looking for. He's dead."

FRANK TOOK A CAB TO BELLEVUE HOSPITAL, WHERE THE city morgue was located. For some reason, he didn't feel strong enough to make the walk across town, even in the cool morning hours. News of Freddie's death had really taken the starch out of him.

He found the coroner, Doc Haynes, in his office.

"Malloy, I'm sorry to call you out like this, but the boy had your card in his pocket."

"How did he die?"

"Strangled. Some drunk stumbled over him in an alley in the Bowery in the middle of the night last night. When I saw the card this morning, I called your office to see if you could identify him."

"I guess you told Gino the boy had a maimed foot."

"I did. Poor little fellow. Still, I'd like you to identify him officially, if you don't mind."

"I expected as much."

"How did you know him?"

"I was hired to find him, by his brother."

"Then he does have a family, at least."

"I'm not sure about that. The man claimed to be his brother, but I now have good reason to doubt it."

"Could he be the one who killed the boy, do you think?"

Frank's shock was wearing off and suddenly, he was furious. "I don't know, but I'm going to find out. I promise you that."

Doc Haynes nodded and sent Frank down to the basement where the bodies were kept.

The room was dark and dank, lit by feeble electric lights and cooled by the water they kept dripping over the bodies to slow decay until they could be identified. The attendant took him to one of the slabs, where Freddie's body lay. Stripped naked and bloodless in death, he looked much smaller than he had in life. Like most boys who lived on the streets, he hadn't enjoyed regular meals or even real meals, unless he was eating at the lodging house. His ribs stood out on his narrow chest, and his limbs looked like twigs.

"Wonder what happened to his foot," the attendant remarked. He was a big fellow who walked with a stoop. His face was creased in a perpetual frown.

"Trolley car."

"Oh, that makes sense. Is the boy who you thought he was?"

"Yes. Freddie Bert, or at least that's the name I knew him by. He also went by Two Toes."

The attendant nodded, confirming the logic of the nickname. "I don't suppose you know that one," he added, jerking his thumb in the direction of a female body lying on the next slab. She was young and had been lovely once. In spite of the dripping water, her body was mottled with the beginnings of decay. Soon even her own family would not recognize her.

"No, why would I?"

"She was found in the Bowery, too, not far from your boy here, and strangled just the same."

"A prostitute then," Frank said, thinking she looked much too young and pretty for that neighborhood. The Bowery was a girl's last stop, when she was too old and diseased to work anywhere else.

"No, her clothes are too good. She's from quality, which makes it strange nobody's come looking for her."

"Somebody's mistress, then, and he dumped her in a place where nobody asks questions."

"You're probably right," the attendant said. "Just seems a shame, that's all."

Frank made his way back upstairs to give Doc Haynes the boy's name and tell him what he knew. "I'll inform my client, and if he's the one who killed the boy, I'll make sure he gets arrested for it."

"Good. Did you see our young lady down there?"

"I did. Harvey said they found her in the Bowery."

"Yes, early Sunday morning, but she didn't belong there. Her clothes were too good and her teeth, too. She had a good life up until now."

"And she was strangled, like my boy, but that's a pretty common way to kill someone."

"It is, unfortunately. No weapon or preplanning required. Somebody took some time with her afterward, though. She was stuffed into a trunk and carried down a back alley. She might've been there for days in another neighborhood, but some street arabs saw the trunk and thought what a good place it would be to live. It was too heavy to carry, so they opened it up to empty it and found her. She hadn't been there more than a few hours, which is lucky. In this heat, she wouldn't have been recognizable after a day."

"And yet nobody has come looking for her."

Doc shrugged. "Maybe the only one who would miss her is the one who killed her."

"Was she raped?"

"There wasn't any sign of it, or of violence at all except her neck and some broken fingernails, which probably happened when she was killed. Oh, and she's with child. I'd say about three months gone."

"Which might be why she was murdered. You should put her picture in the newspapers. Someone will recognize her."

"The Wrecking Crew was here and did a sketch of her Monday, but I haven't seen a story about her." The Wrecking Crew was the portion of the *Journal*'s staff dedicated to tracking down sensational stories. It included a photographer and a sketch artist.

"Probably because you haven't seen a copy of the *Journal* this week," Frank said. "The newsies are on strike, remember?"

"Which means her family didn't see it either, I guess."

"Or anybody else who might've recognized her."

"That's too bad. Maybe while you're nosing around down there, you'll hear something about her, too."

"If I do," Frank promised, "I'll let you know. Meanwhile, I've got to find out who killed this boy. Oh, and I'll take care of his funeral."

"I thought you said he was a newsie."

"He was."

"They'll probably take care of him themselves, then."

"What are you talking about?"

"The newsies, the ones without families at least, when one of them dies, they all contribute to pay for the funeral. They're like a family. They look out for each other."

But many of the boys were on strike and not earning any

money. "I'll put the word out to them, but if there's any shortfall, I'll take care of it."

Doc nodded. "That's nice of you, but maybe the brother will pitch in."

"If he really is the brother. All I know is the boy was just fine until I started looking for him, and now he's dead. If something I did caused it, I'm going to do everything I can to make up for it."

4

"YOU'VE GOTTA CALM DOWN, MR. MALLOY," GINO SAID.

He was right, of course, but Frank couldn't seem to even sit still for a minute. The more he'd thought about that boy lying on a slab in the morgue, the madder he got. Fury boiled inside him, and he was more than ready to take it out on Will Bert or whatever his real name was. If Bert had anything to do with Freddie's death, Frank was afraid he'd take matters into his own hands. The law, he knew, could be a fickle thing and didn't always punish the guilty.

At least not the way Frank wanted to see them punished.

Frank paced all the way around his office once more and then tried sitting down in his chair again.

"If he sees you're this mad," Gino warned, "he's going to hightail it out of here before we can even ask him a question."

"I'll be fine, Gino. Don't worry. I just need to get some

of this out of my system or I'll punch him right in the face the minute he walks in the door."

Gino grinned at that. "He probably deserves it, too, if not for this then for something else."

"You're probably right. I'll keep that in mind."

Frank found he still couldn't sit still, but after he'd taken only a few more turns around his office, the outer door opened, and Will Bert tentatively stuck his head in, as if unsure of his welcome.

"Mr. Bert," Gino said, hurrying to greet him. "I'm so glad you could make it. Come in, please. Mr. Malloy is waiting for you."

Bert grinned stiffly. "Good news, I hope."

Neither man answered him, but Gino ushered him rather forcefully into Frank's office and into a chair, closing the door to Frank's office on his way.

Bert looked up in alarm at the sound of the door clicking shut, but Frank distracted him with a friendly greeting.

"So you've found Freddie again?" Bert asked. His grin was wobbling now, as if unsure of its position on his face.

"We have," Frank said, sitting down behind his desk.

He seemed surprised at this, but Frank couldn't judge exactly why. Was he genuinely surprised they'd found him again so quickly or did he already know the boy was dead? "Where is he then?"

Frank waited, watching him glance uneasily at Gino, who stood with his back to the closed door, blocking any possible exit. Finally, he said, "You can claim his body at the morgue at Bellevue Hospital."

Bert blinked a few times and his grin slid completely off his face. "Morgue? What do you mean?"

Frank was now sure Will wasn't really Freddie's brother,

so he felt no obligation to be kind. "I mean the boy is dead. Someone murdered him last night."

Bert glanced at Gino again, then back to Frank. "You don't think I had anything to do with that, do you?"

"Could you have killed your beloved younger brother?" Frank mused. "What do you think, Gino?"

"I think the boy isn't his beloved younger brother, for one thing."

"What? That's ridiculous. Of course he's my brother." Bert had started to sweat. The room was hot but not that hot.

"And I think," Frank said, "that neither one of you ever went anywhere on the Orphan Train."

Bert squirmed in his chair. "But why would I say that if it wasn't true?"

"To get our sympathy. It worked, too. I guess you didn't know how easy it would be to check, though."

Bert stared at Frank for a long moment as the sweat thickened on his brow. Finally, he said, "All right then, we didn't go on the Orphan Train. You're right, I made that part up, but I figured if I told you I just lost track of my brother, you might not help me."

"And now I've told you that your brother is dead, but you don't seem real sad about it."

"I'm sad! But how do I even know you're telling me the truth?"

"Why would I lie about that? It's easy enough to check."

Bert perked up at that. "You're right. I'll go check." He jumped to his feet, but Gino stepped over and pushed him back down into his seat.

"Not so fast, Mr. Bert or whatever your name is. We have a few questions for you first," Gino said.

"What kind of questions?" He glanced uneasily up at Gino.

"Oh, like what *is* your name, for one?"

"I told you—"

"And I told you, I don't believe you. Now what's your name?"

He looked up at Gino again. "Arburn."

"Willy Arburn?" Frank asked, remembering his conversation with the bouncer at the Devil's Den.

"Yeah," he admitted warily. "They call me that."

"You're a guide," Gino said. "You take people slumming in the Bowery."

"So what if I do? It's legal."

"I'm sure it is," Frank said. "So what's your story now? You've made your fortune taking swells slumming and now you want to find your brother and give him a good home?"

"Look, this wasn't my idea. None of it was my idea."

"Are you saying you're not even the one who wants to find Freddie?"

"I . . . I'm helping a friend."

"Maybe you'd tell us that friend's name."

"And maybe I won't."

"Then we'll have to take you down to the police station and have them lock you up for murdering Freddie Bert."

Arburn's eyes widened in terror. "I didn't murder that little dago."

Gino took offense at the slur and cuffed him on the ear. Frank ignored his howl of protest. "Then who did?"

"How should I know? It's the Bowery. Somebody gets murdered there every night."

"Not quite, but why would somebody kill a kid? He didn't have any money, and he couldn't be a threat to anyone."

Arburn just sat there and glared.

"Or maybe he could be a threat to someone," Frank mused. "Is that it? Did he see something or know something and you had to get rid of him?"

"Not me! I told you, I didn't touch the kid. I didn't even know where he was. You wouldn't tell me, remember?"

"But you figured it out, didn't you? And then you found him and you choked him to death."

"No! I swear, I never even saw him!"

"But you did tell somebody where he was."

"I told you—"

"And I'll tell you again, I don't believe you. If you weren't after the boy, you were working for somebody who was. Who are you working for, Arburn?"

For some reason, the question scared him more than Frank did. The blood drained from his face and he pressed his lips together until they disappeared into a thin line.

"It's Black Jack Robinson, isn't it?" Gino said softly.

Arburn's head jerked up at that. "Jack wouldn't hurt the boy, either! He just wanted to find him."

"Why?" Frank asked.

Arburn swallowed. "Because of the girl."

Frank exchanged a glance with Gino. "What girl?"

"Jack's lady friend. She . . . she disappeared. The boy would've been there that night, though, and Jack was sure he'd seen something."

"Why was he so sure?"

Arburn swallowed. "Because he slept there, at the flat, most nights, and when Jack was there, the boy would sleep outside under the steps."

"At the Den," Gino said.

"How'd you know that?" Arburn demanded in surprise.

"We're detectives," Frank said mildly. "The boy slept in the flat with the lady friend?"

"No, not with . . . She didn't live there. She only came when . . . when she wanted to."

"When did she disappear?"

"Saturday night."

Gooseflesh rose on Frank's arms. "What does this lady look like?"

"I don't know."

Frank just gave him the glare he'd perfected while interrogating suspects for the New York City Police.

Arburn swallowed again. "She's got blond hair, kind of curly. Pretty. Small boned but with . . ." He gestured over his chest to indicate an ample bosom.

"She comes from a good family, too," Frank said. "A family with some money."

"How'd you know that?" Arburn demanded.

Frank felt no obligation to reply. "How would Black Jack Robinson meet a girl like that?"

When Arburn didn't reply, Gino guessed, "Slumming."

"Don't look at me like that! It wasn't my doing," Arburn said, his voice shrill with panic.

"You took a respectable young lady to the Bowery to meet a gangster?" Frank asked in wonder.

"It wasn't like that," Arburn insisted. He pulled out a handkerchief to wipe the sweat now dripping down his face. "She's not . . . respectable."

"What is that supposed to mean?" Gino asked with just the proper amount of outrage. There was hope for the boy yet.

"Just what I said. She might come from uptown, but she wasn't a lady, not that one. The first time she came on a tour with me, she was dressed like a man. Nobody was fooled, but they all got a thrill out of taking a lady to those places. I guess I did, too," he added sourly.

"And she came back again?"

"Again and again. She couldn't get enough. She had this fellow she came with."

"A lover?"

"No, some family connection, I think. She'd hardly even talk to him, though. She just needed him to bring her. And one night she met Jack."

"And then she didn't need to go on tours anymore," Frank said.

"That's right," Arburn said with obvious bitterness. "She just toured Jack's flat."

"Until she disappeared. What happened to her?" Frank asked, very much afraid he already knew.

"That's all I know. She just disappeared. She was supposed to meet Jack and he was late, and when he got there, she was gone. He went crazy. He told me to find the boy, because he was gone, too."

"Maybe she just went home."

"Don't you think he checked? Like I said, she disappeared."

"What's her name?" Frank asked.

"Her name?"

"Yes, stupid, her name," Gino said, cuffing him again.

"Estelle," he said, rubbing his ear.

"Estelle what?"

Plainly, he hated giving this information. "Longacre," he said through gritted teeth.

"And what about the gent she came with on the tours?" Frank asked. "And don't pretend you don't remember."

"Tufts. Norman, I think."

"Any idea where they live?" Frank asked.

"Not hardly. It's not like they invite me in for tea or anything."

"Where do you meet them?"

"At the boardinghouse where I live. People can leave messages for me, if they want a tour. I have a regular schedule."

"And Robinson owns all those buildings around the Den," Gino said. "He's got them set up for the tours."

"Yeah, the locals get a kick out of playacting for the swells."

"I guess you wouldn't want one of your customers to end up dead because you took them to the wrong place," Frank said.

"That's right," Arburn agreed uncertainly.

Even Gino frowned.

"So the boy's really dead?" Arburn asked after an awkward silence.

"Yes, he is."

"Who killed him?"

"I thought you did," Frank said.

"I didn't, I swear."

"You already swore you didn't. I still don't believe you."

"Why would I kill him? Jack wanted to know what he saw, what happened to the girl."

"To Estelle."

"That's right. He just wants to find her."

"I think I know where she is."

Arburn gaped at him. "How could you? You didn't know anything about her a few minutes ago."

"I'm a detective."

Arburn snorted his derision. Even Gino gave him a funny look.

"You go back to Robinson and tell him the boy is dead and that I'm going to find the girl for him."

"I . . . I can't do that."

"Why not?"

"Because . . ." Arburn was squirming again. "He doesn't know I hired you. I was supposed to find the boy myself."

Gino gave a bark of laughter, and Frank shook his head in dismay. "You better tell him then, because he's going to be real interested in my report."

"But—"

"You can go now," Frank said.

"I can?"

Frank nodded to Gino, who opened the office door and stood back. "Yes. Get out."

Arburn jumped to his feet and hurried out, not even looking back.

"You think that's the girl Freddie was talking about?" Gino asked.

"I'm pretty sure, and there's a good chance she's dead, too."

"What makes you think so?"

"There's a girl's body in the morgue with Freddie. They found her in a trunk in the Bowery, and she fits the description of Estelle Longacre. Not many pretty young girls in fine clothes get killed in the Bowery."

Gino gave a low whistle. "Are you going to ask Black Jack to identify her?"

"Not on your life. I'm going to see if I can find her family first. If she's been missing since Saturday night, they must be going crazy."

"Why haven't they checked the morgue then?"

"They probably didn't expect her to get herself murdered in the Bowery."

"True. Do you think Mrs. Malloy or her parents will know the family?"

Sarah's family were members of New York society, and Sarah's mother knew everyone who mattered in that world. "I don't know, but they're probably in the City Directory, at least."

"Do you think Longacre Square was named after them?" Located above 42nd Street on Broadway, Longacre Square was home to Oscar Hammerstein's Olympia Music Hall, but otherwise, the neighborhood was known as Thieves Lair.

"Let's hope not."

"Are you going to tell them their daughter is dead?"

Frank sighed. "If I have to."

GINO HAD COME FOR DINNER THAT NIGHT, AND AS AL-ways, the children were delighted to see him. Sarah was proud of the way Catherine showed off her growing knowledge of American Sign Language to keep her new brother, Brian, informed of what others were saying and to tell everyone else what Brian said in return.

When Catherine's skills fell short, Malloy's mother would help. Mrs. Malloy accompanied Brian to the school he attended, New York Institution for the Deaf and Dumb. The students there came from all over the country, and most of them lived in, but Mother Malloy escorted Brian and stayed with him all day, learning to sign along with him while she helped as a volunteer.

Catherine had just turned six, so she'd be attending school in the fall, too. Sarah remembered what Malloy had said the other day about Catherine being adopted. Sarah had tried to adopt her when she'd first taken in the abandoned child, but unmarried females were not permitted to adopt. She'd called herself Catherine's guardian, although she had no legal papers to prove it. Now she was no longer unmarried, though, and they knew Catherine's parents were dead, so they should really begin the process. She'd have to remind Malloy when they were alone.

"Time to get ready for bed," Mrs. Malloy told the children as they left the dining room, signing the words for Brian.

Both children protested. They didn't want to be separated from Gino.

"I'll carry you upstairs," Gino offered, lifting a squealing

Brian onto his shoulders and then hoisting Catherine onto his hip. "Let's go."

Maeve followed, unable to conceal her grin. Gino was a good man, and he'd make a good husband when the time came. Of course he was Italian and Catholic and Maeve wasn't, so his family would have something to say about it, but Malloy was Catholic and Sarah wasn't and they'd managed.

Mrs. Malloy told Sarah, "I'll go up and put the children to bed so the young people can come back down."

She didn't wait for Sarah's response, because of course, she didn't need Sarah's approval and she didn't want to give the impression that she did. Sarah bit back a smile. "Thank you, Mother Malloy," Sarah called after her.

Mother Malloy waved away her thanks, not even glancing back.

Frank was chuckling as they went into the parlor.

"What's so funny?" Sarah asked.

"The way she still pretends she's doing us a favor by being here."

"She *is* doing us a favor by being here. If she lived somewhere else where she couldn't see Brian every day, she'd drive us crazy."

"She'd drive me crazy, you mean."

"And she'd be very unhappy, which is why she'd make us unhappy, too, but this way, she's very helpful and gets to see her grandson grow up."

"And she got a granddaughter into the bargain."

"Which reminds me, we need to get started on adopting her."

"I know. As soon as this case is over, I'll see about it." He pushed open the front windows to let in whatever breeze might be lingering on Bank Street. "We should have gone to Newport or something this summer."

"Dear heaven, I never thought I'd hear you say something like that," Sarah said.

"And I never thought I'd say it, but New York is unbearable in the summer. Why don't your parents leave?"

"My father likes to keep an eye on his business, and my mother likes to keep an eye on the children, I think."

"That makes sense, but if we went somewhere, we could take your mother with us."

"And yours."

Malloy gave her a look before slipping off his suit coat and draping it over a chair. "I'm sure I'm breaking several rules of etiquette by taking off my jacket, but it's too hot to keep it on."

"I'll never tell," Sarah assured him. She continued to chatter about the children's activities so he wouldn't suddenly remember the dead boy, at least not until they absolutely needed to discuss him. Frank had tried to cover the depth of his grief, but she'd seen it in his eyes when he told her the boy in the morgue was definitely Freddie.

When they returned to the parlor, Gino looked very pleased and Maeve looked very coy, and Sarah noticed they chose to sit next to each other on the sofa.

"Now," Maeve said, "tell us what happened with your case."

Malloy and Gino took turns describing their day. Malloy stoically described identifying Freddie and discovering the dead girl in the morgue. Gino took up the tale with an account of their meeting with Will "Bert" Arburn and his unwitting identification of the girl.

"How horrible," Maeve said. "I know she was asking for trouble when she went on those tours and then took up with a gangster, but still . . ." She gave a delicate shudder. "I can't stand the thought of her lying in that morgue all alone."

"What I don't understand is why a girl like that would do the things she did," Gino said.

"Don't make the mistake of thinking just because someone has money that they're happy," Sarah said. "You should have learned by now that even rich people can be miserable and cruel and their children can be desperately unhappy."

"So she did it because she wasn't happy?" Gino said doubtfully.

"Or because her life was incredibly dull or really horrible," Maeve said, "and she wanted to do something that made her feel alive."

"Or no one cared what she did, so she decided to shock them into paying attention," Sarah added.

"Oh," Gino said weakly, more than overwhelmed by their reasoning.

"So you're going to visit the girl's family?" Sarah asked.

"Yes, if I can figure out which Longacre family is hers," Malloy said. "Do you know them by chance?"

Sarah shook her head. "Although my mother might. She pays much more attention to knowing people than I do."

"Do you think Longacre Square is named for the family?" Gino asked.

Sarah smiled. "Longacre Square is named for a square in London, I think. Some foreign city, I know. So, no, this Longacre family is not that important."

"Thank heaven for that," Malloy said. "And before we go any further, I want to make sure the girl isn't safely at home. If she is, then we'll know she doesn't have anything to do with why Freddie was killed," Malloy said.

"But you don't think you'll find her safely at home," Sarah said.

Malloy sighed. "No, I don't. That body in the morgue is too much of a coincidence."

"But if she's been gone . . . how many days is it?" Maeve asked.

"Five days now," Gino said. "Since Saturday night."

"If she's been gone for five days with no word, why hasn't her family gone to the police? They would've found her body in the morgue within an hour."

"I can think of at least one reason they wouldn't go to the police," Sarah said.

"The scandal," Malloy guessed.

"Yes. They might think she just ran off with someone and wanted to keep it quiet. She might even have left a note or something."

"But wouldn't they at least look for her?" Maeve insisted.

"If they knew what she'd been doing and who she'd been doing it with, they might be relieved that she left," Sarah said.

"But what if she really did run off?" Gino said. "She might've met somebody she liked better than Black Jack."

"That's possible, I guess," Malloy said. "And if she did, her family will find out when they go to identify the body that it isn't her. There's very little chance of that, though, which is why I'm not looking forward to visiting her family."

"You need to take Mrs. Frank with you," Maeve said.

Sarah looked up in surprise. Not from the title. Their maid and cook called her Mrs. Frank to distinguish her from Mother Malloy, so Maeve had adopted it as well. She was only surprised to hear Maeve echoing her own thoughts.

Malloy was already protesting, but Sarah interrupted him. "She's right. Even if the family was happy to see the last of this Estelle, they'll be shocked to find out she's dead."

"You think she's got an invalid mother who'll faint or something?" Malloy scoffed.

"I think if Estelle felt such a strong need to rebel in such a scandalous way, her family has definitely failed her, but that doesn't mean there won't be someone who feels her loss very deeply."

"And it's still possible she's not missing at all," Maeve said.

Gino stared at her in amazement. "I thought that was the one thing we were sure of."

"Why? Because that lying Arburn fellow told you the gangster checked to make sure she wasn't at home? Maybe he did, but how? He couldn't go knock on their front door and ask to see her."

"I see what you mean," Malloy said. "He'd have to rely on spying or gossip."

"And he wouldn't have any friends in that neighborhood to help," Gino said, taking up the theory.

"So maybe her family sent someone after her to bring her home," Sarah concluded. "And they're keeping her locked up or something."

"And if that's the case," Maeve said, "they aren't likely to admit it to Mr. Malloy."

"Do you think they'll admit it to me?" Sarah asked in surprise.

"I think they're much more likely to confide in you than in Mr. Malloy."

Sarah glanced at Malloy, who shrugged. "As much as I hate involving you in this, I think Maeve is right. I wouldn't let you go alone, of course, but if we go together, you'll be perfectly safe."

"Yes," Gino agreed with a grin. "It's not like he's taking you to the Bowery to interview a gangster or anything."

"Which reminds me," Sarah said. "Do you think this gangster—what's his name?"

"Black Jack Robinson," Gino offered.

"This Black Jack, do you think he's the one who killed the girl?"

"He seems like the most likely suspect," Malloy said.

"And it would explain why he wanted to find Freddie, who was a witness," Gino said.

"Why would he kill her, though?" Sarah asked.

"Maybe he got tired of her," Maeve said.

"He wouldn't have to kill her to get rid of her," Frank said. "More likely he was jealous. Maybe she had another lover."

"You said she brought a man along on the tours," Sarah said.

"Arburn didn't think she cared about him, but maybe he was wrong," Gino said.

"Or maybe Robinson got the wrong impression," Maeve said.

"What if Arburn killed her?" Gino said. "Maybe he was jealous of Robinson and killed her out of spite, and he was looking for the boy himself, so he could get him before he told Robinson."

Malloy nodded his approval of their theories. "So which one of you is going to ask Black Jack if he killed the girl?"

"I think Mrs. Malloy should do it," Gino said, earning a swat from Maeve and a laugh from Sarah.

"Don't even joke about that," Malloy said. "It's bad enough she's going with me to see the family."

"Do you want me to ask my mother if she knows any Longacres?" Sarah asked.

"I don't suppose it would hurt, although we're not taking your mother along."

Sarah almost laughed at the prospect. "Of course not, although she'd be thrilled to help."

"She'd be thrilled to be working on another case," Gino clarified, "but after what happened last year, Mr. Decker made us swear we wouldn't let her do that again."

"I'm fairly certain he didn't get Mother to swear she wouldn't do it again," Sarah said, "so don't be surprised if she does. But I'll make the case sound very dull when I ask her. We should probably go over there first thing in the morning. I'll telephone to let her know, so she's dressed."

"Can't you just ask her about the family on the telephone?" Malloy asked.

"With operators listening?" Sarah scoffed. "If Estelle's family hopes to avoid scandal, that's the last thing they'll want. Besides, Mother would just say she'd have to think about it and use that as an excuse to come over here to deliver her report."

Gino pretended to cough to cover his laugh, and Malloy glared at him, but only halfheartedly.

"All right," Malloy said. "Sarah and I will go to see her mother tomorrow morning, then try to figure out which Longacre family in the City Directory is the right one and go see them."

"And if it turns out the body in the morgue is Estelle Longacre?" Gino asked.

Malloy's expression hardened. "Then we find out who killed her and why, because then we'll know who killed poor little Freddie."

5

Frank figured he'd never cease to be amazed when Elizabeth Decker greeted him with delight and a kiss on the cheek. She certainly had no reason to be delighted that her only living daughter had married an Irish Catholic (former) policeman, and yet she always seemed to be.

"Sarah said you needed help with a case," Mrs. Decker said when she'd seated them in the back parlor and served them coffee. This was the room the family used most, and it was filled with comfortable, overstuffed furniture and no valuable knickknacks that could get knocked over.

Frank pretended not to notice how excited Mrs. Decker was at the prospect of helping them with a case.

"We just need to know if you are acquainted with a family named Longacre," Sarah quickly explained. "The name came up in one of Malloy's investigations, and he needs to locate a young woman named Estelle Longacre. She may have witnessed a crime."

"Longacre? Like the Square?"

"We assume so, yes," Sarah said.

"And is the family in society?"

"We aren't certain," Sarah said. "All we know is that the young lady came from a respectable family and wore expensive clothes."

"That seems like an odd thing to know about someone, if that's the only thing you know." Which was Mrs. Decker's way of asking why they didn't know more, and if they did, why they weren't telling her.

Sarah valiantly refused to explain. "I told you, she may have witnessed a crime, and that was all the other people had observed about her."

"That and her name," Mrs. Decker mused shrewdly.

"That's right." Frank admired the way Sarah kept her voice so calm, as if this were of little importance. "And we don't want to bother people if it's not the right family, but there are several Longacres listed in the City Directory."

"Let me check," Mrs. Decker said, going to her desk. She was still a fine-looking woman, even though her blond hair was turning silver and age had softened her features. Sarah had inherited her beauty and her spirit, too, although Mrs. Decker had never had the opportunities to exercise hers quite as much as her daughter had. At least not until lately.

Mrs. Decker rummaged in a drawer and pulled out the small book in which she kept addresses of her friends and acquaintances. She started flipping through it as she walked back to her seat. "That's odd," she mused when she had found the page she wanted.

"What's odd?" Sarah asked.

"I have a Winifred Longacre listed, but her name is crossed out."

"Why would her name be crossed out?" Frank asked.

Mrs. Decker frowned. "Usually, it means the person died."

Before either of them could think what to say to that, Mrs. Decker got up and went back to her desk. This time she returned with a book.

"The Social Register?" Sarah asked.

"I know you don't care about these things, but it can be quite helpful," Mrs. Decker said, not even glancing up. She paged through. "Yes, here it is. Longacres still at the same address as poor Winifred, although I'm not sure what Horace Longacre might have done to retain his listing here. I remember them now. Winifred died years ago, in child-birth, I believe, or shortly afterward. There's a Miss Estelle Longacre listed at the same address, so that may be her daughter." She handed the book to Sarah.

Frank leaned over to see a listing of names, apparently in alphabetical order, followed by incomprehensible abbreviations along with their street addresses. He pulled out the small notebook he always carried and a pencil and jotted down the address beside the names of Horace and Estelle Longacre. "What do those letters after his name mean?"

"They indicate club membership and college attended, I believe," Sarah said, looking to her mother for confirmation as she handed the book to Frank.

"Yes, there's a list of the abbreviations in the front. I haven't seen Horace in years. He was never very amiable, and after Winnie died, well, I'm sure someone may have invited him somewhere, but not anywhere I went."

"He belongs to a yacht club," Frank reported, having found the list of abbreviations. "Does that mean he has a yacht?"

"A yacht doesn't have to be some enormous, seagoing vessel," Mrs. Decker said. "Just a boat of some kind, although I can't imagine him with the boating set, unless he's changed a lot. But you don't want to hear what I thought of him. You just want to find your witness."

"And it looks like we have, Mother," Sarah said. "I can't thank you enough for your help."

"Maybe you'll reward me by telling me why you wanted to find this girl," she asked hopefully.

"I promise we will, but we don't know very much at the moment, and it may all come to nothing." Sarah deftly changed the subject to the children's latest antics, which successfully distracted Mrs. Decker until they had stayed long enough to leave without giving offense.

"How do you get a copy of the Social Register?" Frank asked as they walked away from the Decker home.

"You have to subscribe, I believe. They update it four times a year."

"I can see it would be handy to have. If we subscribed, we wouldn't have had to tell your mother anything about the case."

As he had expected, Sarah smiled at this. "I can see that would be a definite advantage."

"I'll have Gino find out how to subscribe."

The Longacres' house was only a few blocks away, so they walked over. The July air was still tolerable at this early hour. On the way home, they'd probably have to take the elevated train. The El wasn't particularly cool, but it was fast. He'd have to remember not to complain about the heat to Gino. The boy would start telling him that was another reason he needed a motorcar.

* * *

THE LONGACRE HOUSE ON THE UPPER WEST SIDE WAS one of a score of identical town houses sitting side by side behind wrought iron gates that enclosed the tiniest patch of ground that could, with a straight face, be called a front yard. The patch in front of the Longacres' home wasn't particularly well tended, and the front steps did not appear to have been swept recently, Sarah noticed.

A surly maid answered their knock. Sarah gave her the haughty look she had learned, at a young age, to use with unruly servants. "We are here to see Miss Estelle Longacre."

Sarah offered her calling card, but the maid made no effort to accept it. "Miss Estelle, you say?"

Sarah felt a pang at the lies, knowing Estelle was most likely dead, but there was no sense in alarming anyone if that wasn't really the case. "That's correct. I realize it's early, but we'll wait if she needs a few minutes."

The maid went from surly to distressed in a matter of seconds. "I don't know if she's home," she tried.

As Sarah well knew, people could simply have their servants claim they were not at home if someone called whom they did not wish to see. "I'm sure she will be at home for us." She offered the card again and this time the maid looked at it as if it were a poisonous snake. Sarah glanced at Malloy, who gave her a slight nod. Then she started walking forward, right into the house, giving the maid the choice of backing up and allowing it or getting knocked down.

The maid backed up, scuttling out of Sarah's way. Malloy came in behind her.

"If you'll tell Miss Longacre we are here," Sarah reminded the maid, offering the card once again.

This time, the woman took it and scurried off, leaving them standing in the foyer with the front door hanging open.

"We don't appreciate Hattie nearly enough," Malloy said, pushing the door closed.

"A good maid is to be treasured," Sarah agreed.

After the sunshine outside, the foyer seemed quite dark, but even when Sarah's eyes had become accustomed, she realized it was still too dark. Maybe they were trying to hide the collection of dust, she decided, spying some gathered in a corner.

"What if they won't see us?" Malloy asked.

"They'll see us. If Estelle is here, she'll be dying of curiosity, and if she's not here, they'll want to know why two strangers are looking for her."

The maid returned, descending the stairs with marked reluctance. When she reached them, she grudgingly said, "Miss Longacre will see you."

She turned on her heel and started back up the stairs, not even bothering to invite them to follow. Sarah exchanged a surprised glance with Malloy and shrugged in response to his silent question. Was it possible Estelle Longacre was indeed here?

They wouldn't find out unless they went upstairs, so Sarah hurried to catch up with the ill-mannered maid. Malloy was right behind her.

These stairs hadn't been swept in a while either, Sarah couldn't help noticing. Everything about the Longacre house looked neglected and sad, and the neglect was not recent either. Wallpaper was curling in spots along the stairway, and rugs had been worn patternless where feet had tracked across them over a period of years.

Upstairs, the maid went to an open doorway and stepped in to announce them. "Mrs. Malloy and . . . some man."

Without so much as glancing at them again, she stepped out of the room and headed away down the hall.

Sarah had to cough to cover a laugh that would have ruined her credibility. Then she stepped into the room to find a middle-aged woman nervously awaiting her. She was small with mousy brown hair pulled back in a severe, unflattering bun. She might once have been pretty, when youth would have put roses in her cheeks, but those cheeks now were drawn and pale and traced with fine lines. Her faded blue eyes looked Sarah and Frank over anxiously and more than a little fearfully. Her dress was an ugly brown and hung on her, as if she'd recently lost weight. One hand convulsively clutched and unclutched the fabric of her skirt while the other fiercely gripped Sarah's calling card.

"Miss Longacre?" Sarah asked when the woman failed to greet them.

"Yes."

This couldn't be right. No gangster would take this woman as his mistress, and she was much too old to be described as a "girl." "Miss *Estelle* Longacre?" Sarah tried again.

The woman stiffened as if Sarah had slapped her. "Of course not. I'm Penelope Longacre. Who are you and what do you want?"

"As you know," Sarah said, gesturing to the card the woman held, "I am Mrs. Frank Malloy, and this is my husband."

"And what are you wanting with Estelle?"

"We'd like to speak to her about a private matter," Malloy said.

Miss Longacre made a rude noise. "I'm sure you would. But you won't see her today. She's not home."

"Do you know where she is?" Sarah asked.

Fear sparked in her eyes again, but she said, "Of course I do."

"Then perhaps you'll tell us where we can find her." Sarah

softened her tone to one of genuine concern. "You see, we are also trying to make sure that she's safe."

"Safe from what? And you still haven't said why you want to see her."

"She isn't here, is she?" Sarah said gently. "In fact, she's been missing since last Saturday."

The woman's eyes widened, but she shook her head in silent denial.

"And you have no idea where she might be," Sarah said. "Or perhaps you do, but it's not a place you care to go to retrieve her."

"Who *are* you?" the woman demanded desperately.

"I'm a private investigator," Malloy said.

She frowned in confusion. "A private . . . ? Did Horace hire you?"

"No, I was hired by someone else to find someone else, but in the course of my investigation, Miss Longacre's name was mentioned, and we have reason to believe she might be in some danger."

Now Miss Longacre was terrified. Her watery gaze frantically darted between the two of them. Finally, she said, "What kind of danger?"

"If you don't mind my asking," Malloy said, "what relation are you to Miss Estelle Longacre?"

The woman drew an unsteady breath. "She's my niece. My brother's girl."

"Maybe we should speak to him, then," Malloy said. "If he's at home."

"He's ill," she said almost angrily, as if she could hardly forgive him for being sick. "This is his house, and that's why I'm here. The girl disappeared, and he didn't have anybody to do for him, so he sent for me. That's the only time he thinks of me, when he needs something."

"Do you think he's well enough to see me?" Malloy said.

"Why would he want to?" she snapped.

Malloy was holding on to his temper with difficulty, Sarah could see, but he kept his voice level when he said, "I have news about his daughter that I think he'll want to hear."

"Nothing you tell him about her will be something he wants to hear, but I can see you're not going to give up until you get your chance," she said in disgust, pushing past them as she walked to the doorway and yelled, "Marie!" startling them both. Seeing their shock at her uncouth behavior, she said, "The bell's broken. He never fixes anything. Why should he? He says he won't be around much longer, so why should he care about somebody else's comfort?"

"Is he dying?" Sarah asked.

"He claims he is, although I don't see any sign of it yet." She sounded disappointed.

Sarah was getting a clear idea of why Estelle Longacre might want to escape her life.

The unhappy maid appeared in the doorway after an uncomfortable wait.

"Take Mr. . . ." Miss Longacre glanced at the card she still held. "Mr. Malloy up to see Mr. Longacre."

"He won't like it," the maid warned.

"Mr. Malloy has news of Miss Estelle."

"Then he surely won't like it," the maid said.

Miss Longacre sighed long-sufferingly. "Take him up anyway. If he complains, tell him I made you do it."

The maid shook her head at such foolishness, but she said, "Come on then," and took off with Malloy on her heels.

When Sarah turned back to Miss Longacre, she was rubbing her forehead as if it ached.

"Perhaps we could sit down," Sarah said.

"Yes, of course," she said absently, and moved to a grouping of upholstered chairs in front of the cold fireplace. The furniture in here matched the rest of the house, and Sarah could see that no one had changed anything in this room for a generation. The upholstered pieces were worn and faded, and the decorations hopelessly out of style.

Miss Longacre sat in one of the sagging chairs, and Sarah chose one opposite so she could watch her reactions.

"I can't offer you any refreshment," Miss Longacre said. "Marie either won't bring it or it will be inedible when it arrives. She even manages to ruin tea."

"I understand your brother is a widower," Sarah tried, hoping to get a conversation started.

"Yes, Winifred died right after Estelle was born. That was almost twenty years ago."

"And he's never remarried?"

Miss Longacre looked up, her gaze sharper, less watery now. "Why should he? He had the girl."

So all he'd wanted was a child. Most men wanted a son and heir, of course, but perhaps Longacre was content with a daughter. If she'd grown up in this house, she hadn't had much in the way of amusement, though. "Has Mr. Longacre seen a doctor? I should have mentioned that I'm a nurse, and I'd be happy to—"

"There's nothing a nurse can do except clean up after him," she said, not bothering to hide her disgust. "He's seen more doctors than you can shake a stick at, and not one of them can help."

"I'm sorry to hear that."

Miss Longacre's frown said she doubted that very much.

"I suppose it's been lonely for Estelle, growing up without a mother."

"I don't know how much company a mother would be, but my Norman takes her places."

Sarah's skin prickled at this, knowing the places Estelle

had been going of late and that someone named Norman had accompanied her. "Norman?"

"Yes, Norman Tufts. He's my ward. A cousin's child. He was orphaned very young, and I took him to raise."

Malloy had said Arburn thought Tufts was a family connection, and it appeared that he was. "That was very kind of you."

She didn't seem to know how to accept the compliment. "He's a good boy, and he was always a companion to Estelle."

How much of a companion? Sarah wondered. If he was the one who had escorted her to the Bowery dressed as a man, was that something a "good boy" would do for his cousin?

"Your husband," she said before Sarah could think of something else to ask. "He said he knew where Estelle is. You might as well tell me. Horace will tell me himself soon enough."

And Malloy would want to see her response, which they wouldn't be able to do if Horace told her. Sarah glanced at the door, which still stood open.

Miss Longacre waved away Sarah's concerns. "Don't worry. Nothing happens here that Marie doesn't know about."

Sarah took a moment to decide exactly where to begin. "We were investigating a missing newsboy. His brother was trying to locate him."

"Somebody paid a detective to find a newsboy?" she scoffed.

"The brother had come into some money and wanted to give the boy a home."

Miss Longacre was still not impressed.

"During the course of our investigation, we learned that the boy worked for a gangster."

Her eyes widened in surprise, but Sarah couldn't be sure what part of that statement had surprised her. "What does all this have to do with Estelle?"

"Estelle was seen visiting the gangster on numerous occasions."

Miss Longacre seemed genuinely surprised, but perhaps not as surprised as she should be. "That's . . . impossible."

"I hope this won't come as too much of a shock to your brother."

She ignored Sarah's concern. "Is that where she is? With this gangster?"

"Unfortunately, no. It seems he is looking for her as well."

Miss Longacre took a moment to consider this information. If she'd known about Robinson—and Norman might have told her—then they'd probably thought she'd run off with him. "Then where is she? You said she's in danger."

"We are very much afraid . . . And I'm sorry to tell you this, but we have reason to believe that she's dead."

"Dead?" She said the word as if uncertain of its meaning.

"Yes, we think she was murdered."

"Dead," Miss Longacre said again, as if savoring the word. Then she leaned back in her chair and smiled like a cat who had gotten in the cream.

THE MAID LED FRANK UP TO THE SECOND FLOOR. ALL the doors were closed along the hallway. She stopped outside one and rapped loudly. Without waiting for a reply, she opened the door and stepped inside.

"There's a Mr. Malloy here to see you about Miss Estelle."

As she had done downstairs, she stepped out again without waiting for a reply and walked off, even though Mr. Longacre was clearly replying, loudly and not happily.

"Get back here, girl, and listen to me!" he shouted as Frank stepped into the room. The curtains were drawn, and the air was suffocating.

"She seems to have gone," Frank said, finding Longacre not in bed but sitting in an upholstered chair, his feet resting on an ottoman. He wore a stained dressing gown, and his spindly bare legs stuck out from beneath it, white and hairy. His slippers had seen better days.

"Who are you and what the devil do you want with me?" Longacre asked, eyeing Frank balefully. He was almost completely bald, with only a few wisps of white hair sprouting forlornly from his scalp. His face was haggard, cheeks and eyes sunken, skin unnaturally pale. Still, his eyes glittered with life. And anger.

"Like your maid said, I have some information about your daughter, Estelle." Frank handed him a business card.

"Private detective, eh? I had you pegged for a cop."

Frank merely smiled.

"And what do you have to tell me about Estelle, eh? Nothing good, I'll warrant."

Frank glanced around the untidy room, noticing the stacks of newspapers and piles of unopened correspondence on every flat surface. The bed was unmade, the covers half off. He spotted a straight-backed chair nearby. He went to it, removed the stack of papers from the seat, and carried it over so he could sit down facing Longacre.

"It has come to my attention, during the course of an investigation, that your daughter, Estelle, was in the habit of visiting a man named Black Jack Robinson."

He did not seem surprised by this information. "And what business is it of yours who my daughter visits?"

"Ordinarily, none, but this Robinson lives in the Bowery, and a young woman who matches the description of your daughter was found dead in the Bowery early Sunday morning."

If Frank had expected grief or even anger, he would have been disappointed. Instead, Longacre's glittering eyes narrowed shrewdly. "And you think this dead girl is Estelle?"

"I know she was supposed to meet Robinson on Saturday

night, but she never showed up. I know girls like her don't usually turn up in the Bowery at all, much less dead. So I came to see if I could find Miss Longacre, because if she was safely at home, that would mean the dead girl was someone else. But it appears that she's not safely at home."

"Who told you that? Not Marie."

"Miss Penelope Longacre," Frank said.

Longacre snorted. "Penny never did know when to keep her mouth shut."

"So if Miss Estelle has indeed been missing since Saturday night, you might want to check the body in the morgue to see if it is your daughter."

This time Longacre's face did reflect anger. "Look at me! Do you think I can go traipsing all over the city looking at dead bodies?"

"Your sister did say you were ill."

"Ill? Is that what she calls it? I'm dying, Mr. Malloy. Slowly but surely."

"I'm sorry to hear that," Frank said, not bothering to sound sorry.

Longacre glared at him for a long moment. "I could send Penny, I guess."

"The morgue is no place for a lady, Mr. Longacre."

"All the more reason to send her," Longacre said viciously. "But we can't have her fainting, can we? No, indeed. I'll send Norman. It'll make a man of him."

"Norman?" Arburn had said a man named Norman had accompanied Estelle.

"Yes, my sister's . . . ward or whatever she calls him."

"Then I can assume your daughter has been missing since Saturday, and you don't know where she is?"

"If she's missing, then I wouldn't know where she is, would I? I also don't know about any of this nonsense with a fellow named Black Jack something, either. What kind of a name is that for a man? Does he think he's a pirate?" He gave a bark of laughter at his own joke. Didn't he realize how inappropriate that was since Frank had just told him his daughter was probably dead?

"And if this dead girl is your daughter, aren't you interested in how she died?"

That sobered him instantly. "But I'm not sure it's her, am I?"

"I was sure enough that I tracked you down, Mr. Longacre."

His bloodless lips flattened to a straight line. "But I'm not sure until Norman sees her. You can tell me all about it then."

"If it's her, then the police can tell you all about it," Frank said, rising from his chair. He'd had enough of Horace Longacre.

"She was murdered then," he mused. "Tell Penny to get that brat of hers to the morgue so we can settle this."

Frank found Sarah and Miss Longacre staring at each other in awkward silence in the parlor.

Miss Longacre looked up expectantly. "What did he say?"

He hesitated, not sure how much Sarah had told her.

"She knows," Sarah said.

"He said to send Norman to the morgue to identify the body."

"Norman! He can't expect that poor boy to go to a horrible place like that!"

"Norman Tufts is Miss Longacre's ward," Sarah explained, and Frank nodded to tell her he'd made the connection.

"Your brother wanted to send you, but I convinced him it was no place for a lady," Frank said.

Miss Longacre gasped in outrage. "That fiend. I should have known he'd do something like this."

"Is Mr. Longacre too ill to go himself?" Sarah asked him.

"He says he is," Frank said. "What's wrong with him, if you don't mind my asking?"

Miss Longacre pulled a face. "Pernicious anemia."

Frank glanced at Sarah for an explanation. "It's a blood disorder, debilitating and ultimately fatal, although the person can linger for a long time."

"He'd go to the morgue if he could get there on his yacht," Miss Longacre said bitterly. "Instead he wants to send my poor Norman."

"I'll be glad to go with the boy," Frank said, glancing at Sarah to find her biting back a knowing smile.

Miss Longacre glared at him suspiciously, but he gave her only his most innocent smile in return. Sarah said it wasn't really all that innocent, but it worked on Miss Longacre. "I suppose it would be better than having him go alone. He'll be very distressed, seeing his cousin dead."

"Perhaps it isn't her," Sarah said.

Miss Longacre sighed. "She left here on Saturday and hasn't been seen since. She would've come home by now if she could."

Plainly, Miss Longacre was not a romantic who imagined her niece had eloped or something like that.

"How can I get in touch with Norman, Miss Longacre?" Frank asked.

"Fix a time, and I'll have him meet you there," she said. "Where is this place?"

NORMAN TUFTS WAS AN UNPREPOSSESSING YOUNG MAN in his midtwenties. He wore an ill-fitting plaid suit and a derby hat he obviously thought looked jaunty but which just looked silly. It sat too low on his head and made his ears stick out. Tall and gangly, he hurried across the street at a clumsy lope to meet Frank in front of Bellevue. "Mr. Malloy?" he asked.

Frank shook his hand.

Sarah had explained the young man's relationship to the family. He bore a slight resemblance to Horace Longacre, but his eyes lacked the lively glitter of intelligence and were a little too far apart.

"I've never done anything like this before, Mr. Malloy."

"Don't worry. All you have to do is look at her face and tell them if it's her or not."

"Then she's not . . ."

"Not what?"

"Aunt Penny said she'd probably be . . . decaying."

Aunt Penny was a morbid sort. "You can still recognize her."

Frank escorted Norman down to the basement, where the attendant readily accepted Frank's explanation of why they were there.

"I'm glad somebody's going to claim her," the attendant said, and indicated the two men should go on in and take a look.

"She's naked," Norman cried in horror, covering his face with both hands. "They're all naked."

"Just look at her face," Frank said. "Is that her?"

Norman had turned a little green, but he obediently lowered his hands just enough. "Oh dear heavens, yes, it's her. That's Estelle." Then he turned and ran.

The attendant was ready with a bucket when Norman lost his lunch. "Happens all the time," he confided to Frank.

While Norman waited on a bench in the hallway, his head in his hands, Frank gave the attendant the name and address of the next of kin and promised they would send for the body.

"I see the boy's body is still here," Frank said.

"Yeah, but some of the newsboys came by to say they'll

claim him. Did you know they take up a collection to pay for the funeral when one of them dies?"

"Yes, I did." Frank handed him one of his cards. "Tell them to see me. I'll make a donation."

Since Norman was still too unsteady to go home, Frank took him to a nearby bar for a little fortification.

And a few questions.

When he and Norman had downed their first drink and were on their second, Frank led him to a table. The place was quiet in the midafternoon, with only a few truly dedicated customers, so they could talk easily.

"That was a hard thing to do, Norman," Frank said.

Norman shuddered. "Aunt Penny told me I had to, because there was no one else. Uncle Horace is too sick, and I couldn't expect her to do it, could I?"

Which sounded exactly like what Penny would have said to him. "No one wants to see a family member like that."

"They should cover them up. It's not decent."

"Yes, they should."

Norman finished his drink, and Frank signaled the bartender for another. "So you and Estelle were cousins."

Norman's head came up at that, as though the question were suspicious in some way. "That's right."

"And Miss Longacre raised you."

"My parents died when I was very young. I don't even remember them." He said it like he was reciting something memorized in childhood.

"That's unusual, isn't it? For a maiden lady to take in a child, I mean."

"I don't know. She said she wanted to give me a home. She sacrificed everything for me."

Another thing she had probably told him many times over the years. "She must be very kind."

Norman frowned, looking a little confused. He also didn't agree.

"I guess you and Estelle saw a lot of each other growing up," Frank tried.

He shrugged and sipped his drink.

"How about lately? Have you been called on to escort her places now that she's grown?"

Norman choked on his whiskey, and Frank had to slap him on the back a few times before he could get his breath again. When he did, he gave Frank a wary glance and started to rise. "I really should be going—"

But Frank was ready for him. "You went with her on those tours in the Bowery, didn't you?"

Norman's chin dropped and his eyes popped so far open, Frank thought they might roll out of his head. "I never!"

"Of course you did. Lots of people saw you, including the guide, Will Arburn."

"Willy!" Norman sank back down into his chair. "Is he the one who told you? I'll . . . I'll . . ." Unfortunately, he couldn't seem to think of anything he might do to avenge himself on Will.

"Whose idea was it to go on the tours, Norman?"

"Hers! I swear. I don't even know how she knew about them. She was an evil girl, Mr. Malloy. If you don't believe me, ask Aunt Penny."

"Who could have told her about the tours?"

"I don't know. She reads the newspapers, though. Maybe she saw it there. They're always doing stories about things like that."

"And she dressed up like a man to go on the tours."

"They don't take women, and why would a female want to go? They take you to bars and gambling dens and whorehouses."

"But Estelle wanted to go. And you took her."

Norman sighed. "I thought she'd change her mind when she found out what it was like."

"Had you been on the tours before?"

"I . . ." Norman's pale face turned crimson. "Once or twice. I thought she'd be scared and start crying and beg me to take her home."

"But she didn't."

Norman slowly shook his head, still marveling over Estelle's behavior. "She loved it. She even went upstairs with a whore once."

"You took her more than once?" Frank said, unable to keep the astonishment out of his voice.

"Yes," he admitted, not willing to meet Frank's eye.

"Did the other men on the tour know she was a woman?"

"Of course they did. She thought she was so clever, but she didn't fool anybody."

"What did Will think about taking a female along?"

This time Norman's face darkened with anger. "He thought it was fine, especially when she went off with him after a tour."

"Went off with him?"

"Yes, back to some flat he knew about where they could be alone. She didn't come home until morning. After she did that, I told her I wasn't going to take her on the tours anymore."

"Who did she go with then?"

"She didn't. She just started meeting Will, or at least that's what he told me. He wanted to make sure I knew what they were doing."

"Why?"

"Because Estelle and I were supposed to get married."

6

"THEY WERE ENGAGED?" MAEVE ASKED IN WONDER.

Frank had finally put a slightly tipsy Norman Tufts into a hansom cab and headed across town to the welcome refuge of his own home. Gino had valiantly agreed to meet him there, knowing he'd be forced to spend time with the children and their lovely nursemaid while he waited. Frank would have to commend him for his self-sacrifice.

Now Mrs. Malloy had taken Catherine and Brian up to the nursery so Maeve could hear Frank's report along with Gino and Sarah in the parlor.

"They weren't actually engaged," Frank said. "He told me they were supposed to get married, so of course I asked him some more questions. It seems Miss Penelope Longacre had always told him his duty was to marry Estelle."

"Did Estelle know this?" Sarah asked with unusual skepticism.

"Norman claimed she did, although she wasn't nearly as enthusiastic about the idea as Penelope was."

"What about Norman?" Gino asked. "Was he enthusiastic?"

"He didn't seem to be. In fact, he seemed almost relieved that Estelle was dead."

"Relieved? Are you sure that's what he was feeling?" Sarah asked.

"I'm not positive, but he certainly didn't act like a man who had lost the love of his life."

"But you did say he seemed jealous of Will," Gino reminded him.

"Which doesn't make any sense," Maeve said. "I thought she was seeing that Black Jack fellow."

"Norman didn't seem to know anything about Robinson. From what he said, Estelle flirted shamelessly with our friend Will Arburn during the tours, and when Arburn invited her to go home with him, right in front of Norman, she did. Arburn bragged to Norman afterward, too, so it's possible she really did have an affair with Arburn before she met Robinson."

"How did she meet Robinson then?" Sarah asked.

"Maybe Arburn introduced them," Maeve said.

Sarah frowned. "Would a young man introduce his new girl to a man who was more powerful and apparently more attractive than he is?"

"I wouldn't," Gino said.

"Or maybe she wasn't ever Arburn's girl at all," Frank said. He'd had the entire walk home to think about it. "What if Arburn was just procuring her for Robinson?"

"Do men do that?" Maeve asked with obvious distaste.

"Do you mean he's a cadet?" Gino asked.

"Not exactly. Cadets recruit females for prostitution, and Estelle Longacre wasn't a prostitute. She was apparently

Robinson's mistress, though, and she must have met him through Arburn, somehow."

"So either Arburn found her first and Robinson took her from him, or Arburn found her and brought her to him," Sarah said.

"Does it really matter which way it was?" Gino asked.

"It does if Arburn was jealous and killed Estelle," Frank said. "So I guess we need to find out."

Sarah frowned again. "How will you do that?"

"We'll have to ask Arburn, of course."

"He'll lie," Maeve said.

Frank nodded. "Men always lie about women. But we'll also ask Robinson and see if their stories agree."

"Do we have to ask Robinson?" Gino asked uneasily. "If he's the one who killed her, he won't be happy to see us."

"But if he didn't kill her, he'll probably want to help all he can."

"Maybe he'll even hire you," Maeve said with a grin.

"I'm not counting on it," Frank said. "And don't forget, whoever killed her also killed the boy. Estelle Longacre may have put herself in danger by going to the Bowery in the first place, but Freddie was completely innocent."

That sobered all of them.

"So you're going to do whatever you have to in order to find this killer," Sarah said. "What's next?"

"Next, we question Will Arburn again and then we find Jack Robinson."

BUT BLACK JACK ROBINSON, A MAN WHO OWNED BROTH-els and saloons, was probably not an early riser, especially on a Saturday, and neither was Will Arburn, so Frank and Gino met at the office the next morning to discuss strategy. By the time Frank arrived, Gino had already opened up and a client was waiting.

"Kid Blink, isn't it?" Frank said when he saw the young man sitting in one of the chairs they'd optimistically put in the front office for clients to sit in while they waited.

The Kid jumped to his feet and pumped Frank's offered hand. "Yes, sir, Mr. Malloy. They told me down at the morgue that you wanted to help out with Two Toes's funeral."

"Come into my office and let's talk about it."

The Kid seemed surprised, but he followed Frank into his office and took the offered chair. He looked around, taking in every detail of the modestly furnished room with his one good eye. Frank had decided he didn't need to impress anyone, and a lavish office might scare off the more interesting clients who might not have much money to spend on detectives.

When Frank had taken a seat behind his desk and Gino had sat down on a chair in the corner so he could take notes, Frank said, "I'm very sorry about Freddie. I'm afraid I might have led his killer to him."

"You found him then?"

"I did. A newsboy, Raven Saggio, arranged for me to meet Freddie in an alley behind some tenements in the Bowery. I think it was where Raven usually sleeps."

"I know the place. Why were you looking for Two Toes?"

"I thought I told you. His brother had come into some money and wanted to give Freddie a home."

"Yeah, that's what you told me, but did you really think anybody would believe that whopper?"

Frank shrugged. "I believed it when Will Arburn told it to me."

"Arburn?"

"Yeah. You know him?"

"Everybody knows him." But not everybody liked him, Frank guessed from the Kid's tone.

"He told me his name was Will Bert, though, and he gave me a story about being Freddie's brother and the two of them going out West on the Orphan Train. Supposedly, Freddie got sent back, but Will stayed and made his fortune."

"That's funny, you don't look like a rube," the Kid said with a sly grin.

Frank grinned back. "I'm not usually, but I didn't have any reason to doubt him at first. It sounded like it could be true, but we found out pretty quick that they were never on the Orphan Train. That got me curious as to why this Arburn fellow wanted to find Freddie, so I decided to ask him. Freddie didn't tell me much, though."

"But you told this Arburn where he was?" the Kid asked, angry now.

"No, I didn't, but I did tell Arburn we'd located Freddie and that Freddie didn't want to see him. I don't think I told him anything that would have helped him locate Freddie, but somebody found him and killed him, so I feel responsible. That's why I want to help with the funeral."

"We don't need your money, mister, and we don't need your help. That's what got Two Toes killed."

Frank was very much afraid he was right. "I'm not trying to excuse myself, and I'm not finished. I'm a detective, so I'm going to find out who killed Freddie and why, and then I'm going to make sure he pays for it."

Kid Blink blinked furiously. "You are?"

"Of course I am. Now anything you can tell me about Freddie would help."

The Kid needed a minute to decide. "He didn't have no brother."

"We've already figured that out. And we know he slept

in Black Jack Robinson's flat over the Devil's Den Saloon when Robinson wasn't using it."

The Kid nodded. "He'd keep an eye on things, make sure nobody snuck in. Black Jack didn't like to leave it sitting empty at night."

"So Robinson didn't live there all the time."

"No, he gots a place uptown, real fancy, I hear."

"And where did Freddie sleep when Black Jack was using the flat?"

"Under the stairs. They run up the side of the building, and there's a nice spot underneath that's dry unless it's really raining hard."

"So Freddie would be nearby even when Black Jack was using the flat."

The Kid shrugged. "A lot of nights, I guess. If it was cold or stormy, he'd go to the lodging house, same as the rest of us, though."

Freddie had gone there recently, on a bad night, but he didn't go often, as Gino had learned. "Did he get along with Robinson?"

"He let the boy sleep in his place," the Kid said, which of course told Frank all he needed to know.

"So you don't think Robinson killed him?"

"Why would he?"

Why, indeed? But Frank knew about Estelle Longacre and Kid Blink didn't.

"Do you know anybody who might wish the boy harm? Somebody he got into a fight with, for instance?"

"Or maybe he stole somebody's corner," Gino added, surprising the Kid, who'd apparently forgotten he was there.

"Not that I heard. Besides, none of us is selling papers right now. And everybody liked Two Toes. But if I hear anything, I'll let you know."

"We'd appreciate that." Frank reached into his pocket and pulled out some bills. "Put this toward Freddie's funeral."

The Kid took the money and quickly counted it. "This is more than enough for the whole thing."

"Then use the rest to make sure no newsies go hungry during the strike."

"I will."

"And let me know when the funeral is. I'd like to attend."

REMEMBERING WHAT THE BOUNCER AT THE DEVIL'S DEN Saloon had said, Frank and Gino found the boardinghouse at the corner of 6th Street and Second Avenue where those wishing to take one of Will Arburn's Bowery tours could reach him. It was a seedy-looking place, and even late in the morning, the shades were still drawn.

"Do you think anybody's home?" Gino asked as they climbed the sagging porch steps.

"They're probably still asleep." Frank raised his fist and pounded loudly on the front door.

A prune-faced old woman opened the door and glared at them with rheumy eyes. Her wiry gray hair stood out around her face like a perverse halo, and she clutched a dingy silk wrapper to her bony chest with a clawlike hand. "What's all the fuss?"

"We'd like to see Will Arburn," Frank said.

"He ain't available, but if you want to go on a tour, the book's inside here on the table. Just sign up and pay your fee. You're too late for tonight, but the next one's on Monday."

"We aren't here for a tour. We need to see him on some personal business."

She looked them up and down contemptuously. "Will pays the roundsman every week, so don't try to shake him down for more."

Frank sighed. Why did people always think he was a copper? And even worse, a copper looking for a bribe? "We're not here to shake him down."

"Then come back later," she said, and made to close the door, but Frank was ready. He slapped his hand against the peeling wood and gave it a shove. The old woman staggered back a few steps, giving Frank and Gino the opportunity to step inside. She called them some names that no little old lady should know, but Frank didn't take it personally.

"Will you tell him we're here or do we have to go room to room until we find him?"

Her glare could've drawn blood on a rock. "Your knees are younger than mine. He's on the second floor, first door on the right."

"I'll go," Gino said.

"You hurt the boy, and you'll be sorry," the old woman warned Frank. "He works for Black Jack Robinson."

"I know he does. I'm not going to hurt him. In fact, I work for Will. He hired me to find his brother," Frank tried, curious to see her reaction.

The old woman reared back at that. "Brother? Will ain't got no brother."

"How would you know?"

"Because he's my grandson."

Now, that was interesting. Gino was pounding on the door upstairs, making the old woman wince. Frank said, "You don't think he had a half brother he didn't know about?"

"No, I don't."

"You should ask him why he hired me to find one, then."

Arburn was awake now and swearing at Gino for disturbing him. Gino's voice was a calm rumble in between Arburn's curses. Arburn quickly ran out of steam, though, and then the two men came back down the stairs, Arburn in the lead.

He'd pulled on a pair of trousers, but he was barefoot and shirtless. The house was already stifling, and Frank found himself wishing he could remove his shirt and suit coat, too. "I don't know why you had to wake me up," Arburn was grousing. "Why couldn't this have waited until later?"

Frank saw no reason to answer him. "Mind if we use the parlor?" he asked the old woman, then gave Arburn a gentle shove toward the doorway without waiting for a reply.

Now the old woman was cursing, although much more softly than Arburn had. "Should I get somebody, Willy?" she asked.

"No, Granny. Go back to bed."

"You sure?"

"I'm sure."

The old woman walked away grumbling while the three men went into the shabby parlor. The curtains were closed, but sunlight would not improve this room. A few stuffed chairs with sprung seats were scattered around. The smell of stale cigarette smoke hung heavy in the air, and overflowing ashtrays cluttered dusty tabletops. Arburn sank down into the nearest chair and gazed up at them with bloodshot eyes, absently scratching his bare chest. "Just tell me what you want and get out."

"We thought you'd be interested to know we found Estelle Longacre," Frank said.

Arburn's stubbled face twitched at this, but he pretended to be unimpressed. "Where has she been? Mr. Robinson'll be real happy to see her."

"She's been in the morgue at Bellevue."

"The morgue?" he echoed stupidly.

"Yes, she's dead. She's probably been dead since Saturday night."

He sighed wearily. "I should've known. She was asking

for trouble, coming to the Bowery at night like that. I guess she ran into the wrong person."

"The thing is, we also found Norman Tufts."

Arburn's eyes snapped open at this. "Tufts? Is he dead, too?"

"Not at all."

"Then is he the one killed her?"

"Why would you ask that?" Frank asked.

Arburn blinked a few times. "I . . . Because he was the one who brought her in the first place. He knew her before."

"And they were going to be married," Frank said, watching for Arburn's reaction.

He snorted in derision. "That's what Tufts thought."

"But you didn't?"

"She wasn't going to marry somebody like him."

"No, not when she had a real man like you," Frank said.

"What?" Arburn frowned. "What are you talking about?"

"Tufts told us you were having an affair with Estelle Longacre, that you took her to your flat one night after a tour." Frank glanced around in distaste. "Is this where you took her? Somehow I can't imagine your Granny playing hostess to Miss Longacre."

"Oh no, he'd want to impress her," Gino said. "I bet he took her to Jack Robinson's flat."

"I bet you're right, Gino," Frank said. "He'd know if Robinson was using it or not, and all he'd have to do is send the newsboy out, the one who watched the place when Robinson wasn't there."

"I never . . . I didn't . . ." Arburn tried, but his brain was still sluggish from lack of sleep, and he couldn't seem to form a coherent argument.

Frank continued without him. "So you took Estelle to Robinson's flat after one of your tours. How many times did you take her there afterward, Arburn? How long did you have her before Robinson took her away?"

Arburn glared at him. "That's not what happened."

"What did happen?"

"She . . . I got tired of her."

Frank raised his eyebrows to demonstrate his disbelief.

"It's true! She was . . . a tease."

"A tease? You mean she didn't submit to your advances?"

"Of course she did!" he said, insulted by the very suggestion. "But she didn't . . . I thought . . . She wasn't . . ."

"She wasn't what?" Frank asked, genuinely confused.

"She acted like she was . . . interested. Like she'd be fun."

"And she wasn't *fun*?" Frank asked, still confused.

"Not at all! She just . . . She'd just lay there. She wouldn't even look at me!"

Frank and Gino exchanged a glance.

Arburn didn't like the glance. "It wasn't my fault! She wanted me. It was her idea to go with me the first time."

"How did she get involved with Robinson then?"

Arburn worked his jaw a little before he replied, like he had to force the words out. "He came to the flat one night when she was there. She was waiting for me, but I was late."

"So she threw you over for him?" Gino said, earning a black look from Arburn.

"I was glad enough to see her go. I could see he was taken with her, just like I was at first. We don't see many girls like her in the Bowery."

"You don't see *any* girls like her in the Bowery," Frank said.

"You'd be surprised," Arburn said bitterly. "But Black Jack was smitten, so I left her to him."

"Didn't she have any say in it?" Gino asked.

"Oh, she wanted him, too, or at least she pretended like she did, the way she did with me at first. He's the boss, ain't he? A big man. She liked the idea of being with a real gangster."

"How long ago was this?" Frank asked.

"I don't know. Three weeks or a month, I guess."

"And didn't Robinson get tired of her, too?" Frank asked.

"Maybe she had more fun with him than with Arburn here," Gino said when Arburn didn't answer.

"I don't know anything about it," Arburn insisted angrily.

"You know Robinson was upset when she went missing," Frank reminded him. "Or did you make that up?"

Arburn crossed his arms and looked away.

Gino gave Arburn's foot a nudge with his own, reminding him they weren't just having a friendly chat.

"Yeah, he was upset," Arburn snapped. "He . . . he really cared about her, for some strange reason."

"So he sent you out to find the boy," Frank said.

"Yeah. He thought Two Toes might know what happened to her, why she left that night. He was crazy about her. Black Jack, I mean. I couldn't figure out why, but he was. The way he talked, I thought he might even marry her."

"But she was engaged to Norman Tufts," Frank tried.

Arburn looked up in surprise. "Did Tufts tell you that? Because she couldn't stand him. I know that much, at least. I told you, she wasn't going to marry Norman Tufts."

Frank was sure he was right. "We need to talk to Jack Robinson."

"Why are you telling me?" Arburn asked.

"Because you work for him."

"I'm not his secretary."

"Are you afraid to tell him we're looking for him?"

"I'm not afraid of anything," Arburn lied. "It's just . . . He's a little mad at me right now."

"Because you hired a private investigator to find the boy?" Frank guessed.

Arburn shrugged.

"Just tell us where we can find him then."

"You can ask at the Devil's Den, but I doubt they'll be much help."

"So I guess you're going to tell Robinson yourself that the girl is dead."

Arburn looked up, his eyes wide. "I . . . I can't do that."

"Why not? He's already mad at you, so what harm can it do?"

"I'll . . . If you see him, you can tell him yourself, can't you?"

"Yes, we can."

"Then I'll find out where he is and I'll let you know."

On Monday morning, Sarah left a very disgruntled Malloy behind as she and Maeve made the trip to an attorney's office to take possession of the house that would become a maternity hospital.

"Poor Mr. Malloy," Maeve said. They were tucked inside a cab making its way through the crowded city streets. "Do you think that Arburn fellow was lying when he said he'd find his boss?"

"I have no idea, but maybe Arburn is having as much trouble finding him as Malloy and Gino. According to them, when they didn't hear from Arburn by yesterday, they asked practically everyone in the Bowery for information, but they came away no wiser."

"Sunday in the Bowery is a pretty lonely place. They probably didn't even see anyone who really knew anything."

"How do you know what the Bowery is like on Sunday?" Sarah asked.

Maeve simply smiled. "I've heard rumors."

"I just can't believe this Jack Robinson is so difficult to find."

"I'm sure he just doesn't want to be found," Maeve said. "If he killed Estelle Longacre, he has a good reason to make himself scarce, doesn't he?"

"But if he killed her, why did he send Arburn out to find the boy?"

"Maybe he just wanted to know if the boy saw anything. He wouldn't want any witnesses, would he?"

Sarah hadn't considered that possibility. "I don't suppose he would. But to kill a child . . ." She shuddered.

"I know. That's horrible. But if he's the kind of man who could do that, we probably don't want Gino and Mr. Malloy to find him either."

"That's true, although I'm not sure we can convince them to give up trying."

"I'm afraid you're right." Maeve sighed out her frustration. "Let's talk about something else. Tell me more about the house. I'll get to see it now, won't I?"

They chatted about Sarah's plans for the house until they reached the attorney's office. Sarah paid the cab driver, and they rode up an elevator to the seventh floor to a remarkably luxurious set of offices.

A well-dressed young man escorted them into the office of Odell Cavendish, Esquire. Mr. Cavendish was a distinguished, middle-aged gentleman and not at all what Sarah had expected Mr. Bartholomew's attorney to look like. Sarah introduced Maeve, identifying her as her associate. If Mr. Cavendish thought it odd such a young woman would be anyone's "associate," he didn't say so. Instead he invited them to sit in two of the three leather upholstered chairs situated in front of his desk.

"Will Miss Smith be a part owner in the property?" Cavendish asked.

"No. She'll just be helping to manage it," Sarah said.

He nodded, as if this were a common occurrence, although Sarah was willing to bet he had never before sold a property to a lone female either.

"Is Mr. Bartholomew here?" she asked.

"Uh, no, he— Ah, here we are," Cavendish said, rising to his feet to greet the man who had just stepped into the office.

He was about forty, a tall, well-built gentleman in a tailor-made suit and handmade shoes. He wore his dark hair brushed back from his handsome face, and he was clean shaven except for a well-trimmed mustache. Cavendish came from behind his desk to shake the man's hand, and then he turned back to Sarah and Maeve.

"Mrs. Malloy, Miss Smith, may I introduce Mr. John Robinson?"

Robinson stepped forward and sketched a small bow. "My friends call me—"

"Black Jack," Maeve murmured, although he plainly heard her.

"My *friends* just call me Jack," he said with a small smile.

"I'm very pleased to meet you, Mr. Robinson," Sarah said, wondering if this encounter could possibly be a coincidence. "What brings you to see Mr. Cavendish this morning?"

"Mr. Robinson owns the house you wish to purchase, Mrs. Malloy," Cavendish quickly explained.

"How odd. Mr. Bartholomew presented himself as the owner when I looked at the property."

"Mr. Bartholomew does so with my permission," Robinson

explained. "I find people are sometimes reluctant to do business with me, you see."

"And why would that be?" Sarah asked.

Mr. Robinson gave an elegant shrug. "I have no idea."

"Well, now," Mr. Cavendish said, rubbing his hands together. "Shall we get started?"

"By all means," Robinson said, and took the vacant chair beside Sarah. "I must say, I'm surprised your husband isn't with you, Mrs. Malloy."

Did he know who her husband was? Had he hoped to meet Malloy today? "Do you think a woman isn't capable of conducting business without her husband's help?"

"Oh no," he quickly assured her, "but few men would allow their wives to purchase property by themselves."

"My husband and I agree that having a man own a building where women go for refuge might raise questions, so I should be the sole owner of the property."

"And yet his money is paying for it."

Sarah decided not to take offense. "I can't believe that is any of your business, Mr. Robinson."

Most men would have found her remark impertinent at best, but Jack Robinson apparently was not easily offended. "You are absolutely right. All that should concern me is whether or not you are paying."

"And I am, so you have nothing to fear."

"Oh, I wasn't afraid, Mrs. Malloy," he assured her with another smile.

Cavendish distracted them then with a stack of papers requiring one or both of them to sign. He carefully explained each of them, and when they were finished, Sarah pulled the bank draft out of her purse and presented it to Mr. Cavendish. He examined it and nodded his approval.

"Bartholomew told me you drove a hard bargain," Robinson said.

"Did he? I'm glad to hear it. I hope you made a profit."

"I won the house in a poker game, so anything would have been a profit. I'm just glad to see it go to someone who will do some good with it."

"We hope to. I've been a midwife in the city for a long time, and I know there's a great need in that neighborhood."

"So you're really going to have a maternity hospital there?"

"Of course. What did you think?"

"I won't insult you by telling you what I thought." He turned to Cavendish. "Are we finished?"

"Yes. I'll just have my secretary divide up the documents and prepare packets for each of you. If you wouldn't mind waiting for a few minutes . . ."

"Of course not," Sarah said, and Robinson also agreed.

"Miss Smith," Mr. Cavendish said, "perhaps you'd like to wait in my secretary's office."

Maeve, who had been eyeing Jack Robinson warily through the entire meeting, now looked up in alarm. "Why?"

Cavendish obviously hadn't expected to be challenged. He glanced nervously at Robinson, and suddenly, Sarah understood. "I believe Mr. Robinson wishes to speak with me privately. Is that correct?"

Robinson nodded. "It is."

"It's all right, Maeve," Sarah said. "Go with Mr. Cavendish."

"If you need anything, Mrs. Malloy, you need only call out," Cavendish assured her before escorting a very reluctant Maeve through the door.

"Will I need to call out, Mr. Robinson?" Sarah asked.

"Not on my account, Mrs. Malloy."

Sarah studied his face for a moment. Like most powerful

men, he was very good at hiding his emotions, but she thought she saw something in his dark eyes, something vulnerable. She chose her words carefully. "I can't believe it is merely a coincidence that I am buying property from the very same man my husband has been looking for these past three days."

"And of course it is not. When I heard a few weeks ago that a woman wanted to buy a house in that neighborhood for a maternity hospital, I didn't believe it for a moment. Who would go to so much trouble in that part of the city? So I sent Will Arburn to find out who you were and why you really wanted a house."

"And you discovered I was telling the truth?"

"I discovered you were the daughter of one of the oldest families in the city, and that you had recently married a very rich Irish policeman."

"Who now amuses himself by working as a private investigator."

Robinson's expression hardened. "Will didn't tell me that part of the story until a few days ago, when he had to explain that poor little Freddie is dead."

"I'm very sorry. I understand you knew the boy well."

"He worked for me, but I'd grown fond of him."

Sarah thought it was more than that, but she wasn't going to probe that wound any more than necessary. "My husband was quite upset when he learned of Freddie's death, and he intends to find the boy's killer and bring him to justice."

"Justice?" Robinson echoed with some bitterness. "How does he intend to do that?"

"I don't know, and I have no intention of asking him. I'm confident that he'll do what's right, though."

"I think I'll like your husband, Mrs. Malloy. When I heard he was looking for me, I was hoping to meet him here. I find it works to my advantage to catch people by surprise."

"He might have come if he wasn't so busy hunting for you, Mr. Robinson. May I ask why you wanted to meet him?"

"I want to hire him, Mrs. Malloy. I want him to find someone."

"Miss Longacre?"

She'd surprised him. "How did you know?"

"My husband is a very good detective."

He smiled grimly. "Then perhaps he's already found her."

Sarah winced, hating the thought of causing him more pain. "He has, Mr. Robinson, and I'm so sorry to have to tell you, but she's dead."

7

His expression did not change a bit, but the color drained from his face and tears gathered in his unblinking eyes. Sarah glanced quickly around and saw a tray with liquor decanters and glasses sitting on a side table. She jumped up and poured a generous measure of whiskey into a glass and brought it to him.

"Drink this."

He snatched the glass from her hand and downed it in two swallows. Then he pressed the fingers of his free hand to his eyes, squashing away the tears he was too proud to shed. He set the glass on Cavendish's desk with a clunk and drew an unsteady breath. "I must have known that was it. She couldn't have just disappeared. She wouldn't have gone off without telling me."

He seemed very confident of that, although Sarah knew nothing of Estelle Longacre that would justify such confidence. "I'm very sorry."

"How did you . . . ?" He gestured helplessly.

"Her name came up when my husband questioned Arburn after Freddie died. Malloy can be rather persistent when obtaining information."

"So I've heard."

"Arburn told us she had disappeared and you were trying to find the boy to see if he knew anything. Is that part true, Mr. Robinson?"

He frowned, a sight that probably struck fear into most people he encountered. "Of course it is. Why do you ask?"

"Because Freddie is dead."

"And you think I killed him?" he asked, outraged.

"I had to ask. When he questioned Arburn, Malloy had already been to the morgue and identified Freddie's body. They'd called him when they found Malloy's card in Freddie's pocket."

Robinson nodded. His pain was so palpable, Sarah could hardly meet his eyes.

"When Malloy went to the morgue, they also asked if he recognized a young woman who was there. Her body had also been found in the Bowery. They hadn't been able to identify her, and no one had reported her missing even though her clothes were obviously of good quality."

"Her family wasn't even looking for her?" he asked in wonder.

"No." Sarah didn't want to get into the subject of her family just yet. "But when Arburn told Malloy about Miss Longacre, we thought perhaps . . . So we contacted her family, and they have claimed her body."

"No!" Robinson jumped to his feet. "I won't let them have her."

"I'm not sure how you can stop them. They have every legal right—"

"I don't care about their legal rights. She hated them, and they're not going to have her." He began to pace.

"Mr. Robinson, I know this must be very painful for you. You obviously cared for Miss Longacre—"

"Cared for her? I loved her. I was going to marry her if she'd have me."

No wonder he was so distraught, but of course he hadn't yet proposed and she hadn't accepted. Would Estelle actually have married a gangster? Would her father have allowed it? Probably not, but Sarah knew rich girls were perfectly capable of defying their families and eloping. She'd done it herself. But Sarah knew nothing about Estelle to indicate that she returned Robinson's affections or even if she deserved his devotion.

Although Sarah had to remind herself that the devotion of a gangster also might not be worthy. What a muddle. Still, the man before her was most certainly genuinely bereft.

"You have my sincere sympathy, Mr. Robinson, and I can promise you that my husband is determined to find Freddie Bert's killer. Since it seems likely his killer also killed Miss Longacre, we can get a measure of justice for her as well."

"And I should like to hire your husband to do just that, Mrs. Malloy."

"It isn't necessary, I assure you."

"Yes, it is. I want him to tell me what he finds, and I have learned through experience that paying a man greatly increases the chances that he will do what I want."

"I'm sure that's true. At any rate, my husband wants to talk with you. The more information he has, the more likely he is to find the killer."

He reached into his waistcoat pocket and drew out a calling card. "This is my home address. He can find me there."

* * *

"THAT'S A PRETTY FANCY ADDRESS FOR A GANGSTER," Malloy said when she gave him the card.

"What exactly is a gangster?" Sarah asked. They were alone in their private sitting room, so she didn't have to worry about anyone overhearing. "I mean, I know he's a criminal, but what does he actually do?"

They were sitting on the love seat, and Malloy studied the card for a long moment before he replied. "I suppose it depends on the gangster himself. I probably don't know half of what Jack Robinson does, but I do know he owns several saloons and gambling hells. He probably runs some brothels as well. He'll also deal in stolen goods or at least take a cut when crimes happen in the neighborhoods he controls."

"Is he a killer?"

"Personally? Not now. He might've killed someone along the way, when he was building his reputation for being tough. Most likely he just frightened people by beating them up, though. Now he'd have his flunkies do the actual beating."

"And the killing?"

"If it's necessary, although men like Robinson don't like to resort to murder. A dead man can't make you any money. And if he did need to kill someone, he'd have one of his men do it, I'm sure."

"Unless it was his mistress."

"And he killed her in the heat of passion."

"Which is how most men kill women, I assume, but why would Robinson have been that angry with Estelle?"

Malloy sighed. "There's one thing I haven't told you about Estelle Longacre, and it might have made Robinson mad enough to kill her. She was expecting a child."

"Oh my! That's a pretty serious thing to keep to yourself."

"I didn't keep it to myself on purpose. Doc Haynes mentioned it when I went to the morgue to identify Freddie's body. I didn't know who she was then, though, so it didn't seem important, and it slipped my mind until this morning when I was going over everything I knew about her."

"But if the child was Robinson's, he would probably be thrilled because Estelle would almost certainly agree to marry him."

"But it wasn't his. She was about three months along, and she only met Robinson about a month ago."

"So that gave him a good reason to be angry."

"Possibly angry enough to kill her." Malloy's dark eyes turned cold. "I hate that he met with you alone."

"I told you, he expected you would be there, too, and he behaved like a perfect gentleman. I have to admit, that surprised me, that and the way he was dressed. He dressed like a perfect gentleman, too. I suppose he must be rich from all his criminal activities, and he certainly looked it today. And his attorney is quite respectable, as well."

Malloy held up Robinson's card. "And he lives in a fashionable neighborhood."

"All he lacks is a wife whose name is in the Social Register."

"So he must have been thrilled to find her waiting for him in his flat that first time."

Sarah shook her head. "Maybe that's what he saw at first, but I'm sure he really cared for her, Malloy. You didn't see his face when I told him she was dead."

"But even if he did love her—especially if he did love her—he would've been angry to find she was carrying another man's child."

"But if he killed her, why would he want to hire you to find her murderer?"

"Good point. I'll be sure to ask him that when I call."

"And when will that be?"

Malloy grinned. "As soon as we've had lunch."

BLACK JACK ROBINSON LIVED IN AN IMPRESSIVE TOWN house on Lexington Avenue. In distance, it wasn't so very far from his Bowery flat over the Devil's Den Saloon, but socially, it was in another world.

A maid answered Frank's knock and made him wait only a few minutes while she announced him. She took him upstairs, past portraits of at least a century's worth of ancestors who couldn't possibly be Robinson's, and led him to a room at the back of the house that turned out to be a library. Even though Sarah had warned him, he was surprised by Jack Robinson. Well-groomed and well-tailored, he actually looked like he belonged in this book-lined room where expensive cigars were smoked and aged brandy was consumed. Today he'd been drinking whiskey, if Frank's nose did not deceive him.

Robinson's handshake was firm. "Thank you for coming, Mr. Malloy."

"Thank you for letting me find you."

"I don't let many people know where I live. Please, sit down." He motioned to two easy chairs positioned for convenient conversation in front of the cold fireplace. A table between them held a bottle of whiskey and two glasses. One was half-full. "Would you like a drink?"

Frank sat down in one of the chairs, finding it surprisingly comfortable. "I don't drink when I'm working."

"Some lemonade then?"

"That sounds good."

Robinson rang and the maid came almost instantly to receive his orders. When she had gone, Robinson took the other chair and sighed wearily. "Your wife is quite a lady. You are a lucky man."

"I know. She tells me you cared very much for Miss Longacre."

A spasm of pain flickered across his face, and Frank knew Sarah was right. Robinson really had loved Estelle Longacre. "We hadn't known each other very long, but the first time I saw her, I knew she was the one."

"How did you meet her?"

He stiffened at that. Defensively, Frank thought. "What did Arburn tell you?"

"I want to hear your version."

Robinson sighed and drained the half-full glass of whiskey. "I'm sure Arburn told you he had her first." He looked up, his dark eyes glittering with suppressed fury. "She wasn't an angel, but there were reasons."

"I'm sure there were."

"She was desperately unhappy, and she was young. She didn't understand the risks she was taking. Her cousin, that idiot, he had no business taking her to the Bowery no matter what she said she wanted."

Frank knew better than to offer an opinion. His silence invited confession, and Robinson was drunk enough to give it.

"She wanted some excitement in her life. It made her feel alive, she said. That's why she dressed up like a man and went on Will's tour. Everybody knew she was a woman, though, and she enjoyed that, too. She'd never known anyone who wasn't a member of society, and she thought Will was fascinating and dangerous. That's why she went with him."

"But he wasn't as dangerous as you," Frank guessed.

Another spasm twisted his face, and he poured himself

another glass of whiskey. The maid knocked at the door just then and brought in Frank's lemonade. He took a long swallow, wishing he wasn't so strict with himself and could add a dollop of Robinson's whiskey to it. This interview was going to be even more difficult than he'd imagined.

"Will was using my rooms over the Den to meet Estelle. He hadn't asked my permission, so I had no idea I might encounter anyone there. She was as surprised as I was, of course. She knew who I was, too, but she wasn't afraid of me."

That fact seemed to still mystify him. He was probably so used to people fearing him that he didn't know how to react when they didn't. "So you took her away from Arburn."

But Robinson shook his head. "You make her sound like property. Will didn't own her. She'd chosen to be with him, and then she changed her mind. That night, when I found her waiting for him, we just talked. I thought she was Will's girl, and even though I was going to let him know what I thought of him using my place without permission, I wasn't going to do it in front of her. I didn't want to embarrass her, you see. She was so . . . so delicate."

That wasn't a word Frank had heard anyone use about Estelle. "And you wanted to protect her," he said.

"Of course. She was a lady. You could see that right away. The way she carried herself and the way she spoke."

Ladies didn't dress up like men and go slumming in the Bowery and give themselves to men like Will Arburn, but Frank decided not to mention that. "So you protected her from Arburn."

"When he finally showed up, he was pretty scared to find me there, but Estelle sent him on his way, so I couldn't be too mad at him. If he hadn't brought her there, I never would've met her."

"So she started seeing you there instead of Arburn."

"I know what you must think of her, but she wasn't . . ." He took another swallow of whiskey. "I know what she did with Will, but she was still pretty innocent. She didn't even know she could enjoy it. No one had ever really made love to her."

This was getting uncomfortably personal. Frank regretted even more his decision not to drink. "My wife said you wanted to marry Miss Longacre."

"I did. I wish I'd told her. In fact, I wish I'd just married her. She'd still be alive now." He ran a hand over his face.

He was probably right, but there was no reason to make him feel worse by saying so. "Did you know she was with child?"

Plainly, he had not. "What? Are you sure? Who told you that?"

"The coroner. He said she hadn't been interfered with, but that she was expecting a baby and was about three months along."

"Three months? Can they know that for certain?"

"He seemed pretty sure. I'm guessing it wasn't yours then."

"No, three months ago . . . it couldn't have been." He'd gone ashen. Did he think she'd known and had been trying to trap him somehow?

"That's still very early, though. Girls like her are kept pretty ignorant about such things, so she might not have even known herself."

"Is that true?"

"It's what my wife told me, and she's a midwife, so she should know." He hadn't really discussed it with Sarah, but he'd learned a thing or two about pregnancy since meeting her.

This time Robinson sipped his whiskey slowly, thoughtfully. "Even Will hasn't known her that long."

Which meant she was even less innocent than Robinson wanted to believe. "I'm going to find out who killed Freddie Bert, and I think he was killed because he knew something about what happened to Miss Longacre. I'll understand if you don't care anymore—"

"Do you think I'd stop loving her because of that? It wouldn't have mattered. In fact, it would've made her more likely to marry me if she was pregnant. She'd be grateful to me for saving her from disgrace, and I'd be grateful to her for making me respectable. That's why I got this house, you know. Because I wanted to be respectable. One of my clients signed it over to me to satisfy his gambling debts. All I needed was the right wife. With Estelle by my side, we'd have ruled New York society."

Frank wasn't going to explain it would take far more than someone like Estelle to make him socially acceptable to people like Sarah's parents. "I just meant that you don't have to hire me. I'm going to investigate anyway."

"As I told your wife, I want to know everything you find out, so I *am* going to hire you."

"And I'll accept you as a client if you agree to share with me everything you know or find out, too."

"Of course!"

"I mean it. If you find out who the killer is before I do, I don't want you to throw him in the East River before I have a chance at him."

"Are you going to put him on trial?" Robinson scoffed. "Imagine what the newspapers would do with that."

"I don't know what I'll do. It depends on who it is and why he killed them. But I want the chance to make that decision while the murderer is still alive."

Robinson didn't like it, but he said, "All right. I agree."

Frank gave him a moment, waiting to see if he was going to squirm or otherwise indicate he didn't really mean his promise. Seeing no betraying signs, he said, "Now tell me everything you know about Miss Longacre. You said she hated her family."

"Is that really necessary? What can it matter now?"

"It might help me figure out who killed her. If she had another lover before Arburn, he might've killed her when he found out she was seeing you."

Robinson refilled his whiskey glass, draining the bottle, and took a fortifying sip. "I never met any of her family."

"I have," Frank said. "I've met her father, her aunt Penelope, and Norman Tufts. Norman told me he and Estelle were supposed to be married."

Robinson was already shaking his head. "That was Penelope's idea, and she'd been drilling it into Norman his entire life."

"Why?"

"Who knows? The aunt is a little crazy, I think."

Penelope Longacre was many things, but not crazy. "Did Estelle's father want them to get married?"

"No. He and his sister didn't get along. There was something about an inheritance when their father died. Penelope didn't get anything or maybe not as much as she thought she had coming. But definitely, it was about money. Estelle thought she was pushing for the marriage so Norman could get his hands on all the money when the old man died and left it to Estelle."

"Norman told me he's an orphan and the aunt took him to raise."

"Estelle didn't talk about them much. She just called Norman her cousin, and I knew he lived with her maiden aunt."

"Do you think Norman might have fathered her child?"

Robinson made a rude noise. "Not with her consent. I told you, she hated all of them."

"Maybe she hated him because he'd raped her."

Plainly, Robinson hadn't considered this. "I guess that's possible, but he gave her up to Will without a fight. That doesn't sound like a man willing to rape a woman to get her to marry him."

And Norman didn't seem like the kind of man to rape a woman at all. "You're probably right. Did she ever mention any other men?"

Robinson smiled grimly at this. "To me?"

No, Frank didn't suppose she would've discussed her previous lovers with Black Jack Robinson. "You said she was desperately unhappy. Do you know why?"

"Why is anybody unhappy?"

"She was a rich girl. She lived in a big house and had plenty of clothes and she never went hungry. Thousands of people in this city live with far less than that and manage to be content."

Robinson didn't like being challenged. "It was her father."

"What about him? Did he beat her or something?"

"I don't know. She wouldn't talk about him, but he was the reason she hated her life."

Frank remembered the sick old man. Living with him had to be unpleasant. And yet . . . "She had the freedom to go to the Bowery whenever she wanted."

"Norman brought her. She lied about where she was going."

"Did Norman keep bringing her when she started meeting Arburn? Did he bring her to meet you?"

"No," Robinson reluctantly admitted.

"How did she get away, then? It's not easy for an unmarried girl like her to go out. She has to protect her reputation. She has to be chaperoned." Unless no one is paying attention, and who would have been, in that house? The aunt lived elsewhere, and her father was too sick and too selfish to even notice what his daughter was doing.

"I didn't think of that." Probably because the other women he knew didn't have reputations to protect.

"Not to mention the danger for a lone female coming to the Bowery at night."

"She didn't come at night, not after she started seeing me. I knew it was too dangerous. We'd meet in the afternoons. She could get a cab to bring her in the daylight, and I'd make sure she got one to take her home."

"But what about that last time? I thought you were meeting her in the evening."

"That was unusual. She'd sent me a message. She wanted to meet me at the Den that night."

"Why?"

"She didn't say, but it was a telegram, so she couldn't say much." He was right. Ten words that other people would also see made that impossible.

"Where did she send it?"

"Here, to my house. She knew where I lived, although we'd never met here. I didn't want my neighbors to see her coming here before we were married."

How oddly considerate of him, but of course he wouldn't want to give them reason to gossip about his wife if he was marrying her to gain respectability. "Had she ever contacted you here before?"

"Once, when she couldn't meet me as we'd planned. I thought it was strange she wanted to meet so late in the day . . . Well, it wasn't really late—six o'clock—but much later than we usually met. But now that it's summer, it's daylight much later."

"But you didn't meet her."

He drew an unsteady breath and the hand that reached

for his whiskey glass trembled slightly. After he'd swallowed some more whiskey, he said. "I didn't get the telegram in time. I was out of town on business all day, and it was almost nine o'clock by the time I got home. I went straight down to the Den then, but she wasn't there. I figured she'd gotten tired of waiting and wanted to get home before dark."

"You didn't notice anything unusual in the flat?"

"I could tell she'd been there, if that's what you mean. She'd opened the windows and moved some things around."

"Did you notice anything missing?" Frank asked, remembering Estelle's body had been found hidden in a trunk.

"You mean stolen? I don't keep anything valuable there."

"No, I mean furniture, something that wasn't where it should be."

He frowned, trying to remember. "I don't think so."

That was strange, but maybe Robinson just wasn't very observant. Or the trunk had come from someplace else. "Did you see Freddie that night?"

"No. He would've made himself scarce if he saw Estelle there, and it was a nice night. He could've slept anywhere. But now that I think of it, it wasn't even nine thirty when I got to the Den, so even if he intended to stay at the flat, he probably would have still been out with his friends. The boys like to go out to a show or to have some fun, especially on Saturday night."

What a strange thought, a bunch of newsboys attending a play. But they probably liked to be entertained, just like everyone else. "When did you realize Miss Longacre was missing?"

"The next day. We usually met on Sunday afternoon. When she didn't come, I thought maybe she was mad at me for not meeting her the night before. I sent Will out to see if Freddie had seen her on Saturday and if she'd said anything to him. I already knew nobody in the Den had seen her, because I'd asked that night."

"And when Will didn't have any luck finding Freddie, he hired me."

Robinson nodded. "I also sent somebody to her house on Monday morning with a package addressed to her. I put a note in it, telling her why I hadn't come on Saturday night, but she never responded. That's when I started to get worried. By Thursday, when Will told me Freddie was dead, I was actually hoping she'd run off with another man."

If only she had. "Would you take me to your flat? I need to see it for myself."

"Now?"

"If you don't mind."

Robinson rubbed his face again. "I haven't been back there since last Sunday. That's where she was killed, wasn't it?"

"We don't know for certain. You don't have to go in if you don't want to, though."

"Let's go then."

"This just doesn't seem right," Mrs. Ellsworth said as Velvet set the tray with a silver coffee service and a plate of coconut macaroons on the breakfast room table.

"I expect your cookies are better than mine, Miz Ellsworth," Velvet said. "But when you is here, you gotta expect to get waited on."

Sarah bit back a smile. Her cook was being modest only to spare her neighbor's feelings. No one made better macaroons than Velvet.

"I'm sure your cookies are better, Velvet," Mrs. Ellsworth responded, prepared to be even more modest than the cook, "if only because I didn't have to make them."

"I always find that's true, ma'am," Velvet said. "You enjoy these now."

Mrs. Ellsworth assured her that she would. When Velvet had returned to the kitchen, Mrs. Ellsworth said, "Did you find it hard to adjust to having servants again?"

"I'd like to say I did, and that I really enjoyed doing everything myself all those years, but I've been only too happy to have someone to look after the house and prepare the meals. With so many of us living here now, I wouldn't have time to do anything else." Sarah picked up the coffeepot and poured a cup for each of them. She knew better than to put cream or sugar into Mrs. Ellsworth's cup for her. Mrs. Ellsworth was sure to point out that doing so would bring bad luck to her or Sarah or someone close to them. Just about everything brought either good luck or bad, according to her superstitious neighbor. Sarah placed the cup and saucer in front of Mrs. Ellsworth.

"Oh my, bubbles in your cup, Mrs. Malloy," Mrs. Ellsworth said, pointing. "That means money is coming."

Sarah saw there was indeed a row of bubbles floating along the rim of her cup. "That's always good news. How are the wedding plans coming along?"

Mrs. Ellsworth's son, Nelson, had recently become engaged. "Oh, the mother of the groom is hardly involved at all, as I'm sure you know. We are planning a small dinner for the wedding party and the families, but aside from that, my duties include wearing a dress that is slightly less attractive than the bride's mother's dress and showing up at the church on time."

"Malloy and I would like to have you and Nelson and his intended over for dinner one evening. We want to get to know her since she'll be our neighbor as well."

"I'm sure they'd both be thrilled to be invited. After all you've done for Nelson . . . but of course Theda doesn't know anything about that unfortunate incident."

"She certainly won't hear about it from us either."

"Which reminds me, are you working on any interesting cases?"

"Sadly, yes. A young woman was found murdered in the Bowery."

"That sounds like a police matter." Mrs. Ellsworth chose a macaroon from the plate and examined it carefully before taking a bite.

"It should be, of course, but it wasn't what you'd think. The girl comes from an old New York family."

"What on earth was she doing in the Bowery, then?"

"It seems she'd gone slumming."

"Slumming? Is that as bad as it sounds?"

"I'm not sure how bad it sounds, but probably. For reasons I will never understand, wealthy young men enjoy hiring guides to take them on a tour of Bowery saloons and gambling dens and, uh, other places of ill repute."

"Good heavens! But you said young *men* do this, and that's understandable. There's no telling what trouble a young man will get himself into, but you said it was a young woman who was murdered."

"Yes, she had apparently dressed up like a man and gone on one of these tours. In fact, she'd gone on more than one. Then she'd taken the tour guide as her lover."

"A girl from a good family, you said? How shocking! It's a wonder the newspapers haven't reported it. This is just the type of story they love, although I suppose they very well might be reporting it and we'd never know because the newsboys aren't selling the papers."

"That's true, although I don't think the newspapers know about it yet. Her family didn't even know she was dead until a few days ago."

"How could they not know she was dead? Didn't they notice when she didn't come home?"

"Her mother is dead and her father is very ill. I gather he didn't pay much attention to her even before he became ill either, so the poor girl was free to do as she liked, from what we have learned. I believe they thought she'd eloped or something."

"The poor thing. No good comes of allowing young women too much freedom."

Sarah could have argued with her, but she knew it would be a waste of energy. Besides, Estelle Longacre did rather prove the rule. "I guess the newsboys' strike is good for something if it prevents her story from becoming public."

Mrs. Ellsworth had just selected another macaroon. "That's true, although I do miss the Yellow Kid. That cartoon always makes me laugh. Tell me, do you have any idea who might have murdered this poor young woman?"

"I'm not sure if we do. She was spending time in a very unsavory part of town, of course, so her killer most likely encountered her there, but . . ."

"But?" Mrs. Ellsworth echoed, her eyes glittering with interest.

"But her family is rather unsavory as well."

"I thought you said they were society people."

"A listing in the Social Register doesn't guarantee good character."

"Oh dear, I know that perfectly well. What was I thinking? So what is it about this family that makes you doubt their character?"

"Her father is rather unpleasant, for one."

"Ill people often are. They tend to think only of themselves as well."

"I have a feeling her father was unpleasant long before he became ill."

"Ah." Mrs. Ellsworth nodded knowingly. "What about her mother?"

"She apparently died young, probably in childbirth."

"How tragic, especially for a girl. Who raised her then?"

"She has an aunt, the father's sister, although I don't know how involved she might have been. The aunt and the father don't get along."

"If the aunt was involved with her own family, she would have been too busy for the girl, in any case."

"The aunt has never married, although she does have a ward."

"A ward?"

"Yes, a young man who was a cousin of some kind. When he was orphaned, she took him in."

"That's unusual."

"Malloy and I thought so, too, but apparently, she's devoted to him."

"I'm sure she is. I wonder if the boy had a legacy of some kind from his parents. It's amazing how kind people can be when they're being recompensed."

"I hadn't thought of that, but it would explain why a maiden lady would assume responsibility for a child."

Mrs. Ellsworth sipped her coffee thoughtfully. "There might be another reason, too."

Sarah leaned forward. "What reason?"

"It's unusual, of course, but it might also explain the dead girl's behavior. Blood will tell, you know."

"What do you mean?"

"Moral weakness. It's in the blood. You say this aunt is devoted to her ward, a boy with no family whom she took to raise. What if the boy were more closely related to the aunt than being a cousin? What if the whole orphaned-cousin story was invented to explain his existence and give the aunt an excuse to raise him as her own?"

Of course. "Because he was her own," Sarah said.

8

FRANK DIDN'T FIND THE BOWERY QUITE AS THREATENING with Black Jack Robinson beside him.

"Afternoon, Mr. Robinson," the enormous bouncer called from the doorway of the Devil's Den Saloon.

Robinson stopped and introduced Frank to the bouncer, whose name was Tiny. "Mr. Malloy is doing some work for me, so if he asks for anything, he gets it."

"Yes, sir," Tiny said with an uncertain frown. "He's the one who was looking for Freddie."

"I know. He's going to find out who killed him."

That seemed to satisfy Tiny, much to Frank's relief.

Robinson led him around the side of the building to a narrow alley. About halfway back were the stairs that ran up the side of the building to the second floor. "That's where Freddie would sleep." He pointed to the area beneath the stairs. Tucked in there, the boy would be hidden from the street, especially when the alley was dark.

After taking a fortifying breath, Robinson began to climb the stairs. Frank followed, giving the man a little space. Robinson pulled a ring of keys from his pocket, found the right one, and unlocked the door. He pushed it open and hesitated only a moment before entering. By the time Frank entered, Robinson was standing in the center of the front room, looking around thoughtfully. The flat apparently had two rooms. This one was furnished as a sitting room. Lace curtains, the ones he and Gino had noticed before, hung at the windows. A horsehair sofa and matching chair sat at one end of the room. A kerosene lamp perched on a small table between them. An old-fashioned buffet took up another wall. On it stood a collection of liquor bottles and glasses. A sink and some shelves along the last wall formed a kitchen area of sorts, and a small, round table with two chairs took up the center of the room.

Except for a little dust, the place was immaculate, making Frank wonder who cleaned it. Probably whoever cleaned the saloon, if such a thing ever actually happened. Frank had never given much thought to such matters.

"Nothing is missing," Robinson said. "I've been thinking about that since you asked me. I didn't really look around last Sunday when I came, but I would've noticed even then, I'm sure. There's just not that much here."

"What about the other room?"

Robinson led the way. As Frank had expected, it was a bedroom, much smaller than the other room. The iron bedstead had been neatly made up with a slightly faded quilt covering the linens. A washstand stood against one wall and a row of pegs on another wall provided what closet space might be necessary. Nothing hung there now. Robinson studied the room for a moment, then looked behind the door.

"The trunk," he said in surprise, closing the door to reveal the space. "I had a trunk sitting there." The outline in the dust was plain to see, as were the drag marks where it had been pushed or pulled from its corner.

Frank nodded. Just as he'd suspected.

"What is it?" Robinson demanded.

"She was found in a trunk about a block from here. Whoever killed her tried to carry her away, but he probably decided it was too much trouble and just left the trunk in an alley. Some boys who wanted to steal the trunk found her."

Robinson had to close his eyes for a moment as he absorbed this new horror. When he opened them again, they were shining with fury. "But how could he have gotten the trunk down the stairs with her inside?"

"He must've had help."

"So there was more than one of them?"

"Not necessarily. He may have left and come back with help or maybe he found someone outside. A stranger wouldn't have asked what was in the trunk."

"But who . . . ? It could've been Freddie," he guessed after a moment. "He might've been right outside."

"It's possible. That would explain why he was killed, at least. The killer would've been afraid Freddie would tell on him."

"But why wait? Why didn't they kill him right away?"

"Maybe the boy ran off. Maybe someone saw them together and the killer didn't want to take a chance just then. Who knows? I've been thinking the boy must have seen something that put him in danger, though. He must've known it, too, because he was hiding out with his friend Raven."

"Maybe this Raven knows something."

"I'll find out. Do you remember if the trunk was here on Saturday night when you arrived?"

Robinson frowned as he tried to recall. "I came into the flat. The lamp was still burning in the front room, I remember."

"Did you look in the bedroom?"

"Of course I did. I called for her, and when she didn't answer, I looked in. I thought she might've fallen asleep or something. The room was dark, but I could see well enough to know she wasn't there."

"And did you see the trunk?"

"I . . . I don't know. I may have glanced behind the door, just to make sure she wasn't there. But she'd have no reason to hide from me, so I probably didn't."

"And if the trunk was missing, would you have noticed? In the dark?"

"I . . . Probably not. I'm not even sure I looked. But if it was there, that means she wasn't dead yet."

"Not necessarily."

"I . . ." The color drained from his face, and his eyes widened in horror. "Oh dear God, do you think she was here, in the trunk, when I got here? That I could've saved her?"

Frank grabbed his arm and steered him back to the front room, where he could sit down. "Estelle was strangled. If she was in the trunk, she was already dead, and there was nothing you could've done. You said yourself the trunk might've been gone by then, too."

"But how? It hadn't been dark very long when I got here. The killer couldn't take a chance of being seen stealing something from my flat."

"How long were you here?"

"Not long. As soon as I realized she'd gone, I went downstairs to see if she'd left me a message or if anybody in the Den had seen her. Nobody had, and Freddie wasn't around, so I locked the place up and went home. I thought I'd see her the next day at our regular time."

"Who has a key to this place?"

"Me. Estelle, so she could come whenever she wanted. Freddie, because he stayed here. And the bartender keeps one downstairs. He sends somebody up to sweep it out now and then."

"That's all?"

"Yes."

"How did Arburn get in?"

"I . . . He might have used the bartender's key or . . ."

"Or had his own key made." Which meant he could've come and gone whenever he liked.

"One more thing I need to discuss with him," Robinson said.

"When you got here Saturday night, was the door locked?"

He hesitated, trying to remember. "Yes, it was. I tried the knob, and then knocked when it wouldn't open. I thought Estelle was there and would let me in. When she didn't answer, I used my key."

"You said you locked it when you left that night."

"Yes, I always lock it. This is the Bowery, after all."

"And it was still locked when you returned on Sunday."

"Yes. Why are you so worried about whether it was locked or not?"

"Because the killer was very careful. He must've used Estelle's key to lock up behind himself." Or his own, but Frank wasn't going to bring that up. "I'm just trying to figure out when he might've moved her out. I think you're right. He probably came back after dark so no one would see him. It would've taken two people to carry the trunk down the stairs and as far away as it was found. Freddie was a good-sized boy. He might've been the one who helped. Do you think he would have helped somebody taking a trunk out of your flat?"

Robinson rubbed his temples as if they ached. "He wouldn't have helped somebody steal from me."

"What if he thought the person was acting on your orders?"

"He'd do it then, but why would he think that?"

Another reason to think it was Arburn. "I don't know yet. I'm just trying to figure out what might've happened. It was late at night and dark and Freddie came here looking for a place to sleep and he saw somebody trying to get a trunk down the steps. It would take a lot of nerve for somebody to steal from Black Jack Robinson."

Robinson looked up at that. "Yes, it would."

"So maybe the person lied and said you'd sent him. Maybe you wanted the trunk moved right away for some reason."

"That doesn't make any sense."

"To you, but why would Freddie question it?"

"Because he's lived on these streets his whole life, and he doesn't trust anybody."

Malloy nodded. "You're probably right. So the killer had gone for help, and he and his friend carried the trunk down the stairs."

"But Freddie saw them, and they saw him," Robinson guessed. "But how would he know about Estelle being killed?"

"He wouldn't have, not then. But they told me at the morgue that some boys had found the trunk and discovered her body."

"Do you think Freddie was one of them?"

"If he was, he'd probably have recognized the trunk, but if he wasn't one of the boys who found it, he would've at least heard about it. If he'd seen somebody carrying the trunk away and then heard about the woman's body found in a trunk, he'd probably have figured it out."

"Which is why he was hiding."

"And when he heard you were looking for him, he might've thought you killed her and were after him, too."

Robinson swore. "Stupid kid. I could've protected him."

Frank couldn't argue. "I need to talk to the men who work in the saloon downstairs."

"They already told me they didn't see anything."

"Of course they did, but if they saw something and now your lady friend is dead, you're the last person they'd tell."

Robinson opened his mouth to protest, but he must have realized the truth of that because he stopped himself. "All right. Do what you have to do. Just remember you're working for me now."

"Don't worry. I'll be reporting what I find out, and I may have more questions for you later."

"You know where to find me. You can leave word with the bartender downstairs or at my house, too."

Frank left him sitting there in the room where he'd first met Estelle Longacre and where she had most likely died. If only he could find someone to give him a better idea of what Estelle was really like. Everyone he'd met so far either loved her or hated her. While she had behaved very oddly for a young lady brought up in society, she couldn't have been as bad as some had made her out to be. She'd had reasons for doing what she'd done, Frank was sure. If he could figure out what those reasons were, he might be able to figure out who killed her. He'd at least have a better idea of why she'd died.

The Devil's Den Saloon was starting to fill up, but it wasn't nearly as lively as it would become later in the evening. Tiny the bouncer sat perched on a wooden chair just inside the door, his long, thick legs stretched out before him as he kept an eye on the small crowd scattered around at the battered wooden tables or bellied up to the bar along the rear wall. He would, Frank realized, have no trouble at all carrying a trunk with a dead woman inside down a flight of stairs.

"Mind if I ask you a few questions?" Frank asked.

Tiny grunted, his eyes wary.

"You know that Mr. Robinson's lady friend was murdered a week ago Saturday night."

Tiny's broad, pockmarked face sank into a frown. "That's what I've heard."

"She was supposed to meet Mr. Robinson upstairs that night, only he was out of town and didn't get the message. He got here around nine thirty, and she wasn't there. We figure she was dead by then, and whoever killed her stuffed her into a trunk and carried her out."

"That seems like a lot of trouble. Why not just leave her there?"

"If you killed Black Jack's woman, would you want him to just walk in and find her there?"

"He'd find out sooner or later."

Or would he? Maybe the killer had intended to dispose of Estelle's body in a way that she would never be found. It would certainly explain why he'd gone to all the trouble to get help and sneak her out in the trunk. If she'd just disappeared, would her family and Robinson both have just figured she'd run off? Would anyone have even suspected murder? Any efforts to find her would have been fruitless, and eventually, they would've all given up even trying. "Yeah, I guess he would find out eventually," Frank tried. "But the fact is that the killer took her out in a trunk. I was wondering if you heard anything suspicious that night."

"The boss already asked me. He asked me right after she disappeared, in fact."

"And did you?"

"I told him no, and it's the truth. It gets pretty noisy in here at night. We've got a piano player." He nodded to a disreputable-looking upright behind him. "And people sing if he plays something they like. And when the place is full, everybody's shouting. You have to if you want to be heard."

So if Estelle had screamed, no one would have heard. Still . . . "If somebody was dragging something across the floor upstairs or thumping down the steps . . ."

"I didn't hear anything. I didn't see anything, and that little tart didn't show her face in here, not ever. She was too good for the likes of us once she took up with Mr. Robinson."

"She'd been here before that, though," Frank guessed. "Will Arburn brought her."

"On them tours of his. She come to look us over like we was a circus sideshow or something, her and them rich friends of hers."

Frank could understand how that might cause offense. "But what about Freddie? Did you see the boy at all on that Saturday night or the next day?"

"No, but I wouldn't, would I? He'd sell his papers and go off someplace with his pals and then he'd come back here when he wanted to sleep. Sometimes I wouldn't see him for a week or more. No reason I should."

"Would it help your memory if I told you the same person who killed the girl also killed Freddie?"

Tiny's face hardened. "You mean because I didn't care nothing about the girl, and I did care about Freddie?"

"That's exactly what I mean."

"Sorry, no. I still didn't see nothing or hear nothing. Freddie wasn't a bad kid, but those boys are like rats, running around the alleys all the time. Some of 'em live and some of 'em die, and it's no business of mine."

Frank managed not to sigh. "Did you tell the bartender I'm working for Robinson now?"

"Of course."

Frank went to the bar. The bartender was a burly fellow

whose bald head was freckled and fringed with faded red hair. His bushy sideburns and lush mustache made up for his lack on top. He turned pale gray eyes to size Frank up.

"You the one working for the boss now?"

"That's right." Frank introduced himself and passed the man one of his cards. He eyed it suspiciously. Frank reminded him of the day Estelle had died and asked him the same questions he'd asked Tiny.

"Funny you should ask. Mr. Robinson, he only wanted to know if I'd seen his lady friend or if she'd left a message. Nobody ever mentioned nothing about noises."

"You heard something, then?"

"Yeah, later, though. A while after he left."

"What did you hear?"

"I don't know. Thumping or stomping." He pointed to the ceiling above the bar, which would have been the floor of the bedroom upstairs. "Somebody made a joke about Black Jack and the girl really going at it."

"Did the customers know about her?" Frank asked in surprise.

"Everybody knew. There's no secrets in the Bowery. You see a woman like that down here, everybody remembers. They talk, too."

Of course they did. Frank should've known. "But you didn't see her that night?"

"No. I'd only seen her a couple times. When she'd come, she'd pass by the door, I guess. Tiny would say something and we'd all look. She'd come in the daytime. Not many people around then, but we could see her clear."

"Do you remember what time it was when you heard the thumping?"

"No. I know it was after Mr. Robinson left, but how much longer, I couldn't say for sure. Nobody watches the time here."

"Did you see any strangers around that night?"

"I see strangers every night, mister. This is the Bowery. Everybody who comes to New York wants to drink in the Bowery."

And even if he had seen someone, it had been over a week. One night must seem much like another here. "What about the boy, Freddie? Did you see him around that time?"

"I don't allow kids in here. I know people like to send their kids for beer and such, but we don't let them in here. Mr. Robinson's orders."

"And yet he slept outside."

"He slept upstairs, too. Mr. Robinson didn't like leaving the place empty. You never know when some drunk will move in and mess the place up. Might even die in there. It's bad enough when we find them in the alley. But Freddie didn't come in here."

Frank thanked the bartender, nodded to Tiny, who ignored him, and made his way out into the summer evening. He hadn't learned much, but the few scraps of information he'd managed to glean seemed to confirm his theory about when Estelle had died and what had happened to her afterward. Now all he had to do was figure out who had followed Estelle to the Bowery and strangled her to death.

And why.

WHEN MALLOY ARRIVED HOME, IT WAS ALMOST TIME FOR supper, and the children demanded his attention. Sarah knew he'd told Gino not to stop by this evening. Tomorrow would be early enough for him to learn what they'd discovered today. Besides, as Malloy had whispered to her shortly after his arrival, he needed to consult with her in private before bringing Gino up to date.

Maeve looked a little disgruntled to be left out when Sarah and Malloy retired to their private sitting room after supper, but Sarah would placate her later.

"This is very mysterious," Sarah said when they were settled on the love seat in what had originally been the husband's bedroom of the master suite. Malloy had felt they didn't need separate bedrooms, and Sarah had wholeheartedly agreed, so they'd created this sanctuary for themselves where they could be alone for just such occasions as this.

"I didn't mean to be mysterious, but I needed to get your opinion on something I learned about Estelle Longacre. It's about sex."

"Good heavens!" Sarah said, unable to hide her amusement.

"So of course I couldn't ask you in front of Maeve and Gino."

"Were you afraid they'd be embarrassed?"

"No, I was afraid *I'd* be embarrassed."

Sarah managed not to laugh, although it was a struggle. "I'm sorry. I know there's nothing funny about this."

He gave her one of his stern looks, but that just made her want to laugh more. When she felt that she could control herself, she said, "All right. What is it?"

He sighed long-sufferingly. "Will Arburn was not impressed with Estelle."

"In what way . . . ? Oh, you mean sex."

"Exactly. Apparently, she gave the impression that she was very . . . That she would be an enthusiastic partner."

"And she wasn't?"

"According to Arburn, she'd just lay there and not even look at him."

Sarah frowned. "That's an odd thing for a man to reveal, but perhaps men talk about these things all the time, and I just don't know."

"I thought it was an odd thing for him to reveal to me,

but he did. He was trying to convince me he wasn't angry when Estelle left him for Robinson. I think it was important for him to convince me he didn't care about losing her."

"Ah, pride."

"Yes," he said. "Male pride."

"If he was telling the truth, I suppose it's easy to understand her behavior. She may well have been a virgin and—"

"She was already with child when she took up with Arburn, don't forget."

"That's right, but we don't know how that happened. Maybe she was forced."

Malloy considered this possibility for a moment. "If she was forced, wouldn't she try to avoid any contact with men? Instead, she seems to have sought it out. Arburn said it was her idea to go off with him after one of the tours."

"Of course he'd say that. Male pride."

"All right, maybe he lied about whose idea it was, but she didn't have to go with him, did she? She didn't have to go on those tours at all, but according to Norman Tufts, that was her idea, too. And as for her being a virgin, well, Kathleen was a virgin when we got married, and she was pretty enthusiastic."

Malloy hardly ever spoke of his first wife, who had died when Brian was born, so Sarah needed a moment to register her surprise. "That's nice," she managed.

"I bet you were, too, with your first husband."

Sarah wished she were better at acting demure because she couldn't help her grin. "Because I'm so enthusiastic now?"

"Yes, and I thank God every day. So were you?"

"Enthusiastic with Tom? Well, I was a nurse so I already knew basically what to expect, but of course no one tells you how much fun it is."

"So you were?"

"I'd say I was more eager than enthusiastic, at least at first."

He rolled his eyes. "So just being inexperienced doesn't explain why Estelle would be so anxious to start up an affair and then so . . . so . . ." He gestured helplessly.

"So uninterested?"

"So *uninterested* in actually having the affair."

"I don't suppose you discussed this with Robinson."

"As a matter of fact, he mentioned it, too."

"How amazing! Or do men just naturally discuss these things with each other?"

"Not normally, no."

"I'm relieved to hear it."

Malloy sighed again. "Yes, well, he was remarking on how fragile Estelle was, which is not the way anybody else described her. He wanted to protect her. He didn't even seem to care that she'd already been with Arburn either. Or that she was pregnant by somebody else entirely, and he confirmed that neither he nor Arburn could have fathered her child three months ago. In spite of all that, he still considered her innocent because she didn't seem to know much."

This was even more amazing. "What exactly did he say?"

Malloy cleared his throat and shifted his gaze to the ceiling. "He said she didn't know she could enjoy it and that nobody had ever made love to her before."

Sarah pretended not to notice he was blushing. "Oh dear. But maybe he was just . . . bragging."

This brought Malloy's gaze back to her again. "I did think of that, but you were the one who told me he was in love with the girl, and I think you're right. And there's even more to it than that. He owns a house on Lexington Avenue that one of his customers gave him to pay off some gambling debts. It looks like your parents' house, with expensive furniture and old family portraits on the walls."

"Black Jack Robinson has ancestor portraits?" she asked in wonder.

"Of course not. They came with the house. But he's set himself up there because he wants to be accepted into society."

"What?"

"He's got the house, and he thought all he needed now was the right wife, and Estelle Longacre seemed to be the woman he'd been looking for. She was young and pretty and she came from the right background, and she would probably marry him."

"How . . . sad."

"I'm sure he would've been furious when he found out nobody in society would have anything to do with him, no matter who he married, but that's no concern of ours. All that does explain is why he's so angry to have lost Estelle, though, and why he wants to find her killer."

"And probably why he was willing to forgive her past indiscretions."

"Which brings us back to my original question. Why would a woman who obviously didn't enjoy it be so willing to go with Arburn and then Robinson? Because as soon as she met Robinson, she switched her attentions to him."

"So Arburn didn't procure her for him?"

"Absolutely not. Arburn was using Robinson's flat to meet her, and one day Robinson found her there, waiting for Arburn. According to Robinson, she sent Arburn packing when he finally showed up."

"It's so hard to understand why she did the things she did. If someone raped her, I'd expect her to be terrified of men and avoid any situation where she'd be alone with one, but I know that isn't always how a woman reacts."

"You mean you've known other women who behaved like Estelle?"

"Not exactly, but . . . Well, most of my experience with women who have been raped is with the ones who became pregnant, and I don't always know everything about them, but sometimes, being raped kills something inside of them. I don't know what to call it. Self-respect, maybe. They start to think the only thing about them that has value is their bodies, so they become promiscuous, as strange as that sounds. Perhaps they also felt helpless when they were raped, so by choosing to give themselves, they aren't helpless anymore. I don't know. That's just a guess, and of course Estelle isn't here to tell us what happened to her or why she did the things she did."

"Maybe her family can tell us something," Malloy said grimly.

"Do you really think her father would speak about these things?"

"I'm not even sure he'd know that much about her. He seemed awfully selfish and not at all concerned about her, even though she'd been missing for days."

"Maybe he already knew she was dead."

"All the more reason to go back and question him again."

"What about the aunt and the cousin? What was his name?"

"Norman Tufts. I'm definitely going to question him again, too."

"Do you want me to talk to the aunt?" Sarah asked. "She's far more likely to know things about Estelle, being a woman."

"She struck me as pretty selfish, too, but if you think you can get anything out of her, by all means try."

"That just reminded me. Mrs. Ellsworth has an interesting theory about Penelope Longacre."

"Let me guess—it somehow involves finding a four-leaf clover or throwing salt over your shoulder."

Sarah smiled at that. Mrs. Ellsworth's superstitions were legendary. "No, but she did suggest bad blood might explain Estelle's immoral behavior."

"Bad blood? She sounds like my mother. She was always telling me not to be friends with certain kids in the neighborhood because their families had bad blood."

"I don't make any judgments, but when I told her about Miss Longacre taking in an orphaned cousin, she suggested that perhaps Norman wasn't a distant relative at all. She thought Norman might be Penelope's own illegitimate child."

Malloy raised his eyebrows. "That would certainly explain her devotion to him, but what does it have to do with Estelle?"

"I think Mrs. Ellsworth was insinuating that if the aunt were immoral enough to have an illegitimate child, then the niece might have inherited the same lack of moral fiber. I don't agree with her, of course, but if Norman is Penelope's son, then that's two generations of females in the same family who became pregnant out of wedlock."

"That happens a lot, you know."

"Not in families like the Longacres, where unmarried girls are rigorously chaperoned practically from birth. And if it does happen, the girl is usually married off quickly to her paramour."

"So that means there's something wrong in the Longacre family."

"Well, we don't know for sure about Penelope, but we do know Estelle wasn't chaperoned at all, or at least not adequately. So yes, something at least isn't quite right."

"Do you think you can figure out what it is?"

"I can try."

"And I can help. So that's settled. Maybe Mrs. Ellsworth's theory has some truth in it, unlike her superstitions."

Sarah smiled. "She had a lovely one today. I had bubbles in my coffee and she said that meant I was going to receive some money."

For some reason, this made him grin. "As a matter of fact . . ." Malloy reached into his pocket.

"What's this?" she asked when he handed her a check.

"It's my retainer from Robinson. I told him to make it out to you. It's a donation for your maternity hospital."

FORTUNATELY, SARAH FOUND NORMAN TUFTS AND PEnelope Longacre in the City Directory, living at the same address, so she didn't have to ask her mother to consult the Social Register. Probably, they weren't listed there anyway. Miss Longacre didn't give the impression she was a society matron, if an unmarried female could ever be considered a matron.

The address on Fifth Avenue and 38th Street proved to be one of the apartment hotel buildings, so called because they provided many of the conveniences of living in a hotel. Also called *bachelor hotels*, they were designed for bachelors and young families who could not yet afford or did not wish to go to the trouble and expense of setting up a house. The apartments provided cleaning and laundry services and an in-house restaurant would supply meals, which meant residents could live comfortably without their own servants.

Did someone who lived in one of these buildings observe the strict rules of society when visiting? Did someone no longer considered part of society observe those rules? Sarah decided they probably did not, since she was here much too early for a morning visit and didn't want to be turned away.

The lobby was like a hotel, with a front desk and a lounge area with sofas and chairs, but unlike a hotel, no one sat in the lounge area, smoking cigars and reading newspapers. And unlike a hotel, no one was checking in or out. The desk clerk perked up noticeably when Sarah walked in.

"May I help you?"

"I'd like to see Miss Longacre if she's at home."

"Is she expecting you?"

"No, but I'm sure she'll be happy to see me." She gave him her calling card.

He wrinkled his nose a little at the Irish name, but Sarah gave him her haughtiest glare when he looked up again, which convinced him to announce her. He went to the switchboard and telephoned and when he hung up, he said, "Miss Longacre asked if you would wait about fifteen minutes before coming up. If you'll have a seat . . ."

Sarah figured Penelope Longacre wanted a few minutes to make herself presentable and perhaps tidy up a bit, so she waited the allotted time and then allowed the elevator operator to take her to the seventh floor.

Sarah tapped on the apartment door, and Miss Longacre opened it herself. Sarah hadn't expected to be greeted warmly, but Miss Longacre was glaring, her face blotched with fury.

"What have you done with Estelle?"

9

GINO JUST SAT GAPING AFTER FRANK FINISHED TELLING him what he'd learned about Estelle Longacre. Fortunately, Frank hadn't mentioned the part about how interested or not interested Estelle was in sex. Gino might've fainted dead away.

"So she was expecting a baby, but it couldn't have been Arburn or Robinson who fathered it?"

"So it seems. Sarah is going to question Penelope Longacre to see what she can find out. Hopefully, she'll have some idea who else Estelle might've been involved with."

"Because he might've also been jealous of Robinson and followed her to the Bowery to take his revenge. Could it be Norman Tufts, do you think?"

Frank rubbed his chin thoughtfully. "Robinson didn't think so, and I can't imagine Norman would even know what to do, but maybe I'm misjudging him. Anything is possible, I guess."

"But who else would she have spent time with?"

"I don't know. I'm going to go back and talk to her father again. He might know something, too. Of course, he might not tell me. He seems like the kind of man who enjoys being disagreeable."

"That does sound like fun," Gino said with a grin. "What can I do?"

"I think we need to talk to Raven Saggio again. Find out if he and Freddie were the ones who found Estelle's body in the trunk, and also if Freddie told him anything about seeing Estelle that night or someone hauling the trunk out of Robinson's flat."

"It would be nice if Freddie had recognized him and told Raven who it was, too."

"I'm not asking for miracles, although it's possible that he did recognize the person."

"You think it would've taken two people to get the trunk down the stairs and haul it away, though, so that doubles the chance that Freddie recognized one of them."

"Unless he was the second person. I didn't say anything to Robinson, but another possibility I was thinking about is that Freddie would've helped Arburn if Arburn told him Robinson had asked him to take some things out of the flat."

"Wouldn't he wonder what was in the trunk that was so heavy?"

"Probably. That might be what happened. Freddie kept asking and when Arburn or whoever it was refused to answer, he got scared and ran. That would explain why the killer had to leave the trunk. He wouldn't have gone to the trouble of hauling her body away unless he didn't want her found."

"And if he didn't want her found, he'd never just leave her where he left her, knowing she'd be found almost immediately."

"So I'm thinking your chances of finding Raven this early

in the day are pretty good. He's probably still sleeping, since the newsies are still on strike."

"How long can this strike go on?"

"I don't know, but I read in one of the other papers I picked up that newsboys in all the surrounding states are all refusing to sell the *Journal* and the *World*, too. Somebody has to give in soon."

"I'm thinking it'll be the boys. They've got to be feeling the pinch after almost two weeks with no income."

They'd left the office door open to catch what breeze there was in the hallway, and a ragged young boy they'd never seen before stuck his head in and looked around, wide-eyed.

"Can we help you, young man?" Frank asked.

"Is one of you Mr. Malloy?"

"I am."

"Kid Blink sent me. He said to tell you Two Toes's funeral is this afternoon at two o'clock."

"Where?"

The boy told him the name of the church and the street.

"Thanks." Frank flipped him a dime, and the boy stole away, grinning.

"I'll meet you there," Gino said.

"You want to go?" Frank asked in surprise.

"Of course. There but for the grace of God."

And Gino was right, about both of them. They'd been lucky to grow up in families who were able to keep them. With just the slightest bad luck, they could have ended up living on the streets like Freddie.

"All right. I'll see you there."

SARAH STARED BACK AT PENELOPE LONGACRE. "I HAVEN'T done anything with Estelle, Miss Longacre. What are you talking about?"

"Her body is missing."

Sarah glanced around the hallway, expecting a neighbor's door to open so they could better hear this amazing conversation. "Wouldn't you prefer to have this discussion inside?"

Miss Longacre made a disgusted noise and stood aside so Sarah could enter. The entrance was a long hallway that led past two closed doors, most likely bedrooms, before opening into the parlor. The room looked out on the street below and was furnished with tired-looking pieces that might have been castoffs from Horace Longacre's house. They probably were.

When they reached the parlor, Miss Longacre turned to face Sarah again. "Someone has taken Estelle's body from the undertaker."

"How could that happen?"

"I have no idea. Horace is furious, of course. He hired someone to fetch her from that awful morgue and prepare her for burial. We weren't going to have a funeral since the circumstances of her death were so sordid, just a private memorial service. But when I sent Norman down to the undertaker's office to make the arrangements, he was told that someone else had claimed her body and taken it away."

"Didn't they tell you who it was?" Sarah asked, although she had an excellent idea who it was.

"They wouldn't tell Norman a thing. It was all very mysterious. They insisted whoever took her claimed he was a family member and that we had changed our minds and wanted another undertaker to handle the burial."

"And you think I knew about this?"

"Who else could it be? No one else even knew she was dead. We haven't put an obituary in the newspapers, and thank heaven, the newspapers haven't reported her murder either."

"I assure you we had nothing to do with it. My husband

and I would never dream of interfering in such a matter. Besides, what would we want with Miss Longacre's body?"

Penelope had no reply to that, and Sarah could see that her anger was rapidly mellowing into confusion. "I . . . I hadn't thought of that."

"It might be a mistake of some kind. Perhaps you should go yourself or send Mr. Longacre to straighten it out, if he's able to go." Of course she didn't believe for a minute that it was a mistake. Obviously, Jack Robinson had made good on his threat to claim Estelle's body, but if so, Sarah didn't think it was her place to get in the middle. She'd ask Malloy to speak to Robinson and see if he wouldn't make some sort of compromise.

"Oh dear, you're probably right. It must be some kind of mistake. I'll speak to Horace and let him handle it. She's his daughter, after all. There's no reason for Norman and me to be involved anyway. We were only trying to help."

"I'm sure this is all very distressing to you. You could never have imagined Estelle would be murdered," Sarah said. Sympathy was a good way to win a person's confidence, and she needed Penelope's confidences.

"Absolutely not! Not in my wildest imaginings. Estelle was always a bit of a trial, and she had certainly behaved badly in recent days, but I'm sure she never did anything to deserve such a fate."

"No one does," Sarah agreed. "Uh, perhaps we could sit down for a moment."

"Oh yes, I'm sorry. I'm quite distressed, but that's no excuse for bad manners, is it? Please, sit down. May I offer you something? Tea or coffee?"

"It's much too warm for that, I'm afraid. Could I trouble you for some water, though?"

"Of course." Miss Longacre scurried off through the

adjoining dining room to what must have been the kitchen and returned shortly with two glasses of water.

"I'm feeling very guilty now, Miss Longacre," Sarah said when she'd taken a long drink. "I came today to ask you for some information that might help us find out who killed her."

"You can't believe I'd know anything about that! She was found in the Bowery, I understand, so you'd be better off asking her lover why she was there, but I know nothing about it and neither does Norman."

"Are you sure?" Sarah asked with as much puzzled innocence as she could muster. "Because Norman was the one who first took her to the Bowery."

Penelope looked genuinely shocked. "What are you talking about?"

"We've learned that Estelle started going to the Bowery on tours. It seems people pay money to have a guide take them to dangerous neighborhoods in the city. It's called *slumming*."

"That's impossible," Penelope said weakly. "Norman would never do anything like that."

"You told me yourself that Norman escorted Estelle when she went out. Apparently, one of the places he escorted her to was these tours."

"But surely they don't take young ladies to places like that."

"I'm told that Estelle dressed as a man for the tours."

Penelope stared back at Sarah in horror. "That's impossible."

"More than one person has told us this, and Norman himself confirmed it."

Penelope frowned. "I can't believe Norman would do this voluntarily. He must have been coerced somehow."

Sarah thought this unlikely, but she simply sat there, staring back at Miss Longacre. After a long, uncomfortable moment, Sarah said, "Norman is very fortunate that you were willing to take him in. It must have been difficult for you as an unmarried woman."

Several emotions flickered across Penelope's face too quickly for Sarah to identify them. "I was happy to do it."

"This seems like a very comfortable place to live. Does Norman live here with you?"

"Yes. He looks after me," she said with pride.

"How nice for you. What is his profession?"

It was an impertinent question, but Sarah gave no indication that she was aware of it. She merely smiled and waited. "Uh, he . . . Norman doesn't need to work. Horace has provided for us."

"Oh, of course. I should have realized that. He's very generous to allow you a place of your own. Most families keep their unmarried female relations at home and expect some sort of service in exchange for their keep."

Penelope shifted uncomfortably in her chair. "Yes, well, after Father died, I wanted to be on my own. Horace and I never got along, so he agreed to give me an allowance."

"So you took Norman in after your father died?"

"Yes, he . . . my father, that is, he would never have permitted me to take on such a responsibility."

"Did you know that Estelle was with child when she was killed?"

Apparently, she had not. "Who told you such a thing?"

"The coroner discovered it when he examined the body."

Miss Longacre needed a moment to absorb this information. "Well, I guess I shouldn't be surprised, the way she carried on."

"You mean with the gangster she met in the Bowery."

"Yes, her lover. So it's no wonder she'd gotten herself into trouble."

"The way you did?" Sarah asked gently.

This time the emotion on Penelope's face was clearly alarm. "What do you mean?"

"I mean, it's obvious. You'd been forced to give Norman up, but when your father died, you convinced Horace to support you so you could claim your son again."

Penelope shook her head, but her terror gave her away. "No, you're wrong. I don't know where you'd get an idea like that."

"Don't worry, I have no intention of telling anyone. In fact, I think it's admirable that you found a way to keep him and raise him yourself. You must have loved him very much."

"I do love him. He's the most important thing in the world to me."

"Of course he is. I understand you wanted him to marry Estelle."

Penelope made a visible effort to regain her composure. "Yes, I did."

"That seems odd, since they were really first cousins, even though no one knew it."

"You're right, no one knew it but Horace and me, and it was the only way Norman could get his rightful legacy."

"And did your brother agree? About the marriage, I mean?"

Anger flared in her eyes, but she drew a calming breath and tamped it down, as she had doubtless been trained to do. As all well-bred young ladies had been trained to do. "My brother takes great delight in thwarting me whenever he has the opportunity. And of course, it doesn't matter now. With Estelle dead, she can't marry anyone."

"No, she can't, but the fact remains that she was with child, and whoever fathered that child might be the man who killed her."

"Then you should be looking in the Bowery, since that's where she found her lover."

"Actually, she had two lovers in the Bowery, but neither

of them fathered her child. She was already pregnant when she met them."

Penelope had no answer for this. She simply stared back at Sarah, lips pressed together in a bloodless line.

"We were hoping you might have some idea of who else she might have been involved with."

"Me? How would I know such a thing?"

"I thought perhaps she might have confided in you."

"Confided that she had taken a lover? Hardly! The fact is, I barely saw Estelle these past few years. She'd never confide in me."

"Perhaps she confided in Norman, then. Or . . . Do you think he might have . . . ?"

"Absolutely not! I raised Norman to respect females, not take advantage of them!"

"But if he wanted to marry her and her father wasn't likely to consent . . ."

"Nonsense! Norman is not a seducer."

Malloy, at least, agreed with that. Sarah had no opinion, having not yet met Norman. "I'm sorry. I didn't mean to upset you, but I'm sure you're as eager as we are to find Estelle's killer."

"You won't find him here, as I said before. In fact . . ." Penelope's eyes narrowed in calculation. "If you want to know who fathered her child, ask Horace."

"Horace? Her father?"

"Yes, her father. I'm sure he'll be able to help you. Now I must ask you to leave, Mrs. Malloy. Your visit has been most upsetting, and I feel I must lie down."

"Of course. I'm sorry to have disturbed you. I'll see if my husband can find out who took Estelle's body, too."

"I'm sure Horace will appreciate that, and you needn't bother informing me if you find out. Let Horace worry about the girl for once. Heaven knows, it will be his last chance."

* * *

Gino thought nothing was sadder than the Bowery in the morning. All the detritus of the previous night's revelries littered the streets, along with the bodies of those who had been too drunk to make it home in the wee hours of the morning. Alleys were the worst, since they collected the same litter but no one ever carried it away. Summer heat only increased the misery, as garbage and sewage festered, filling the air with noxious fumes.

The alley where Raven Saggio had his nest was a perfect example. Trash had collected in piles, driven by the wind. Rats and stray dogs investigated the piles, not even looking up when Gino passed. He wondered if living here meant growing used to the smells and the filth. He couldn't imagine it, but it must be true, or people couldn't live here.

The lean-to made of scraps of wood and metal held together by rusted nails, twine, and hope was exactly as Gino remembered it from their visit a few days ago, except Freddie Two Toes wasn't waiting for him. Ordinarily when he was calling on a witness, Gino would pound on the door, hoping to waken his subject and catch him unawares, but Raven's abode had no door, and Gino was afraid pounding on any part of it would bring the whole thing crashing down. He settled for calling out a greeting.

"Raven! Are you in there?"

Something started scrabbling around. It might've been a rat or a dog or a boy. Gino was ready for anything to come barreling out the curtained doorway, but he was going to try to catch it only if it was a boy. But Raven wasn't barreling. He was pouting.

"What do you want?" he asked, rubbing one eye with a

grubby fist. He was fully clothed in a dirty shirt and trousers that hung raggedly short of his ankles, although his feet were bare. He probably saw no need of shoes in the summer in any case.

"I wanted to ask you a few questions, Raven. There's a dollar in it for you."

"Last time you gave me a fiver," the boy reminded him.

"Yes, but last time you found Two Toes for me. This is much easier."

"Yeah, but you woke me up."

"I'm sorry about that, but I wanted to catch you in."

"A dollar, you say?" he asked doubtfully.

Gino remembered the five dollars they had paid him was probably his only income in the almost two weeks since the strike had started. It was also probably more than he would've earned selling papers during that time, but he'd also most likely squandered it by now. "Two dollars, if I like your answers."

"I can't help if you like them or not."

"Well, then, if you *answer* all the questions. Do we have a deal?"

"Two dollars for answering all your questions. All right." He raised a foot and scratched the back of his other calf with his big toe.

"Were you and Two Toes the ones who found the trunk with the dead woman inside?"

Raven's whole body stiffened, and he would've darted away except Gino was expecting him to run, so he caught him around the waist and lifted him off his feet. He started howling and fighting and kicking with his bare feet, but Gino pinned the boy tightly to him and said, "I'm not going to get you in trouble. Three dollars!"

Raven instantly went limp.

"So were you the ones who found her?" Gino asked again.

"Yeah."

"How did it happen?"

"What do you mean?"

"I mean how did you happen to find the trunk?"

Raven thought about it for a long moment, and Gino wished he could've watched his face, which was hanging down and facing the ground, but he didn't dare let go of him. Finally, he said, "Two Toes found it. He came and got me. He said he couldn't carry it alone. I knew there was something wrong. He was acting real strange."

"What do you mean, strange?"

"Nervous-like. Jittery. Couldn't stand still. And when I saw the trunk, it was too nice for somebody to just leave it in an alley, so that wasn't right. Then I saw the hair."

"What hair?"

"There was some hair sticking out of one end of the trunk, where it got caught in the lid. Not a lot. Just a few strands, but it was long and curly. Anybody could see it was a lady's hair. I was gonna run, but Two Toes, he opens the lid. It was a lady's hair, all right, and the rest of her was inside the trunk."

"What did you do then?"

"I still wanted to run, but Two Toes, he said to find a cop and tell him. He said he'd wait there to make sure nobody bothered her."

"And you found a cop?"

"Yeah. It wasn't easy. They don't like to go in the alleys at night. He had to find another one to go with him. By the time we got there, Two Toes was gone."

"So the cops never saw him?"

"No. He was here when I got back, though. He asked could he stay with me for a few days, so that's how I knew where he was when you and that other fellow come asking about him."

"Did he tell you who the dead lady was?"

"No. How would he know that?"

"Did he tell you how he knew the trunk was there?"

"He said he saw a fellow drag it there and then leave. He wanted to get it before the fellow came back for it."

"A fellow? That's what he said? Just one?"

"Yeah, he said the fellow probably went to get help because it was so heavy."

Now, that was interesting, but Gino wasn't going to discuss it with Raven. He set the boy back on his feet and turned him so he could see his face while keeping a grip on his shoulder. "Did Two Toes say anything about seeing something happen at Black Jack's flat?"

"Is that where it happened?"

"Where what happened?"

"I don't know, but Two Toes was really spooked. He'd hardly sleep at night, jumping at every sound, and when he did sleep, he had bad dreams. He said it was finding the dead woman, but we've found dead people before, so I knew it wasn't that."

"Was it because he knew her?"

"Did he? He didn't say."

"She was Black Jack's girl."

Raven swore colorfully. "Did he kill her, then?"

"Who, Two Toes?"

Raven rolled his eyes at such a stupid question. "No, Black Jack."

"We don't think so. It might've been somebody Freddie knew, though. That would explain why he was scared."

"Oh yeah. He'd be afraid they'd come after him." Raven's face fell. "And I guess he was right."

"We want to find out who killed Two Toes and the woman. Did he say anything else that might help?"

Raven's small face screwed up in concentration, but after a minute he said, "I can't think of nothing, I swear, mister. I'd help you if I could."

"If you remember anything or you hear anything, come and see us. There'll be a reward."

Gino fished a fiver out of his pocket along with another of his cards.

"You said three dollars," the boy said suspiciously.

"You were a lot of help. Thanks, Raven."

"Sure."

Gino turned to go.

"Mister?"

Gino turned back. "Yes?"

"You're really gonna find out who killed him?"

"Yes. We're going to his funeral this afternoon, too. Will you be there?"

"We'll all be there."

NO MOURNING WREATH HUNG ON THE LONGACRES' front door. Horace Longacre probably didn't worry about such niceties. The surly maid, Marie, answered Frank's knock. This time he didn't give her the chance to turn him away. He simply walked forward, using his hand to keep her from slamming the door in his face. Since he was stronger, he got inside.

"I don't know what you think you're doing, but you're wasting your time," she huffed.

"I'm going to see Mr. Longacre, if he's still alive."

"He was the last time I checked. I guess you know where his room is, so I don't need to show you." With that she strode off toward the back of the house, where she probably had a comfortable place to sit here on the first floor where it was cooler.

Frank trudged up two flights of stairs to Longacre's bedroom and knocked on the door.

"What do you want?"

Frank took that as an invitation to enter and did so. "Good morning, Mr. Longacre."

Today, he was still in bed, although he'd flung off all the covers in deference to the weather. He lay there, propped up on pillows and surrounded by newspapers. He wore a yellowed nightshirt. "What do you want?"

"I just have a few more questions about your daughter."

"My daughter is dead, and I'll be dead soon, too, so why should I answer any of your questions?"

"Don't you want to see her killer caught and punished?"

"What kind of question is that? Are you trying to make me feel guilty or something?"

"Would it help?" Frank asked, finding the chair he'd claimed the last time and clearing the seat before moving it over near the bed.

"Don't you have any pity for a dying man?"

"Apparently not. I just have a few questions." Frank sat down.

Longacre sighed wearily. "And I have a question for you. What have you done with Estelle's body?"

Frank looked up in surprise. "I haven't done anything with it."

"Norman said you'd taken it away from the undertaker who got it from the morgue."

"I don't know why he'd say that since it isn't true."

"Norman says a lot of things that aren't true. What is true is that somebody took her body and we don't know who or why or where they took it."

"I'm sure it's some kind of mistake," Frank said, wondering if it was possible for Jack Robinson to have done such a thing. Surely, he was the only one bold enough to try it. Unless it really was a mistake.

"Oh yes, I'm sure people go around the city claiming the bodies of people they don't even know all the time."

"Well, I'm not one of them, so I can't help you. I wanted to ask you if your daughter had any suitors."

"You mean besides that gangster she took up with?"

"Yes, besides him. Did she have any gentlemen calling on her?"

"What kind of a question is that?"

"A reasonable one, I think. She was young and pretty and—"

"How do you know she was pretty?"

"I was with Norman when he claimed her body, remember?"

Longacre grumbled something Frank didn't catch.

"She was young and pretty and eligible. Girls like that usually have suitors."

"Not Estelle. She might've gone out looking to find one, but I didn't let any young bucks come sniffing around here."

"Why not?" Most parents wanted to see their daughters married and settled.

"Because I didn't. Her job was to take care of me."

Which was a little selfish, but knowing Longacre as he now did, he wasn't surprised. "What about Norman Tufts? I heard he wanted to marry her."

Longacre's expression hardened and his rheumy eyes narrowed with distaste. "That was all Penny's idea. As soon as she got him, she started bringing him over to visit my girl, and she'd tell Estelle that she and Norman were going to get married someday."

"What did Estelle think of that?"

"Nothing, I expect. Nobody pays attention to Penny."

"I'm surprised you allowed talk like that."

"What do you mean?" Longacre asked, suddenly wary.

"Oh, I know you gave out the story that Norman is a distant relation, but you knew he was more closely related than that," Frank said, testing the waters.

"Where did you get such an idea?" Longacre was angry now.

Anger was a good sign. "Yours isn't the first family to make up a story to cover up an illegitimate birth, but you couldn't allow Estelle and Norman to marry if they're really first cousins."

Longacre's anger instantly dissipated. "First cousins, eh? That's what you think? Well, they weren't going to marry, so it doesn't matter. Estelle couldn't stand the sight of him."

"Are you sure? I understand Norman escorted her sometimes when she went out. Maybe they fell in love."

"Estelle fall in love with Norman? Not likely."

Frank pretended to consider his denial. "That's funny, because we know Estelle was close to at least one gentleman."

"Are you calling that gangster a gentleman?"

"No, I'm talking about someone else. You see, Estelle was with child when she was murdered, and she was too far along for it to have belonged to Jack Robinson."

Longacre registered surprise and something that might have been alarm. "How do you know that?"

"Because I do. And I suspect that whoever it was might've been jealous of her affair with Robinson."

"And you think this mysterious gentleman killed her? Claptrap! The gangster killed her."

"I don't think he did."

"I don't care what you think, and what business is it of yours who killed her?"

"None, but whoever killed her also killed a boy I cared about, so I'm going to find his killer, and I'll get hers into the bargain."

"That's your business, I suppose, but it's not mine. I just need to get Estelle's body back and put it in the ground. She's going to be buried next to me. We'll be together forever." That thought seemed to give Longacre immense satisfaction. Frank had thought he couldn't dislike the man any more, but he'd been wrong.

He took his leave and made his way downstairs again. He hadn't learned as much as he'd hoped, but he knew the servants in houses like this often knew far more than their masters ever suspected. He hadn't bothered questioning Marie before, but maybe he should give it a try before he left. At least that would mean he wouldn't need to come back here again.

Frank went down the hallway and found a door that led to the kitchen, where he found Marie just as he had pictured her. She sat in a Windsor armchair that had probably been transferred from the dining room, shoes off, with her stocking feet propped up on a stool. What he hadn't pictured was the rangy man sitting at the table nearby and tucking into a meat pie.

They both looked up in surprise at Frank's unceremonious entrance. Marie recovered first. "What are you doing in here?"

"Looking for you," Frank said. By then the man had risen to his feet, setting down his fork in the process. "I'm Frank Malloy." Frank offered his hand.

The man was even taller than he'd looked sitting down, and his hand enveloped Frank's in an enthusiastic grip. "Pleased to meet you. I'm Tom O'Day."

"Don't talk to him, Tom. He's here nosing around about Miss Estelle," Marie said.

"Don't mind Marie," Tom said with a friendly smile. "She's just a little out of sorts because her feet hurt."

"My feet got nothing to do with it, Tom O'Day."

"Won't you have a seat?" Tom said. "Would you like some meat pie? Marie is famous for her meat pie."

"He's not getting any of my meat pie," Marie declared.

"No, thanks," Frank said, "although it smells delicious. I was just going to ask for a drink before I go on my way. It's getting hot out there again today."

"Sit right down, then. I'll fix you some lemonade."

"You'll do no such thing, Tom O'Day!" Marie said, but he completely ignored her while he fetched some lemons from a bowl on the cluttered shelves and began his preparations.

"Do you work here, too, Mr. O'Day?" Frank asked, pulling out one of the mismatched chairs that circled the old wooden table.

"That's none of your business," Marie said.

"Oh yes," Tom said, still blithely ignoring her. Frank had already figured out that he must do that a lot. "I used to drive Mr. Longacre's carriage, but then he stopped going places, so he gave it up. He fired his valet, too, but he couldn't fire me because if I go, Marie goes with me, and he has to have his meat pie. Marie is my missus."

Frank nodded, deciding not to glance at Marie, which might encourage her to speak again.

"So I do whatever needs doing around here. It's just me and Marie here now, while Mr. Longacre waits to die." Tom had fetched a glass juicer and was twisting the halved lemons on it to extract the juice. Their tart aroma filled the kitchen.

"So did the old man tell you what you needed to know?" Marie asked suddenly.

Frank had to look at her. "Not really."

"What is it you need to know, Mr. Malloy?" Tom asked

with a pleasant smile. Frank wondered if he had any other expression. He seemed like a very amiable man.

"I was wondering if Miss Estelle had any suitors."

Marie made a disgusted sound, and Tom's pleasant smile vanished, answering Frank's unspoken question about his range of expressions.

"That's a sad thing, Mr. Malloy," Tom said. "Mr. Longacre, he never would let her see any young men."

"Why not?"

"That's no mystery," Marie said. "He wanted to keep her for himself."

10

"WE'RE GOING TO ATTRACT A LOT OF ATTENTION IN THIS carriage," Maeve said, glancing out the window as they slowly made their way through the Lower East Side. Ragged children were already chasing along beside them, calling out for pennies.

"I know, but we shouldn't go to the new house alone, and my mother was only too happy to lend us the use of it."

"And the use of John to guard us," Maeve said with a smile.

Sarah smiled back. "I think the coachman will be busy guarding the coach, but yes, if we happen to need assistance, he'll be there."

"How do you think Estelle got herself to the Bowery? Or got out of her house, for that matter?"

"She probably said she was going someplace acceptable, like a party or a church event. We know Norman Tufts took her when they went on the tours."

"And she dressed up like a man for that," Maeve remembered, "but did Norman take her when she went to meet Arburn and Robinson?"

"I can't imagine he did. If he was planning to marry her or even had hopes of marrying her, he certainly wouldn't take her to meet a lover."

"Or two lovers. So how did a lone female get to the Bowery and home again safely?"

"I guess the lover may have escorted her home, or at least as far as a main thoroughfare where she could get a cab."

"But she'd still have to get there," Maeve said with a frown.

"Let's see, it's the first of August now, and from what we've learned, she started seeing Arburn about two months ago. Even if she visited him in the evenings, it would have been light until around eight o'clock or even later."

"That's right. So if she managed to get a hansom cab to bring her, she would have arrived in daylight."

"Which still would have been risky, but I've gotten the impression that Estelle liked taking risks."

"I got that impression, too," Maeve said.

Sarah glanced over at Maeve and wondered if she should broach the subject she had been considering herself ever since Malloy had raised it to her. She didn't want to shock Maeve or embarrass her. On the other hand, she'd never known Maeve to be shocked or embarrassed, or at least not very much, anyway. "Maeve, would you give me your opinion on something, as a respectable young woman?"

Maeve's eyes lit up at this. She obviously knew Sarah would not have asked if she didn't value that opinion. "Certainly, although I'm not sure somebody raised by a grifter could be called *respectable*."

"Don't be silly. Of course you are."

"Then what do you want to ask me?"

"Malloy told me privately about conversations he had with both Arburn and Robinson."

"Was that why you went off alone together last night?"

"Yes, and I already apologized for not including you, but when I tell you what we discussed, you'll understand why."

"So you really discussed something? I though the two of you just wanted to be alone."

Sarah smiled at that. She wouldn't mention what had happened when they'd finished their discussion last night. "Apparently, Arburn told Malloy that Estelle was very . . . uh, flirtatious with him. He even claimed that it was her idea to go off with him after one of the tours."

"Of course he'd say that."

"Yes, men do like to give the impression they're irresistible to women, but he also said he was very disappointed in . . . Well, let's just say she did not appear at all interested in the actual deed. Now, I know you don't have any personal experience," Sarah hastily explained, "but I also know you met a lot of young women at the Mission who did. I was wondering if you might have any idea why a girl would behave the way Estelle behaved, inviting a man—either by her behavior or by actually inviting him—to take her, and then, well, he said she'd just lie there and not even look at him."

"Oh," Maeve said faintly.

"I'm sorry," Sarah said. "I didn't mean to offend you."

"I'm not offended," Maeve hastily assured her. "I'm just . . . surprised."

"Surprised that a woman would act like that?"

"No, surprised Mr. Malloy would talk about it."

That startled a bark of laughter from Sarah. "I admit, it surprised me, too. But now you understand why he couldn't talk about it in front of you."

"Oh yes, it makes perfect sense now."

"And do you have any ideas?"

"I . . . Well, I don't know for sure, of course, but the girls would talk about that sort of thing at the Mission."

"I know many of the Daughters of Hope had been prostitutes before they found refuge at the Mission. That's the main reason it was started in the first place."

"Yes, and when I heard what some of the girls had been through, I was even more grateful to my grandfather for taking me in. He might've been a crook, but he made sure I didn't end up on the streets."

"I'm grateful to him, too."

That made Maeve smile, but only briefly. "The girls who had to sell themselves, they talked about how they had to pretend they enjoyed it even though they didn't, but this one girl . . . Well, she told us she knew a trick. She'd learned it when she was a little girl and her stepfather used to sneak into her bed at night and have his way with her. She said when he'd come to bother her, she'd just pretend she was somewhere else."

"What do you mean?"

"I'm not really sure, but she said she could just lay there and shut out what was happening and not even feel it, like she wasn't there at all."

"How amazing."

"I'd forgotten all about that until you asked me."

"But she was a child, or at least very young, I guess. Children are good at pretending."

"They're better than adults, but if you'd learned how to do that, I suppose you could always remember."

"But that would probably mean you'd have to have learned it when you were a child," Sarah said, and suddenly she remembered something Penelope Longacre had said that sent chills up her spine: Horace Longacre hadn't remarried because *he had the girl*.

"What is it?" Maeve asked.

"Nothing. I just . . . I was thinking how horrible that would be."

"You said Mr. Malloy also talked to Robinson. Did he say the same thing?"

Sarah shook off the ugly thoughts. "He said that apparently Estelle acted the same way with him at first, but that his, uh, skill as a lover overcame her disinterest."

This time Maeve gave a bark of laughter. "Did he really say that?"

"I don't know what his exact words were, but yes. I did suggest that he might have been bragging, though."

"I'd have to agree with that. I don't have any experience with this, but I do know that men usually try to make themselves look good, so I doubt Arburn would lie about Estelle not being interested in him. That's too humiliating to admit if it wasn't true."

"I agree. And maybe Robinson really is a magnificent lover who won Estelle's heart, but he also confirmed she wasn't particularly interested when they first met. Now we need to figure out if that means anything."

"You think it does."

"What makes you say that?"

"I saw the look on your face a few minutes ago. You thought of something."

"I did, but it's not something I want to discuss with you. You already know too much about the uglier aspects of life."

"I'm so happy that you want to protect me, but it may be too late."

"I'm still going to try," Sarah said. "Oh, looks like we're here."

As the carriage came to a stop, Maeve looked out the window at the house. "Is that it?" she asked in disbelief.

"I'm afraid so."

Maeve gave her a glorious smile. "This is going to be so much fun!"

John the coachman stayed outside with the horses to prevent anyone from stealing them and the coach and to keep the dozens of children who had gathered in their wake from climbing all over it.

Sarah and Maeve climbed the rickety front steps, and Sarah pulled the key Jack Robinson had given her out of her purse and unlocked the door. "Hello!" she called before stepping through the front door.

"Do you expect somebody to answer you?" Maeve asked.

"No, but I saw evidence that people had been squatting in the house. If they're still here, I want to give them a chance to escape."

"I guess I don't have to ask how they got in," Maeve said, pointing to a broken window.

The summer heat had festered in the house, turning the air thick. They left the front door open and started strolling through the rooms as Maeve made mental notes of everything she saw. "This was a nice place once."

"Yes. I like to think a happy family grew up here. There's a pump in the kitchen, so there's water, but we'll have to install at least one bathroom."

They had made it as far as the kitchen and were discussing what needed to be done when a male voice called out. "Hello?"

"Who could that be?" Maeve asked.

"Let's go see."

They found an attractive young man standing just inside the front door. He wore one of those checked suits that young men thought made them look dashing but really made them look silly. His derby sat on the back of his head, so he looked like he'd been buffeted by a strong wind. He'd been scowling until they got close enough for him to see clearly in the shadows of the hallway.

"Good afternoon, ladies," he said with a delighted smile. "Is there something I can help you with?"

"I doubt it," Sarah said. She glanced over to see that Maeve was unimpressed with his charm. Maeve was extremely difficult to impress.

This seemed to disconcert him, but only for a moment. "Do you ladies know this is private property?"

"Yes, it is, and may I ask what you're doing here?" Sarah said.

"I, uh, I'm protecting it for the owner."

"That's a surprise, since I'm the owner."

He blinked a few times while he considered this information. "You . . . But . . . Mr. Robinson owns this house."

"Not anymore. He sold it to me."

His surprise was almost comical, but it lasted only a moment before he remembered himself. He tried his charming smile again. "I hadn't heard that. I'm sorry. One of the neighborhood kids came running to tell me some people were breaking into Mr. Robinson's house, so naturally I came to see."

"And you work for Mr. Robinson?"

"Uh, yeah, I mean, yes, ma'am." He pulled off his derby, nearly dropping it in his haste. "I'm Will Arburn, and you must be Mrs. Malloy."

Of course he would know her name. Robinson had assigned Arburn the task of investigating her before he sold her the house, and that was how he'd found Malloy. "Pleased to meet you, Mr. Arburn. I've heard a lot about you."

Her tone left no doubt that it hadn't been good things she'd heard, but he refused to be intimidated. Instead he nodded to Maeve. "Miss."

"Oh, and this is Miss Smith."

Arburn turned the full force of his charm on Maeve, probably knowing it would be wasted on Frank Malloy's wife. "Pleased to meet you, Miss Smith. We don't see many young ladies as lovely as you down here."

"Mr. Arburn," Maeve said primly.

"Oh, please call me Will."

"No, thank you."

He blinked in surprise, but refused to be discouraged. "I hadn't heard the house was sold."

"I don't suppose Mr. Robinson is speaking to you at the moment," Sarah said.

Arburn also refused to be embarrassed. "He's a busy man."

"Did you intend to run us off?" Maeve asked.

"I intended to find out what your intentions were, but two such lovely ladies as yourselves couldn't possibly mean any harm. And you must know it isn't really safe for you in this neighborhood. But I'll be glad to offer my protection while you're here."

Someone giggled, and Sarah looked past him to see a cluster of children peering in the front door. They must have found him as ridiculous as Sarah did.

Arburn turned and shouted, "Get out of here!"

The children scattered, but Sarah noticed they were still giggling.

"We would be delighted to have your company," Sarah said. This was probably the only opportunity she'd have to get to know him.

"And we'd be so grateful for your protection," Maeve added, although she didn't sound quite sincere. She wasn't really trying, but Arburn was so sure of himself he didn't seem to notice.

"We were just going upstairs," Sarah said.

"Let me go ahead," he suggested. "You never know what you might find in an empty house."

They let him precede them up the stairs.

Maeve stopped to stomp on two or three of the steps, earning a shocked look from Arburn, which she ignored. "They seem pretty sturdy."

"The whole place is sturdy," Arburn said, but as he reached the top of the stairs, his next step made a splintering sound and he stumbled and almost fell when his foot broke through a rotting floorboard.

"Oh my, are you all right, Mr. Arburn?" Sarah said.

"Uh, yes, I'm fine. Just a little . . . a bad board there, I guess."

Sarah and Maeve stepped carefully around it, ignoring Arburn's offered hand. "This is the room with the leak," Sarah said, and they proceeded to explore the rest of the house with Arburn trailing behind them.

"It looks like whoever was squatting here is gone," Sarah observed as they descended the stairs again.

"Oh, Mr. Robinson would've run them off for you, I'm sure. Are you ladies really going to turn this house into a hospital?"

"Yes, a maternity hospital," Sarah said.

"I wouldn't expect you'd get much business in this neighborhood. Nobody here can afford to go to a hospital."

"That's exactly why we chose to put it here. We aren't going to charge our patients."

"So anybody can come?"

"Any woman who is expecting a baby, yes."

"Ah, that's what *maternity* means, then. But how are you going to stay in business if you don't charge the patients?"

"We'll take donations from rich people," Sarah said. "Mr. Robinson has already made a generous gift."

They'd reached the front hallway, and Sarah stopped. This would be a good opportunity to question Arburn some more. "I know Freddie wasn't really your brother, but you must have known him well."

Arburn's charming smile faded. "Not real well."

"But he worked for Mr. Robinson, too, didn't he?"

"If you call what he did working."

"Did he know Miss Longacre? I understand you would meet her at Mr. Robinson's flat over the saloon, so surely, he'd seen her there."

Arburn glanced at Maeve, as if concerned about her reaction. "He might've seen her there a lot of times, I guess, but not with me."

Sarah feigned surprise. "But I thought you were lovers."

Plainly, he hadn't expected a lady like Sarah to say anything like that. "I . . . I only saw her a few times. She had bigger fish to fry."

"I'm sure you were hurt when she threw you over for Mr. Robinson."

"I wouldn't say I was hurt," he hedged.

"But still, you must have been shocked to hear she'd been murdered."

"Or maybe you were glad," Maeve said sweetly. "Maybe you thought she got what she deserved."

Arburn's gaze darted between the two women. "I . . . I wasn't glad, exactly."

"I'm so happy to hear that," Sarah said. "I would hate to think you callous."

"But you had a right to be angry," Maeve said. "She treated you badly. Making you fall in love with her and—"

"I wasn't in love with her."

"But you were angry," Maeve said. "Nobody likes to be humiliated."

"I wasn't humiliated," he insisted, sounding angry now.

"Not even when you found her with Black Jack Robinson and she sent you away with your tail between your legs?"

"She didn't . . ." He paused to regain control, which disappointed Sarah. He was far more likely to blurt out something if he was angry. "I never cared about her. She was the one who started it. We were on a tour, and she slipped me a note. She'd written it out ahead of time. She planned it all."

"And being a gentleman, you couldn't hurt her feelings by refusing her," Sarah said.

He gave her black look. "I wasn't going to refuse her, no. What man would?"

He had a point. But still . . . "Didn't Mr. Robinson laugh at you when she sent you away?"

"No!"

"But they must've laughed when you were gone," Maeve said. "You knew they would, and it rankled, didn't it?"

"Where do you get your ideas? I told you, I never cared for her. I was glad when he took her. She was more trouble than she was worth."

"How was she trouble?" Sarah asked in a voice that demanded a reply.

"She wanted me to marry her."

"What? Are you serious?"

"Yes, she told me that the first time we . . . we were alone."

"Why would she want to marry you?" Maeve asked, which did hurt his feelings, if the look on his face was any indication.

"Because that's what women want. They all want a man to take care of them. She said she wanted me to take her away from her father's house. She never wanted to go back there again."

"You must have been very flattered," Sarah said.

"Flattered? She just wanted to use me. I wasn't going to marry no spoiled rich girl. I wasn't going to marry anybody."

"But you weren't going to let Black Jack marry her either, were you?" Sarah tried. "If you couldn't have her, nobody could."

"What are you saying? Do you think I killed her? I never killed nobody. He could have her and good riddance."

"I think you're right, Mrs. Malloy," Maeve said. "I think Mr. Arburn here couldn't stand the thought that some spoiled rich girl had thrown him over, so when he saw her go into the flat that night, he followed her. He went up there to tell her what he thought of her and things got out of hand and he strangled her."

"I never!"

"Yes, and Freddie saw him go in there," Sarah said. "Maybe he even asked Freddie to help him carry the trunk down the stairs. And when somebody found her body, Freddie was going to hear about it and figure out what had happened, so you had to kill him, too, didn't you?"

"I never killed her and I never killed Freddie, but if you want to find out who did, you should ask Norman Tufts."

"Norman? What does he have to do with this?"

"Just ask him." With that, Arburn turned and was gone, stomping down the front steps with a foolish disregard for how unstable those steps were.

"That was interesting," Maeve said. "I think Mr. Malloy would've been impressed."

"If only we'd learned something important."

"I think we learned that Arburn didn't kill them."

"You may be right, although Arburn is probably a good liar, so we can't be absolutely sure."

"He doesn't have much experience with women, though.

I think he usually just gets by on his charm and never really has to talk to them."

"You're probably right. Did you believe him when he said Estelle gave him a note?"

"I did, actually," Maeve said. "People don't usually lie with so much detail."

What a useful thing to know, Sarah thought.

The children Arburn had scared away were starting to gather again. "Let's go," Sarah said. "We can talk in the carriage." She locked the front door behind them, although she knew that wouldn't really keep anyone out.

John appeared relieved to see them and had them quickly on their way, even though the progress through the crowded streets was slow.

"All right, let's see what we learned," Sarah said. "You think he was telling the truth about Estelle initiating their relationship. But why would she do it?"

"Usually, if a girl goes after a man like that it's because she really likes him. Do we think Estelle really liked Arburn?"

"She couldn't have liked him very much if she threw him over the minute she met Jack Robinson."

"Exactly. Another reason she might go after him is because she—uh, I don't really know how to describe this but maybe *desire* would be the right word—because she *desired* him."

"And you think that would be different from liking him?"

Maeve shrugged. "I've noticed that women often stay with men they don't like, so there must be other reasons."

"Ah, I see what you mean. And do we believe Estelle desired Will Arburn?"

"Having met him, I can't imagine why, and she apparently

didn't enjoy his, uh, attentions, so I have to say no to that as well."

"Then what possible reason could she have had for . . . well, let's call it seducing him, because that was the result of her efforts. Why would she do that if she didn't like him and she didn't desire him?" Sarah asked.

"For the same reason women have always married men they don't love or desire—she wanted a husband."

"Yes, a husband and all that goes with him, a home of her own and a family."

"Arburn said himself she wanted to get away from her father. I can understand that, but how desperate would she have to be to think somebody like Will Arburn could save her?"

Sarah knew one reason Estelle might have been desperate to marry. "She was with child."

"She was? Why didn't you tell me this?"

"I only found out yesterday myself. The coroner mentioned it to Malloy back when he went to identify Freddie's body, but he didn't even know who she was then, and he'd forgotten all about it. She was about three months along."

"So she was already pregnant when she met Arburn."

"Apparently, but not very far along at that point. I don't know if she even realized it yet, but if she did, she'd be desperate to get married and not too particular to whom."

"But what about the father of the baby?" Maeve asked. "Wouldn't she want to marry him?"

"I think we can assume she didn't or why would she have been involved with Arburn and then Robinson?"

"So if she knew about the baby, she really did need to be saved."

"But she may not have known, in which case she must have had another reason. And if we assume that she wanted to be saved, she may have realized rather quickly that Arburn wasn't fit for the task, but then she met Robinson."

"A man with money and power. If she needed saving, he was perfect for the job."

"And he had his own reasons for wanting her."

"What were they?

Sarah sighed. "He thought she'd make him respectable and that he'd be accepted into society."

"Oh my."

"Yes, and Estelle may not have known what he expected, but she knew he could take care of her. And he wanted to. I think he really cared for her."

Maeve wrinkled her nose. "It wasn't exactly a fairy-tale romance."

"How many marriages are?"

"All right. I surrender," Maeve said with a grin. "But who fathered Estelle's baby?"

"We don't know that, and maybe we never will, but if we can figure it out, we might know who killed her."

"At least we know it wasn't Robinson or Arburn."

"I wonder how long she'd been going on these tours," Sarah mused. "She might have met someone else before Arburn."

"That's possible, I suppose. And let's not forget Norman Tufts. Didn't he want to marry Estelle? And he's been around for most of her life, so he was certainly around three months ago."

"Or maybe she was raped. Norman said everyone on the tours knew she was a woman, so they might have considered her fair game."

"Maybe we're getting carried away here," Maeve said. "Let's not forget that who fathered Estelle's baby is only important if he's also the one who killed her."

"Yes, or caused her to be killed in some way. But what other reason could there be?"

"We should be able to figure it out. Why does someone usually commit murder?"

Sarah gave that some thought. "If it's the heat of passion, it can be just about anything that set them off."

"Like jealousy or betrayal."

"Estelle certainly gave men reason to feel both of those. But let's not forget money."

"Estelle didn't have any money."

"Not of her own," Sarah said, "but her father must have some, and he's dying."

"Oh, so she'd inherit. But that only gives somebody a reason to kill him, not her."

"But if she's dead, who is the next heir in line?"

"Oh, I see," Maeve said. "Do you mean the sister?"

"Most likely the sister, although we can't forget Norman, too. I asked Penelope why she wanted Norman and Estelle to marry. She said it was the only way Norman would get his rightful inheritance."

"*His rightful inheritance?*" Maeve echoed. "That sounds like something out of a penny dreadful."

"Doesn't it? And why should Norman have a 'rightful inheritance' if he's nothing but the child of a distant cousin?"

Maeve studied Sarah's face for a long moment. "You know the reason, don't you?"

"I have a theory, courtesy of Mrs. Ellsworth."

"Mrs. Ellsworth? This is so delicious. What does she think?"

"She thinks that Norman is Penelope's illegitimate child."

"What makes her think that?" Maeve asked.

"I mentioned that Estelle was with child and then I told her that Norman was Penelope's ward, and she immediately jumped to that conclusion because of her belief in bad blood."

"What's bad blood?"

"Weak moral fiber, in this case, that runs in families."

"Oh, I see. If Estelle gets pregnant out of wedlock, she must be morally weak, and if she is, she inherited that weakness."

"Which means her aunt might have the same moral weakness," Sarah said. "I'm not too sure about the bad blood, but I do know that bad things keep happening in some families, generation after generation."

"Because bad people in the family make them happen."

"Yes, I think that's a more logical explanation."

"And what do you think is the bad thing that keeps happening in the Longacre family?" Maeve asked. "And don't act like you don't know what I'm talking about. You figured it out on the way over and pretended that you didn't."

"I . . . Well, illegitimate children, of course. First Norman, if what we suspect is true, and after seeing Penelope's reaction when I practically accused her, I'm sure it is, and then Estelle's baby."

"Both fathered by men who can't or won't marry them."

"We don't know that. We don't know the circumstances of either pregnancy. And it's possible the father of Estelle's baby would have married her. She may not have even known about her condition."

"But if she had a lover already, one who'd be willing to marry her, why did she go looking for more? I don't believe for a minute that Estelle would have married her baby's father."

Sarah didn't either, but she wasn't going to agree with Maeve, who would demand an explanation. No, she'd keep her sordid theory a secret until she was certain it was true.

FRANK STARED AT MARIE O'DAY FOR A LONG MOMENT. "What do you mean, Longacre wanted Estelle for himself?"

"Marie didn't mean anything, did you, sweetheart?" Tom said sharply.

"He did the same thing to Miss Penelope," Marie continued, ignoring Tom the way he ignored her. "Kept her at home to look after him until she was too old for any other man to want her. Then as soon as Miss Estelle was old enough, he turned Miss Penelope loose and let the girl take care of him instead."

"She must have known some young men, though." The evidence seemed to prove it. "Maybe at church? Or she met them when she went out."

"Mr. Norman looked after her when she went out, didn't he, Tom?" Marie said.

Tom just kept on preparing the lemonade, pouring the juice into a pitcher of water and adding sugar.

"But Norman didn't always go with her, did he?" Frank said.

Tom looked up warily and Marie smiled slyly.

"Where'd you get an idea like that?" she asked.

"From Norman. And from the other men she used to meet."

"I won't have you saying such things about Miss Estelle," Tom said.

"I'm sorry to have to say them, but it's true. She used to go to the Bowery to meet men."

"If you know all that, why are you asking us?" Marie said.

"I'm just wondering who knew she would sneak out at night."

"Wasn't at night," Tom said. "And she didn't sneak."

"Mr. Longacre, he don't pay any attention to what goes on here if it don't involve him," Marie said. "So Tom's right, she didn't have to sneak."

Tom poured lemonade into three glasses. "And mostly she went out in the afternoon. She went to concerts and museums."

Frank remembered those sad rooms over the saloon. "Who knew she went out?"

"We did," Tom said.

"What about Mr. Longacre?"

"I told you . . ." Marie began, but Tom silenced her with a gesture.

He set one of the glasses in front of Frank with calm deliberation. "He knew."

"Longacre knew Estelle went out alone?"

"Yes. He'd see her leave. His bedroom faces the street. Then he'd ask me where she went."

"And you told him?"

"I told him she went to a concert or a museum, whatever I happened to think up."

"Did she tell you anything before she left? Some excuse?" Frank asked.

"We're just servants. She didn't have to tell us anything," Marie said. "But we'd see her when she came back. We knew she was meeting a man."

"And what about Longacre? Did he know, too?"

Tom pulled himself up to his full and considerable height. "Mr. Longacre doesn't have to tell us anything either."

No, of course he didn't. Frank took a sip of the lemonade. It was very good. "Just tell me one more thing. Does Mr. Longacre ever go out at all anymore?"

"Occasionally, when he's feeling strong enough," Tom said.

"And when was the last time he felt strong enough?"

Tom and Marie exchanged a glance, and some silent communication passed between them. Tom answered for them. "The last time he felt strong enough was a week ago last Saturday, the night Miss Estelle disappeared."

II

THE CHURCH WAS NEARLY FULL WHEN FRANK ARRIVED, packed with row after row of boys and a sprinkling of girls. They'd cleaned up as best they could for the occasion and sat quietly and respectfully, waiting for the service to start. Frank found Gino in the last row, where he could keep an eye on the crowd. Gino moved over to make room for him.

"Freddie had a lot of friends," Frank observed.

"The newsies stick together, and they always take care of one when he dies. Most of them don't have families, and they're all afraid of being put in an unmarked grave in a potter's field."

That made sense. Nobody wanted to think their life hadn't mattered to anyone, even kids. "Who's that family on the front row?"

"Rudolph Heig and his wife and children. He's the super-intendent at the Duane Street Lodging House."

A group of four men entered the church and stopped at the back. "That's Robinson," Frank told Gino. He didn't have to say which one. Robinson was the obvious leader. The others, probably brought along for protection, hung back from him, eyeing the crowd for potential danger. He saw an empty pew and headed toward it, his men following closely behind.

"I don't see Arburn," Gino said.

"He's probably staying out of Robinson's way for now."

No sooner had Robinson and his men seated themselves than the pallbearers entered carrying the small casket. Frank picked out Kid Blink and Raven Saggio. The Kid hadn't seemed to know Freddie when Frank and Gino were looking for him, so maybe he'd been chosen because of his position as leader of the strike. Raven was too small to offer much actual help, and he kept swiping at his red eyes with his shirtsleeve.

The pallbearers set the casket on a stand at the front of the church, and Kid Blink took his place at the pulpit. He began by praising all the newsboys for their strength and courage, both during their normal activities and especially during the strike. He truly was a gifted speaker. When he had the boys cheering for themselves and one another, he finally mentioned the dead boy.

"Freddie 'Two Toes' Bertolli was a good friend to everybody who knew him," he began.

"Bertolli?" Frank whispered to Gino.

"Pop Rudolph said he thought Bert wasn't his real name."

Frank nodded and continued to scan the crowd as he'd been doing since he sat down. Freddie's killer might be in this room, although most of the more likely suspects wouldn't even know the funeral was being held.

When Kid Blink was finished, he invited others to come and speak. Several newsboys had a story to tell about Freddie helping them out or being a good friend. When everyone who wanted to had spoken, Kid Blink took the pulpit again.

"It's a dirty shame that Freddie got himself murdered. The coppers don't care and they ain't gonna be looking for who did it, but I'm here to tell you that somebody cares. Mr. Frank Malloy and his partner, Mr. Donatelli, are looking for the killer. Would you gentlemen please stand up?"

Frank and Gino exchanged a glance and stood up. Surprisingly, the boys cheered them enthusiastically.

"These men is private detectives, and if you know anything about who killed Freddie, you can tell them. We can't let one of our own get killed without doing something about it, can we, boys?"

More cheers and more speech making and finally Kid Blink announced that Freddie would be laid to rest in the Linden Hill Cemetery in Brooklyn. Whoever wanted to follow the hearse across the bridge was welcome.

The pallbearers once again lifted their small burden and carried it down the aisle. The children followed them out, with remarkable reserve. Mr. Heig stopped to shake Gino's hand and be introduced to Frank on his way out. Finally, Frank and Gino were left alone in the church with Jack Robinson and his men.

Frank and Gino waited while he approached. "That was clever, getting Kid Blink to point you out to all of them," Robinson said.

Frank decided not to mention it hadn't been his idea. Let Robinson think well of him. "I doubt anybody knows who killed Freddie, but they might hear something."

"Have you found out anything yet?"

"One thing that you might want to know."

Robinson stiffened, then turned to his men and motioned for them to move away. They did so, gathering by the door that stood open to the street, waiting. "What is it?" Robinson asked softly.

"Longacre says somebody took Estelle's body from the mortuary."

Robinson smiled slowly. "Is that right?"

"Yes. He thought I did it."

"Why would he think that?"

"Because I was the only other person who knew who she was, I guess. Anyway, he wants her back."

"Does he? Well, he isn't going to get her. She's going to be buried in a nice cemetery with a beautiful marker."

"Longacre wanted to be buried next to her."

Robinson's fury was instant. "Well, he won't be."

"Should I tell him that?"

"I don't care what you tell him, but he isn't going to get his hands on her."

"Do you know why she hated him so much?"

Robinson hesitated just an instant too long. "No."

"All right, and don't worry, I'm not going to tell him you have her. I just wanted to make sure it was you and not somebody we don't even know about."

"Did you find out anything else?"

"Nothing definite, but I'll let you know the minute I'm sure of anything."

Robinson's eyes were cold. "You'd better."

As Robinson left, followed by his men, Frank couldn't help thinking Robinson had been putting on a show for them. He wouldn't want his men to see him the way Frank had seen him at his house, drinking to dull the pain of losing a girl he had no right to even know.

"Is that true? Did he really steal her body?" Gino asked.

"So it seems. And I'm sure he didn't steal it. He probably

paid a pretty penny for the privilege of taking it. He also knows why Estelle hated her father."

"But he said he didn't."

Frank smiled. "He was lying."

"Oh," Gino said in admiration. "Did you find out anything else this morning?"

"Oh yes. How about you?"

"I'm not sure. I'll let you decide when you hear it."

"And Sarah might have some news as well. Let's go home and find out."

Upon their return home, Sarah and Maeve had stripped off their street clothes, sponged off the sweat and dirt accumulated during the trip downtown, and changed into light cotton housedresses. After paying Catherine and Brian a visit in the nursery to give Mrs. Malloy a brief respite, they let her resume supervising the children when they heard Gino and Malloy arrive home.

At Sarah's urging, the men took off their suit coats, rolled up their sleeves in deference to the heat, and greedily consumed the cold beer their maid Hattie served. The ladies received iced mineral water.

The parlor was cool, with the heavy drapes pulled shut against the afternoon sun, and when everyone was settled, Sarah said, "Someone has stolen Estelle's body from the mortuary."

"It was Jack Robinson," Malloy said. "We saw him at Freddie's funeral this afternoon, and he admitted it."

"Oh dear, I didn't know his funeral was today," Sarah said.

"A boy came by our office this morning to tell us. Gino and I both went."

"Was it very sad?" Maeve asked.

Malloy shook his head. "Not as sad as I expected. The boys talked about Freddie. He was a good kid. Anyway, Robinson has Estelle's body," he continued, making it obvious he didn't want to talk about Freddie's funeral anymore.

"What is he going to do with it?" Maeve asked.

"Nothing too scandalous," Malloy assured her. "He wants to bury her and put up a fancy headstone, but he doesn't want her family to know where she is."

"I was afraid of this," Sarah said. "He threatened something like that when I met him in the attorney's office. Do you think we should at least tell her family?"

"Ordinarily, I'd say yes, but in this case, I'm not sure," Malloy said. "Longacre said he wants to be buried beside her, but is that what she would've wanted?"

"I doubt it," Sarah said. "Maeve and I have decided she must have been desperate to get away from her father to do what she did."

Malloy let them discuss the proprieties of it for a minute. Then he said, "I think we can solve this pretty simply. We just wait until Robinson has buried her. He's not going to tell us where she is, because we aren't even going to ask, so we can't tell the Longacres. All we can say is that we think he took her and let them ask him if they still want to."

"And of course he'll refuse to tell them. Well done, Malloy," Sarah said. He nodded to acknowledge her compliment. "Now, who wants to go first?"

"Ladies first. Tell us about your visit with Penelope."

"Oh, we had another interesting visit today as well, but you'll have to hear about Penelope first," Sarah said. She told them what Penelope had said about living on an allowance from Horace, and Penelope's reaction to hearing that Estelle was pregnant and to Sarah's theory that Norman was her son.

"But she didn't actually admit that he was," Malloy said.

"No, and I don't think she ever would, but I'm sure it's true. It would explain everything."

"Including Longacre giving her an allowance," Gino said. "I doubt he'd be willing to support his sister if she'd just decided to take in somebody else's kid, but if he knew it was her child, he might feel obligated."

"Knowing Longacre, I don't think he'd feel an obligation," Malloy said, "but he might do it to placate her, so she didn't cause him any trouble."

"How could she cause him trouble without ruining her own reputation?" Maeve asked.

"She couldn't," Sarah said, "but she could hardly be more of a social outcast than she is now, and any scandal would also touch her brother. He'd want to keep his listing in the Social Register, and they drop you pretty quickly if there's a scandal in your family."

"Did Penelope have any idea who the father of Estelle's baby was?" Gino asked.

"Only that she was sure it wasn't Norman, although that might've just been wishful thinking. He was certainly close enough to Estelle, at least. But," Sarah added, "she did say if I wanted to know who the father of Estelle's baby was, I should ask Horace."

"Which I did," Malloy said, "and he claimed he didn't know either. All right, so who else did you visit today? I thought you were just going to take Maeve to see the house."

Sarah nodded to Maeve, indicating she should be the one to tell. "We saw Will Arburn."

"What? How did you manage that?"

"Someone—he said it was a child—ran to tell him two females were breaking into Mr. Robinson's house, so he came to deal with us."

"And how did he deal with you?" Gino asked grimly.

Maeve shook her head at his disapproval. "Not very well. He claimed he didn't know the house had been sold."

"Which he wouldn't have if Robinson is still mad at him about hiring a private detective without telling him," Malloy said.

"That's exactly what we said to him," Maeve happily reported. "And then we accused him of killing Estelle and Freddie."

"You did what?" Gino asked, horrified.

"Isn't that what you would have done?" Maeve asked.

They all knew it was, so Gino was spared from admitting it.

"And what did he say when you accused him?" Malloy asked.

"He denied it, of course, and Mrs. Malloy thought he was telling the truth, and so did I, but of course he's probably a good liar, so we couldn't be absolutely sure. He also told us Estelle wanted to marry him."

"Do you think that's true?" Malloy asked.

"It's possible," Sarah said. "Maeve and I can't figure out why she would want to be involved with him unless she was desperate to get married and was willing to settle for just anyone."

"Because of the baby, you mean?"

"We don't know if she even knew she was pregnant when she took up with Arburn," Sarah reminded them, "but it does seem that she wanted to escape the Longacre household, and marriage to anyone at all might have seemed the only way out."

"But Arburn claimed he didn't care anything about Estelle and certainly didn't want to marry her," Maeve added. "He says he was glad when Robinson took her away, so why would he be jealous or want to kill her? And then he suggested we should talk to Norman if we want to know who killed her."

"Norman?" Malloy echoed. "Did he say why?"

"Of course not."

"But I think we need to see him anyway, don't you?" Sarah said. "He might know more about Estelle than anyone else. He spent a lot of time with her, after all."

"We need to make sure Penelope isn't around when we talk to him, though," Malloy said.

"Of course. So what did you find out from Raven, Gino?" Sarah asked.

"He and Freddie were definitely the ones who found Estelle in the trunk. Or rather, Freddie was. He came to Raven and claimed he'd found a trunk and needed help. He acted like he didn't know what was in it, but Raven said he was very nervous, and Raven noticed some hair sticking out of the lid, so he knew before they opened it there'd be a body inside."

"If he noticed it, then Freddie probably did, too," Maeve said. "He probably would've recognized it as Estelle's hair, too. That would explain why he got scared and ran away from the killer."

"If he was the one helping the killer carry the trunk," Malloy said. "But maybe he did just find the trunk in the alley. He would've recognized it, and if he saw the hair sticking out, he would have guessed it was Estelle's."

"So we still don't know anything for sure," Gino said with a sigh.

"Did Raven tell you anything else?" Malloy asked.

"Just that Freddie was scared and asked to stay with Raven for a few days. We already knew that. What did Longacre say?"

"Not much. He accused me of taking Estelle's body, and I think I convinced him I didn't. He said he wants to be buried beside her."

Everyone groaned. "That settles it," Sarah said. "No one is going to tell him where she is."

"Indeed. He also said he didn't allow Estelle to be courted, so she didn't have any official suitors. He didn't know Estelle was pregnant, and he was pretty upset to hear it. He was sure Norman wasn't the father, but he had no idea who could be. I let him know I thought Norman was Penelope's son, and he didn't deny it. I wondered why she'd want Norman to marry Estelle since they were first cousins, and he said it didn't matter because he never would have allowed it."

"You're right, that's not much," Sarah said.

"But I also talked to Marie."

"That awful maid of Longacre's?"

"And her husband, who seems like a very nice man."

"What on earth did they have to say?" Sarah asked.

Malloy turned to Maeve and Gino. "Sometimes servants won't talk about their masters, or at least they won't say anything bad. Marie is about the rudest maid I've ever seen, though, so I thought she might be willing to talk."

"And her master is dying, so she doesn't have to stay in his good graces much longer," Maeve said.

"So I asked them both what they knew about Estelle. They confirmed that she didn't have any suitors and that Norman was the only young man who came to the house."

"So they didn't tell you anything new," Gino said.

"Yes, they did. They told me they knew Estelle was going out to meet a man, and they also told me that Longacre knew she was going out alone."

"He knew she was meeting someone?" Maeve asked.

"I don't know what he suspected, but they said he could see her leaving from his bedroom window. He must have known something wasn't right."

"But he didn't stop her," Sarah said.

"No, and I found out one more thing that's very interesting. It seems Mr. Longacre sometimes still goes out, when he feels up to it, and the last time he went out is the night Estelle was killed."

"We hadn't even considered him because we thought he was too sick," Gino said.

"But would he have been able to carry her body and the trunk down the stairs and through the alley?" Sarah asked.

"I don't know, but after I talked to Robinson, I worked out what I think happened the night Estelle died," Malloy said. "See if this makes sense to you. Estelle left home and went to the flat. She'd sent Robinson a telegram, asking him to meet her there at six o'clock, but he was out of town and didn't get the telegram until around nine."

"Is that how they normally set up their meetings?" Sarah asked.

"No. I gathered that they had regularly set times they would meet. In fact, they were supposed to meet the next day. Sunday afternoon was their regular time, he said. He also said they usually met during the day, so it would be safer for her to come to that part of town."

"That makes sense," Maeve said. "Mrs. Malloy and I were wondering how she managed to get there safely."

"So for some reason Estelle needed to see Robinson that night, for something that couldn't wait until the next day."

"But why?" Gino asked.

"Maybe she just realized she was having a baby and wanted to tell him," Maeve said.

"But why not just wait until the next afternoon?" Sarah asked. "One day wouldn't make any difference. And it can't have been convenient for her to get out to send the telegram either."

"So for whatever reason, Estelle went to the flat that night.

She had a key and let herself in to wait. Then she had a visit from someone she wasn't expecting."

"Her killer," Maeve said. "But why would she let him in?"

"Maybe she thought it was Robinson," Gino said.

"Or maybe it was someone she knew and wasn't afraid of," Sarah guessed.

"Whatever the reason, she let him in. Then something happened. Maybe an argument, or maybe he just came there already intent on killing her. Now she's dead and he has a body to dispose of."

"But why bother?" Gino asked. "It's not like she's lying on the street where anyone can see her or might've seen him. Nobody even knew he'd been there, so all he has to do is leave."

"And yet he puts her body into a trunk that's in the bedroom," Malloy said.

"And somehow carries it down the steps," Gino said.

"Not yet, because it's still daylight. Somebody might see, and everybody knows that's Black Jack's flat, so they'd question why he was taking something out of it."

"Maybe, or maybe they'd remember seeing him with a trunk and when Estelle went missing, they'd make the connection," Gino said.

"So he just leaves her there?" Maeve asked.

"That's my theory. He leaves her there in the trunk for a while, probably waiting for it to get dark. Jack Robinson gets home and finds the telegram around nine o'clock. He goes straight over to the saloon, but she's not there. He's sure he looked in the bedroom, and he's pretty sure he would've noticed if the trunk was gone."

"And it's just gotten dark by then," Sarah said. "So the killer hasn't had a chance to move the trunk yet anyway."

Malloy nodded. "Jack goes downstairs and asks the bouncer

and the bartender if they saw her or if she left a message, and they both say no. The bartender told me he heard some noises from upstairs later, though, after Jack left. He didn't think anything of it at the time."

"So that was the killer coming back for the trunk," Gino said.

"I think so. He would've had a hard time carrying it by himself, so he must've either brought help or maybe he got Freddie to help him."

"Because Freddie would've come back to the flat to sleep by then," Gino said.

"And he must have seen whoever moved the trunk, because why else would someone have killed him?" Sarah said.

"And now we know that Longacre went out that night," Malloy said.

"He could have followed Estelle," Gino said.

"But could he have carried her body away?" Sarah asked.

"And why would he want to?" Maeve asked.

"Because he wanted to be buried beside her," Malloy said.

"And he killed her because he didn't want anyone else to have her," Sarah said. "Especially not someone like Jack Robinson."

"You make him sound like a spurned lover," Maeve scoffed.

"I'm afraid he is."

Everyone gaped at Sarah, speechless for a long moment. Finally, Maeve said, "Do you think he . . . ?"

Sarah nodded. "We've been trying to figure out who could have fathered Estelle's child, but there's one man we haven't considered who was always in that house and who always had the opportunity to be alone with her."

"That's horrible," Gino murmured.

"But it would explain why she was so desperate to get away

from her father that she'd be willing to marry someone like Will Arburn," Maeve said.

"And especially Jack Robinson," Sarah said. "It would explain a lot of things."

"But how did he manage the trunk?" Gino asked.

"He's got a very big manservant who might've helped him with the trunk," Malloy said.

"All right," Gino said, "but how did he find Freddie? How did he even know who he was?"

"I don't know, but maybe Freddie's death wasn't connected with Estelle's after all and he was killed by someone else entirely. Or maybe Longacre got lucky and found him by accident."

"But you said that night was the last time Longacre left his house," Sarah said, "so he couldn't have killed Freddie himself."

"He might've had someone else do it, or like I said, maybe Freddie wasn't killed because of this. We need to go back to the Longacre house and ask some more questions," Malloy said.

"Are you going to ask Longacre if he raped his daughter?" Sarah asked, shocking Gino with her boldness. "Because he'll certainly deny it. There must be another way to figure it out."

"Maybe Penelope knows what went on in that house," Maeve said.

"Or the servants, if they'll admit it," Gino said.

"Or maybe Jack Robinson knows," Malloy said.

"Do you think Estelle would have told him?"

"I think he knows something. He acted strangely when I asked him if he knew why Estelle hated her father so much. He said he didn't, but I was sure he was lying. I guess I should talk to him first, before I see Longacre, so when I accuse him, I already know."

"And I should go with you," Sarah said.

"Absolutely not!"

Sarah glared at him the way he always glared at her when he was trying to intimidate her. It never worked on her, and it looked like it wasn't going to work on him either.

But then he said, "Why do you think you should go?"

"He was very gentlemanly when I met him. I think he's a little in awe of women he considers ladies, and I believe he'd answer my questions while he might not answer yours."

"She's right," Maeve said. "I think he'd do anything Mrs. Malloy asked."

Malloy didn't care for that one bit, but he said, "All right, we'll try it, but Gino will go along and wait outside, so if Robinson doesn't behave himself, I can send you home."

"What about me?" Maeve said.

Malloy looked at her for a long moment. "You're a nursemaid. You shouldn't even be here."

"Can I resign as your nursemaid, then?"

"No." Malloy turned back to Sarah. "Should we try to see Robinson this evening?"

"Do you think he'll be at home? I don't know what kind of schedule a gangster keeps."

"I think he's still mourning Estelle, so he probably isn't going out much. He might be on the telephone, so I'll try to telephone him to see if he's home. If I can't reach him, we'll go in the morning."

"THIS WOULD BE SO MUCH EASIER IF YOU HAD A MOTORCAR," Gino said, helping Sarah down from the hansom cab and leaving Frank to manage himself. Gino had followed them to Robinson's house in a separate cab, since there was room for only two in each. And now he'd sent his own driver on his way, while Frank asked his to wait. Gino took a seat in the remaining cab, prepared to escort Sarah home again if necessary. Early-evening shadows were growing long in the streets, and the heat of the day was slowly dissipating, so the horse and driver were pleased to find a shady spot to rest.

The Malloys were expected, and a maid opened the door almost instantly after Frank knocked. Robinson was waiting for them in the parlor. The room, like all the others in this house, reflected the good taste of the previous owner and his ancestors. Robinson's clothes were impeccable, and he looked much less drunk and grief-stricken than he had on Frank's first visit. "Mrs. Malloy, what an unexpected pleasure," he said.

"Thank you. I've been wanting to offer my condolences. I'm afraid I didn't really do that at our last meeting."

"I appreciate your concern. Malloy, I didn't expect to see you again so soon. I hope you have some news for me."

"Not yet, but I have a few more questions. When I have the answers, I'll be much closer to having the information you want."

"Then let's sit down. I've asked my maid to bring us some iced tea, but if you'd prefer something else, I'm sure we can provide it."

Frank and Sarah agreed iced tea would be a refreshing novelty. Not many people in New York served it. When they had been served and the maid was gone, Robinson said, "All right. You said you had questions for me."

He looked at Frank, but by previous agreement, Sarah was the one who began. "Mr. Robinson, I know you cared very much for Estelle. You told me you wanted to marry her, which I believe proves your true feelings for her. I know it must be difficult for you to speak of her at all, but especially about things in her life that were unpleasant."

Robinson's expression hardened but not with anger, as Frank had expected. "But you're going to ask me about something unpleasant anyway, aren't you?"

"I'm very sorry, but I also know you want to find out who killed her, and we need this information in order to do it."

"I understand." He held himself very stiffly, as if expecting a blow.

"First let me ask you if you have any idea why Estelle wanted to see you that night instead of just waiting until the next day when you'd already arranged to meet?"

"No, I don't. She didn't say anything in the telegram, of course, and I couldn't imagine . . . I thought something must have happened."

"What did you think could have happened?"

His body had gone rigid. "She . . . I thought maybe . . . maybe she had argued with her father."

"Argued about what?"

"They didn't get along. It could've been about anything."

"But it would've had to have been something terrible for her to send a telegram like that when she could have just waited until the next day. You didn't think it was just an argument, did you?"

"Really, Mrs. Malloy . . ."

"Mr. Robinson, you don't have to worry about my sensibilities. I've worked as a midwife in the tenements. Very little can shock me, although many things horrify me. We have learned that Estelle was with child before she met you and Arburn. We have also learned that her father did not allow anyone to court her, so she had no male visitors at her house except her cousin Norman. Do you believe Norman could have fathered Estelle's child?"

Robinson had gone pale. "No. Not Norman. I'm sure of that."

"How can you be?" Frank asked.

"She . . . she was fond of him in an odd way, the way you're fond of a pet, I guess. And she pitied him. She wouldn't have felt like that if he'd abused her in any way."

"Did Estelle tell you who could have fathered the child?" Sarah asked.

"I didn't know about the child," he hedged, plainly more than uncomfortable with the subject.

"But you knew she wasn't innocent when she started coming to the Bowery."

"If you mean she wasn't a virgin, then yes, I did know that, but she was still innocent." He was angry now, although his instinctive good manners wouldn't allow him to raise his voice to Sarah.

"I'm sorry. That was a poor choice of words. You're right, she was innocent in so many ways. But I think someone she should have been able to trust had betrayed that trust. Do you know who that was, Mr. Robinson?"

"She never told me," he tried.

"But you figured it out, didn't you? And you were as horrified as we were when we realized it, too. Did you come to understand that her father had violated her?"

He flinched as if she'd struck him, and Frank understood that she had in a way. "Yes," he said through gritted teeth. "That son of a . . . He doesn't deserve to live."

"And he'll die soon in any case. The question is, did he kill Estelle?"

"Why would he have killed her?" he asked bitterly.

"Perhaps because she was going to escape him. Or because she'd taken a lover. You must have thought he'd abused her in some horrific way that day, and you may have been right. That would certainly explain why she was so desperate to see you that she couldn't wait even one day."

"When she wasn't at the flat that night, I thought she'd

gone home," Robinson said, angry again. "I was relieved, because surely she wouldn't have gone home if it was as bad as I thought. But how could the old man have killed her? He's too sick to leave the house."

"We're still trying to figure that out," Frank said quickly, before Sarah could reply. "Are you sure she didn't give you any hint at all about why she wanted to meet you that night? What exactly did the telegram say?"

"Just that she wanted to meet me that night instead of Sunday."

"Do you still have the telegram?" Sarah asked.

"Of course."

"May we see it?" she asked gently.

He sighed. "If you think it will do any good. Excuse me."

He rose and left the room.

"What do you think the telegram will tell us?" Frank asked.

She shrugged. "I don't know, but it can't hurt to take a look."

Robinson returned with the small square of paper. He handed it to Sarah. She needed only a moment to read the typewritten words, and then she looked up with a puzzled frown.

"What is it?" Frank asked, reaching for it.

"It's worded very oddly."

Indeed it was. It merely said, "Change time today six instead." The signature was only her initials.

"I thought she just didn't want anyone to guess what it was about so she said as little as possible," Robinson said.

"You're probably right," Sarah said, although she still looked puzzled.

Frank reached into his pocket and pulled out a small notebook and a pencil.

"What are you doing?" Robinson asked.

"Just copying it down. I assume you want to keep it."

"Of course I do. It's the last message she sent me."

When Frank had finished copying all the information, including the identifying letters and numbers at the top, he handed the paper back to Robinson.

"Do you really think the old man could've killed her?" Robinson asked.

"We're going to find out," Frank said, rising to his feet. "Just don't you kill him until we do."

12

WHEN SARAH AND MALLOY CAME OUT OF ROBINSON'S house, Gino eagerly climbed out of the hansom cab and demanded to know if their theory was right.

Sarah nodded and Malloy glanced away, his expression grim.

Gino frowned his dismay. "What do we do now?"

"You will go home and get a good night's sleep, and so will we," Malloy said. "I'll see you at the office sometime tomorrow."

"But won't you need me? If you're going to visit Longacre again . . ."

Sarah exchanged a glance with Malloy, and they silently agreed about Gino's involvement.

"I'll telephone you at the office if I have something for you," Malloy said.

"But—"

"I can't afford to wear out my welcome with Longacre," Malloy said. "We won't find out anything if I do, so it's better if I see him alone."

Gino grudgingly agreed, wished them good night, and strode off into the evening to find another cab.

Malloy helped Sarah into the waiting one and gave the driver their address on Bank Street.

"I suppose this means we don't need to speak to Penelope," Sarah said as the cab pulled away from the curb.

"Not yet, at least."

Sarah shivered, in spite of the warmth of the evening. "I was hoping I was wrong about Longacre."

"I was, too."

She slipped her hand into his. He squeezed it, and she knew a moment of pure joy that they had found each other.

"I hate that you know about these things," he said.

"I knew about a lot of them before I ever met you. I just never knew people killed over their secrets. Do you think I could be of any help at the Longacre house?"

"You certainly can't question Longacre in his bedroom."

She smiled at the ridiculous thought. "Of course not, but maybe I could talk to the servants while you're busy with Longacre. They might tell me even more than they told you, especially Tom."

"I'm sure you could utterly charm Tom. I'm not too sure about Marie, though."

"Was she charmed by you?"

"Not that I noticed."

"And yet look how much she revealed to you. I think I know how to handle her."

"All right then. We'll both go tomorrow."

* * *

AT FIRST GINO COULDN'T FIGURE OUT WHY SOMEBODY had left a bundle of rags outside the door of their office. Admittedly, the hallway was dim, with only the morning sunlight filtering through the frosted glass of the doors lining it, so he couldn't see very clearly. When he got closer, the bundle of rags took on a more recognizable form, though, and when he nudged it with his foot, it sat right up and glared at him.

"Hey!"

"Who are you?" Gino asked.

"I'm . . ." He caught himself. "Never mind who I am. You're one of them detectives, ain't you? The ones looking for who killed Two Toes."

"That's right. Do you have some information for me?"

"I might."

"Well, whether you do or whether you don't, you need to move so I can get into my office."

The boy scrambled to his feet and stepped back so Gino could unlock the door. His visitor was a runty little fellow, all knees and elbows. His dark eyes were enormous in his thin face, but they looked like they'd seen way too much in his short life.

"Have you been here all night?" Gino asked.

"Yeah. It seemed like a good place, and I didn't want to miss you."

Gino had to admit, the boy was resourceful. "Have a seat." He pointed at the chair beside his desk. The boy sat down warily while Gino took his usual seat behind his desk and found some paper and a pencil in the top desk drawer. "All right then, what do you have to tell me?"

The boy squinted at the paper from beneath the brim of his battered cap. "What do you need that for?"

"I'll write down what you tell me if I think it's important."

"Everything I'm going to tell you is important."

"Even your name?"

"I ain't no fool, not after what happened to Two Toes."

"I see." And he did. "Did you see something? Or hear something?"

"Both. I mean . . . Well, it was Wednesday, I think, last week. Somebody was looking for Two Toes."

"Somebody besides me and Mr. Malloy, you mean?"

"Yeah, somebody besides you."

"Do you know who it was?"

"Yeah."

Gino was going to have to work on his interrogation skills. "So who was it?"

"Willy Arburn."

Gino laid down his pencil. "Arburn is the one who hired us to find Two Toes in the first place."

"Oh . . . But if he hired you to do it, why was he looking, too?"

Gino considered that for a moment. Why *would* Arburn have been looking? "This was Wednesday, you said?"

"Yeah, I'm pretty sure. The day before I heard he was kilt."

"What time of day was it?"

"Late. We ain't selling papers, so we was all just hanging around under the bridge, pitching pennies and shooting craps."

A very dangerous activity, but Gino knew the newsies would say it was only illegal if you got caught. "And Arburn just asked if any of you had seen Two Toes?"

"No, he pulled me aside 'cause he knows I'm pals with Two Toes."

"And what did you tell him?"

The boy's dirty face nearly crumpled at this, but he managed not to cry. "I didn't know what was gonna happen, did I?"

"No, you didn't, and you shouldn't blame yourself. You're not the one who killed Freddie, are you?"

"No!" he nearly shouted, outraged.

"Well, then, it's not your fault. The man who did it is the one to blame. Just tell me what you said to Arburn."

The boy swallowed. "I said I ain't seen Two Toes in a few days, but Raven would probably know where he was."

Gino managed not to wince. He didn't want to confirm the boy's worst fears that he had led Freddie's killer right to him. In fact, Gino didn't know if he had or not, because why would Arburn want to harm the boy?

"He said I done good and give me a nickel," the boy added sadly.

"We know Arburn was looking for Two Toes, but that doesn't mean he's the one who killed him. What you said probably didn't cause any harm to anybody."

"Do you really think so?" the boy asked hopefully.

"Of course. I guess a lot of people know Raven and Two Toes were pals, not just you."

"I guess."

"And a lot of people know where Raven's place is."

"Yeah, they do."

"So anybody could've been looking for him, and anybody could've found him."

The boy dragged his sleeve across his mouth. "I reckon you're right."

"I appreciate you coming to tell me. And here's your reward." He pulled a dollar from his pocket. The boy's eyes lit up.

"Thanks, mister."

"And if you hear anything else, be sure to let me know."

The boy was halfway to the door when he stopped and turned back. "You won't tell Arburn I told you, will you?"

"What can I tell him? I don't even know your name."

The boy grinned hugely at that, and then he was gone.

Gino leaned back in his chair to consider what the boy had said. Maybe he'd been telling the truth when he assured the boy that Arburn probably wasn't the killer, but maybe not. Why would Arburn have gone looking for Freddie the very night they'd told him he'd been found? And after they'd assured him they would keep working on the case? There was only one way to find out for sure.

Gino picked up the telephone earpiece and jiggled the switch hook to summon the operator. He gave her the Malloys' number and waited for Maeve to answer. She'd let Mr. Malloy know where he'd gone if the Malloys went home first. He'd leave a note here if Mr. Malloy came to the office looking for him.

"You're like a bad penny, ain't you?" Marie said when she saw Frank and Sarah standing on the Longacre doorstep that morning. "And don't think I don't know this is way too early in the day for visitors."

"This isn't a social call," Sarah said in that authoritative voice she'd used on Marie the last time.

This time, Marie didn't even pretend she wasn't going to admit them, though. When she'd closed the door behind them, she said, "He's awake if you want to go on up, although I wouldn't take no lady with me if I was you."

"I thought I'd wait down here with you," Sarah said. "We could chat."

"Chat, is it? I suppose you'll be wanting something cold to drink, too. Come along, then, if you're not too grand to sit in the kitchen." She turned and started toward the back of the house, not even bothering to see if Sarah was following.

Sarah gave Frank a satisfied grin and went after her.

Malloy wondered if he would merit something cold to drink when he was finished with Longacre. With a sigh, he started up the stairs to the dark, stuffy sickroom.

He knocked loudly, so Longacre would know it wasn't Marie, and then he opened the door to find Longacre glaring at him from his chair this time. He wore the same stained dressing gown and disreputable slippers. "Can't you leave a man alone to die in peace?"

"Are you planning to die today? I wouldn't have come if I'd known."

"Don't be daft. Of course I'm not going to die today, but dying is hard work, and I don't have any energy left for you and your questions."

"That's too bad. I'd think you'd want to see your daughter's killer caught and punished before you go."

Longacre had no answer for this, as Frank had suspected he wouldn't. If he'd killed Estelle, he certainly didn't want to be caught and punished.

Without waiting for an invitation to sit that was probably not going to come, Frank again cleared a chair and straddled it, resting his arms along the back of the chair and meeting Longacre's steady stare.

"Aren't you going to ask me if I found out who took Estelle's body?" Frank asked after a long moment of silence.

"I figured that's why you came and you'd tell me in your own good time."

"That's not why I came, but I believe it was Jack Robinson who took her."

"I thought as much, after you told me he's the one Estelle was meeting. What does he think he's going to do with a dead body?"

"He doesn't confide in me. You'll have to ask him yourself."

Longacre snorted in derision.

"I also thought you'd ask me if I've found out who killed Estelle."

"You'd look a lot happier if you had."

Frank thought he was probably right. "I did find out some new information since I saw you last, though. I found out you sometimes go out."

Longacre's eyes narrowed. "So what if I do?"

"I just thought it was interesting that one of the times you went out was the night Estelle died."

"I suppose Tom told you that. Well, he'll find himself out of a job for his trouble."

"And you'll find yourself with no servants to take care of you in your dying days," Frank said. "Have you tried to hire a new servant lately? It's not easy to find one who won't take advantage of you, especially when you're sick." Frank had no idea if this was true or not, since he'd never hired a servant in his life, but he was gratified to see Longacre believed him, if the sudden panic in his eyes was any indication. "And of course there's Marie's meat pies, which I am told are delicious."

"She told you that herself, I guess."

"So where did you go that night?"

"Where do you think I went?"

"I think you probably followed Estelle, which would mean you went to the Bowery."

Longacre gave no indication he'd even heard. He simply stared back, expressionless.

"When did you first realize Estelle was sneaking out?" Frank tried.

Silence.

"Ah, so she outsmarted you, then. She and Norman Tufts.

You didn't know what she was doing and you didn't care either. You probably—"

"I knew! And I cared! What man wouldn't care if his daughter was making herself a harlot?"

"That's a harsh judgment."

"And a correct one, too. What else would you call it? She goes gallivanting off at all hours of the day and night to meet her lovers."

"Did you think Norman Tufts was her lover?"

"Norman?" he scoffed. "I don't think there's a drop of man's blood in his whole body. Penny leached it out of him long ago. No, he wouldn't know what to do with a woman. Estelle just used him until she didn't need him anymore."

"Do you know where Norman took her?"

"Tom said they went to the Bowery. I had him follow them once."

Tom hadn't mentioned that to Frank, but he probably hadn't wanted to tell Frank he'd spied on poor Estelle and then betrayed her to the old man. Frank couldn't blame him.

"It was maybe the second or third time Estelle left here dressed in men's clothing." Longacre continued, rubbing a hand over his face. Frank realized he looked even paler than usual. Questioning him like this was probably cruel, but Frank had no choice if he wanted to find out who killed Estelle and Freddie. "I can see who comes and goes from that window." He jerked a thumb at the large window, now heavily draped, that faced the street. "The first time, I saw Norman arrive. He visited Estelle a lot, probably because Penny made him. She wanted them to get married, that witch. She couldn't see that nobody was ever going to marry Norman."

"So Norman arrived," Frank prodded.

"Yes. He didn't stay long, and when he left, there was

another man with him. I didn't recognize him and I'd never seen him come in, so I thought it was odd. I sent for Estelle to ask her about him, but Marie said she'd gone out with Norman. That's when I figured out she'd dressed in men's clothes to go wherever they were going."

"That must have concerned you," Frank said, trying not to sound too sarcastic.

"It made me mad as the devil, I can tell you. I don't know when she got home that night, but the next day I told her I knew and that she was forbidden to leave the house like that again."

Frank raised his eyebrows to show his amazement. "She must have misunderstood you."

"She laughed at me, that little tart! Said she'd do whatever she wanted or she'd . . . Well, she'd do what she wanted. And I guess she did."

"Didn't you tell your servants to lock her in her room?"

"They don't pay any attention to me, as you know. So I told Norman he couldn't come here anymore. The servants weren't to let him in the house. That didn't stop him calling for her, though. And she'd go off with him. At least, she did a few more times. And then I thought it had stopped, because Norman didn't come anymore."

"But it hadn't stopped."

"Oh no. She just went out alone, during the day. She'd found someone. A man. You could see it. She was different somehow. And when I told her she was a fool, she laughed at me again." His face pinched up with pain.

"You must've been awfully jealous."

Longacre's head jerked up at that. "Jealous?"

"That she'd taken a lover."

"Why would I be jealous?" he asked, suddenly wary.

"Because you wanted her all to yourself, just the way it

has always been. Well, maybe not always. How old was she when you took her the first time?"

Alarm brought life to his bloodshot eyes. "What are you talking about?"

"I think you know what I'm talking about. Sexually violating a child is an ugly thing, Mr. Longacre, and when it's your own child, it's unspeakable."

"You don't know anything about it!"

"I think I do. That's why you didn't allow any young men to court Estelle, isn't it? You didn't want to lose her."

"Who told you that? It was Penny, wasn't it? She thinks she's so clever, but she won't get another dime from me, not now!"

"Are you saying your sister knew and didn't do anything about it?" Frank asked in disgust.

Longacre gaped at him, his eyes owlish. "It wasn't Penny?"

"No, it was Black Jack Robinson who told me. Estelle confided in him, you see."

"She was lying," he tried, nearly frantic now. "She lied about everything."

"But she wasn't lying about being pregnant, was she? And she was already pregnant when Norman took her to the Bowery the first time. Who could have done that to her?" Frank asked with all the venom he felt. "Not one of her suitors, because you wouldn't let anyone court her. Not Norman, because you already said he wouldn't know what to do with a woman."

"I wasn't . . . That isn't true . . . about Norman, I mean. He wanted Estelle. He's always wanted her. He must be the one who . . ."

"Who what? Raped her? Forced her to submit to his lust? And then afterward she asked him to take her to the Bowery so she could find another lover? That doesn't make sense."

"Nothing that girl did made sense," he insisted. "She was just trying to hurt me. To make me jealous."

At last! "How? By taking a lover? By trying to find a man who would rescue her from you?"

"She didn't need to be rescued! I loved her!"

"You loved her so much, you forced her to submit to you, and that was the last straw for her, wasn't it? She finally decided to do whatever she had to in order to get away."

"No, she didn't. She couldn't!"

"She couldn't what? Get away from you? Of course she could, if she found a man willing to marry her. But what was different about that time? Why did she suddenly decide to take action after so many years?"

"I don't know what you're talking about!"

"You know exactly what I'm talking about. And you raped her again just before she died, didn't you? That's why she left the house that night. She was going to tell Robinson what you'd done and ask him to take her away."

Frank glared at Longacre, expecting his sputtered denials and guilty excuses. Instead, Longacre just frowned in confusion. "But I didn't . . . What do you mean? She didn't leave the house that night because of me."

UNLIKE THE REST OF THE HOUSE, THE KITCHEN WAS TIDY and fairly clean. A very tall man rose from where he'd been sitting at the kitchen table shelling peas, to greet Sarah.

"That's Tom," Marie said without looking at either of them. She disappeared into the pantry.

"I'm Mrs. Malloy," Sarah said.

"Ah, so that's who was at the door. Has Mr. Malloy gone on up to see Mr. Horace, then?"

"Yes, he has." Sarah sat down so Tom could, too.

Marie emerged from the pantry with a brown crockery jug. "Chip off some ice, Tom."

While Sarah watched, Tom produced the ice and distributed it into three glasses, which Marie filled with a brown liquid. "Sassafras," was all she said when she placed a glass in front of Sarah. The drink was delicious.

"Mrs. Malloy is supposed to bother us while her husband annoys Longacre," Marie informed Tom.

"I thought Mr. Malloy found out everything he needed to know when he was here before," Tom said.

"Sometimes during an investigation, we find out something new and then need to go back and ask some more questions," Sarah said.

"Are you a detective too?" Marie asked with a doubtful frown.

"Not officially, but sometimes I help out."

"I'm sure you're a big help, Mrs. Malloy," Tom said.

Sarah expected to see the glitter of scorn in his gray eyes, but he seemed to be perfectly sincere in his compliment.

"So you found out something new, and now you're back," Marie said. She turned to Tom. "I guess she found out about the baby."

Sarah didn't even bother to hide her surprise. "You knew about Estelle's baby?"

"Of course I did. I do the laundry. I knew right away when her monthly stopped."

"Marie, that's not something you say to a lady like Mrs. Malloy."

"That's all right," Sarah said. "I'm a midwife, so I don't shock easily. Do you think Estelle knew?"

Marie shook her head. "That girl knew a lot, but she didn't know about babies. How could she?"

"So you told her," Sarah guessed.

"No, I didn't! It ain't my place to tell her something like that."

Sarah gaped at her. "You weren't even going to warn her?"

"I tried. I asked her about it, but she didn't have no idea what it meant. She was just happy she wasn't bleeding."

"So you let her go on in ignorance?"

"I told you, it ain't my place, but I did tell Miss Penelope."

Sarah couldn't argue with that strategy. Penelope was Estelle's nearest female relative, after all. "And did Miss Longacre tell her?"

"I don't have any idea. It's none of my business, is it?"

Of course it wasn't, but Sarah figured Marie usually made everything her business. "Did Miss Estelle act like she knew?"

Marie pouted at being challenged, but Tom said, "We don't think she knew. If she did, would she still go off to meet her lover looking like she didn't have a worry in the world?"

She wouldn't unless she thought Robinson was the father and would be happy and willing to marry her. But Sarah knew he wasn't. "Who do you think fathered the child?"

"It ain't our place to wonder about things like that either," Marie said, too quickly.

"But it would be that man, wouldn't it?" Tom said. "The one she went off to meet."

Sarah held Tom's gaze for a moment and saw no deceit there. When she turned to Marie, however, she saw something completely different. "But it wasn't that man, was it, Marie? She was pregnant before she ever met him."

"It ain't my place—"

"It may not be your place, but you couldn't help noticing. You also know everything that goes on in this house, don't you?"

"That she does," Tom said, earning a black look from his wife.

"You know what happened. You know what's been happening here for years."

"Not *for years*," Marie snapped. "He'd stopped."

Sarah needed a moment to recover. "He'd stopped what?"

"You know what. Bothering that poor girl. He never had a wife, not since the girl was born, so he used her instead, from the time she was little. But he'd stopped, finally."

"How long ago?"

"Years. Three or four, at least. Maybe longer. She said he wasn't interested in her now that she was grown."

"Oh, Marie." Tom covered his face with both hands.

"It's true," Marie insisted. "It ain't my fault what he does."

"And then he suddenly did it again," Sarah guessed.

Marie gave a little shudder. "He was like a crazy man. Went into her room one day, and she was screaming and fighting, but he had his way. I went in, after. I expected she'd be crying, and she was, but mostly she was angry. She told me she thought it was over, but now she knew it would never be over, and she had to get away from him for good. It was just a few weeks later that she went off with Mr. Norman dressed up like a man. I didn't know what she was up to, but she wasn't going to listen to me. And by then I knew about the baby, so I told Miss Penelope to see if she could help."

"I wonder what set him off that day," Sarah mused.

"The doctor," Tom said, and both women turned to him. "The doctor told him he was going to die. I thought he'd be sad. That's how I'd feel, I guess, but not him. He was mad, railing at God and the doctors and everything else he could think of."

"So he took out his fury on Estelle," Sarah said. "And he did it again right before she died."

But Marie just stared back at her blankly. "Did he?"

Suddenly, Sarah wasn't so sure. Marie would know, wouldn't she? "I thought . . . We know something happened the day she disappeared, because Miss Estelle made special, last-minute arrangements to meet Mr. Robinson that Saturday night. It must have been urgent, because she was already supposed to meet him the following afternoon. So what could have caused her to change their meeting time?"

"Nothing that I know about," Marie said. "The old man wasn't doing anything that day except being cantankerous as usual."

"She did get a telegram," Tom said.

Once again, both women turned to him in surprise.

"She did?" Marie demanded. "You never told me."

"I didn't think it was important."

"How could it not be important? She never got telegrams."

"Do you know what it said or who it was from?" Sarah asked.

"Of course not," Tom said, affronted by the very thought that he would read someone else's telegram.

"When did it arrive?" Sarah said, undaunted.

"I don't know exactly. Late afternoon, I think."

Which meant it was sent earlier in the day, perhaps even the morning, although Western Union did try to be prompt with their deliveries. "Do you suppose she kept it?" Sarah asked Marie.

"I never saw nothing like that, but I ain't touched her room since she's been gone."

Marie hadn't touched any of the rooms, Sarah was sure. "Will you allow me to go up to look for it?"

"What good will it do now?" Tom asked.

"I'm not sure, but it could be very important."

"I don't expect it'll do any harm if you look," Marie allowed.

Sarah jumped to her feet before Marie could change her mind.

* * *

As Gino had expected, Will Arburn was still sound asleep when Gino arrived at the house on the corner of 6th Street and Second Avenue. Arburn's grandmother wasn't pleased to see him, but she let him in. Gino tried his charm again, and it served him well enough.

"You know where he is," the old woman said, and shuffled off back to wherever she'd been when he'd knocked on the door.

Gino took the stairs two at a time and then pounded much more loudly than he needed to on the door.

"Go away!" Arburn shouted.

Since that meant Arburn was awake, Gino took the liberty of going on in. Arburn sat up at the intrusion and cursed Gino roundly. When he was finished, Gino closed the door behind him and grabbed the lone chair in the room. Dumping the clothes piled on it, he straddled it. "Sorry to bother you, but I have a few questions."

"But I don't have any answers, so get out of here and leave me alone."

"It won't take long and then you can go right back to sleep."

Arburn cursed again. "At least hand me my pants." It appeared Arburn was naked under the sheet. His hair was tousled, and he hadn't shaved in a couple days.

"You won't need them. I missed you at Freddie's funeral yesterday."

"I don't like funerals."

"The newsies had a lot of nice things to say about Freddie."

Arburn scratched his bare chest. "He was a good kid."

"Kid Blink pointed me and Mr. Malloy out to the crowd. He told them we're trying to find Freddie's killer and they should tell us anything they know about it."

Arburn's eyes narrowed. "That was a good idea. Maybe one of them knows who did it."

"I expect the killer was smarter than that, but a few of the boys remembered that you were looking for Freddie the night he was killed."

"Why would I have been looking for him? You and Malloy had already found him."

"I know. That confused me, so I figured I should just ask you about it. Did you go out that night looking for him?"

"Of course not."

"Because lots of people saw you." Gino didn't know that for sure, but it was probably true.

"I . . . Oh yeah, I forgot," he said, not very convincingly. "I did go out that night. I figured if I could find the boy, you and Malloy wouldn't have to, and I could stop paying you. Can't blame me for wanting to save a few bucks, can you?"

"No, I can't," Gino agreed. "But I don't think that's really why you were looking for Freddie."

"All right, I wasn't trying to save money. I was trying to find Freddie as fast as I could. Black Jack was crazy to find Estelle, and he thought the boy might know what happened to her."

"And did you find him that night?"

"No, I didn't, but I wasn't the only one looking for him."

"You mean me and Malloy?"

"And Black Jack. He'd told me to find him, but it had been days. He probably got tired of waiting."

"Are you saying Robinson was out looking for the boy himself?"

"I'm saying he's the reason I was looking, so maybe he told some of his other men to look, too. Maybe one of them found him."

"Found him and killed him? Is that what you were supposed to do?"

"Of course not! I was just supposed to bring him to Jack."

"And you think Jack sent someone else out to kill the boy?"

Arburn groaned and rubbed both hands over his face. "No, you idiot! Jack . . . Jack just wanted to talk to him, but maybe somebody got a little excited or misunderstood and the boy ends up dead."

That was possible, of course, but Arburn was certainly lying about something. Gino just had to figure out what. Maybe he should try a little bluffing. "We know what happened to Estelle."

Arburn's head jerked up. "What do you mean?"

"I mean we've figured it out. See, she decided she needed to see Robinson that night, so she sent him a telegram, telling him to meet her. Unfortunately, he wasn't home, so he didn't get the telegram until late that night."

"What . . . ? What do you mean, Jack wasn't home?"

Arburn was surprised. Now wasn't that interesting? "Just what I said. Jack didn't get the message until late, and by the time he got to the flat, it was after nine o'clock and she was gone."

For some reason, Arburn found this information very disturbing. He needed a long moment to recover. "So what happened when he didn't come? Did she just . . . leave?"

"No. We think she waited for him, and someone else showed up instead."

"Who?" He really didn't know.

"We don't know, but that person killed her."

"Are you sure?"

"Well, someone did, and we're pretty sure it wasn't Jack Robinson."

Arburn groaned and rubbed his face again.

"What is it? What's wrong, Arburn?"

"Nothing," he claimed. "Keep going. What do you think happened next?"

"For some reason, the killer put her body in a trunk that was in the bedroom. We aren't sure why, but we suspect he decided to get rid of the body. Maybe he didn't want Jack to find it and figure out he'd killed her or something. Anyway, he left and came back later, when it was dark, and carried the trunk out."

Arburn was starting to look sick, and Gino wondered if he was hungover. Maybe he should get a bucket just in case. He glanced around and saw a chamber pot sitting just under the bed. That would do in a pinch.

"What happened next?" Arburn asked hoarsely.

"The trunk must've been pretty heavy, so we think he got Freddie to help."

Arburn nodded his understanding, so Gino continued.

"The two of them carried the trunk away, but Freddie must've gotten suspicious and figured out what was in it or something. Whatever it was, Freddie got scared and ran off and decided to hide until he could figure out what to do. So the killer had to leave the trunk where it was. Maybe he intended to come back for it or something, but Freddie made sure the police found it before he could."

Arburn was staring off into space like he'd been poleaxed. Gino gave him time to think about it, and at last Arburn said, "Yeah, that's pretty much how it happened."

13

FRANK STARED AT HORACE LONGACRE FOR A LONG MOment, trying to judge if he was telling the truth about not having done anything to send Estelle fleeing to the Bowery the day she died. "What did happen, then? I know something happened."

"What makes you think so? Estelle left the house at all hours, whenever she wanted."

"But she was murdered that night. And I know you went out that night, too. Did you follow her or did you already know where she was going?"

"I didn't follow her!"

"So you already knew."

"No! I didn't know, and I didn't follow her. I didn't even know she'd gone out."

"Where did you go, then?"

"Nowhere."

"I doubt that very much."

Longacre drew a long breath, as if to steady himself. "I felt good that day, better than I had for a while. I thought . . . I wanted to go to my club one more time. I wanted to see everyone and feel important one last time."

"What club was that?"

"The Yacht Club. It doesn't matter, though, because I never got there."

"Why not?"

"Because . . . because I fainted. I was walking to the corner to find a cab, and I fainted before I got there."

"Did anyone see you?"

The color had risen in his face, and Frank wondered if he was feverish or simply embarrassed. "Tom did. He'd followed me. He was worried, he said."

Why hadn't Tom finished the story when he told Frank that Longacre had gone out that night? But then, Frank hadn't even thought to ask. He'd assumed the servants wouldn't have known where he went.

"Tell Penny she's too late," Longacre said bitterly.

"Too late for what?"

"To ruin me. That's what she wants, I'm sure, to shame me in front of my friends, but it's too late. By the time she manages it, I'll be dead, and she'll be the only one left to suffer."

"What does that mean?"

"She'll know. Just tell her."

As they climbed the stairs to the second floor, Sarah asked Marie, "Was Estelle sick at all with the baby?"

"Not that I ever knew, although she might've been and just not told me. Something changed about her, though."

"Maybe she was just in love."

Marie made a rude noise. "Not that one. She didn't believe in fairy tales. She might've been happy if she found a man who wouldn't be afraid of her father, though."

"I don't think Jack Robinson is afraid of very much."

"That's it, then. Here we are." Marie opened one of the closed doors along the second floor hallway.

Estelle's room looked as if she'd just stepped away for a few minutes. The bed was made but rumpled, and clothes lay draped over it and various other pieces of furniture. She'd probably tried on several outfits before settling on what she would wear for the evening. The furniture itself was newer than that in most of the rest of the house. It had probably been purchased especially for her and was suitably feminine and delicate with gold leaf trim and porcelain knobs. The wardrobe stood open to display a jumble of dresses and skirts and jackets. Her dressing table was cluttered with bottles of different sizes and shapes and scattered hairpins and combs.

Sarah surveyed the room. Would Estelle have hidden the telegram? Or put it in a safe place? She didn't see anything resembling the white square or the envelope it would have come in, so she moved to the dresser and began her search.

"Can I help?" Marie asked, and Sarah noticed the woman's toughness had disappeared. She was gazing around the room with what could only be described as sadness.

"You could hang up the clothes, in case the telegram is under something. And check the pockets before you put them in the wardrobe in case she stuck it somewhere."

While Sarah sifted through drawers, Marie eagerly began to gather Estelle's garments and carry them to the wardrobe. As she lifted the last item off the bed, something fluttered to the floor. "Here it is."

Sarah hurried over. The telegram looked exactly like the

one they'd seen at Robinson's house, except the message was different. This one said, "Meet usual place Sat five." The signature was "J.R." and the date was July 22, the same as the other telegram. The day Estelle had died.

How strange.

"What is it?" Marie asked, apparently alarmed by Sarah's expression.

"Nothing," Sarah said, schooling her face to show less emotion. "I guess I expected it would say more."

"Maybe he was afraid other people would see it."

"That's probably it, and Estelle understood the message, which is all that would matter."

"So he sent for her that night, the man she was seeing. Does that mean he killed her?" Marie was angered at the thought.

"We don't think so. He's actually hired Malloy to help find her killer."

Marie frowned in confusion, but before she could manage another question, Malloy stuck his head in the door.

"Is this Estelle's room?"

"Yes," Sarah said.

"Did you find anything interesting?"

"We did, although I haven't searched the whole room yet. Are you finished with Longacre?"

"For now. I'll meet you in the kitchen."

"Fine."

When he'd gone, Marie sighed and looked around again. "She was a good girl. Never gave me a minute's trouble."

"Did you know her all her life?"

"No. We've been here about ten years. Tom wanted to leave when I found out what was going on, but I couldn't leave that girl all alone, could I?"

"You could go now."

Marie's grief hardened into resolve. "Not yet. We'll wait until he's too sick to do for himself anymore. We'll go then."

Frank found Tom O'Day in the kitchen, sitting at the table with his head in his hands. He looked so beaten, Frank didn't have the heart to berate him.

"Why didn't you tell me what happened the last time Longacre went out?" he asked gently.

Tom looked up in surprise. "He begged me not to say a word. He cried like a baby that night. Didn't want anyone to know how weak he was. Marie says I'm too soft."

"She may be right, but I have to say I'm a little relieved. As evil as Longacre is, I'm glad to know he didn't actually murder his own daughter."

"I'm relieved for Miss Estelle, too. I expect it would be too horrible to spend your last minutes on earth knowing your own father wanted you dead."

Frank sat down and sniffed the empty glass sitting there. "What's this?"

"Sassafras tea. We drink it cold. I'll get you some."

A few minutes later, Sarah and Marie returned.

Marie didn't even glance at Frank. She just slumped down into one of the chairs. Both she and Tom were spent, and since Frank knew what Sarah had questioned them about, he could understand why.

"Are you ready to go?" Sarah asked.

They thanked Tom and Marie for their help and let Marie show them out.

As soon as they were away from the house, Frank said, "It wasn't Longacre. He didn't follow Estelle that night. He was going to his club, but he fainted on the way. Tom had to bring him home."

Sarah said, "But someone sent Estelle a telegram that day, asking her to meet at the usual place that night, which I assume meant Robinson's flat."

"So that's why she went out. Who sent it?"

"The signature was Robinson's initials, but we know he didn't send it. He wasn't even going to be in the city at five o'clock."

"Five? I thought it was six."

"Robinson's telegram said six, but hers says five."

They'd reached the corner, and they had to stop so Frank could hail a cab. That took a few minutes, and the instant they were settled in it and on their way, he said, "Do you have the telegram?"

"Of course." She pulled it out of her purse and handed it to him.

The message definitely said five o'clock and the initials were Robinson's, but who could have sent it and why?

"Someone wanted her to go to the flat that night," Sarah said. "Someone who knew she was seeing Robinson and where they usually met."

"And that someone wanted to kill her."

"We don't know he intended to kill her," Sarah reminded him, "but at least he wanted to lure her there."

"But wouldn't he be worried about Robinson show-ing up?"

"No, because Robinson wouldn't know anything about it."

"But he got a telegram, too," Frank insisted.

"No, don't you see? The killer—or someone—sent Estelle this telegram to get her to the flat, but it came late in the day. She must have needed to change the time, to make it later. I think she wanted to get dressed and fix her hair. Her room looked as if she'd been very careful about her appear-ance that night, so she must have thought she was meeting Robinson. But for whatever reason, she wanted Robinson to know she'd be later than he'd requested, so she sent him a reply."

"And if she hadn't sent the reply, he wouldn't have even known they were supposed to meet."

"That also explains the odd wording of the second telegram," Sarah said. "What did it say again?"

Frank pulled out his notebook and read the words aloud, "Change time today six instead."

"We read it to mean change the time of their meeting to 'today at six o'clock' instead of tomorrow at two or whenever they usually met."

"But because there aren't any punctuation marks in telegrams, it could also mean to change the time of the meeting today to six instead of five."

"And if Robinson had sent the first telegram, it would make perfect sense to him. But of course he didn't. So now all we have to do is figure out who sent the first telegram. Can we do that?"

Frank nodded. "We can start by finding the office where it was sent."

"How do we do that?"

"By using this code here." He pointed at the series of letters and numbers at the top of the message.

Frank reached up and knocked on the roof of the cab. The driver, seated high on the back of the cab, opened the trapdoor and peered down at them. "What is it, mister?"

"Can you take us to the nearest Western Union Office on the way?"

"WHAT DO YOU MEAN, THAT'S PRETTY MUCH THE WAY IT happened?" Gino asked, every nerve in his body tingling the way it did whenever he knew he was onto something.

Arburn rubbed his face again. "Can you give me my pants at least? If I promise to answer you?"

Arburn would be far less likely to run without the pants, but he might also be more cooperative if he could regain a little dignity. Gino snatched up the pants in question and tossed them over. When Arburn had donned them, he sat down on the bed again and put his head in his hands.

"Are you saying you killed her?" Gino asked cautiously.

Arburn's head jerked up. "No! She was dead when I got there."

"All right," Gino said even more carefully. "Start at the beginning."

Arburn sighed wearily. "I was going to meet a girl at the flat that night. A different girl."

"Who?"

"Her name is Opal, and you can ask her. She'll tell you. We were supposed to meet about eight o'clock. I got there a bit early. I wanted to make sure the room wasn't messed up or anything. Girls don't like it if it looks like somebody was there before them."

"Right," Gino said, although he had no idea. "And was the room messed up?"

"Not much, except that Estelle was laying on the floor, dead."

"Any sign of her killer?"

"No, and she was cold when I found her. Whoever did it was long gone."

"And who do you think did it?"

Arburn sighed again. "I thought it was Jack, but you said he wasn't in town that day."

"That's right. He said he didn't get back until late."

"Maybe he's lying, though. Maybe he just said he was away so you wouldn't suspect him."

"Maybe, but you thought he killed her," Gino prompted.

"Who else could it be?" Arburn wailed. "He was the only one who'd meet her there. She wouldn't dare use those rooms with anybody else."

"Except you."

"That was different. That was before he met her. And I was the one who set it up because I knew when Jack was going to be there and when he wasn't."

"And you knew he wasn't going to use the rooms that Saturday night."

"He never went there on Saturday. He was too busy checking on his businesses."

"So you found Estelle dead, and you thought Jack had killed her. What did you do then?"

"I figured he must've panicked and taken off. Nobody was going to come in and find the body right away, or at least that's what he'd think, but I knew Opal was coming any minute. I remembered the trunk in the bedroom and that it was almost empty, so I put her in it."

"That was a good idea," Gino said by way of encouragement.

"I thought so. Then Opal showed up. It took me nearly an hour to finish with her and get her out again."

Gino gaped at him. "Wait. You took her to bed with Estelle's body in the same room?"

"Yeah. I guess it does sound strange when you say it like that, but she didn't know so . . ." He shrugged.

Gino shook his head to clear the images. "So when you were, uh, finished, you sent Opal away?"

"I took her away. We went to a dance house, but I kept thinking about Estelle and how pleased Jack would be if she just disappeared and he never had to think about her again. I'd be sure he knew it was me who took care of it for him, too. He'd be grateful."

"And he'd always know you knew about the murder, too."

Arburn shrugged again. "He'd have to reward me."

Or kill him, but Gino didn't bother to point that out. No use upsetting Arburn. "So you went back."

"I had to act like nothing was wrong, for Opal's sake, so I stayed awhile at the dance house. But I had business to take care of, so I finally picked a fight with her and walked out."

"And when you got to the flat?"

"I realized I couldn't carry the trunk away by myself, but luckily Freddie was already there. He knows Jack doesn't use the rooms on Saturday, so he was going to sleep there."

"And you asked him to help you."

"I told him Jack wanted to get rid of the trunk."

"Didn't he notice how heavy it was?"

"Of course, but I told him I didn't know what was in it. I just knew Jack wanted it moved and it was locked. I told him I'd pay him so he helped me."

"When did he notice Estelle's hair sticking out of it?"

"How'd you know that?" he asked in amazement.

"I'm a detective."

"Oh. Well, yeah, he saw it when somebody opened a door in the alley and there was some light for a minute. He dropped his end pretty quick."

"He knew who it was?"

"I don't know what he knew. He didn't stay around long enough for me to ask. He just kind of yelped and dropped the trunk and took off running."

"That ruined your plan, didn't it?"

"I didn't know it then, but yeah, it did. I went to get somebody else to help me, but by the time we got back, the cops had found the trunk and it was too late."

"And what did Jack say when you told him how you helped him?"

"Are you crazy? I never told him a thing. On Sunday night he ordered me to find Freddie because Estelle was missing and nobody'd seen her or Two Toes and maybe the boy knew something. I knew Two Toes would never come out of hiding if he heard I was looking for him, but I also knew Malloy was a private detective, because Jack had asked me to find out about the woman who wanted to buy a house in the neighborhood and turn it into a hospital. So I decided to hire you to find the boy."

"Didn't you think it was strange that Robinson wanted to find Freddie? If he'd killed Estelle, I mean."

"No, I figured he was afraid the boy knew he'd done it and wanted to get rid of him, too. In fact, if you think about it, you only have Jack's word that he didn't kill her and the boy."

SARAH WATCHED FROM THE CAB AS MALLOY WENT INTO the Western Union office. He showed the clerk the telegram from Estelle's room and the page in Malloy's notebook where he'd copied down the information from Robinson's telegram. After just a few minutes of conversation, Malloy reached into his pocket and rewarded the clerk with enough money to make him smile.

This time Malloy gave the cab driver the address of his office.

"I gather the clerk was helpful," she said when they were on their way.

"More than helpful. I was right, the telegrams have a code on them that tells which office they were sent from. The one Robinson got was sent from this office, which is the closest one to the Longacre house. It was sent at around four o'clock, which explains why she changed the time of the meeting.

She probably wouldn't have been able to get to the Bowery by five if she had to primp first."

"Just changing her clothes would've taken an hour, as you well know, Malloy."

"It goes much faster when I help," he said with a grin.

"Yes, but you never help me put them back on again."

He sighed, not wanting to concede her point. "Anyway, the telegram Estelle got was sent from an office that was nowhere near Jack's house or the Bowery or even the Lower East Side."

"Which isn't surprising, since he didn't seem to know anything about it. Which office was it sent from?"

Malloy gave her the address on Fifth Avenue.

"You'll never guess who lives near there," she said.

"I think I will. Is it Penelope Longacre?"

"WHERE COULD GINO HAVE GOT TO?" MALLOY ASKED AS he unlocked the office door. "I told him to stay here until he heard from me."

"He wouldn't have left if it wasn't important," Sarah said.

They stepped inside to find the windows still open to catch whatever air might be circulating outside, but no sign of Gino.

"Oh good, he left a note." Malloy picked it up off the desk and read it.

"What does he say?"

"He went to see Will Arburn. It seems a newsie came by to tell him Arburn was looking for Freddie the night he was killed."

"Is that important?"

"I don't know, but Gino thought it was."

"But we already knew Arburn wanted to find Freddie. That's why he hired you in the first place."

"Yes, but let me think, when did we tell Arburn that we'd found the boy? I think it was the very day he was murdered."

"Did you tell Arburn anything that would've made him go after Freddie himself?"

"Not that I know of, but now I'm wondering if we told him something that made it easier for him to find Freddie. We were careful not to mention Raven or give him any indication of where Freddie was hiding."

"But if you found him, Arburn probably could, too."

They heard the clatter of footsteps hurrying down the hallway, and Gino appeared in the doorway. He was flushed from the exertion or maybe from excitement. "You got my note?"

"Yes. Did you find out anything interesting from Arburn?"

"I found out something *very* interesting. In fact, he answered a lot of our questions."

"Why don't we pull up some chairs and you can tell us all about it?" Sarah suggested.

They gathered in Malloy's office, where the chairs were a bit more comfortable. Malloy sat behind his desk and Gino and Sarah in front of it.

Gino told them what Arburn had confessed about finding Estelle's body and trying to dispose of it. "So that explains why somebody put Estelle in the trunk and tried to carry her body away. It also means her father could've followed her there and killed her, because we know he went out that night."

"Except he didn't," Sarah said. "We found out some interesting things, too."

Gino's face fell, but he leaned forward anxiously. "What?"

"We were right about Longacre abusing Estelle," Malloy said gruffly.

"Apparently, he'd stopped several years ago, but when he found out he was dying, he went crazy and attacked her," Sarah said.

"Dear heaven," Gino murmured.

"Yes," Sarah continued. "This means Longacre must be the father of Estelle's baby."

The horrible truth settled over them like a suffocating fog.

"Let's hope she never realized that, at least," Malloy said, and Gino muttered his agreement.

"But she did know her father had raped her," Sarah said, "and that must have been why she suddenly decided to abandon all pretense of respectability and convinced Norman Tufts to take her to the Bowery."

"Longacre knew what she was doing, and that she'd taken a lover, but he couldn't control her anymore," Malloy said.

"But didn't the servants say he followed her that last night?" Gino asked.

"No," Sarah said. "They only said he went out. He actually tried to go to his club, but he fainted and had to be brought home again."

"So he couldn't have killed her," Malloy said.

"Drat, I was sure he'd done it," Gino said. "So who does that leave?"

"I'm very glad you asked," Malloy said. "Sarah and I have been arguing about it all the way back from the Longacres' house."

"You see, we've discovered why Estelle went out to meet Robinson that night," Sarah said.

"She got a telegram," Malloy said.

Gino frowned, obviously confused. "I thought she sent Robinson a telegram."

"She did, but only after she got one she thought was from him telling her to meet him that night," Sarah said.

"Her message to Robinson was only to change the time of the meeting she thought he'd set up."

Gino was still frowning. "And you're sure Robinson didn't send it?"

"He never said a word about it," Malloy said. "Which made us think he didn't know about it, and when we checked, we also discovered it was sent from a Western Union office that is suspiciously close to someone else's home."

"Whose?" Gino asked with renewed interest.

"Penelope Longacre."

"And Norman Tufts," Sarah added.

"You think her aunt sent her a telegram to send her down to the Bowery?" Gino asked, confused again.

"Or Norman did," Sarah said. "Or both of them together. We won't know until we ask them, of course."

"And if they tell the truth," Malloy added.

Gino rubbed his forehead. "Let me get this straight. You think the aunt and the cousin sent Estelle down to the Bowery so they could kill her?"

Sarah exchanged a glance with Malloy. "That's where we disagree. I can't imagine why they'd want to kill Estelle. Penelope wanted her to marry Norman, because she wanted Norman to get all of Longacre's money when Estelle inherited it."

"But why would they need to trick her into going down to the Bowery unless they wanted to do her harm? I think Penelope wanted Estelle out of the way so she could inherit Longacre's money," Malloy said.

"But there's no telling what Longacre has put in his will," Sarah said. "Maybe it all goes to charity if Estelle dies before he does."

"I should've asked him that when I was there today," Malloy said.

"So what are you going to do now?" Gino asked.

"Visit Penelope and Norman," Sarah said.

"Which is something else we're arguing about," Malloy said. "I think it's too dangerous to take Sarah. I came back here to get you and send her home."

"But it's only dangerous if they're killers, and even if they are, why would they kill us?" Sarah said. "They're certainly not going to inherit any money from us."

"She's right," Gino said. "And they aren't likely to murder you in their own apartment, in any case."

"Gino is right," Sarah said triumphantly. "What would they do with our bodies?"

"Do you realize how crazy that sounds?" Malloy asked with a disgruntled frown.

"Of course I do. I'm only sorry my mother isn't here to hear it."

That made Gino laugh, which drew another disgruntled frown from Malloy, which silenced Gino instantly.

"And there's still the question of Freddie's murder," Malloy said. "Why would Norman and Penelope have killed the boy?"

Gino cleared his throat. "Arburn had a theory about that."

"That's impressive," Malloy said without admiration.

"It was interesting, at least. He pointed out that we only have Robinson's word that he was out of town that day. He could've killed Estelle, even by accident, and run away in panic, leaving Arburn to find her body and dispose of it. When Robinson came back later to deal with it, he saw somebody else had taken Estelle away, so he just pretended that was the first time he'd been to the flat that night."

"And I suppose Arburn also thinks Robinson killed the boy," Malloy said.

"Or had him killed. Freddie obviously saw something or

he wouldn't have been hiding, and Robinson couldn't take a chance on what he'd seen. Robinson didn't know the real reason Freddie ran away because Arburn wasn't going to admit what he'd done."

"So do you think we should go back to Mr. Robinson and ask him if he's been lying to us all along?" Sarah asked innocently.

Both men glared at her, but she only smiled back.

"Ah, so you both agree that we should see Penelope and Norman next," she continued. "And I should go along because Penelope is far more likely to confide in a female."

"Unless she's a killer," Malloy said. "In which case, she's not going to confide in anyone."

"Do you really think someone like Penelope Longacre would take herself down to the Bowery in order to strangle her niece to death?" Sarah scoffed.

"I thought we agreed the killer might not have intended to kill her," Gino said.

"Which means that Penelope Longacre would have tricked her niece into going to the Bowery just so she could meet her there to . . . what? Chat?"

"All right, so Penelope probably didn't do it or at least didn't do it alone," Malloy said. "But she might've put Norman up to it or goaded him into it."

"Assuming she really wanted Estelle to die, because why else would she have gone to all that trouble?" Sarah said. "I'm quite interested in hearing her feelings on the subject."

"Which you will be able to do when we call on her," Malloy said in surrender.

"What about me?" Gino asked.

"Stay here so we know where to find you," Malloy said.

"Unless the killer shows up," Sarah said. "In which case, run."

*   *   *

"GINO HAS BEEN TALKING ABOUT GETTING AN APARTMENT like this," Malloy said as they entered the building where Miss Longacre and Norman lived. They'd stopped on the way to have a quick lunch, so it was now the appropriate time for a social call.

"Wouldn't his mother have something to say about that?" Sarah asked.

"I'm sure she would, and it would be expensive for him, too."

"You pay him pretty well."

"Yes, but he should be saving his money."

"Why do you think he's interested in having his own place?"

Malloy raised his eyebrows at her.

"Maeve is too young to get married," Sarah said.

"How old is she?"

"I don't know exactly. I don't think she does either, but she's still too young."

"I'll be sure to mention that to Gino."

"May I help you?" the man behind the desk asked. "Mrs. Malloy, isn't it?"

"Yes, and this is my husband. We'd like to see Miss Long-acre if she's at home."

"And Mr. Tufts, too," Malloy added.

"Mr. Tufts is out, I'm afraid," the clerk said. "Please have a seat."

"See, nothing to worry about," Sarah said when they'd taken a seat in the lounge area. "If Miss Longacre attacks, I'm sure between the two of us we can fend her off."

"It's not funny. You've put yourself in danger before. You can't blame me for being careful."

Sarah patted his hand. "I know, and I love you for it. I'm sorry to be such a tease."

"Mr. and Mrs. Malloy?" the clerk called. "Miss Longacre would be happy to receive you. You may go right up."

They made the trip up in the elevator, and the operator let them out on the proper floor. Malloy looked around approvingly. "We should have brought Gino so he could see the place."

"And Maeve so she could approve it," Sarah added with a grin.

Miss Longacre opened the door at their knock. "What a pleasant surprise," she said, not entirely sincere but looking more welcoming than she had the first time Sarah had visited. Maybe bringing Malloy along had been a wise decision.

"We're sorry to bother you again, but we have a few more questions for you," Sarah said.

"Of course," Miss Longacre said, leading them down the hall to the parlor. "I'm anxious to hear what progress you've made in solving Estelle's murder."

Sarah didn't dare glance at Malloy for fear her expression might give them away.

Miss Longacre invited them to have a seat. "I asked the restaurant downstairs to send up some lemonade. You must be parched."

"It is warm outside," Sarah agreed.

"This is a very pleasant apartment, Miss Longacre," Malloy said. "Do you like living here?"

"I find it economical, Mr. Malloy, but it's not at all what I'm used to. I always had a lady's maid when I lived in my father's house, and servants at my beck and call. Here, a girl comes in to clean twice a week, and they send our meals up to us. For the rest, we fend for ourselves, I'm afraid."

Sarah didn't mention that many maiden aunts would consider themselves blessed to have such comfortable accommodations. Miss Longacre probably wouldn't appreciate it. "We were hoping to see Mr. Tufts as well. I was looking forward to meeting him."

"Norman had some business to attend to. You said you had some questions." Was she uneasy or simply ill at ease? Sarah couldn't tell, but she was definitely tense. "And if you've been talking to Horace, I expect you do have questions."

14

"As a matter of fact," Frank said, watching Miss Longacre's face closely, "your brother asked me to deliver a message to you."

She stiffened, as if bracing herself. "How odd."

"I thought so, and I didn't understand it, but he said you would. He said to tell you that you are too late if you wanted to ruin him."

She laughed mirthlessly. "Of course he would think only of himself until the very end. His reputation was the only thing he ever really cared about."

"Do you have the power to ruin him, Miss Longacre?" Sarah asked. She sounded so sincere and sympathetic, Frank could believe she actually cared.

Miss Longacre drew her lips back in the parody of a smile. "Every family has secrets, Mrs. Malloy. Ours are probably no worse than anyone else's."

"You mean Norman's birth, I guess," Sarah said. "But how would your child ruin your brother's reputation?"

"You said you had some questions for me about *Estelle's death*," Miss Longacre said firmly. She obviously knew how to change a subject she didn't want to discuss. Did all well-bred ladies study this technique? Frank wondered.

"Yes, we do," Sarah said, answering both his and Miss Longacre's questions at once. "Although this is a bit sensitive, I'll admit. You see, we have learned that you knew Estelle was with child. Marie told you long before Estelle died."

"Not *long* before," she said, obviously annoyed. "Only days before. Perhaps a week at most."

They could check that, of course, Frank thought.

"But you gave me the impression you hadn't known at all," Sarah said.

"What does it matter? The poor girl is dead."

"And you also insisted you had no idea who the father might be, which makes me wonder if you were less than truthful about that as well," Sarah continued relentlessly.

"I do not appreciate being called a liar, Mrs. Malloy," Miss Longacre said in outrage.

"And yet you did lie to me."

Sarah was such a joy to watch. Her polite interrogation was more effective than the third degree would ever be.

Miss Longacre drew a calming breath. "I merely saw no need to air our family's dirty linen to a stranger."

"So you do know that Horace Longacre fathered Estelle's child."

The blood drained from Miss Longacre's face. "How dare you!"

"I apologize, Miss Longacre. I know this must be painful for you, but we're only trying to find out who killed Estelle."

"And do you think destroying her memory will accomplish that?"

"We have no intention of destroying her memory. We're only trying to determine who might have had a reason for killing her."

"Horace had a reason," Miss Longacre said, nearly spitting the words. "He'd ruined her, and she was setting out to ruin him in return by taking up with a gangster."

"He may have had a reason, but he didn't do it."

"How can you know that?" she demanded.

"We have a witness," Frank said. "Two, in fact. Mr. Longacre couldn't have done it."

"And we also know that someone tricked Estelle into going to the Bowery that night by sending her a telegram," Sarah said.

Miss Longacre blinked a few times. "Why would someone do that?"

"We were going to ask you that very thing," Sarah said, "since you were the one who sent her the telegram."

"I . . . What are you talking about?"

"I'm talking about the telegram that you sent from the Western Union office just down the street from here telling Estelle to meet her lover that night."

Just then, a bell rang, startling all of them. Miss Longacre jumped to her feet and hurried off toward the kitchen, where there must have been a service entrance.

"I guess that's our lemonade," Frank said, and Sarah nodded. She'd be angry at the interruption, as was he. Miss Longacre had just been upset enough to blurt out something important.

When Miss Longacre returned with a tray of glasses, she had composed herself. She set the tray down on a table and calmly handed each of them a glass. She did not, Frank noticed, take one for herself.

"I'm afraid I became a little emotional," she said when she was seated again. "I'm still mourning poor Estelle, and I'm too easily upset, I'm afraid. You must be desperate indeed if you think I had anything to do with her death."

"We didn't say you had anything to do with her death," Frank said. "We're just wondering why you sent her that telegram. And we can prove that you did, so don't try to deny it," he lied.

The color returned to her face, turning it an angry scarlet. "All right, I did send it, but I had nothing to do with killing her."

"Why?" Sarah asked in apparent astonishment. "Why did you want her to go to the Bowery that night?"

Miss Longacre drew a steadying breath. "It's very simple and completely innocent."

"I'm sure it is," Sarah said, although Frank was sure it was not.

"You're right, Marie did tell me that Estelle was with child. She also told me what . . . what Horace had done." She closed her eyes for a moment and when she opened them, she looked more determined than outraged. "Marie wanted me to tell Estelle about her condition and to help her. I'm not sure what Marie expected me to do, but I had the perfect solution. I've wanted Estelle and Norman to marry since the day she was born. Their marriage would finally make Norman a recognized member of the family."

"I can see why that would be important to you," Sarah said.

Somewhat mollified, Miss Longacre continued. "Also, Horace was never going to leave any of his fortune to Norman, but if Norman married Estelle, everything she had would be legally his. As I said, it was the perfect solution."

Perfect for everyone but Estelle, who obviously didn't care a fig for Norman, but Frank kept that opinion to himself.

"What does this have to do with sending Estelle the telegram?" Sarah asked with just the right amount of confusion on her lovely face.

Miss Longacre sighed impatiently. "We needed to get her someplace alone so Norman could propose to her. If she didn't know she was with child, he was going to inform her and offer to marry her and raise the child as his own. Her gangster lover wouldn't do something like that. What man would? Especially if he knew who the father was."

"And would you have told him?" Frank asked, frankly curious.

Miss Longacre gave him a quelling look. "If necessary. But I'm sure Estelle would have seen the wisdom of marrying Norman. She wouldn't want anyone to learn the truth either."

"I still don't understand why you had to go to all that trouble, though. Why couldn't Norman just propose to Estelle at her home?" Sarah asked.

"Because Horace had forbidden him to enter the house after he found out Norman was taking Estelle to the Bowery."

"I thought she was still meeting him, though," Frank said.

Miss Longacre's color deepened again. "She was, at first, but once she took up with that gangster, she had no more use for Norman. She wouldn't even reply to his messages or mine."

Sarah nodded her understanding. "I see, so you tricked Estelle with a message she thought was from her lover. I guess Norman knew where Estelle usually met him."

"Yes, he . . . he said he'd heard gossip."

Or Arburn had bragged to him, Frank thought.

"And Norman was to meet her and tell her about the baby and offer to marry her," Sarah said.

"Yes," she said sadly. "It was a perfect plan."

"Miss Longacre," Frank said as gently as he could manage,

"do you understand that this means Norman must have murdered your niece?"

"Oh posh, Norman didn't murder anyone. He didn't even go to the Bowery that night."

"What?" Sarah said.

"That boy . . ." Miss Longacre held her temper with difficulty. "He's such a coward. He told me . . . He promised me . . . But in the end, he didn't go."

"Why not?" Sarah asked.

"He claimed he was afraid to go down there alone. He'd always gone with a guide, you see. I told him he was a fool, that Estelle apparently went down there alone all the time and she was a female. But by the time he confessed to me, it was too late. He'd missed his opportunity, and then we heard that Estelle hadn't come home that night, and Horace sent for me . . ."

She stopped because they'd all heard the front door open and the sound of footsteps coming down the hallway. Norman Tufts appeared in the doorway, obviously surprised to see they had visitors. He wore a slightly rumpled brown suit, and he held a derby in his hand.

Frank rose. "Hello, Norman."

He didn't look happy to see them. "Hello, Mr. Malloy. What are you doing here?"

"They're just asking some questions about Estelle, dear," Miss Longacre said. "Nothing for you to worry about."

"Sarah, this is Norman Tufts," Frank said. "Norman, this is my wife."

Norman nodded uncertainly at Sarah. She smiled reassuringly back at him.

"Won't you join us, Norman?" Frank said. "We were just discussing why you didn't go to meet Estelle in the Bowery the night she died."

Norman turned his startled gaze to Miss Longacre. "You said you weren't going to tell anyone about that."

"She didn't," Frank assured him. "We found out because of the telegrams."

Norman's gaze skittered from Frank to Miss Longacre and back again. "I don't understand."

"I told you, it's nothing for you to worry about," Miss Longacre said. "I've already explained that you didn't see Estelle that night."

Some emotion flickered across Norman's face. Fear? Frank couldn't be sure. "Sit down and join us. We were just offering our condolences on the loss of your cousin. You must miss her very much."

Norman moved cautiously to a chair and sat down slowly, as if afraid it might shatter beneath his weight. "Yes, I miss her."

"I'm sure you do," Sarah said. "You must have assumed your whole life that you'd eventually marry her."

"That was Aunt Penny's idea," Norman said. "I don't think Estelle liked me very much."

"Nonsense," Miss Longacre said quickly. "Estelle was very fond of you."

"Did you like her?" Frank asked.

Norman glanced at Miss Longacre and then glanced away when he saw her frown. "She was pretty."

"You weren't really afraid to go to the Bowery, were you, Norman?" Frank asked. "You'd been there lots of times before, hadn't you?"

"I . . . Well, yes, I'd been there a lot, but always with Willy. He'd take us around so nothing happened to us."

"But it was still daylight, and they knew you down there, didn't they? I mean, you'd been down there many times," Frank tried.

"Of course he hadn't," Miss Longacre said.

But at the same time Norman said, "Not very many."

"So you weren't afraid to go, were you? Not really."

"Of course not," he said proudly.

"Were you afraid of Estelle?"

"No. I'm not afraid of girls."

"So you did go to see her that night."

Miss Longacre made an impatient sound. "Really, Mr. Malloy, I already told you—"

But Frank ignored her. "You weren't afraid, were you, Norman, and you did go to see her. You told her she was going to have a baby and she had to marry you, didn't you?"

"Stop this at once," Miss Longacre said, rising to her feet, but Frank rose, too.

"You told her she had to marry you, and what did she say? Did she laugh at you, Norman? Did she make fun of you?"

"She was always making fun of me," Norman cried, jumping to his feet as well. "Yes, she laughed at me. She said she'd sell herself on the street before she'd marry me!"

"Norman, stop!" Miss Longacre cried, grabbing his arm, but he shook her off.

"And she said we couldn't get married even if she wanted to, not ever!"

"Why did she say that, Norman?" Frank asked. "Why couldn't you get married?"

"Because . . ." He stopped, choking, nearly gagging.

"No, Norman, don't," Miss Longacre begged. "Please—"

"Because Uncle Horace is my father, too!" He turned on Miss Longacre. "She said you're really my mother. She said Uncle Horace raped you like he'd raped her, and that she's really my sister, and I couldn't stand it so I put my hands around her throat to stop her because I didn't want to hear any more, and I squeezed and I squeezed until she was finally quiet and then I left her there."

For a long moment, no one moved. Frank was too stunned to even breathe at first.

Miss Longacre stared at Norman, horrified. Then her knees seemed to give out, and she collapsed back into her chair. "Oh, Norman," she whispered.

"Did you go back later?" Frank asked.

Norman turned to him in surprise, as if he'd forgotten Frank was there. "No, of course not."

"Did anyone see you?"

"I . . . I don't know. I ran down the stairs and through the alley. I don't remember seeing anyone."

"A boy? Did you see a boy?"

"No, of course not. What would a boy be doing there?"

"Oh, Norman," Miss Longacre wailed. "You told me you were afraid to go down there."

"I didn't want you to know the things she'd said, Aunt Penny. Why would she say those awful things?"

Because they were true, Frank thought, but he wasn't going to be the one to tell Norman.

"Miss Longacre," Sarah said, "we have to tell the police."

"What?" she said. "No, you can't. He's just a boy!"

But of course he wasn't a boy at all. "He killed Estelle."

"I didn't kill her," he said. "I just made her stop talking."

Was it possible he really didn't know what he'd done? The boy must be even more simple than he'd seemed. But Sarah was right, he'd definitely committed murder.

Suddenly, Frank remembered the promise he'd made to Jack Robinson. It had seemed perfectly reasonable then, but now he was no longer sure. "Sarah, we have to go."

"But—"

"We aren't going to report this to the police for a day or two," Frank said. "That will give you time to find an attorney." An attorney who would help them figure out who to bribe to keep Norman from being charged, assuming Horace was willing to provide the funds. That seemed doubtful, but if Norman really was his son, perhaps he'd consider it, even though his son had murdered his daughter.

Sarah was on her feet, and Frank took her arm and led her down the hallway to the front door. "What are you doing?" she asked in a whisper.

He didn't answer her until they were out in the hallway, waiting for the elevator again. "I promised Robinson that I would tell him who the killer is before reporting it to the police."

"Oh."

"Yes, oh. That was before I knew who it was, though."

"Norman may be pathetic, but he did kill Estelle. We can't just excuse him," Sarah said.

"You're right, but can we turn him over to Robinson? I mean, I can, but can you? You know what he'll do to him."

"Let me be the one to tell Robinson. If it's possible to convince him to show mercy . . ."

"You're the only one who could do it," Frank said with a weary sigh. "I hope you understand that Jack Robinson is the last gangster you are ever going to meet."

Sarah just smiled.

When they left the building, they walked to the corner to find a cab, and to their surprise, newsboys were everywhere, shouting the headlines and selling newspapers to eager readers.

"What happened?" Sarah asked.

Frank snagged the nearest newsie and bought a copy of the *World*. "Is the strike over?" he asked the boy.

"Yeah, Pulitzer and Hearst gave in," the boy reported with a grin.

"Is that possible?" Sarah asked Frank.

He held up the paper, looking for a story. "Ah, it says here that the price the newsboys pay for the papers will remain the same, but the newsies will be able to get a refund on any unsold papers."

"So the moguls can claim they didn't give in but the newsboys get something, too," Sarah said.

"Looks that way. I guess Kid Blink and his friends will be heroes now."

"Good for them," Sarah said, but he could see the sadness in her eyes. She was certainly thinking of Freddie, too, and that he hadn't lived to see their triumph.

Frank managed to flag down a cab, and he gave the driver an address.

"Where are we going?" Sarah asked.

"You wanted to be the one to tell Jack Robinson. Now you'll get your chance."

"Good, and on the way we can talk about something I just realized."

"What's that?"

"We still don't know who killed Freddie."

GINO SIGHED INTO THE STILL AND SILENT AIR OF THE office. Waiting was not a skill he had mastered, so he'd pulled some paper and a pencil out of his desk and started doodling. The doodles quickly became a list of what Will Arburn had claimed happened the night Estelle Longacre died. It all made sense, as the truth usually did. It also explained some things they hadn't been able to understand, such as why Estelle's body had ended up in the trunk in an alley in the

Bowery. In fact, it explained everything except the beginning of the story and the end.

The beginning was Estelle getting killed in the first place, and of course Arburn would deny doing that. Now that they knew about the telegrams and the planning the killer had done to get Estelle to the flat that night, Arburn no longer looked like a good suspect anyway. Arburn might've killed her in a fit of passion if he found her there, but why would he go to the trouble of luring her to the flat so he could do it? And was he even smart enough to figure all that out? Or to send the telegram from a Western Union office near Norman Tufts's apartment? No, that seemed much too complicated for Arburn to have planned. Which meant someone else had killed Estelle. They'd narrowed it down to either Norman or Miss Longacre or the two of them together, or maybe Jack Robinson. Robinson might've been clever enough to send the telegram from that particular Western Union office, and maybe he'd had an argument with Estelle that night and killed her, but why would he hire Mr. Malloy to find Estelle's killer if he'd done it himself?

But if either Norman or Robinson had done it, then Arburn's story fit nicely with the facts they knew about Estelle's body ending up in the trunk. It even explained why Freddie had gone into hiding. In fact, it explained everything up until the very end. The very end was Freddie getting killed. Mr. Malloy had suggested that maybe Freddie's death had nothing to do with Estelle's. That could be true, of course. People got killed in the Bowery for many reasons and sometimes for no reason at all. Street arabs like Freddie, boys with no home or family, died regularly in the city, although hardly ever from being murdered. Still, it could happen.

But what were the odds that Freddie would somehow find out Estelle Longacre had been murdered and then turn up murdered himself a few days later without the two being connected? Not very likely. But if Norman Tufts had killed Estelle, why would he have killed Freddie? Did Freddie see something? And even if he had, how would Norman know who he was and how would he have found him days later to kill him?

No, whoever killed Freddie had to know who he was and then had to work hard to find him. Gino and Mr. Malloy knew just how hard. And why would they need to kill the boy at all? Because he knew about Estelle's murder, of course. Arburn had said that himself. And Freddie probably thought Arburn had done it. But Arburn thought Jack Robinson had done it, or so he claimed.

Now if Jack Robinson had killed her and knew Freddie had seen him coming out of the flat or something, then he'd naturally want Freddie dead. That would certainly explain why he ordered Arburn to find the boy, and Arburn did believe Jack had killed Estelle, so he probably thought Jack would want to get rid of the boy, too.

Arburn, by his own admission, was trying to help Jack. How far had he been willing to go to do it?

Gino found a clean sheet of paper and left Mr. Malloy another note. He was supposed to wait here, but now he couldn't wait any longer. Will Arburn knew they were close to figuring it out now, and he might not stay around until they did.

THE MAID TOLD MALLOY AND SARAH THAT MR. ROBINSON had a visitor and asked them to wait, offering them a seat on the chairs in the foyer. When she was gone, Sarah reached over and Malloy took her hand. How well he understood her. She did want justice for Estelle, a girl whose whole life had been tainted by her father's selfish lust, but how much justice did she want? Norman's life had been tainted, too.

In a few minutes, Robinson's visitor came down. He was a middle-aged man in an expensive suit, carrying a briefcase, and Sarah recognized him at once. "Mr. Cavendish."

"Hello, Mrs. Malloy. How nice to see you again."

Sarah introduced the attorney to Malloy.

"I hope you're still pleased with the house," Cavendish said.

"Very much so. Thank you again for your assistance."

Cavendish wished them well and allowed the maid to show him out. Then she escorted them upstairs.

Robinson received them in the parlor again. He had apparently just put on his suit coat and was still adjusting it when they entered. He looked like he hadn't slept since their last meeting.

"I'm sorry to keep you waiting," Robinson said. "My, this must be very serious if you brought your wife," he added to Malloy.

"It is. She thinks she can talk you out of doing something rash."

Sarah gave Malloy a reproving look, or at least she hoped it was reproving. "The story we have to tell you will be painful for you to hear, and I'm afraid you'll be very angry when you've heard it."

"I've understood that from the start, Mrs. Malloy, and rest assured, I didn't get to where I am today by being emotional. Please, sit down. I've sent for some iced tea, but I believe I'll have something stronger myself."

He poured himself a tumbler of whiskey while Sarah and Malloy took a seat on the sofa. Robinson took the chair opposite and downed a healthy swallow before inviting Sarah to begin.

As gently as she could, she told him that Horace Longacre

had raped his daughter after learning he was dying, and that they suspected she had become pregnant as a result. Then she explained how the maid, Marie, had told Penelope Longacre about the pregnancy and Penelope had decided to use that information to arrange a marriage between Estelle and Norman so Norman would eventually get control of the Longacre fortune.

"You see, Penelope had been in the same situation herself, unmarried and expecting a baby," Sarah said. "That baby was Norman Tufts."

"Good God!"

"Yes, so naturally, Penelope thought Estelle would be grateful when Norman offered to marry her."

"But wait, if Norman was her son, that would make him Estelle's first cousin, and cousins can't marry."

Sarah didn't dare even glance at Malloy, because of course, it was much worse than that. "Penelope didn't seem to think that would matter, since no one knew Norman was her son." Which was true as far as it went. She couldn't tell him the truth just yet.

Robinson had been right when he said he could control his emotions. Although fury burned in his eyes, his voice was calm. "All right. Go on."

Sarah told him about the telegram to draw Estelle to the Bowery, and what they believed had happened when she sent a telegram to him to change the time. "Norman told us what happened when she arrived at the flat. We don't know if she already knew she was expecting a baby or not, but she knew she couldn't marry Norman. She told him they could never marry because Penelope Longacre was his mother and Horace Longacre was his father, too."

Robinson stared at her in horror for a long moment, then muttered a curse, too overwhelmed to even realize he should apologize. "Was it true?"

"Yes, but Norman didn't believe it. Perhaps he couldn't allow himself to believe it. In any event, he was furious at Estelle for saying those things and he killed her."

Robinson tossed back the rest of his drink and then rubbed his eyes. Sarah's heart ached for him.

She waited, giving him time to come to terms with the shock of it.

Finally, he nodded once, as if to acknowledge all she had told him. "And then he took her away in the trunk, I suppose. What did he think he was going to do?"

"No, he wasn't the one who took her away," Malloy said more gently than Sarah had expected. "He just left her there."

"That doesn't make sense. Who else would've carried her away?"

"The story gets even more complicated from there," Malloy said. They'd agreed he should tell this part. "It seems Will Arburn had planned to meet another girl at the flat that night. He knew you wouldn't be using it, so he thought it would be safe."

"He did, did he?" Robinson said coldly.

"And of course he found Estelle's body there. He didn't have any idea what had happened, so he assumed that you had killed her."

"What?"

"You have to admit, he couldn't possibly have imagined the sequence of events that got Estelle there in the first place," Sarah said, needing him to understand. "The only reason he could imagine she would be there was to meet you."

"And he thought I'd murder a young woman and just leave her there?"

Malloy shrugged, obviously unwilling to excuse Arburn any further. "Whatever he thought, he decided he would help you by disposing of Estelle's body. He's the one who put her into the trunk, but it was still light outside, so he decided to come back later to remove it. The other girl was still coming, of course, so he had to get her away before she suspected anything, and when he came back, after you'd been there and gone, Freddie had arrived. He was going to sleep there, so Arburn convinced the boy to help him carry the trunk out. He told him you wanted to get rid of it."

"And Freddie figured out what was in the trunk," Robinson guessed grimly. "He always was a bright boy."

"He must've thought Arburn killed Estelle, so he was hiding from him."

"And then I sent Arburn after him," Robinson realized with renewed horror.

"Arburn told us he knew Freddie would never come out of hiding if he heard Arburn was looking for him, so he hired me to find him. Arburn also told us that when you sent him to find the boy, he was sure you'd killed Estelle and that Freddie knew it. He said he thinks you found the boy yourself and killed him."

"He said that?" Robinson stared at Malloy for a long moment. Malloy nodded very slowly. "But you know I didn't kill Estelle, so why would I want to hurt the boy?"

"That's what Mrs. Malloy and I were wondering," Malloy said. "It didn't make sense to us either."

They both waited while Robinson put it all together as they had on the drive over.

"Arburn killed Freddie."

"That's what we think," Malloy said. "I don't know if I told him anything to help him find Freddie, but we do know another newsie sent him to see Raven, the one who was hiding Freddie. However it happened, he found the boy. He thought he was doing you a favor."

"He thought I'd kill a boy? He thought I'd kill the woman I loved?"

They had no answer for that. Sarah could hardly stand to see his pain.

"I promised I'd tell you who the killer was before I went to the police," Malloy said. "And now I've done that."

"Are you going to tell the police?"

Malloy considered the question, but Sarah already knew what he wanted. She wanted the same thing. "I'd like to see justice done."

Some silent communication passed between Malloy and Robinson. "But we both know the law doesn't always administer justice," Robinson said. "What will happen to these two if the law gets hold of them?"

"That depends on who has the money to bribe the proper people," Malloy said. "If Horace Longacre dies soon and his sister gets his money, then there's a good chance Norman Tufts will go free. She'll pay off the prosecutors and his case will get pigeonholed and will never come to trial. If Horace's money isn't available for a bribe, Norman will probably go to trial. In that case, the newspapers will find out every piece of gossip they can to blacken Estelle's name and make up even worse things. It won't be hard, since her conduct was quite unusual for a girl with her background. They won't accuse her father of incest, of course, because they can't put that in the newspapers, but by the time they're finished, everyone will despise Estelle, and Norman could find himself freed by a jury of self-righteous hypocrites."

"And what about Arburn?"

"Will Arburn might be able to bribe his way out of trouble, too, if he's got anything put aside or if he has important friends."

"This important friend isn't going to help him," Robinson said.

"But he knows some rich men from his tours. He might blackmail them into helping him. If he goes to trial, he'd explain how he met Estelle, and it would get pretty sensational. None of the men who took the tours would want their names in the newspapers."

Robinson turned to Sarah. "Mrs. Malloy, do you really expect me to stand by and watch these men go free?"

"We just wanted you to understand how this happened and how the sins of Horace Longacre caused it all," Sarah said.

"Did you think I would feel sorry for Norman Tufts?" Robinson asked in surprise.

"Not at all. He killed Estelle. And Arburn killed an innocent boy for no reason at all."

Robinson frowned, obviously confused. "Then you aren't asking me to leave them to the police?"

"We can't stop you from whatever you decide to do. We're only asking you to show mercy, whatever mercy you feel is deserved," Sarah said. "And we're asking you to remember who is really responsible for all of this agony."

He held her gaze for a long moment. "I understand," he said at last, then turned to Malloy. "Does Arburn know you suspect him?"

"My associate questioned him this morning, and he confessed to being the one who took Estelle's body away. He tried to put the blame for killing Freddie on you, but he'd be a fool not to at least suspect that we'd eventually figure it out."

"Then we need to find him right away, before he has a chance to leave the city. Mrs. Malloy, the Bowery is no place for you. I'll have my driver take you home in my carriage. Mr. Malloy and I will make better time on foot anyway. Will's house isn't that far from here."

15

GINO COULD HEAR THE SHOUTING BEFORE THE CAB EVEN stopped outside Will Arburn's house. Because of the weather, all the windows stood open, and he noticed people on the street had stopped to listen. He paid the driver and jumped out, wondering what was happening.

No one even glanced at him. They were too concerned with trying to make out what the argument was about. Gino decided this would be the perfect time to question Arburn again, since angry people usually forgot to be discreet. He bounded up the front steps and listened for a moment.

"You can't just leave! What will become of me!"

"I can't stay here, Granny!"

Good thing Gino had decided to come when he did. He knocked politely.

As he'd expected, the occupants didn't hear him, so he

let himself in. "Hello!" he shouted, and the argument ceased abruptly. "Anybody home?"

Gino waited. Would they pretend they hadn't heard? That nobody was home? Who would believe it? But he knew people who carried on like that seldom realized how loud they were or that they were providing entertainment to everyone in the neighborhood. After a minute or two of what was probably whispered conversation, someone appeared from the back of the house. The small figure of Will Arburn's grandmother made her way cautiously down the hall toward him.

"What do you want?"

Gino tried the charm that he'd used before. "I'm here to see Will again. Is he home?"

Her beady eyes glistened with hatred, so obviously his charm wasn't working today. "No, he's gone. Don't know when he'll be back."

"That's funny. I could've sworn I heard you and him talking just now."

She couldn't deny that. "You better leave."

"But I need to talk to Will. Maybe you could tell him I'm here."

She thought that over. "All right. You wait here. I'll see if he's come back yet."

But Gino had caught movement out of the corner of his eye, and the moment she turned away, he glanced over to the open window in the parlor, where he could see the top of Arburn's head moving past. He was sneaking down the alley, probably intending to get away. Did innocent people try to run?

Not usually.

Gino backed up silently and then slipped out the front door, just as Arburn rounded the corner of the house.

"Arburn!" he cried happily. "Your grandmother said you'd be right back. I'm so glad I waited."

Before Arburn could react or even realize he should run, Gino had grabbed his arm and started dragging him back to the front door. He looked around wildly for assistance, but the crowd that had gathered to listen to the argument had already begun to disperse. Those still lingering were happy to simply enjoy the show.

"I was just . . . I was out and . . . I just got back . . ." Arburn stammered, although the fact that he was barefoot and in shirtsleeves gave the lie to his claims.

"That's all right," Gino assured him, still smiling. "I didn't have to wait long."

And then they were back inside. Gino propelled him into the parlor and down onto a sprung overstuffed chair in the corner.

"Hey, no reason to get rough!"

"I only want you to be comfortable," Gino said.

"What's going on here?" the old woman demanded from the doorway.

"Nothing, ma'am," Gino assured her. "I just needed to talk to Will about something."

"I told you to leave. Get out or I'll . . ." She stopped, obviously at a loss.

"Or you'll call the police? By all means, do that, ma'am. You'll save me the trouble."

"You don't need no police," Arburn said with forced confidence. He even managed a smile. "Granny, you leave us now. Me and Mr. Donatelli need to have a little talk, and then everything will be all right."

Granny frowned doubtfully. "You sure?"

"Of course I'm sure. Me and Gino are good pals."

Gino did not contradict him, and the old woman finally

turned away, although Gino figured he didn't have much time until she got someone to help. And it probably wouldn't be the cops.

He closed the door behind her and turned back to Arburn, who still smiled with his phony assurance. "What is it now? I already told you all I know about Estelle's death."

"But not all you know about Freddie's death."

Arburn's smile vanished. "I told you, Jack was the one who wanted the boy dead."

"No, you said that's what you thought when you believed Jack had killed Estelle."

"I suppose Jack claims he didn't kill her."

"He didn't have to claim it. Did I mention that he hired Mr. Malloy and me to find her killer? Why would he do that if he'd done it himself?"

Something very much like panic flickered in Arburn's eyes, but to his credit he didn't surrender to it. "Because he's smart. He'd know that would be the best way to convince you that it wasn't him."

Gino couldn't agree with that reasoning, but he played along. "I never thought of that."

"Of course you didn't. Black Jack Robinson is the smartest man I know."

"How did he find Freddie, though? It took me and Mr. Malloy days to find him."

"He's got men working for him all over the city. You think you're the only ones who were looking?"

"And you were looking, too."

"I was just trying to help. I wanted to get back in Jack's good graces. But he had everybody looking for the boy. I'm telling you, he had to have killed Estelle. Why else would he have wanted the boy so bad?"

"Then why were you the only one asking about him that night he died?"

That shocked him, and before he could think of an answer, Gino heard the parlor door open behind him. He turned to see Granny barreling toward him with a cast iron skillet raised high above her head.

Instinctively, he threw up his arm to ward off the blow, and the skillet struck the arm with a sickening crack and a blinding pain that drove him howling to his knees.

"Run, you idiot!" the old woman cried. "I'll take care of him."

Gino had grabbed his arm, desperately trying to ease the agony, but some small part of his brain still screamed that he couldn't let Arburn escape.

Arburn jumped to his feet and tried to dodge around Gino, but Gino released his broken arm and caught Arburn's ankle, sending him sprawling to the floor in a hail of curses. Before he could scramble back up, Gino threw himself on top of him, using his weight to pin him down while Arburn bucked and twisted like a demon.

"Granny, help!" Arburn shouted.

The old woman made a grunting sound, as if lifting something heavy, and Gino remembered the skillet. He threw himself to the side just as the skillet rushed past his cheek and landed on Arburn's face with a horrible crunch.

Arburn howled and blood spurted everywhere and the old woman started screaming and Gino writhed on the floor in agony because he'd landed on his broken arm. Then somebody came running into the room, and Gino couldn't see who, because he was blind with pain, and he was sure it was all over for him when Mr. Malloy said, "What on earth is going on here?"

* * *

IN THE END THEY HAD TO TIE THE OLD WOMAN TO A chair to keep her from attacking someone again. Robinson wasted no time sending a bystander to the Devil's Den for a couple of his men. In the meantime, Frank found some rags and made a sling for Gino's arm and rounded up some whiskey for the pain. The boy was holding up pretty well, all things considered.

For his part, Robinson examined Arburn's broken face, wiggling his smashed nose and exploring his crushed cheek with a probing finger, until Arburn admitted between screams that he had indeed found Freddie "Two Toes" Bertolli that night. He hadn't believed Freddie's claims that he hadn't seen Black Jack at all the night Estelle died and had no idea Jack had killed Estelle. But when Two Toes admitted he thought Arburn had killed her, Arburn had choked the boy to death to ensure he never made that claim to another soul. When he heard that, Frank began to regret that he had conceded all retribution to Robinson.

Once he had the information he wanted, Robinson said, "We don't need the police for this." By then the old woman had stopped struggling, but she watched through narrowed eyes as Robinson's men half carried a bloody Arburn away, and she cursed Robinson eloquently. He didn't seem to notice.

"I'm in your debt, Mr. Malloy," Robinson said, "and yours, too, Mr. Donatelli. I'm sorry we haven't met before now."

"I hope you'll excuse me for not shaking hands," Gino said with his usual spirit, even though his face was a little gray from the pain.

"You don't owe us anything," Frank said. "All I wanted was justice for Freddie."

"And now you'll have it. I've got a hansom cab waiting outside for you both," Robinson said. "You'll want to get that arm fixed up."

"What about . . . the others," Frank asked.

"We won't need the police for them either. Please tell your lovely wife that I will take her information into consideration."

Frank nodded. "Before you make any plans for Horace Longacre, I suggest you consult his servants, Tom and Marie O'Day. They already have some ideas."

Robinson smiled mirthlessly. "Thank you, Mr. Malloy. I'll be sure to do that."

FRANK HADN'T FELT MUCH LIKE GOING INTO THE OFFICE the following Monday. The summer heat still lay heavily over the city, and he had seriously considered not going in at all. But Gino's mother and Sarah had conspired to make sure Gino took a few weeks off to rest after breaking his arm, so Frank thought he ought to open the office for a few hours, at least, in case a client appeared.

The person who did appear wasn't a client, though.

"What have you done with Norman?" Miss Longacre demanded when she stormed into his office.

Frank sighed. Black Jack Robinson must have dispensed his justice. "I haven't done anything with him. Please, have a seat."

She plunked herself down into one of the visitor chairs in front of his desk and glared at him. "Just tell me where he is. I must warn you, I don't have any money to pay a ransom with, but I'm told Horace has taken a turn for the worse, so I should have some very soon."

"You don't need to pay a ransom. I told you, I have no

idea where Norman is." Which was perfectly true, as far as it went. "Tell me what happened."

"Nothing happened. Norman went out yesterday, as he often does. He likes to walk in the park. But he never came home again."

"Have you asked his friends if they've seen him?"

"No one has seen him," she reported through clenched teeth.

And no one ever would, Frank was sure. "Why have you come to me?"

"Because I know you've had him arrested or something. He shouldn't go to jail. He didn't mean to kill Estelle. It was all a terrible accident, and he's very sorry."

"I didn't have him arrested. I didn't tell the police anything."

"Then where is he?"

Should he prepare her? It would be a kindness, he decided. "You say he's very sorry. I'm sure it haunts him. He was very upset when he had to identify her body, I know."

"That was horrible. Norman is much too sensitive for an ordeal like that."

"Then maybe he decided he couldn't live with it anymore."

Miss Longacre stiffened at that. "What do you mean?"

"I mean lots of people decide they can't live with something they've done, and they take their own lives."

"Suicide? Is that what you think?"

"I don't know, but it's something to consider."

"Norman would never do a thing like that! He knows how much I depend on him."

Did everyone in the Longacre family think of only themselves? Of course they did. This woman in front of him was actually hoping to marry her son to his half sister. "You know him better than I do, but he might've had an accident or something. If you don't hear from him for a few more days, you might check at the morgue, just to be sure."

"Are you trying to tell me he's dead?" she asked, her voice high with terror.

Frank cursed his clumsiness and wished Sarah were here to handle this. "Not at all. I really don't know where he is, but people have accidents all the time in the city. If he didn't have any identification with him, they might not have been able to notify you."

"Is that what they're going to say? That he had an accident?"

Frank decided not to make matters worse by responding. "How is your brother getting along?"

"He's still dying, I hope. I tried to visit him. I need to know if he's changed his will now that Estelle is dead. I should inherit everything now, you know. But they wouldn't let me see him."

That seemed odd. "Marie wouldn't have turned you away unless your brother told her to."

"Marie isn't there anymore. It was someone I didn't know. He claimed he was taking care of Horace now."

Robinson hadn't wasted any time. "I see. Well, I don't know what to tell you then."

"You can tell me where Norman is, but I can see you aren't going to help me." She stood up and left in a huff before Frank was completely out of his chair.

He sat back down wearily. He really shouldn't have come to the office today. And maybe he should go over to Bellevue to see if they had any unidentified bodies there. He was still trying to decide when Black Jack Robinson showed up.

* * *

"You must have been surprised to see Robinson," Maeve said. They were all sitting on the back porch, enjoying the cooling evening air after the children were in bed. Gino had joined them for dinner and had basked in the attentions of the ladies, who were most solicitous of his comfort, finding cushions to support his arm and offering him every delicacy they could find in the house. Even Frank's mother had made a fuss.

"I was surprised," Frank admitted. "But Robinson thought I'd want to know what he'd done."

"And did you?" Sarah asked archly.

"Not at all, but I knew you'd be curious."

They all laughed at that, knowing he was just as curious. The laughter died quickly, though, because they also knew what Robinson had come to report.

"Are they all dead?" Gino asked.

"Arburn and Norman are, but he wanted you to know he did show Norman some mercy," he told Sarah.

His mother made a huffing noise to demonstrate her disbelief, but he ignored it. "Norman was chloroformed before they dropped him into the river. It will look like a suicide, Robinson assured me, although I don't think that will be any comfort to Penelope."

"But it will keep the police from investigating," Sarah said, "so she should appreciate that."

"Is it better to have a son who committed suicide or one who committed murder?" Maeve asked.

"Not much of a choice," Frank's mother muttered, and he had to agree.

"Actually, Miss Longacre had already visited me this morning. It seems Norman never came home yesterday, and she thought I'd had him arrested. I suggested he might not have been able to live with himself, but she didn't like that idea much."

"And what about Arburn?" Gino asked. "I hope he didn't get any mercy."

"I didn't ask for details, and Robinson didn't offer any, except to say that Arburn's body might also turn up in the river."

"He got what he deserved," Maeve said.

Frank nodded. Nothing would really give Freddie justice, but at least his killer had been punished. "And he also is making sure Horace Longacre gets what he deserves."

"Is he planning to kill him?" Sarah asked. "That would actually be a mercy, since he's already dying."

"Which is why he isn't going to kill him. I didn't tell you, but Tom and Marie O'Day—they're all that's left of Longacre's servants," Frank added for those who didn't know, "were planning to leave him as soon as he got to the point where he couldn't care for himself anymore. That was going to be their revenge for what he'd done to Estelle. I suggested that Robinson consult with them before deciding what to do."

"And did he?" Sarah asked.

"He did. He sent his attorney in as well to see what Longacre's will said. He'd pensioned them off in the will, and left everything else to Estelle. The attorney explained that since Estelle had died before him, the estate would go to Horace's surviving next of kin."

"Which would be Penelope," Sarah guessed.

"Yes, although I think she's going to be disappointed. Horace wasn't a very good manager, and he's not leaving much except the house and his yacht."

"Didn't she expect Norman would be rich if he married Estelle?" Maeve asked.

"That's what she said," Sarah said. "I imagine she could sell the house and the boat and continue to live as she has, very comfortably, although I'm sure that's not what she dreamed of."

"What about those servants?" his mother asked. "What'll happen to them?"

"Like I said, they'll get a nice sum that will provide a pension for them. Robinson said he's going to see they keep getting paid until Longacre dies, and in the meantime, he's put his own man in the house to make sure no one comes to comfort him."

"That should please everyone who knew Longacre," Sarah said, "although it's little enough to repay the suffering he caused his sister and his daughter."

"Which is why there's a hell," Frank's mother said, earning a startled look from Maeve and an amused glance from Gino.

"Maybe that's why Robinson has decided to reform," Frank said.

"What do you mean?" Sarah asked.

"Remember when we went to see him the last time, he'd been meeting with his attorney?"

"Yes."

"He's decided to sell off all his businesses. He's already rich, and now he wants to be respectable."

"That was why he wanted to marry Estelle," Sarah said, remembering. "He thought she would do that for him and they would be accepted into society."

"Would it have worked?" Maeve asked.

"There's a lot of new money in the city nowadays," Sarah said. "It won't buy you friendship with the old families, but if you've got enough of it, you can make your own respectability."

His mother said, "If Francis can do it, anybody can."

"Ma!" he protested, but everyone laughed because it was true.

"Let's talk about something more pleasant now," Sarah suggested. "Maeve has hired the contractors to work on the new maternity hospital."

"When will it be ready?" Gino asked, his eyes dancing with mischief because everyone knew how hard it had been to get the Malloys' house refurbished.

"They said it will be ready by Christmas," Maeve said, "but I told them it had to be done by Thanksgiving. I don't think they take me seriously yet."

"They will," Gino said.

THAT NIGHT, WHEN THEY WERE ALONE IN THEIR ROOMS, Sarah stopped brushing her hair when Malloy came back from his dressing room, ready for bed. "I've been remembering my conversations with Penelope Longacre. I'm afraid I missed some things. She'd been trying to tell me about Estelle, or at least point me in the right direction."

"I think we all missed some things along the way."

"This was so obvious, though. She said that the reason Horace never remarried was because 'he had the girl.' Those where her exact words. I took it to mean he had only wanted a child, so he didn't need a wife anymore."

"And that was apparently true, although not for the reason you thought."

"No, incest isn't the first reason I think of for anything, I'm happy to say. She also told me to ask Horace if I wanted to find the father of Estelle's baby. Nothing could be clearer than that."

"But I asked him, and he claimed he didn't know," Malloy reminded her.

"I just feel like I should have done more."

"You did what you could," he said. "I think what you really want is to save Estelle, and it's far too late for that. She was dead before you ever knew she existed."

"You're right, I do. I look at Maeve and I think of all the young women in the city with no one to help them."

"You can't help them all. You have to accept that."

"I know, and we have the Mission and soon we'll have the hospital, too."

"By Thanksgiving, if we can believe Maeve," Malloy said with a grin.

She smiled back. "Yes, and we'll save some of them."

"That's enough regret for one night. Come to bed now. I'll make you forget everything else."

And he did.

Author's Note

I FOUND A LOT OF REALLY INTERESTING HISTORICALLY accurate things to include in this book, so here are my explanations to save you the trouble of asking, "Did this really happen?"

The newsboys did strike both the *World* and the *Journal* in late July of 1899, and Kid Blink was one of the leaders of the strike. They managed to halt the sale of those papers not only in New York City but all over the East Coast. They didn't get William Randolph Hearst and Joseph Pulitzer to lower the cost of their papers to the newsboys, but they did get them to agree to buy back any unsold papers, which was a huge victory. The story was dramatized in the movie *Newsies*, which contains many historical inaccuracies but is a fun movie to watch.

The newsboys and newsgirls—yes, some girls sold newspapers, but there weren't nearly as many newsgirls as newsboys—could rent a bed for the night in one of the

Newsboys' Lodging Houses located in the city. As I explain, the children often preferred to sleep on the streets, but when the weather was bad, they appreciated having the option, although they had to pay for the privilege.

The Orphan Trains were also real. From 1854 to 1929, over a quarter million children were placed on the Orphan Trains and taken out West, where they were "put up" for adoption, literally put up on a stage for people to see so they could choose the child they wanted. Many of these stories ended happily, with children finding loving homes. Other children were abused and exploited, and a few returned to New York permanently.

The Orphan Trains and Newsboys' Lodging Houses were operated by the same charity, so the orphans were often recruited from the lodging houses. The newsboys, most of whom had no families or had been abandoned by their families, looked after one another, and they even paid for one another's funerals, as I depicted in this book. Their greatest fear was dying unmourned and being buried in a pauper's grave.

Finally, Bowery tours were also real. Rich "swells" could pay a guide to take them on a tour of the rougher parts of the city. Often the people they observed in the gambling dens, saloons, and brothels were merely actors, since real people don't appreciate being gawked at and were likely to demonstrate their disapproval by attacking the gawkers. It was sort of like reality TV before we had TV: It looked real but it wasn't exactly real.

If you're wondering about the way the telegrams were worded, why there was no punctuation and why I didn't use the word *stop* to indicate a period, here are the answers. Early telegrams had no punctuation because Morse code did not include a code for periods and commas. Only later, when World War I made it absolutely necessary to have clarity in military orders sent via telegram, was the word *stop* used to indicate the end of a sentence.

I hope you enjoyed *Murder in the Bowery*. Please let me know how you liked it. You can contact me through my website at victoriathompson.com, or follow me on Facebook at facebook.com/victoria.thompson.author, or on Twitter @gaslightvt.

Keep reading for an excerpt of the first book in
Victoria Thompson's new Counterfeit Lady Novels

CITY OF LIES

Available now in hardcover
from Berkley Prime Crime

Jake LOOKED MUCH TOO SMUG.

Elizabeth's hand itched to smack the smirk off his face, but well-bred young ladies didn't go around smacking people in hotel dining rooms. Since she was pretending to be a well-bred young lady at the moment, she made herself smile pleasantly and threaded her way through the mostly empty tables to where he was sitting.

He jumped to his feet and pulled out her chair, because he was pretending to be a well-bred young man. "Good morning, dear sister. Did you sleep well?"

"Did you drop the leather?" she asked.

"Of course, and he just came into the dining room. Oh, wait. He stopped to talk to someone."

Elizabeth glanced over, turning her head only slightly so she wouldn't be caught watching their mark. Jake had done the same thing.

"It's a woman," Jake murmured.

"Shhh." She could see that. She needed to hear what they said. If he had a friend in the city, someone who might advise him . . .

"Hazel, how nice to see you," Thornton said, although a trace of strain in his voice indicated it wasn't really so nice to see her at all.

"Oscar," the woman said. Her back was to them but her tone was unmistakable. Elizabeth almost shivered from the frost in it. She'd have to practice that tone. It might come in handy someday.

"What brings you to Washington City?" Thornton asked with obviously forced enthusiasm. He'd also felt the chill and was trying to pretend he hadn't.

The woman rose to her feet, and even though she was much shorter than Oscar Thornton, she seemed to tower over him. How did she do that? "I can't believe that is any of your concern." She laid her napkin down on the table and walked away, making Thornton look like a dog. How on earth did she do that? But Elizabeth couldn't worry about that now. She had to salvage Thornton's pride.

"Start talking," Elizabeth whispered.

"So I told him I wanted to order a dozen pair," Jake said a little louder than necessary so Thornton would know they'd been talking to each other and hadn't noticed that woman cutting him dead so beautifully. Never embarrass a mark. "And he looks down his nose at me, the way those clerks in those fancy stores do, and he says, 'Sir, you will never have use for a dozen pair.'"

"He didn't!" Elizabeth said, outraged on behalf of her brother in this imaginary conversation.

"He did. So I told him I'd take two dozen instead."

She laughed the little tinkling laugh she'd practiced so many times and said, "Father will be furious."

"Why do you think I did it?" Then he looked up in apparent surprise to see Thornton approaching their table. "Good morning, Thornton. Won't you join us?"

Elizabeth looked up, too, and gave him a delighted smile that told him how pleased she was to see him, because she was pleased, if not for the reason he thought. His face was still scarlet from the woman's snub, but she gave no indication she noticed. "Yes, do join us and save me from having to listen to any more of my brother's silly stories."

Jake pretended to be affronted, but they soon had Thornton seated and responding to Elizabeth's subtle flirting. He probably hadn't forgotten that woman, but he was thinking about Elizabeth now, which was all that mattered.

"Oh dear, are those women still marching at the White House?" she asked, seeing the headline in the newspaper Thornton had carried with him.

"Yes, even though they're getting arrested almost daily now," Thornton said. He'd cleared the last of the humiliation out of his voice, she noticed with relief.

"I don't know why women would want to vote anyway. Would you, Betty?" Jake asked, using the name they'd chosen for this job.

"I can't imagine why," Elizabeth said. "Politics is so boring." She didn't have to lie about her opinion of politics, at least.

"And not something a lady should concern herself with," Thornton said with the condescending smile that set her teeth on edge.

Thornton told them the details of the suffragettes' latest brush with the law while the waiter in his spotless white gloves served them eggs and potatoes and bacon and refilled their coffee cups. When they were nearly finished, Elizabeth said, "Oh, I'm sorry, Mr. Thornton."

"For what, my dear?" he asked. He thought he was charming, and she let him think so.

"I stepped on your foot."

"No, you didn't," he assured her.

Elizabeth frowned in confusion. "It must have been you then, Jake."

"No, it wasn't," he said.

"Well, I stepped on something," she said, pushing her chair back a bit and looking down at the floor. "What could it be?"

She couldn't see because of the tablecloth, so Thornton obligingly bent down to help look. Then he reached under the table and came up with a man's wallet.

"You've dropped your pocketbook, Perkins," he told Jake.

Jake patted his jacket. "No, I haven't. Mine's right here. It must be yours."

Thornton patted his own jacket and shook his head. "It's not mine, either."

"Someone's going to be very upset," Elizabeth said. "Look how much money is in it."

Thornton had opened the wallet and discovered a large amount of cash inside.

"How much is it, do you think?" Jake asked.

"Several hundred at least," Thornton said.

"We need to find the owner and return it," Jake said. "Is there anything in there with a name on it?"

Thornton started emptying the wallet, which was stuffed not only with money but other papers as well. He laid the items out on the table, and Elizabeth and Jake moved the dishes aside to make room.

Jake picked up the stack of money and counted it while

Thornton laid out several telegrams, a paper with a row of letters and numbers written on it, and a newspaper clipping.

"There's over six hundred dollars here," Jake said. Two year's salary for an average working man.

"What does the newspaper clipping say?" Elizabeth asked.

Thornton read it to himself. "It's about some fellow named Coleman making a killing in the stock market."

"These telegrams are to someone named Coleman, too," Jake noticed.

"Is that his photograph?" she asked, peering at the clipping in Thornton's fat fingers.

"For all the good it does." He turned it so she could see. The photograph was of a man holding his hat to cover his face.

"We don't need his photograph if we have his name," Jake pointed out. "He's probably staying at the hotel. Let's take it to him. I want to see his face when he gets it back."

Thornton glanced over at her. "How do you feel about going to a strange man's hotel room, Miss Perkins?"

She gave him a mischievous smile. "It's scandalous, I know, but I'll be thoroughly chaperoned."

"Indeed you will," Jake said with a grin.

While Jake stuffed everything back into the wallet, Thornton rose and pulled out her chair for her. She thanked him with a coy little smile that promised things she would never in this world deliver. Jake went on ahead to the front desk to see if Mr. Coleman was registered at the hotel. Which he was, of course, and he also happened to be in his suite at that very moment, the clerk reported after telephoning to find out.

Elizabeth should have been pleased. Everything was going perfectly. Jake was doing his part and she was doing hers. So why did she have that hollow feeling in her stomach every time she pictured how it would end?

The two men allowed her to go before them to the elevator, and Elizabeth felt Thornton's gaze on her like a slimy hand. She and Jake were pretending to be members of an "old money" family, but she was sure Thornton knew they weren't. She'd gathered that his late wife had come from one of the old New York families, so he'd know the difference. That didn't matter, though. Actually, it was better if he thought they weren't rich. He only needed to believe she was interested in him, and a young woman of limited means would certainly be interested in a single man of apparently unlimited means, no matter if he wasn't particularly handsome or very young.

And Jake had determined that Thornton had the means while they chatted in the smoking car on the train down from New York. If he was green in other areas, Jake was a master at getting marks to talk.

The elevator operator deposited them on the top floor.

"The rooms up here are pretty nice," Jake remarked as they walked down the hall. "I wanted to get a suite, but Betty wouldn't hear of it."

"It's a waste of money," she said, reinforcing Thornton's suspicions that they weren't actually rich.

"This is it," Thornton said when he found the room.

"Betty, you stand out of sight," Jake said, "in case this fellow doesn't take the news in a friendly way or something."

Elizabeth gave him a surprised look, but Thornton said, "Stand behind me and slip away if things get ugly."

"All right," she said, stepping back to allow Thornton to protect her. He was probably hoping they did have to slip away. Left to his own devices, he most likely would have just pocketed Coleman's cash and left the wallet for the hotel staff to find, so they'd get blamed for stealing the money.

Jake knocked.

After a few moments, the door opened a little and a suspicious man peered out at them. "Yes?"

"Mr. Coleman?" Jake said.

"Who wants to know?"

"I'm Jake Perkins and this is Oscar Thornton. We—"

"Stop bothering me. I already told you, I'm not giving any more interviews."

He started to close the door but Jake threw up a hand to stop him. "We found your wallet downstairs in the dining room, and we're returning it."

The man frowned at the wallet Jake held up. "I haven't lost my wallet."

"Are you sure?"

He patted his jacket impatiently, just the way Thornton had downstairs, but he didn't find the telltale bulge he was expecting. He patted some more and felt around in all his pockets. "You're right, I do seem to have lost my wallet. I'm sorry to be so rude, but I thought you were newspaper reporters. They hound me all the time, which is one reason I came to Washington City. I thought I could get away from them here. Please, come in, gentlemen." He held the door open. "Oh, and young lady," he added when Thornton stepped aside to allow Elizabeth to precede him.

"My sister, Miss Perkins," Jake said.

"Pleased to meet you," Coleman said with a nod. "Come in, all of you."

The suite was even nicer than Elizabeth had expected, with a view of the White House grounds across the way.

"I guess you can identify this," Jake said, holding up the wallet again.

"Of course. Let's see, I had a few hundred dollars, five or six, I think. Some telegrams, and a list of ciphers. Oh, and a newspaper clipping. Is that close enough?"

"Yes, it is," Jake assured him. He handed over the wallet with a little flourish he probably thought was cute. Elizabeth managed not to roll her eyes.

She watched Thornton's surprise when Coleman didn't count the money to make sure it was all there the way Thornton probably would have. Instead, Coleman pulled out the piece of paper with the rows of letters and numbers and tossed the wallet with its wad of cash carelessly onto the table. "I can't thank you enough for returning this. I wouldn't have missed the money at all, but without this paper, I'd be out of business."

"We were wondering what that was," Thornton said. "What did you call it? A cipher?"

"That's right. Say, can I offer you fellows a drink? And some sherry for you, miss? I know it's early, but I feel like celebrating. Please, sit down and join me."

Jake gave Thornton a questioning look, and Thornton shrugged. She was sure he never turned down a free drink.

Coleman poured a generous amount of whiskey into three glasses and a small amount of sherry into a stemmed glass for her and handed them around.

"You have good taste in whiskey, Coleman," Thornton said after a taste.

"What kind of business are you in that you need a cipher?" Jake asked. "I don't even know what that is."

"Oh, it's all very hush-hush, but I think you folks have proved you're trustworthy. I work for a combine of Wall Street brokers who are trying to break up the branch stock exchanges and the bucket shops. They control the rise and fall of large blocks of stock, and they send me around the country and tip me off when to buy and sell. You probably saw those telegrams in my wallet. They're written in code, telling me what stocks to buy and sell. Without this cipher,

I wouldn't know what they were saying, and I'd probably lose my job."

"And they pay you to do that?" Jake asked in amazement.

"No, they don't," Coleman said with a wink. "But they do let me keep the money I make when I sell the stocks. Say, I feel like I should give you some kind of reward for returning my wallet since you saved my bacon. I know you don't need the money, but how about if I give each of you fellows a hundred to cover your expenses while you're in town at least?"

"That's awfully sporting of you, Coleman—" Thornton started to say, probably thinking a hundred sounded good, but someone knocked on the door and called, "Telegram!"

"Excuse me," Coleman said and went to answer.

"Say, Thornton, did you ever hear of a scheme like this?" Jake whispered while Coleman was busy with the bellhop.

"Sure," Thornton said, although he was most certainly lying. "Those Wall Street types are always manipulating the market somehow." Which was probably true, at least.

Coleman tipped the bellhop and sent him on his way. Then he hurried over to the desk and consulted his cipher to translate the telegram he'd just received. When he'd finished, he said, "I've just gotten instructions to buy some stocks, so I'm going to have to go to the brokerage right away. Before I do, though, I want to give you fellows your reward."

"We couldn't take a reward," Jake said, completely ignoring the black look Thornton was giving him. "Anybody would've done the same thing."

Thornton wouldn't have, Elizabeth was certain, but Coleman said, "Don't be too sure of that, young fellow. I know you're both honorable men, but I still think I owe you something. Tell you what—why don't I take the two hundred I was going to give you and buy stock with it for each of you?

This order I just got is going to pay off big, and I'm going to sell by the end of the day, so you can keep the original investment and whatever your share earns. It should at least double."

Even Thornton smiled at that prospect. "I think I could live with that, Coleman."

"I don't know much about stock, but it sounds good to me," Jake said. "If it's going to double, I have a notion to give you fifty of my own, too, if you wouldn't mind."

"Oh, Jake, do you really think you should?" Elizabeth said with a worried frown.

"You're right to be careful, Miss Perkins, but in this case, you can't go wrong," Coleman said. "I can guarantee your brother will double his money."

Before Elizabeth could protest again, Jake pulled out his wallet and passed Coleman a fifty.

"How about it, Thornton?" Jake said. "Don't you want to get in on this deal?"

"Mr. Thornton is as careful as your sister," Coleman said with a smile when Thornton made no move for his own wallet. "I don't blame him for hesitating. But I think I'll have your confidence by the end of the day. Can I meet you gentlemen in the hotel bar at around six o'clock to give you your earnings?"

They agreed that would be satisfactory, and Coleman tucked their money into an envelope. Then he thanked them again and sent them on their way.

"I can't believe you gave him your own money," Elizabeth scolded her brother when they were in the elevator.

"Do you think I made a mistake?" Jake asked Thornton.

"I guess you'll find out," Thornton said, apparently gratified that Jake was finally asking his advice.

"And maybe you'll be sorry you didn't give him anything yourself," Jake said with a grin.

"OH, JAKE, HOW COULD YOU HAVE BEEN SO FOOLISH?" Elizabeth cried, blinking back tears. Two days had passed since they'd found Mr. Coleman's wallet, and Coleman's stock deals had turned the original two hundred reward dollars and Jake's fifty into over a thousand. Thornton had even given Coleman some of his own money to invest the last time. This success had led Jake to sign a check for a hundred thousand dollars he didn't have in order to purchase stock that Mr. Coleman had recommended.

And now he was in trouble.

"It's not foolish, Betty," Jake said. They were sitting with Thornton in the empty hotel dining room in the middle of the afternoon, discussing the situation. "This Coleman knows what he's doing, and the stock he told us to buy with that check did exactly what he said it would. We made a fortune! Just think what the Old Man will say when he finds out," he added, his eyes literally sparkling with glee at the prospect. She only wished she thought the Old Man would really be pleased by any of this.

"Then why can't you just collect your money? Wouldn't that cover the check, too?" she asked.

"Miss Perkins," Thornton said gently, "it's really nothing to concern yourself about. The brokerage is just being careful, and we did give them a worthless check when we bought the stock."

"We just didn't realize they'd contact the bank and find out we didn't even have an account there," Jake said, as if this were some unimportant detail.

"I told you not to put your name on a check so large," Elizabeth said, sniffling again. "You heard me say it, Mr. Thornton, but you let him do it anyway."

"All we have to do is come up with the cash to cover the check, and we can collect our profits," Jake said. "Betty, we made over a hundred and fifty thousand dollars."

"But only if you have a hundred thousand in cash to cover the check. How on earth will you manage that?"

Jake nodded at Thornton. "Our friend here is going to help."

Elizabeth let him see her admiration. "Oh, Mr. Thornton, we hardly know you. We couldn't ask you to do that."

"Why not?" he asked. "Jake and I are partners."

"And Oscar and I are going to split the profits," Jake said.

"Oh," Elizabeth said. "I didn't realize."

"Which is why I'm putting up half of the money to cover the check," Thornton said.

"But where will the other half come from?" Elizabeth asked.

"I've got those bonds Grandmother gave me that I can sell for about thirty," Jake said.

"But what will Father say?"

Jake waved away her concerns. "He'll never know, because I'll buy them back when I get my money. And I thought we could use your inheritance, too."

"You want me to help you?" she cried, suddenly furious. "But that's the money Aunt Mabel left me for my dowry."

"It's only for a few days," Jake said.

"And you'll get back more than double what you had," Thornton said. "The stock had a return of a hundred and fifty percent."

"But I only have about ten thousand," Elizabeth argued. "That still isn't enough to cover the check."

"Mr. Coleman offered to lend us the rest of it," Jake said. "He's a good fellow."

"He must be," Elizabeth said, still not quite convinced. "Oh, Mr. Thornton, I don't know what to think. Tell me what I should do."

Thornton smiled and patted her hand where it lay on the table. It took all her willpower not to jerk away. "Miss Perkins, you should lend your brother the money. In a day or two, you'll be a very wealthy woman, and I'll be an even wealthier man."

"Are you sure?" she asked.

"Of course I'm sure, and then we can celebrate by taking a ship down south to where it's warm. Didn't you say that's what you'd like to do if you could?"

Elizabeth blinked the tears from her eyes. "Oh my, yes, that sounds wonderful." She turned to Jake. "All right, then, I'll help you. But, Jake, you must promise never to get into another fix like this again."

Jake gave her an unrepentant smile. "She says that every time, but this time you won't be sorry, my girl. Now, we'll need to go down to the bank and open an account. Mr. Coleman will help us. They know him down there."

"It'll be just a matter of days before we have our money transferred into the account," Thornton said. "Then we'll take it down to the brokerage and pick up our profits."

"Take it down to the brokerage? You mean you'll be carrying all that money around with you in cash?" Elizabeth asked, horrified anew. "Isn't that dangerous?"

"You worry too much, Miss Perkins," Thornton said. "I'll have my boys watching us."

A frisson of alarm shivered over her. "Your boys?"

"Yes," he said with that superior grin he always gave her when he was explaining something he thought she was too simple to understand. "I always travel with bodyguards. They've been bored these past few days, so they'll be glad to have something to do."

Elizabeth had her bag packed, and she'd been pacing her hotel room, looking out the window each time she reached it. Not that she expected to see anything. All she had was a view of the rear of the hotel, where the deliveries came in. They hadn't wasted money on a better room, since Thornton wasn't going to be coming to see her here, much as he might want to.

Finally, someone knocked on her door, but it couldn't be Jake. She'd given him a key. Her apprehension hardened into fear.

"Lizzie, it's me. Open up!"

She hurried over and opened the door to Coleman. "What's wrong? Where's Jake?" she asked as he closed the door behind him.

"You need to get out of here, Lizzie. It came hot and Thornton went wild when Jake told him it blew up."

"You were supposed to cool him off," she cried.

"I warned you—when you play it against the wall, there's no way to cool off the mark. You just get out the best way you can. Thornton slugged Jake, so he ran."

"You were supposed to hit Jake!"

"I told you, Thornton went wild. He sucker punched the boy before I could do a thing. And when Jake ran, Thornton sent his goons after him. He's probably going to come looking for you next, so you need to get out of town."

"But he let you go?"

"Of course. Jake might be a fool, but he knows how to do

a switch. Thornton still believes I was conned, too." Switching a mark's allegiance from the roper to the inside man was crucial to a successful con, and Elizabeth had to admit that Jake was particularly good at it.

"What about Jake?" she asked, picking up her suitcase.

"Just leave that. I'll bring it to you in New York with your share of the score. What the . . . ?" he said, looking out the window. Elizabeth hurried over to see. They were on the second floor, so they had a clear view of Thornton's two bodyguards finally catching Jake near the loading dock of the hotel.

"They're going to kill him!" she cried as the two men began to beat him.

"I'll take care of it, Lizzie," Coleman said, his voice high with terror. "But I can't save you both. You need to get out of here and go straight to the station. Get yourself on the first train out. It doesn't matter where. You can get back to New York from any place. Do you need money?"

"No, I—" She cried out as one of the men landed a particularly vicious blow and Jake doubled over.

"Hurry," Coleman said, pushing her toward the door. "Thornton is probably already trying to get the desk clerk to tell him where your room is. He'll be here any second." He grabbed her shoulders and looked straight into her eyes. "You're a woman, and you know they won't be satisfied with just beating you. Now go."

He checked the hallway and then sent her out. She didn't wait for the elevator, instead racing down the stairwell, nearly tripping over her skirts in her frantic haste. She took a deep breath before pushing open the door and entering the busy lobby. She didn't want to call attention to herself, but she couldn't resist the urge to at least hurry. She was nearly running when she reached the front door. The doorman had already opened it for her when she heard Thornton call, "Betty!"

She didn't turn. She didn't slow. She ran for her life.

Keep reading for an excerpt of
Victoria Thompson's next Gaslight Mystery

MURDER ON UNION SQUARE

Coming May 2018 in hardcover
from Berkley Prime Crime

"**W**HAT DO YOU MEAN 'WE CAN'T ADOPT CATHERINE?'" Sarah asked the attorney.

Michael Hicks gave her a look that told her he shared her frustration. "I'm sorry—"

"I thought Mr. Wilbanks settled all of this in his will," Sarah's husband said. Frank Malloy reached over and took his wife's hand, giving it a reassuring squeeze. They'd come to Michael's office today expecting good news. Plainly, they were going to be disappointed.

"I thought David had settled everything, too," Michael said. "And I know he certainly intended to as well. My father-in-law was a very careful man, but you see, I didn't draw up his final will. Estates are not my area of expertise, and it would be unethical for me to prepare a will for a family member in any case, so I referred him to a colleague of mine, Bill Jonson."

"Are you saying this colleague made a mistake?" Malloy was angry now but trying not to take it out on poor Michael. Sarah understood completely.

"Not a *mistake*." Michael was being very diplomatic. "My father-in-law was careful but also very private. He didn't believe he needed to tell Mr. Jonson all the sordid details about Catherine's birth."

"Which ones did he leave out?" Malloy asked.

Michael winced. "I, uh, I've asked Mr. Jonson to join us, if you don't mind, so he can explain it all to you." He got up and went to his office door to admit a man who had obviously been waiting for this summons.

Michael introduced Mr. Jonson, who was a distinguished-looking man of middle age wearing a conservatively cut, tailor-made suit and immaculate shirtfront. When they were all seated again, Michael said, "Bill, I have informed Mr. and Mrs. Malloy that they cannot adopt Catherine, but I haven't explained exactly why yet. I thought you could do that better than I."

"Of course." Mr. Jonson gave them his best reassuring smile. "You see, Mr. Wilbanks told me that Catherine was the illegitimate child he had with his mistress, an actress named Emma Hardy. However, he didn't think it necessary to explain that Emma Hardy also happened to be married to a Mr. Parnell Vaughn at the time of their affair. He probably thought it was none of my business."

"But what difference does that make?" Sarah asked. "Even Mr. Vaughn admitted he couldn't possibly be Catherine's father because he and Emma were separated when she met Mr. Wilbanks."

"Which is why Mr. Wilbanks didn't think it necessary to mention Mr. Vaughn at all," Jonson said. "Unfortunately, the law is rather unforgiving when it comes to matters of paternity."

"What does that mean?" Malloy asked.

"It means that the law considers a woman's husband to be the father of her children, regardless of any evidence to the contrary."

"But that's ridiculous," Sarah tried.

"In some cases, yes, but it is nevertheless the law."

"So you're telling us that the law considers Parnell Vaughn to be Catherine's father?" Malloy asked, no longer bothering to hide his anger.

"Yes," Michael said. "And that's one reason why David decided to leave part of his estate to Frank rather than directly to Catherine."

"You mean he knew about this paternity law?" Sarah asked.

"No, I'm sure he didn't," Mr. Jonson said. "And I certainly didn't explain it to him because I had no idea Miss Hardy was ever married to Mr. Vaughn. Rest assured, I would have made sure to settle the matter prior to Mr. Wilbanks's death. Even without knowing about Mr. Vaughn, I was already very concerned that if he left Catherine a great deal of money in her own right, she'd be a tempting target for any greedy family members of Emma Hardy or anyone willing to pretend to be her family member. A large inheritance would also make her a target for fortune hunters later in life."

"But after seeing how much you loved Catherine, Frank," Michael said, "David decided you were the man who could and would protect her from both of those dangers."

Malloy winced and glanced at Sarah. "He should have left the money to Sarah."

"I'm afraid David was also old-fashioned. He would never

trust a female with so much money, and besides, Sarah had already told him she wouldn't accept it." Michael smiled slightly. "I must also tell you that Mr. Jonson did not approve of David making you one of his heirs, Frank."

"I certainly did not," Jonson said. "Even though Mr. Wilbanks's will instructed you to become Catherine's legal guardian, there was no way to compel you to do so. Such a provision causes an attorney great concern."

"Yes, it does," Michael said. "Bill was almost apoplectic about it."

"So was I," Malloy said. "I wish I'd suspected he was going to do it so I could have threatened to refuse it like Sarah did."

"Which is why he never informed you, I'm sure," Michael said.

Mr. Jonson still looked distressed. "You see, after you received your inheritance, you could have abandoned Catherine completely, and even now you have no obligation to share any of the money with her."

"But we would never abandon Catherine," Sarah said.

"David believed that, I know," Michael said, "which is why he did what he did, but the fact remains that he has put you in a difficult position. You can't adopt Catherine as long as Vaughn is legally her father."

"You might get a judge to name you as her official guardian," Jonson said, "but it would mean a court case and publicity you'd find distasteful and a scandal that could follow her all of her life. You'd probably win in the end, although there's no guarantee of that, but even if you did, you still wouldn't be able to adopt Catherine, and Vaughn would always be there."

"You might never hear from him again, of course," Michael said. "But whenever there's money involved, people do tend to make nuisances of themselves. There's no telling what he might do, and after what happened before . . ."

"You don't think he'd try to kidnap her?" Sarah asked in alarm, remembering the horror of her first encounter with Catherine's blood relatives.

"It wouldn't legally be kidnapping," Michael said. "In the eyes of the law, he's her father, so he could be entitled to custody."

Sarah couldn't help groaning.

"So what can we do about this?" Malloy asked impatiently. "I know you lawyers always have an answer for everything."

Michael glanced at Jonson, who said, "We do try, but there isn't always an easy answer for everything. In this case you would need Vaughn to relinquish his parental rights. I could have the documents drawn up, and when he has signed them, you could then proceed with the adoption."

"And Vaughn couldn't come back later to reclaim Catherine?" Sarah asked.

"No, he couldn't."

"I wonder how much he'll want in exchange for his signature," Malloy said.

"Uh, that's another thing we need to discuss," Michael said uneasily. "It's illegal for you to pay him to give up custody."

"What?" Malloy nearly shouted. "Why would that be illegal?"

"Because it's considered selling a child, and selling human beings is illegal in the United States, I'm happy to say."

Sarah wanted to weep. "So we're supposed to convince Mr. Vaughn to sign Catherine over to us out of the goodness of his heart?"

"I'm afraid so."

"And if he doesn't have any goodness in his heart?" Malloy asked.

Michael and Mr. Jonson exchanged looks again. "Let's just hope he does."

"WHAT ARE WE GOING TO DO?" SARAH ASKED MALLOY the moment Michael's office door closed behind them.

"We're going to find Parnell Vaughn and convince him to sign Catherine over to us."

"What are the chances he'll do it?"

Sarah didn't like Malloy's expression one little bit. "Very small, I'd guess."

Sarah wanted to weep again. "He'd do it if we paid him, I'm sure."

"I know, which is why I think we'll have to pay him."

"But Michael said that's illegal!"

"Which means we're stuck either way."

"What do you mean?"

"I mean, when Vaughn finds out he's legally Catherine's father, he'll probably decide he'd be a fool to sign her over. He'll know that as long as he has the right to claim her, we'll be willing to keep paying him off to keep him from doing so."

"But if he signs the papers . . . ," Sarah said.

"Which he won't do unless we pay him, and if he knows that's illegal, he'll always have that over us, too. If we don't keep paying him, he'll accuse us of 'buying' Catherine and try to get her back again."

"So, we're back to my original question: What are we going to do?"

"I'm going to find Vaughn. We can't decide anything until we've talked to him."

He was right, of course. "He's probably touring in some theater company, though." Vaughn was an actor, too, which was how he'd met Emma Hardy. "How will we track him down?"

"Same way we did before, and with any luck, we'll find out he drank himself to death since we last saw him."

"Oh, Malloy, we don't really wish him dead," Sarah said, although she couldn't help thinking how Vaughn's death would make everything so much simpler.

"Mr. Malloy is right," Maeve said. "If Vaughn was dead, that would make everything so much easier."

Sarah gave her nanny a look meant to chasten her, although she was sure such efforts were wasted on the girl. "We do not wish Mr. Vaughn ill, Maeve. We simply want him to sign some papers." Sarah had gone straight home after their meeting with Michael Hicks, while Malloy had gone to find out what he could about Parnell Vaughn. Maeve had just returned from the Lower East Side where she was supervising the workmen who were turning the old house Sarah had purchased into a maternity clinic that would provide services free of charge to women in need. She'd wanted to tell Sarah how she'd outsmarted the workmen yet again and terrorized them into doing exactly what she demanded, but she'd forgotten all that when Sarah told her about their meeting with the attorney.

"Oh, no, I don't wish Mr. Vaughn any misfortune," Maeve assured her with just the right amount of sincerity. "But I'm afraid your lawyer is right. People act strangely when money is involved."

"Then we'll deal with that when we must. In the meantime tell me how the clinic is coming along."

"Women are still coming to the door every day wanting to know when we're going to open," Maeve said.

"I know. You've told me that before. I'm sure everyone knows the midwives have moved in, too, so that probably doesn't help."

"Those two women you hired are going to be perfect, and having them move in to make sure the place is occupied at night was a very good idea. They're already making home visits, and Miss Hanson delivered a baby last night."

"She did?" Sarah couldn't have been more delighted. "Oh, I do miss those deliveries." Sarah had made her living as a midwife for years before her marriage.

"I already told them they'll need to let you deliver a baby every now and then."

"Thank you," Sarah said with a grin.

"Oh, and I almost forgot; you'll never guess who I saw today."

Sarah didn't particularly care, since her mind was still focused on Catherine and their situation, in spite of Maeve's best efforts to distract her. "Who?"

"That fortune teller, Seraphina Straface."

"Seraphina? Really?" Sarah asked in surprise. "How long has it been since we saw her?"

"A couple years, I think."

"What did she want?"

Maeve gave her a pitying look. "The same thing all the other women want."

"Oh!" So Seraphina was expecting.

"Yes. Apparently, she's still telling fortunes or whatever it was she did."

"She's a medium."

Maeve rolled her eyes at such a notion. "So she says. Then

I guess she's still a medium, but I gathered she's looking for a private place to have her baby."

"I suppose she married her young man, Mr. DiLoreto."

"You can suppose that all you want, but when she told me her name, she said it was Straface."

"Oh, dear." The world was not kind to unwed mothers. Then she remembered. "In Italy women don't take their husband's name."

"Really?"

"Yes, really."

"That's interesting. But I guess in America, actresses don't either. Emma Hardy didn't."

"You're right, she didn't. So Serafina is interested in using the clinic?"

"I think she was just interested in using you as a midwife. She said she went to your old house, and they sent her to the clinic to find you."

"Our neighbors have been very good about not telling people where we live now," Sarah said.

"Yes, they have, and it sure cuts down on the number of people coming here looking for a handout," Maeve said with a smirk. "She didn't tell me when, uh, she'll need the clinic, but she seemed glad to hear it should be ready in a few days."

"Do you think so?" Sarah asked in surprise.

"If I have anything to say about it, it will. I have those workmen terrified of Mr. Malloy, especially after they tried to pretend they didn't know they were supposed to fix the wall in the back today."

"Maeve, you missed your calling."

"I know. I should've been a man. I would've been good at it, too. Better than most men, anyway."

Sarah couldn't help laughing in spite of everything, which

she guessed had been Maeve's intention. "I didn't mean that. I meant you should have been a . . ."

Maeve waited a few seconds while Sarah tried in vain to think of some profession to which a woman could aspire that would use Maeve's talents. "See? You can't think of anything. I was right. I should've been a man."

"But instead you're going to help other women."

"I suppose, and maybe someday Mr. Malloy will let me work for him."

FINDING PARNELL VAUGHN TURNED OUT TO BE MUCH easier than Frank had anticipated. As an actor, Vaughn often worked for touring companies, and he might have been anywhere in the country. The last time they'd tried to locate him, he'd just been returning to New York from a tour. Frank tried the theatrical agent who had helped him then, only to discover that agents represented shows, not actors, and Vaughn was no longer appearing in any of that agent's shows. Frank only had to visit a couple more agents, however, before he found his quarry.

"Oh, yes, Parnell Vaughn," Mr. Dinsmore said with obvious distaste. "He's having quite a successful run with Mrs. Hawkes at the Palladium Theater."

"Mrs. Hawkes?" Adelia Hawkes was one of the most famous actresses in the country. "Are you sure? It's Parnell Vaughn I'm looking for. Maybe you have him confused with someone else."

Mr. Dinsmore smiled grimly. "I see you know Mr. Vaughn."

"We're acquainted, yes."

"Then you probably know that he has always been a very talented performer."

"I've, uh, never actually seen him on the stage," Frank admitted.

"Well, then, let me assure you that he is." Oddly, Mr. Dinsmore didn't seem pleased to admit this. "But like many creative individuals, he has a serious problem with, uh . . ."

"Yes, he drinks," Frank said, sparing Mr. Dinsmore from finding a polite way of saying it.

"Or rather, he did. It seems he's turned over a new leaf in the past year or so. He met a lady who has been a stabilizing influence on him, and his career has prospered as a result."

So much for Vaughn drinking himself to death. "I'm glad to hear it. He's performing at the Palladium you say?"

"That's right. I'm sure you can find him there Tuesday through Saturday evenings and on Wednesday, Saturday, and Sunday for matinees."

"Would you happen to know where he lives? He might not want to discuss our business at the theater."

"I wouldn't have any idea. Actors are notoriously migratory."

"How do you find them when you need them then?"

"Oh, they stop by weekly when they're in town. They check in with all the agents, just to let us know they're available. Then when we have a need, we send them to audition."

"That doesn't sound like a very efficient system," Frank observed.

Dinsmore did not seem to appreciate Frank's opinion. "Perhaps not, but it works."

Frank thanked him for his time and made his way back to the street. Like most of the agents, his office was in a building just off Union Square, which was the central location for theaters as well. He couldn't see the Palladium Theater from here, but he knew where it was. He wondered if Sarah would like to see a play tonight.

*   *   *

"I THOUGHT SHE WAS SUPPOSED TO BE HIS MOTHER,"
Malloy said in disgust as they waited in their seats for the
crowd to disperse when the show was over. "And then he
started making love to her."

"Everyone knows Mrs. Hawkes always plays the romantic
lead," Sarah said. "I thought Mr. Vaughn was very good."

"He'd have to be good to make people believe he was in
love with a woman twice his age."

Sarah glanced around and was relieved to see no one was
close enough to have overheard. Most of the audience had
gone and the remaining few were moving toward the exits.
It hadn't taken long, since the crowd hadn't been large to
start with. "I don't think she's *twice* his age."

"She's got at least fifteen years on him though."

He was right, so she didn't bother to dispute it. "I think
we could head backstage now."

They rose from their seats and made their way to the front
of the theater. A few generous tips to crew members bought
them directions to Parnell Vaughn's dressing room. The door
stood open and the sound of laughter spilled out into the
hallway. Two young women emerged. Sarah recognized them
as minor characters from the play. They gave Sarah and Malloy a curious glance before making their way to their own
dressing rooms.

Sarah stepped up to the open doorway and saw a comfortable but cluttered room. Vaughn sat in a slipper chair, his
back to the mirrored dressing table littered with pots and
jars, and a young woman lounged on a worn love seat nearby.
They both looked up in surprise. Sarah recognized the young
woman from her role as the maid in the play. Vaughn got to
his feet. He obviously didn't know who Sarah was, and of

course, he wouldn't since they had never met. Then Malloy came in behind her, and Vaughn's expression changed instantly.

"Mr. Malloy, isn't it?" he said, putting out his hand. He'd stiffened ever so slightly, but he was a good enough actor that his expression revealed only pleased surprise at his visitor. They had not parted on the best of terms at their last meeting.

"Yes. It's nice to see you again, Vaughn. May I introduce my wife, Sarah?"

Vaughn took her outstretched hand, but instead of shaking it, he sketched a little bow and gallantly kissed it. He was a strikingly handsome man with soulful dark eyes and a mane of dark hair artfully styled. He was even more impressive up close than when he was on the stage. When he raised his head, Sarah realized she had fallen completely under his spell.

Then his expression, designed to charm, changed slightly to recognition. "Sarah, did you say? Are you by chance the little girl's, uh . . . ?"

"Foster mother? Yes, I am." Couldn't he even remember Catherine's name?

His gaze darted from her to Malloy and back again as he put the clues together. "And you and Mr. Malloy have married."

"Yes, we have," Malloy confirmed.

Having overcome his initial surprise, Vaughn now eyed them both more critically, taking in Sarah's expensive gown and Malloy's tailor-made suit. "And you've obviously prospered in the meantime."

Sarah blinked in surprise. They'd assumed Vaughn would know what had happened and that Malloy was now a wealthy man, but it seemed he did not.

Fortunately, Malloy also realized this. He smiled broadly. "Yes, we have. I've started my own detective agency." He pulled out a card and handed it to Vaughn.

"Nelly, who are these people?" the young woman on the love seat demanded crossly.

"Oh, pardon me, my dear. May I present Miss Eliza Grimes? Eliza, Mr. and Mrs. Malloy."

Eliza rose gracefully from her seat and offered Malloy her hand quite regally. Malloy made a point of not kissing it, Sarah noted fondly.

"His fiancée," Miss Grimes informed them, slipping her arm through Vaughn's possessively.

Did Vaughn wince a tiny bit? Sarah wasn't sure, but she found it odd he hadn't identified her as his intended when he introduced her. Seeing them together, Sarah couldn't help thinking they probably shared about the same age difference as Vaughn and Mrs. Hawkes, or nearly so. Eliza Grimes certainly hadn't reached her twentieth birthday yet.

"Congratulations," Malloy said without much enthusiasm.

"You also seem to have prospered, Mr. Vaughn," Sarah said quickly.

He brightened at that. "Did you see the show?"

"We did indeed and enjoyed it very much. We thought you were excellent."

"Thank you, Mrs. Malloy. It's a great honor to work with Mrs. Hawkes."

"I'm sure it must be. She's legendary."

"But much too old, of course, to continue playing the romantic lead," Eliza said.

"Now, Eliza," Vaughn said gently.

"And you are an actress, too, Miss Grimes," Sarah said.

Eliza lifted her chin. "Yes, I am. I'm Mrs. Hawkes's understudy."

And much more suited the role, age-wise, but Sarah didn't say that.

"Eliza has a bright future ahead of her," Vaughn said.

"I'm sure she does," Sarah agreed.

No one had a reply to that, and an awkward silence followed. Finally, Eliza said, "Now, who are you really, and what do you want with Nelly?"

Vaughn patted her hand where it was wrapped around his arm. "You remember I told you about Emma's little girl."

Eliza rolled her eyes. "Oh, yes, *Emma*."

"Yes, well, Mrs. Malloy is the lady who took her in."

"Then he must be the copper who arrested you," Eliza said, unimpressed.

"And I'm also the copper who let him go," Malloy said with a small smile.

"But that doesn't explain what you're doing here now," Eliza said.

"No, it doesn't," Malloy said. "We need to discuss something with you, Mr. Vaughn."

"About the little girl?" he asked with a frown.

"About Catherine, yes," Sarah said, unreasonably annoyed that he couldn't say her name.

"But maybe you'd like to meet at my office tomorrow," Malloy said. "Since it's a private matter."

"No," Eliza said before Vaughn could answer. "You're here now, so you might as well get it over with."

Malloy looked at Vaughn who reluctantly nodded. Plainly, he didn't want to talk to them at all.

Malloy glanced at the girl. "Is it all right to speak in front of Miss Grimes?"

"Of course it is," she replied for him again. "We're going to be married. We have no secrets."

Sarah doubted that very much, but she said, "We should

at least close the door. I'm sure you don't want anyone else knowing your business."

Malloy, being the closest, did the honors. Vaughn found a straight-backed chair half-hidden by the rack of costumes along one wall. Malloy took it while the two women sat on the love seat and Vaughn sat back down in the dressing table chair.

"You make this sound ominous, Mr. Malloy," he said with a strained smile.

"Not at all," Malloy said. "Now that Sarah and I are married and Catherine's parents are both dead, we would like to adopt her legally."

"That's very kind of you."

"But why are you telling us about it?" Eliza asked, still suspicious.

Malloy cleared his throat. "It has come to our attention that, even though you and Miss Hardy weren't living together at the time, because you were married to Emma Hardy when Catherine, uh, came along, the law still considers you Catherine's father."

"What?" Eliza cried, turning on Vaughn. "You swore to me that child wasn't yours."

"She isn't," Vaughn assured her. He turned to Frank. "I can't take care of a child. Surely you can see that."

"That's not what we're asking, Mr. Vaughn," Sarah said quickly. "In fact, it's just the opposite. We do want to take care of Catherine. We want to adopt her as our own, but we can't because of this legal technicality. However, our attorney assures us that it's possible for you to relinquish your parental rights by simply signing a paper. That would free you of all responsibility for Catherine and allow us to adopt her."

Vaughn needed only a moment to consider. "Oh, well, in

that case, I'd be more than happy to help you. I don't suppose you've got the paper with you?"

"Wait a minute," Eliza said, and all of them turned to her. "What's in this for Nelly?"

"I'm doing them a favor, Eliza," Vaughn said.

"Yes, you are, so they should do something for you in return."

This was exactly what Sarah and Malloy had been afraid of. "What did you have in mind, Miss Grimes?" Malloy asked. He wasn't using his friendliest tone, but Eliza didn't seem intimidated.

"You want this little girl, but you can't have her without Nelly's help, so I think you ought to give him some token of appreciation."

Vaughn sputtered a protest, but Malloy stopped him with a gesture. "How big of a token would you consider appropriate?"

Plainly, Eliza had not expected to succeed so easily. For a moment her mouth hung open in shock, but she recovered quickly. Without so much as a glance at Vaughn to confirm her decision, she said, "A thousand dollars."

Equally plainly, from the requested amount, neither of them had an inkling of just how wealthy Malloy had become. For his part, Malloy managed to wince, probably because it hadn't been too very long since such an amount would have been impossible for him to raise. A thousand dollars probably equaled Parnell Vaughn's annual income as an actor, but only if he worked regularly.

"But we can't—" Sarah began, but Malloy stopped her with a gesture.

"That's a lot of money, but Catherine means a great deal to us."

"Really, Mr. Malloy, there's no need . . . ," Vaughn said faintly.

"You're entitled to it," Eliza insisted. "You could refuse to sign their paper and then where would they be?"

"We appreciate your help in this matter, Mr. Vaughn," Malloy said, his expression suitably grave. "Our attorney can have the papers drawn up by Wednesday. Can I meet you here before your matinee and get your signature?"

"And we'll get our money, too?" Eliza said.

"Of course," Malloy said.

"Then yes, we'll meet you here on Wednesday afternoon, won't we, Nelly?"

Parnell Vaughn looked far from committed. "I . . . I suppose so."

Before anyone could reply, the door burst open.

"Parnell, darling, I've been wait—" Adelia Hawkes stopped mid-word at the sight of Vaughn's visitors. She did not appear to be pleased by it. "I didn't realize you were having a party."

Frank and Vaughn had risen to their feet. Sarah had to resist the urge to do the same. Adelia Hawkes seemed to fill the room with her presence and demand obeisance. She'd changed from her costume into an ensemble most would have considered outlandish. Her lavish brocade coat glittered with gold threads and an intricately wound turban of patterned silk completely covered her hair and sported a peacock feather that trembled with her every move.

"It's hardly a party, Adelia," Vaughn said. How odd, he sounded a little defensive. "These are some . . . old friends who came to see the show tonight and wish me well."

"Old friends?" She eyed Frank and Sarah much the way Vaughn had done earlier.

"We were so impressed when we heard Mr. Vaughn was

appearing with you that we had to come," Sarah said. "You were absolutely fantastic in that role, Mrs. Hawkes."

Her disapproval vanished. "Did you think so? How lovely. One can never judge one's own performance."

"Oh, yes, and Mr. Vaughn was just telling us how honored he was to be cast as your leading man."

Mrs. Hawkes cast Vaughn a fond look before turning back to Sarah. "Perhaps your friends would like to join us, Parnell. A few of us usually have a little supper together after the show," she added.

"Thank you, but I'm afraid we're committed elsewhere," Sarah said. It wouldn't be a good idea to get too cozy with these people. Someone might figure out who they really were and tell Vaughn. Or worse, tell Eliza.

"A pity. Perhaps next time. Parnell, are you ready?"

"Almost," he said.

"Good. We'll go on ahead then. Lovely to meet you," she added to Sarah, and then she was gone.

For a second she seemed to have taken all the air in the room as well, but they recovered quickly.

"I'm afraid I must go. Duty calls," Vaughn said with forced brightness.

Eliza made a rude noise, and Sarah realized Mrs. Hawkes had not even acknowledged her. For her part, Eliza had sat perfectly still, almost as if frozen, during Mrs. Hawkes's brief visit.

"You know you're welcome to join us, Eliza," Vaughn said.

"Oh, yes, so the great Mrs. Hawkes can subtly insult me all during the meal. No, thank you. I'll see you later." She rose and started for the door, but she stopped when she reached Malloy. "Don't forget to bring the money when you come. Otherwise, you can go whistle for your signature."

When she was gone, Vaughn tried a conciliatory smile.

"She's very young and hasn't learned the art of discretion yet."

Malloy nodded. "Mr. Dinsmore—do you know him? Wylie Dinsmore, the agent?—he told me you'd met a lady who had been a good influence on you and that your career had flourished as a result."

Vaughn didn't seem pleased that Dinsmore had shared confidences about him, but then his expression cleared. "Oh, you mean Eliza. Yes, she has encouraged me, and she wants me to succeed. I don't think Emma ever did."

"We're very happy for you, Mr. Vaughn," Sarah said. "And I know you want to stay in Mrs. Hawkes's good graces, so we'll be on our way now. Thank you for being so understanding about the situation with Catherine."

"I'm happy to help. I have nothing to offer a child, especially one who isn't even my own."

"We understand completely," Sarah assured him.

"And Mr. Malloy," Vaughn added a little sheepishly. "I couldn't take a payment for helping you, so just ignore what Eliza said."

If Malloy was surprised, he didn't show it. They arranged a time to meet next Wednesday before the matinee.

Sarah and Malloy took their leave, and one of the stagehands escorted them out a side door into an alley where the other actors were making their way to suppers or entertainments of their own.

"Why do you suppose she calls him Nelly?" Malloy asked when they were out on the sidewalk and away from anyone who might be interested in their conversation.

"I think it must be a nickname for Parnell, at least in her mind."

Malloy shook his head. "When Dinsmore told me Vaughn

had found a woman who helped him, I was picturing somebody like you."

Intrigued, Sarah said, "Like me in what way?"

"Oh, I don't know. Somebody sensible, I guess. And nice, at least. Instead, she's just like Emma except she's convinced Vaughn he's a good actor instead of convincing him he's not, just to keep him in line."

"Do you think that's what Emma did?"

"She never had a kind word to say about him, as far as I could see, and she encouraged him to drink. Why would a woman do that if not to keep a man under her control?"

Sarah couldn't imagine doing that to someone she loved, but then, she wasn't Emma Hardy, either. "You're probably right. At least Miss Grimes's influence has had good results."

"She's still trying to keep him under control, though. Did you notice the way she answered for him?"

"Of course, and did you notice she's the one who said they're engaged?"

"And he didn't look too happy when she did," Malloy said. "I wonder how long it will last, though."

"What do you mean?"

"You couldn't see Eliza's expression when Mrs. Hawkes came in. She might have inspired Vaughn's success, but she's jealous of it, too."

"Oh, I understood that perfectly," Sarah said. "Those remarks about Mrs. Hawkes being too old for the part were telling."

"They were also perfectly true. I can't imagine Mrs. Hawkes likes having Eliza around to remind her that she's getting a little long in the tooth."

The image surprised a laugh from Sarah. "You don't think Eliza says that to her face, do you?"

"No, she's too smart for that, but she doesn't need to say anything. She just needs to sit there and smile."

Sarah sighed. "She won't be smiling if we don't pay Vaughn the thousand dollars."

"Don't worry. I'll have it with me just in case."

"But if we pay Vaughn to sign the papers—"

"I said, don't worry. I won't be paying Vaughn. If Eliza insists, I'll give the money to her, not him. That way, if they come back later and try to blackmail us, I'll remind her of that."

"Do you think that's all right legally?"

"I think it's legal enough to convince them. And if Vaughn continues to be successful, he probably won't need to come back to us anyway."

"I hope you're right. He really does seem to be a good actor."

"He is if Eliza can keep him from drinking."

"And he'll have to help her become successful, too." Sarah shook her head. "That's a lot of uncertainty."

"I think all actors live with uncertainty, so he's probably used to it."

"I suppose so, and if he's willing to sign that paper, I will wish him all the best."

Malloy smiled. "So will I."

THE NEXT MORNING SARAH AND MAEVE TOOK THE EL-evated train down to the Lower East Side, so Sarah could see for herself how close they were to opening.

The two midwives were out doing home visits. After Maeve and the foreman had taken Sarah on a tour, the two women settled down in the newly completed kitchen for a cup of tea.

"There doesn't seem to be much left to do, and all the furniture is here. How soon do you think we can open?" Sarah asked.

"A few days, I'd say. They're just finishing that last room and they'll have to clean up, although the midwives and I have been doing a lot of that ourselves. I've already had to turn people away, but they know they can return as soon as we hang out the sign." Maeve nodded to the neatly painted board leaning against the wall by the back door.

"Should we have some sort of event to announce that we're open?"

Maeve smiled. "I don't think that will be necessary. Everybody in the neighborhood knows we're here and what we do."

"I guess they're as anxious to get started as we are. My goal is to never turn anyone away."

The sound of footsteps drew their attention, and they looked up to see a young woman standing in the doorway.

"Mrs. Brandt, I was hoping you'd be here," she said.

Sarah rose and looked more closely, not quite trusting her eyes. "Serafina, welcome. Maeve told me you'd stopped by."

They had met the beautiful Italian girl a few years earlier when a séance she'd been conducting had ended in murder. Serafina stepped into the room. Even though the September weather was still pleasant, she wore a cape and had buttoned it closed in front. Then Sarah remembered what Maeve had said about the girl, and she knew what Serafina was hiding.

"I'm afraid we haven't opened the clinic yet, but if you need a place to stay . . ."

"Oh, no, I do not need a place to stay. I am still living in the same house on Waverly Place."

"Still doing séances?" Sarah asked.

"Of course. I have some very loyal clients, and I have done well for myself even after . . . Well, since I saw you last."

"Is Mr. DiLoreto still helping you?" Sarah asked, deciding that was the most tactful way to inquire if Serafina and the young man she had been in love with were still together.

But Serafina's polite smile vanished and her eyes filled with tears. "No, I . . . Nicola has died."

"Died?" Sarah echoed in surprise. "I'm so sorry. I had no idea. Please, come over here and sit down and let us get you a cup of tea."

When the girl was settled, still wearing her enveloping cape and sipping her restorative tea, Sarah said, "Was Mr. DiLoreto ill?"

"Yes, he . . . he was very sick. We called in a doctor, but there was nothing he could do. We were planning to marry, but I was so busy with my clients and we did not think we needed to hurry . . ." She shook her head. "After he was gone, I found out about the baby." She opened her cape to reveal her swollen stomach.

"And you've continued with your work?" Sarah asked, wondering how she had explained her condition and the absence of a husband to the society people who came to her for help contacting dead loved ones.

Serafina smiled sadly. "I wear robes now. Flowing robes. And I have stopped going out."

"Except to come here," Maeve reminded her.

"My time is getting close. I cannot give birth at my house. Everyone will find out and my clients will stop coming."

"What are you going to do?"

"I have told my clients that I will be going on a holiday soon. I had hoped to come to you and stay until the baby is born. Then I found out you were opening this clinic. If I could come here, no one would know. I would pay you, of course. I do not need charity. Then, when I am well again,

I will return to my home. I will hire a servant who has an infant that she will bring with her into my house."

"Oh, Serafina, that is such a wonderful plan. I was afraid you were going to give your baby away."

"Never. And did Maeve not tell you? I have changed my name. I am Sarah now, too. Sarah Straface. I want to be completely American."

"It's a lovely name," Sarah said.

Serafina smiled, but her smile quickly became a grimace, and she clamped a hand to her side.

"What is it?" Sarah asked. "Is the baby kicking?"

"No, I . . . I have been having pains. I know you are not ready yet, but I could not stay at home." Her lovely dark eyes were pleading.

"Oh, dear!" Sarah said, but she wasn't thinking "oh dear," not at all. Excitement skittered through her at the realization she was going to deliver a baby again after all these months. "Maeve, can we get a room ready?"

Maeve's eyes were like saucers. "Of course. I'll go make up the bed."

ON THE APPOINTED WEDNESDAY AFTERNOON, FRANK arrived at the theater just after noon. Early enough, he hoped, to be in and out before most of the cast arrived to prepare for the matinee. He entered through the side door the cast used. The door was unlocked and although a stool stood nearby, obviously for a guard who would monitor who went in and out, no one was around. In fact, the halls were eerily quiet, in stark contrast to the busy bustle he'd encountered after the performance the other night. He caught a glimpse of a woman disappearing into one of the dressing rooms at the end of the hallway, but he saw no one else before he reached Vaughn's dressing room.

Frank hadn't noticed the other night that the door bore Vaughn's name and a small wooden star had been nailed beneath it. Frank knocked and waited, but no one responded. He tried again, more loudly. Still nothing. He glanced up and down the hallway to see if Vaughn was in sight, but he still saw no one. He tried the door and the knob turned easily. Thinking he'd simply wait for Vaughn inside, he pushed the door open.

The first thing he noticed was the sharp metallic odor, and then he registered the body crumpled on the floor. And the blood. So much blood. Vaughn stared up at him, his eyes wide with terror and a silent plea for help. Frank went to him instinctively, kneeling down, heedless of the blood pooled around Vaughn's head. But Vaughn's gaze didn't move. He still stared fixedly up at the door, and when Frank felt for a pulse, he found none. The body was still warm, though, which meant the killer might still be nearby. They should seal off the theater in case he was hiding somewhere.

Frank pushed himself to his feet and started toward the door. Just as he reached it, Eliza Grimes appeared in the doorway.

"Mr. Malloy," she said with some satisfaction. "I hope you don't think you're finished with your business. I know what Nelly said, but—"

"Miss Grimes, we need some help. Can you go find a guard or someone in authority?"

"A guard? What for? What's going on? And don't think you can trick me into leaving you alone with Nelly!"

"Miss Grimes, please," he tried, reaching out to her, but that was a mistake. His hand was covered in blood.

"What's that? What's happened? Nelly!" she shouted and tried to push past him.

"Don't go in there!" He tried to hold her, but she wrenched free and managed to get her head around him enough to see.

"No! Nelly!" she cried and began to scream.

In moments people appeared from every direction. Actors still in street clothes, stagehands still carrying their tools, and an officious looking man in a suit who demanded to know what all the fuss was about.

Before Frank could tell him, Eliza threw herself into the man's arms. "Oh, Mr. Hawkes, he's killed Nelly!"

NATIONAL BESTSELLING AUTHOR

VICTORIA THOMPSON

"Victoria Thompson shines."

—Tamar Myers, national bestselling author
of *Tea with Jam and Dread*

For a complete list of titles,
please visit prh.com/victoriathompson